DEATH AT CASTLE COVE

MARY GRAND

With best wishes

Mary Grand

B
Boldwood

First published in Great Britain in 2023 by Boldwood Books Ltd.

Copyright © Mary Grand, 2023

Cover Design: Head Design

Cover Photography: Shutterstock

A CIP catalogue record for this book is available from the British Library.

Paperback ISBN 978-1-80426-907-7

Large Print ISBN 978-1-80426-903-9

Hardback ISBN 978-1-80426-902-2

Ebook ISBN 978-1-80426-900-8

Kindle ISBN 978-1-80426-901-5

Audio CD ISBN 978-1-80426-908-4

MP3 CD ISBN 978-1-80426-905-3

Digital audio download ISBN 978-1-80426-899-5

Boldwood Books Ltd
23 Bowerdean Street
London SW6 3TN
www.boldwoodbooks.com

To Adèle: Thank you so much for all your friendship, kindness, and love. Thank you for being there through the highs and lows, and for the many smiles and slices of cake we have shared. xxx

NOTE TO READERS

Ventnor is a holiday town on the Isle of Wight. Some details of the geography of the town have been changed to suit the story. The street where Susan lives is fictitious as is The Glanville Hotel and the nursing home. In the same way all the people in this story are completely fictitious.

Freshwater, likewise, is a town on the Island, but the hotel, The Seashells, is fictitious as are the people working in it

St Hilda's and Bishopstone are fictitious places, although their geographical layout is based on real villages. The people in both are fictitious.

PROLOGUE
SUNDAY, 11 OCTOBER

This is a secret place. Safe and cosy by day, but tonight it feels isolated and eerie. Not many people know of Castle Cove, inaccessible to cars, it is one of those hidden magical places here on the island.

Enormous boulders have been placed to protect the land from the waves that crash into and erode it, and yet Colette, huddled among them, appears vulnerable and alone on this cold October evening.

Suddenly her white-blonde hair catches the wind. I don't need to see her face to be reminded of how much her beauty hurts me. She is a fool to be down here on her own.

However, she is oblivious to the threat gathering in the sea salt air, making it too easy for me.

If only she'd stayed away from the island, left me alone with my secrets and my past. But she came, and she won't stop digging until all my secrets have clawed their way out. She has left me no option, she has to die.

1

SATURDAY, 10 OCTOBER – ONE DAY EARLIER

Susan glanced at her young lodger as they left the house. Naturally very fair, Colette looked ghost-like today and Susan was concerned about her. Their cocker spaniels Rocco and Libs pulled impatiently on their leads as they began the steep descent to Ventnor beach to meet up with a group of fellow dog walkers. It was soon after sunrise on one of those crisp autumn mornings that Susan loved.

'How are you feeling today? I can take Libs down if you want a lie-in. You had a late shift at the hotel.'

'Nah, I need some fresh air,' Colette replied and breathed in deeply. 'It's so cool I can just walk down to the beach whenever I want. It's brilliant for Libs, she loves it here.'

Susan looked down at the little black cocker spaniel, head up and tail wagging in anticipation, and knew Colette was right.

'The island suits you both.'

'It does. I've not been back to the mainland once since I arrived. Sometimes I think I might never leave.' Colette gave Susan a quick smile. 'Don't worry, I'll not camp out with you forever.'

Susan grinned. 'I've really enjoyed having you and Libs living with me over the past few months.'

'Do you know what I'd really like to do?' asked Colette, her voice quieter, less confident now.

'Tell me.'

'I'd like to study psychology. I want to work with children who have been abused and feel forgotten, I want them to know someone cares and understands them.'

'That's wonderful, Colette.'

'I looked it up online, to see what I'd need. I managed to get my maths and English at GCSE, and I liked biology. I would have to do A levels first—'

'You can do it, I'm sure. I know people who work at the college on the island. You could talk to them. I would support you in any way you need.'

'Really? You don't think I'm mad?'

'Not at all. You are very bright; I am sure you could do anything you put your mind to. Now, are you working at the hotel today?'

'Not cleaning, just the bar at lunch time. I've got this evening off. By the way, I had a call from the nursing home here, they want me to go up this morning.'

'Really? Why's that?'

'They think they have found Gran's locket.'

Susan stared in amazement. 'Not the one you told us about on Thursday?'

'Yes. The gardener found it when he was digging a new border yesterday morning.'

Susan blinked. 'Didn't you say your grandmother died something like three years ago? It would be quite remarkable for it to turn up now, but it would be wonderful for you if it has.'

'Bit of a coincidence, isn't it – you know, it turning up the day after I told our dog-walking group about it?'

Susan caught the ironic tone in Colette's voice and looked over at her. 'Sorry, am I missing something here?'

Colette shrugged. 'I'll have to see if it's Gran's locket first.'

Before Susan could ask her any more, she realised they were about to cross the road to go on to the Ventnor beach.

Susan, an islander by birth, had now lived in Ventnor for forty years. The town had been built following the steep zig-zag roads winding down from St Boniface Down to the beach below. Susan loved bringing her dog down here, either to walk on the beach or along the esplanade from the fishing haven at one end to the Spy Glass Inn at the other.

Ahead of her on the beach this morning, Susan saw some of the group of dog-walking friends.

This small group of friends met up, in some combination, most mornings. Apart from Susan and Colette, the group consisted of Nikki and Nathan, the owners of the hotel, The Glanville, with their chefs, Trystan and Torri. The only other members were Beatrice, a retired jeweller, and Robert, a retired police officer.

Today Susan could see just Nikki and Torri from the hotel standing with Beatrice.

Nikki looked over at them as they arrived and started frantically waving to them.

'Now, I wonder what Nikki is so excited about today?' commented Susan.

'Oh, god – I think I know—'

Susan heard the tension in Colette's voice, but before she could comment, she saw Nikki was running towards them, hand outstretched.

As usual, Nikki was wearing her faux fur coat. Her red hair and voluminous leather bag were flying wildly in the wind. Her docile black Labrador, Duke, followed quietly behind her.

'What do you make of this?' Nikki asked breathlessly. She thrust her left hand in front of Susan.

'Oh, Nikki, congratulations.'

'Thanks, yes, we're finally engaged. Nathan gave me this late last night. We've had the hotel for three years and now we're becoming proper grown-ups at forty! I've finally given in to the charms of my surfer boy.'

The small diamond ring on a thin gold band was far more delicate than any of the garish dress jewellery on her wrists and fingers. 'I know, it's miniscule.' Nikki took her hand away. 'One day, Nathan will replace it with a giant ruby or diamond but, until then, this is all I have.'

'It's a beautiful ring.' Susan smiled up at Nikki.

Beatrice and Torri came to join them. Beatrice was a smart older lady in a silk headscarf, perfect make-up, mackintosh, and Hunter boots. She and Susan were both in their early sixties but couldn't have looked more different. Unlike Beatrice, Susan had simply pulled on comfy jeans and a jumper, and thrown on an old parka. Her shoulder-length brown curly hair had the odd streak of grey, and her deep brown eyes now looked out from behind her smart new blue-framed Varifocals that replaced the numerous cheap pairs of reading glasses that were scattered around the house.

Beatrice leant forward and gently pulled Nikki's hand towards her. She examined the stone in the ring and then, unsmiling, she let go of Nikki's hand.

'It may be modest but at least it is a genuine diamond.'

Nikki blushed. 'You should be glad Nathan's not embezzling hotel funds to buy me a decent ring.'

Beatrice pursed her lips. 'I am sure Nathan would never do such a thing. You two have a lot more to lose than me if the hotel fails.'

Nikki turned to Colette. 'Do you approve?'

'Of course, congratulations,' Colette replied quietly.

Susan glanced at Colette and wondered why she saw consternation in her eyes.

Beatrice suggested they let the dogs off their leads. Her Dalmatian, Biddy, went rushing off, tearing aimlessly but joyfully about. Nikki's Labrador, Duke, didn't go far, preferring to stay close by. Susan and Colette's cocker spaniels ran to join Torri's terrier, Max, and the three dogs, noses down, went off to dig holes and sniff out seaweed.

'And are you going to tell us when the big day will be?' asked Torri quietly, her soft Welsh tones coating her words. Torri was the pastry chef, working with her partner, Trystan, the inspirational and ambitious head chef at the hotel. Torri was huddled inside a large full-length waterproof, and you could just make out her grey eyes and red nose from under an orange woollen hat and scarf.

'We're not going to need you to make a huge cake if that's what you're thinking,' laughed Nikki.

Susan noticed Torri didn't laugh but looked down at the sand.

'We're not having anything like that,' continued Nikki, oblivious to Torri's feelings. 'We've given notice to the registry office; we will get married in a month. It will all be very quick and understated – no guests or parties.'

Susan was surprised at Nikki's plans for such a quiet wedding. Despite Nikki having maintained a pretty cynical view of marriage, Susan had assumed that if she ever did have a wedding, it would be some big, fancy occasion, with Nikki enjoying every moment of being in the limelight.

'I know I seem the kind to have a big splash, but I don't want that. I am getting married because it's important to Nathan, that is all. We'll pop and get married and back to work.'

'But surely you'll have a honeymoon?' asked Beatrice.

'Nathan had ideas of surfing in Portugal, but I told him we can't be taking time away from the hotel at the moment. Now, tomorrow afternoon, Nathan and I are having little celebration over at Steephill Cove, but for something far more significant. It will be three years to the day that the hotel opened and I expect you all to come. We'll meet at the Falaise car park at about two.'

'Is that why you closed the kitchen tomorrow evening?' asked Torri.

'Yes, we've so few guests this weekend, I've decided they can find places around here for a meal, the B team can cope with providing sandwiches and snacks if needs be. Susan, you must make sure Robert comes.'

'Shall I ask Trystan to make some nibbles?' asked Torri. 'And I could make my *pastéis de nata* if you would like?'

Susan recognised Torri's signature dish; a delicious Portuguese egg custard tart sprinkled with cinnamon.

'Great,' replied Nikki, 'and we'll provide the bubbly.' She paused and looked at Colette. 'You must come as well, you're part of the family now, aren't you?'

'Thanks,' Colette answered.

Beatrice started to walk away, heading towards her Dalmatian, who was trying to pinch a stick off Colette's dog, Libs, and Colette went to join her. Torri, spotting her terrier running into the sea, ran off alone after him.

Susan stayed walking with Nikki, whose Labrador continued to be content walking quietly by her side.

'Thank you for inviting Colette to the cove tomorrow,' Susan said.

'Of course, like I said, she's part of our family now.'

Susan looked over at Beatrice and Colette, who, having sorted out the dogs, now seemed to be in the midst of a very intense conversation. 'Beatrice appears to be reprimanding Colette. Has something happened?'

Nikki stepped closer, her eyes bright, as always, at the prospect of gossip. 'Beatrice told me she'd caught Colette snooping when she was there cleaning. I told her not to fuss. I mean, I would have a nose about if I were cleaning, wouldn't you? I know Colette rummages among my things, but I lock anything valuable away, or bury it in the wardrobe. Beatrice should just be glad Colette fits her in on top of her hotel work. It's so hard to get anyone to clean nowadays.'

Susan glanced over again, the conversation still looked pretty heated. 'I agree, and I am sure Colette doesn't mean any harm. I find her to be very trustworthy and I'm enjoying the company. It's been so interesting. I've never watched much TV, as you know, but Colette has introduced me to *Married at First Sight* and *First Dates*.'

Nikki laughed. 'I can't imagine you watching them. It's not as if they are going to talk about climate change or politics.'

'No, but it is about relationships and how we treat each other,' Susan laughed. 'And we do enjoy guessing who is going to get together with who.'

'I'm glad Colette living with you is working out so well. I'm sure it's persuaded her to stay on longer and I'd hate to lose her now. To be honest, she's surprised me. I know this isn't fair, but somehow you don't expect someone that good-looking and fragile to work so hard. She only came to clean staff and communal areas and now she covers the bar and the guests' rooms if needed – she'll do anything I ask. I am giving her more and more responsibility.'

'And I know she appreciates it.'

'Good. And so Beatrice had better not upset her. These young girls can be so sensitive and Colette could just up sticks and leave the island. You know how severe Beatrice can be, she even frightens me sometimes. I really appreciate her supporting us with the hotel, but I always said to Nathan that I'd not want to get on the wrong side of her.'

Susan laughed. 'I know she can be rather frank, but she's been a good friend to me. And she's been here about five years now, hasn't she? Not long in island years, I know, but I think she has tried to fit in. She told me it's been a fresh start for her.'

'I don't know, I sometimes imagine that if you strip away the posh voice and the headscarves, you'd discover someone quite different. Maybe she was the head of some gang in London, planning heists and ordering hit men about.'

Susan rolled her eyes. 'Honestly, Nikki, I can see why you are so good at acting, you have such a vivid imagination. I don't think a respectable jeweller is going to have had that colourful a past. And she does have a soft side. Look at the way she is with Biddy. When Biddy had to go into the vet's for a scan on her leg, she was a wreck. Beatrice dotes on her.'

'That's what we all have in common, isn't it – we're all dotty about our dogs. Colette and her little dog Libs are so close, aren't they?'

'Libs is like her family. I have an idea her parents died when she was young. She's only told me about her grandmother, who she used to stay with over here as a child.'

'Yes, and fancy her grandmother being a resident at the nursing home I worked in. I don't know why Colette didn't mention that before Thursday. I knew her grandmother, Pam, very well. She was a lovely lady, quiet, always so polite.'

'Oh, something quite intriguing has happened. Colette has just told me that the nursing home phoned her last night, and they think they might have found her grandmother's locket that went missing after she died.'

'No! Fancy it turning up after all this time.'

'It does seem rather extraordinary, doesn't it? It would be lovely for Colette. Does Colette remind you of her grandmother at all?'

'Despite the age difference, I can see a likeness between them. They have that fine bone structure, lovely blue eyes. I could see her gran had been very pretty in her youth.' Nikki paused. 'It's so strange to be talking about my nursing home days, it seems a life-time ago now.'

'That's because the hotel is your life now. Nathan and you must be so proud. The Glanville is a real success.'

'To be fair, it's been a team effort. It was like fate brought the five of us together at the nursing home and gave us the dream.' Nikki glanced at Torri, who was walking towards them, grim-faced and clutching her coat. Nikki laughed. 'Well, it might not have exactly been Torri's dream, to be fair, but fortunately, she will always follow Trystan.'

Torri approached them. 'I'm going to make a move. I need to wash Max's paws before I get on. It's so cold, I hate the idea of another long winter ahead of us.'

'Well, we've got palm trees and our own botanic gardens, what more could you want?' Nikki gestured to the hills behind them.

Torri glanced at Nikki. 'Sunshine? Still, Trystan is settled for now. I have to live in hope; as my mam used to say to me, you can never tell what tomorrow will bring.'

Nikki and Susan watched Torri and her terrier walk away.

'Blimey,' exclaimed Nikki. 'What's got into her?'

'I feel sorry for her, it's not easy putting her life on hold for Trystan like this. I wonder why she puts up with it?'

'Because she is completely besotted with Trystan. In any case, she's not doing so badly. Coming to the hotel has given her huge opportunities as well. She's gone from someone washing up to a pastry chef, and she's good at it. She may have a load of academic qualifications, but she had no skills for the workplace, we've given her a big break.'

Susan smiled. 'I'm not sure she sees it like that.'

'Well, she needs to wake up and be grateful. As for Trystan, this is going to be the making of him. I always knew he was a great chef. When he was working in the kitchen at the nursing home, he couldn't resist busting the budget, but the food was gorgeous.'

'They must have been sorry to lose him.'

'It was pretty obvious he was going to move on to bigger things. If I hadn't asked him to come with us to the hotel, someone else would have snapped him up. Still, I'll admit it was a blow for them. The home lost me, Trystan and Torri at the same time. And, of course, my Nathan was their handyman. Anyway, as I said, that all seems a lifetime ago now.'

Ahead of them, Colette had called Libs over and they were leaving the beach. Rocco, having lost his friend, came running back to Susan.

Beatrice stayed ahead of them, throwing a ball for Biddy.

'How are things going between you and your Robert?' asked Nikki, grinning.

'He's not my Robert,' Susan replied sternly.

'You went to a concert up at Medina, didn't you?'

'We went with a group to an orchestral concert. To be honest, I am sure Robert was bored rigid by the whole thing.'

Nikki laughed. 'Ah, the things men do for love.'

Susan gave her a mock scowl. 'There is nothing like that going on. In any case, I am still officially a married woman, my decree absolute is not through yet.'

'But you've been on your own for a few years now. You should go out, meet someone new, get on one of those dating sites.'

'I will never do that, in fact, I'm not sure I'll ever want to commit to a long-term relationship again. I'm quite happy on my own,' Susan replied firmly.

'Good for you. However, I'll be a married woman soon. No more one-night stands for me.'

They had caught up with Beatrice, who was putting the lead back on Biddy. 'It's time we made our way home.'

'You and Colette were having a heavy chat,' Nikki said. 'What was going on? Were you having a go at her for snooping?'

Beatrice's eyebrows shot up. 'Certainly not. No, we were simply talking about possibly increasing her hours, but of course, she is doing a lot of extra work for you now.'

Susan was sure that wasn't true. It had clearly been a far more serious conversation than that.

Nikki, however, let it go and said, 'Susan was telling me Colette has heard from the nursing home about that locket that had gone missing, apparently they might have found it.'

Beatrice screwed her up eyes up. 'How strange. I really don't understand what is going on. Last Thursday, Colette suddenly tells us about her grandmother being up at the nursing home, and now there is all this business with the locket.'

'It could be that Colette hadn't realised any of you'd had any connection with the nursing home. She has only been here a few months,' said Susan.

'She knew I went up there with Biddy, and I'm sure Nikki must have mentioned about working there in the past,' argued Beatrice. 'No, it's strange. She is very secretive; you never know quite what she is going to come out with next. I thought she seemed quite innocent and charming when I first met her, but now I'm not so sure.' There was a heaviness to her tone that Susan didn't quite understand.

'That's the problem with people coming from the mainland. You know nothing about them when they arrive, they can spin any old story. Still, we usually find out their secrets in the end.' Nikki laughed as she spoke, but there was an edge to her voice.

'But it's not quite fair to assume us mainlanders have the monopoly on secrets, is it?' Beatrice retorted sharply.

Susan watched as the two women held each other's gaze, a tight smile on each of their faces, pretending it was a game but clearly deadly serious. She wondered who would break first, the tension was unbearable, like someone slowly pushing a blunt pin into a balloon.

It was Nikki who gave in, but she spoke with a forced casualness. 'I think we could all do with going home and getting a decent cup of coffee.'

Beatrice nodded but didn't smile. They called the dogs and left the beach together.

Susan began the long climb back up to her house, stopping a few times to catch her breath. As loath as she was to admit it, this ascent was definitely getting harder; she would be glad to get home.

It had been a strange time on the beach. Usually, the meet-ups were pretty relaxed, the usual chat about the weather, their dogs and the like, but today it had been different. Something was wrong, what was it she'd felt in the air down there? Susan paused again and looked down at the beach. And then she knew exactly what it was. It had been fear. She'd seen it in their eyes, but why? What was everyone so scared of?

2

Later that evening, Susan was standing in her kitchen, looking out of the window at Colette, who was sitting on a seat high up the steeply terraced garden. It was dark, and she could only make out the silhouette of Colette, from the solar lights, and the burning end of her cigarette.

Susan had not managed to talk to Colette since the dog walk that morning and still didn't know how she'd got on at the nursing home. In the afternoon, she'd received a text from Colette asking her if she minded taking Libs out for a walk as something had cropped up. And then, about an hour ago, she had heard the front door slam. Colette had gone straight up to her room and then out into the garden to smoke. Susan wondered what was up. Colette's dog Libs was out there with her, but Rocco was tucked up in his bed, close to the log burner.

He lifted his head lazily as if sensing she was watching him and she went over, knelt next to him, and stroked his head. Rocco was a sable roan cocker spaniel, with speckles of blue roan. She loved his black nose, his gentleness and timid disposition. 'Us two are well matched, aren't we,' she whispered. Rocco looked up, his gentle eyes pools of love and trust. 'We look after each other.' She kissed him on the head and Rocco let out a contented sigh and flopped back down in his bed. Susan got up slowly, aware that a few years ago she'd have jumped up easily. Goodness, getting older was hard work, and she still considered herself quite young at sixty-two. Her daughter Zoe had bought her some awful yoga video for Christmas, *Yoga for the Elderly*, maybe she should actually try to do it sometime. From the way her knees were creaking now, maybe it wasn't such a stupid idea.

Susan realised Colette was still outside and decided she should make a drink and go and check on her. She put the remains of her ready meal in the fridge, and once she'd wrapped herself up in an old coat, she went outside.

She carefully climbed the steps.

'Are you warm enough? It's freezing out here.'

Colette didn't reply, or even look at her, but remained staring ahead.

'Do you want to talk? How did it go at the nursing home?' Susan asked.

Slowly Colette turned her head to face Susan, her eyes wide, her lips trembling. She moved along the seat as an invitation for Susan to sit next to her.

Susan breathed in the cold evening air, looked at the sea in the distance. Tonight, a thick black line divided the sea from the sky, which was full of stars, as if someone had sprinkled a black velvet cloth with icing sugar, and the moon was a clear, bright crescent.

She was roused from her thoughts by a slight sniff from Colette. She turned and for the first time saw the tears falling, slow droplets of rain down a sheet of glass. One hand shook as she held the thin rolled-up cigarette; the other hand was clenched into a tight fist in her lap.

'Didn't they have the locket?' Susan asked gently.

Colette held out the clenched fist to Susan like a child scared to share a treasure. Then she turned her hand over. Susan watched as each finger slowly released its grip, until she saw what was hidden inside.

The light by the step picked out the glint of a round gold locket, with tiny birds engraved on it.

Susan gasped. 'Oh, they really had found your gran's locket, but that's wonderful.' She looked at Colette, confused – why was she so upset, this was good news, wasn't it?

Colette stamped out the remainder of her cigarette and then carefully opened the locket.

'That is a photograph of my gran and this, well, this is me. It must have been one of the few photographs my mum gave Gran of me, it's lovely she kept it in here, isn't it?'

Susan held the locket closer to one of the solar lights. The photograph of Colette's gran must have been taken when she was in her twenties and, despite the changes in fashion, Susan was immediately struck by the likeness between Colette and her gran. The photo showed a beautiful woman; fine blonde hair styled in a short bob only accentuated the fine bone structure, wide eyes, and perfectly shaped mouth.

'You look like your gran.'

'Thank you. I would love to think I looked like that.' Collette's face softened into a smile. 'Gran put her looks down to these.' Colette picked up a mug which was on the ground next to her and Susan smelt warm, rich autumn berries. 'Torri gave this to me. Herbal tea is trendy now, and yet my gran drank it every night, even at the nursing home.' Colette looked back at the locket. 'Of course, when I visited Gran as a child, she didn't look like this, she was quite a bit older.'

The smile on Colette's face was warm and innocent. 'Coming over here to see Gran when I was very little were some of the best

times in my life. She was kind and gentle, despite her past.' Colette's
voice tightened.

'What had happened to your gran?'

'Gran's husband was abusive, and she had a very difficult life
with him, but he died young. When their two children, my mum
and uncle, were grown up, my gran came to live over here, but they
stayed on the mainland. My mum married and she would bring me
over to stay with Gran. I loved it.'

Colette sighed and looked ahead. 'It was bliss. I'd sit on the
beach, making sandcastles, the sea twinkling. Gran would bring a
picnic. She read me stories. She didn't once tell me to shut up. She
never hit me, never shouted at me. I believed, you know, she
liked me—'

Susan found listening to Colette talk, as if shouting and hitting
were the norm, heart-breaking. 'It doesn't sound as if your own
home life was very happy.'

'It was awful. Mum had married someone like her own father,
and he abused us both. Mum then fell out with my gran and
stopped bringing me over. Social services became involved with my
family, and I spent the rest of my childhood in and out of foster
homes and in care.'

'You said you came to see your gran the week before she died?'

'I did, Gran was in the nursing home by then. My mum had
died, you see, and so I felt I could come over. I'm glad I did, Gran
died a week later, at least I saw her one more time.'

'I'm very sorry your life has been so hard.'

'You understand, don't you, with all the foster children you've
looked after.' Colette took a long drag on her cigarette. 'The
problem is so many people feel sorry for the abused child, but then
we grow up and we're expected to behave like nothing has
happened, as if we've learnt all the things a normal upbringing
teaches you.' Colette stubbed out the end of her cigarette and

pointed to the picture in the locket. 'That is why this means so much to me: it was my childhood. That's it, the only time I could truly be a child.'

'I can understand why it's so special to you, I am so glad they found the locket.' Susan frowned, seeing the tears and anger she saw etched on Colette's face. 'Is it very difficult being reminded of the past like this?'

'It is, but that's not why I am so upset.'

'What's wrong then?'

'I don't think it was just a lucky coincidence that my gran's locket turned up the day after I mentioned it to our group on the beach. You see, I was laying a trap, seeing if someone would fall into it.'

Susan's eyes widened. 'What on earth do you mean?'

'You are not going to like this. I am sure now someone in our group, most of whom were working in the nursing home when my gran lived there, stole her locket just before she died.'

Susan blinked hard. 'Why ever would you think that?'

'My grandmother kept this in a secret compartment in her jewellery box, with two other items that also disappeared. I saw these things the week before she died, when I visited. There was the locket, a valuable ruby and diamond brooch and a children's book she used to read to me. When my uncle went to collect her possessions from the home the day after she died, all these things were missing.'

'What did the nursing home say?'

'They didn't know anything about them. You see, my gran hadn't told them about them when she went in there. I don't suppose they ever imagined my gran would own something as valuable as the brooch, no one would have checked.'

'But it would have been sensible to put the brooch in the safe at the home.'

'I know, but Gran didn't trust anyone, and she was careful. It was a very clever jewellery box. You have to position a carved flower on the top to find the key. You use this to open a compartment in the base. That is where Gran kept her valuables.'

Colette put the locket in her pocket, and then took out her tobacco and papers, starting the ritual of choosing a paper, adding the tobacco and rolling the cigarette. Only once she'd lit it did she look ready to resume the conversation.

'So, was your grandmother well off?'

'Oh, no. But before she married, she worked for a rich family, and became very friendly with the woman who owned the house. She gave Gran the ruby brooch and the book. Gran read the book to my mum when she was little and then to me. I was very upset when I found they'd disappeared.'

'Did your gran tell anyone else at the nursing home about her hidden valuables?'

'She told Alice, her friend, but no one else. They disappeared between the time of my visit on the Saturday and the day my uncle went to collect my gran's belongings, on the Monday after she died, that would have been nine days later.'

'Did your uncle report this to the police?'

'No, he didn't want to. He didn't believe the brooch was real diamonds or anything like that and so he didn't bother. He had his own issues with my gran, to be honest, he didn't want to get involved.'

'I am very sorry your grandmother's possessions went missing, but I don't see why you are suspecting our friends in the dog-walking group even if they were at the nursing home at the time. A lot of people would have been in and out of the home in those nine days.'

'You're right. However, I have good reason for suspecting one of this particular group. Like I said, when I visited my gran at the nursing home, she showed me her valuables. As she was showing me them, she told me she was worried. A few days before, she'd come back to her room to find someone from the "hotel bunch", as she called them, looking at her jewellery box. Gran said they'd looked very guilty when she asked them what they were doing. I asked her who the hotel bunch were.'

'And what did she say?'

'She mentioned Nikki, who looked after her a lot, and her boyfriend Nathan, who everyone liked. He'd put up some shelves for Gran. Then there was the chef who cooked wonderful food, who I know was Trystan, and his girlfriend in the kitchen, Torri. Gran liked her because she took her cakes. And finally, Gran said there was the woman who brought her dog in, Beatrice. Gran loved dogs and chatted to her a lot.'

'It sounds as if she liked them all. Why on earth did she think one of them would steal from her?'

'That's what I said. Gran told me she had liked them all before this incident with the jewellery box, but that it was as if she'd seen something very disturbing in the eyes of this person, she told me she would be glad when they left. She felt she'd got them all wrong, and she didn't trust them any more.'

'I wonder if she was overreacting a bit?' asked Susan gently.

'I thought that, to be honest. I told her to put the valuables in the nursing home safe and stop worrying. However, she told me she was going to get the brooch valued first, apparently some resident's son was a jeweller.'

'She wasn't sure it was valuable?'

'Gran must have wondered about it, after all, if it was real diamonds and rubies, well, it would have been an incredibly valuable gift for her employer to have given her. I think she'd put off having it properly valued in case it was a fake, she liked living with the dream, I guess, and it was very pretty. I can understand why she wanted to keep it with her, it would have been sad not to be able to look at it and remember happier times whenever she wanted.'

'I suppose that could be true,' Susan sighed, looking out to sea.

'Anyway, whether the brooch is valuable or not, when I found out about it and the other things going missing when I visited my uncle in January, I knew I had to do something about it and I came over. I remembered Gran saying about the "hotel bunch" and it was somewhere to start. Cleaning jobs are always easy to find, and so I got a job at The Glanville. It meant I had a good excuse to search around, as well as get to know the people. I also managed to get a job with Beatrice.'

'And have you found anything?'

'None of my gran's valuables. I was desperate and that is why I decided that I would try one last thing. I would reveal my connection to my gran, and say I was looking for her locket, and that is what I did on Thursday. Now, I knew that this was going to really upset anyone there who had stolen Gran's things. Let's face it, they thought they'd got away with it. My gamble was that if they thought all I needed was the locket returned and then I would leave everything be, they would return it to shut me up. And I was right, the next morning, the gardener very conveniently discovered the locket in the area of the garden where he was clearly working.'

'But maybe it was a coincidence and the locket had been there all along.'

'No way. No, it was put there the night before, I'm sure of it, and it proves to me that one of those people on the beach was the thief.'

Colette sat back, her shoulders relaxed, and she sipped her drink. Susan took a moment to try to unscramble all that Colette had told her. Had Colette really proven that one of her friends in the group had stolen valuables from her gran? It seemed so outrageous somehow. They were all such normal, respectable people, would they really do such a thing?

As if reading her mind, Colette said, 'I know it's very hard for you to accept that one of your friends did this, but I'm sure I'm right.'

Susan shook her head. 'But why would they have held onto the locket all this time and where are the brooch and book?'

'My theory is that the item that was most attractive to a thief was the brooch. It was so beautiful and could have been worth a lot of money. I am guessing the thief took all three objects and examined them later. Now, the book they might have thrown away, the brooch they might have sold, but the locket was more difficult. They couldn't sell it as it was too easy to identify—'

'So why not throw it away?'

'My guess is that it may have been their insurance, something they could use to incriminate someone else if the police had somehow got involved at any point.'

'I suppose it's possible. At least now you have the locket, I'm pleased about that. If you think the brooch and the book have been disposed of, I don't suppose there is much else you can do.'

'But there is, I have to know the whole truth now.'

'But even if it was someone in the group, they're hardly likely to just come out and tell you what they did.'

Colette took a deep breath. 'I realise that they're not going to own up easily, but I have a plan. If they haven't the decency to own up to what they did of their own accord, I will force them out into the open.'

'What do you mean?' asked Susan, alarmed.

Colette took a final hard drag on her cigarette, her hands shaking, her eyes wide with fear and excitement. 'You'll find out tomorrow, you won't like it—'

'What are you going to do? Tell me.'

'No, not now.'

'These are my friends, Colette; they are good people—'

'Are they? If one of them stole from my grandmother, they are not the respectable person you assume they are.'

Susan heard the passion in Colette's voice, saw the way she clenched and unclenched her fist, she looked so young and vulnerable, a child consumed with anger and frustration.

'It might have been a moment of madness, something they really regret now.'

Colette stamped her feet in frustration. 'No, this isn't someone who just slipped up. This is a person who knew my grandmother, knew she trusted them. And yet they were willing to take from her not just money but her most precious possessions, her memories. What kind of person does that? I tell you, Susan, this person is nasty. The more I think about this person, the more frightening I find them.'

'Frightening?'

'Of course. Doesn't it scare you to imagine you that someone can be this dark inside and yet play the part of a respectable, kind person so successfully?'

'Oh, Colette—'

'I mean it, Susan, they are dangerous, and I am going to find this person and make sure everyone knows what they have done.'

A sudden gust of cold night air caused Susan to pull her coat around her. 'It's getting cold, let's carry on talking inside.'

'You're right, poor Libs must be dying to get in the warm.'

They got up and carefully descended the steps down through the garden and went back into the house.

'I'm done in, actually, I think I'll go to bed,' said Colette.

'But wouldn't you like to keep talking? I'm worried about you.'

'I can look after myself, you're not to worry. Thanks for listening to me, it really helped.'

She gave a quick smile, called Libs and the two of them made their way up the stairs.

Susan could see Colette needed some time alone now, and so she went and opened her laptop. There were a few forums she went on, offering advice and support. She also supported some organisations covering a range of things including women's rights, animal rights, conservation, and green issues. Usually, by the time she'd caught up with each, her evening was pretty much done. However, she found it hard to concentrate and instead kept replaying the conversation she'd had with Colette over and over in her head.

Was it really possible that one of her dog-walking friends was a thief capable of stealing from an elderly woman? It was very sinister to think you could have got someone so wrong. Susan shivered. Colette had spoken with such passion and determination about finding this person. But what were these plans she had? It sounded risky, dangerous even, and Susan was very worried about what the next day might bring.

After walking Rocco the next morning, Susan set about making her Sunday morning call to her daughter Zoe, the deputy head of a large primary school on the mainland.

Zoe answered the phone promptly. 'Hi, Mum. How are you?'

'I'm well, thank you. How is school?'

'Manic. Christmas play this year is bigger than ever, my fault, I suppose, but it's exciting. We're working with an amateur dramatic company in town. However, rumour has it that Ofsted are coming in January. They're starting to revisit the schools rated outstanding so there's a mountain of work to do.'

Susan knew it was a waste of time trying to persuade her daughter to work less and simply made sympathetic noises. Zoe soon, however, moved on to talk about her partner, Fay, who had recently started a new job.

'She's loving it and she has so many perks. Subsidised lunches, gym membership, free yoga classes—'

'Her job is very pressurised, she's a manager now.'

'I know, and she's always saying they expect her to be on call twenty-four seven, but I don't see how it's as hard as my job. Still, at least I believe in what I'm doing, I suppose. Now, tell me, how is your so-called lodger? Still there, I assume?'

'Of course, and Colette's fine.'

'You and your strays—'

'Zoe, that's a terrible expression.'

'Only joking. It's good for you to have someone to look after. I hope it's making you cook properly, and stopped you just living on ready meals?'

Susan thought of the remnants in the fridge but simply answered, 'Of course. Actually, yesterday Colette was talking about studying psychology. I'd love her to do some more study, she can stay with me for a while longer if she would like to.'

'I wonder if there are any charities that might support her, it might be worth looking into that. Now, I was wondering if you fancied coming over for the day on Saturday? Bring Rocco. I miss him. The thing is, Dad is coming the weekend after next, and there is something I want to tell you before I see him.'

'What's this about, then?'

'I'd rather chat in person.'

Susan was a bit mystified, but she could tell from her voice Zoe wasn't going to say any more. 'So, you're seeing your dad? That'll be good. You've not seen him for a while, have you?'

She was desperately trying to keep her voice relaxed and upbeat. Susan's husband, Steve, had left her two years ago and Zoe had taken it hard. As hurt as Susan had been, she'd never wanted to break up Zoe's relationship with her father and was genuinely pleased they seemed to be getting on better.

'Dad has been off sailing with Hester in Spain,' Zoe explained. 'He wants to catch up. Now, please, can you come over Saturday?'

'Of course.'

Susan heard the doorbell ring at Zoe's house.

'Sorry, Mum—'

'It's okay, I can hear someone's arrived. I'll see you next Saturday.'

Susan wondered if Zoe was contemplating another move, but she would normally just come out and tell her that. However, as frustrating as it was, Susan knew she had issues she wanted to check up on, and so she opened her laptop again. However, before she could start, Colette returned from her early shift at the hotel.

Libs rushed over to greet her.

'Good morning at work?' Susan asked.

'Not too bad. Nikki reminded me of the celebration this afternoon.'

'Trystan and Torri are providing food, I assume they know about your allergies?'

'I've told them not to worry about me, it's easier for me to cater for myself. You know what it's like, it's not just the obvious things like crab or molluscs, but they cook so much shellfish in the kitchen, I'd prefer not to eat food prepared there, you have to watch out for cross-contamination.'

'That's very sensible.'

'I have to be. You know how I love sweets? I've discovered that some have fish gelatine in, that's made from shellfish. I'm obsessed with labels now.'

Susan closed her laptop. 'How long have you had this allergy?'

'I only found out by accident. I'd never eaten any shellfish really, but then about a year ago we went to this restaurant. I had this awful reaction, anaphylactic shock they called it. It was so quick, it happened there and then in the restaurant. Fortunately, they acted quickly, and an ambulance came. It was the scariest thing in my life, I just couldn't breathe, I thought I was going to die. Anyway, that's why I'm super careful. I always have an EpiPen with me, although I've not had to use it yet, thank god.'

Colette opened her handbag, unzipped a compartment, and

took out what looked like a narrow cosmetic pouch made of bright red velvet, beautifully embroidered with gold thread. 'A friend gave this pouch to me when I was travelling a few years ago, I can just fit my EpiPen in it. The trouble is the zip is broken and so I have to use a rubber band to keep it together. I think he'd like me to use it for something like this, he was always looking out for me. He was very special to me. He died, you see, and this always reminds me of him.'

Colette paused, looked down at the pouch. 'It's a shame it's broken. I reckon I'll replace it with one of those proper medical ones, they are waterproof and everything. But I'll never throw this away.'

Susan could see tears in Colette's eyes, but she clearly didn't want to say any more. Instead, she slid the beautiful velvet pouch back into the compartment and zipped it up. Looking up, she spoke in a business-like manner. 'Now, I'm still really looking forward to this walk to Steephill Cove. As I've not got work tomorrow, I'm going to stay down late, watch films on my phone in the dark.'

'You can't stay down there tonight; it'll be far too cold and anyway, it's not safe.'

'I'll be fine, I've done it lots of times before, I've just never told you. Honestly, Susan, it's magical down there. I usually walk along to Castle Cove, sit by the rocks and I imagine I'm a mermaid.'

'Oh, Colette, you shouldn't be doing this, not now it's autumn.'

Colette flicked her hand. 'I'll be fine, I just need my thickest coat and plenty to eat.'

She took out a packet of marshmallows out of the cupboard. They were in a smart white box, with silver lettering on. 'My luxury, honestly, they are the best, worth every penny and they don't contain fish gelatine. Not like those ones up in the hotel vending machine. I have to watch it there, I'm always picking up a packet of sweets after work.'

'You need more than sweets.'

'You're a fine one to talk. The only time I've seen you eat a proper meal is when I cook for you. Now, I shall take lots of bread and cheese spread.' Colette filled her bottle with water and laughed. 'Us bright young things know how to have fun. Rock and roll.'

'Would you like to take my flask, make a hot drink?'

'No. Water is fine for me, honestly.'

'Fine and, um, Colette—' Susan began nervously. 'Those things we talked about last night, the business with the locket. Be careful this afternoon if you do bring it up. People here like you and want to support you. Don't offend them, will you?'

Colette put her arm around Susan's shoulders. 'If one of them turns nasty, I will set you onto them.' She pointed up to a selection of photographs on the pinboard. 'Look at you on all your marches and protests, fighting war, nuclear weapons, cuts in benefits, you really were a fighter.'

'I was, and I hope I still am. But seriously, Colette, this is not the same. And just say one of them did have anything to do with your grandmother's valuables, then things could get nasty. I worry about you. You've got the locket; I wish you would let it be now.'

'I will be fine; don't you worry about me.' She kissed Susan on the cheek. 'You are really special, and now let me give you a piece of advice for a change. Remember, men are overrated.'

Susan blinked. 'Why on earth are you telling me that?'

'I know how friendly you've been getting with Robert, and he seems a nice enough guy. However, I'm just saying, be careful, I don't want you getting hurt again.'

Susan smiled. 'Thank you for your concern, I promise to look after myself. Now we ought to get ready to go.'

Laughing, Colette left the kitchen and went to change.

Susan went into the living room and checked out of the window. The sky was crisp blue and the sea sparkled; it was a perfect day for the walk, though on the horizon she saw a few thin grey clouds, hovering, waiting. Susan didn't believe in premonitions, but she recognised a feeling of disquiet. Her grandmother had once explained how the barometer in her hallway worked, measuring atmospheric pressure, able to predict a storm was on its way. It seemed to Susan that her body was measuring the growing pressure around her, foretelling a storm. Something terrible was about to happen but, unlike that barometer, she had no idea what it was or when it would happen.

4

Susan was glad to get out in the fresh air and breathed deeply as she walked along the seafront with Colette. They climbed the steep path behind the Spyglass Inn and saw the others waiting for them.

'Susan!' shouted Robert, her name carrying around the car park. It was lovely to be greeted so warmly, even if it was a bit embarrassing. Susan's parents and her husband Steve had all been so reserved. Robert's exuberance was certainly a huge contrast, and she was never quite sure how to cope with it.

Robert came over to her. Even in appearance, he couldn't be more of a contrast to Steve. They were both quite a bit taller than her, but while Steve was slim, with a shock of white hair and wore glasses, Robert was athletic, had closely shaved hair and even a tattoo on his forearm.

He had his two dogs with him. Gem Gem was a stunning liver and white English pointer crossed with a springer spaniel. She had short hair and silky soft ears, was very gentle, and loved flushing out pheasants and chasing rabbits. Dougie was a loving, good-natured black cocker spaniel, with a flash of white on his chest. His coat was like crushed velvet, and despite being thirteen, he was still very active.

The dogs all gave each other a sniff in greeting.

'How ya doing, then?' he asked.

'I'm fine.' She looked over at the others and called to Nikki, 'Looks like we're all here, Beatrice is going to meet us there.'

'Great, let's get going,' shouted Nikki and they set out.

As Susan had guessed, it proved to be a wonderful day for the walk, which followed the coastline. They started high up, and she noticed the concrete shelter up on the grass where she used to sit with Zoe on windy days. Just beside it, the name Ventnor, made out of white rocks, was arranged on a grassy bank. Susan loved the way Ventnor proudly displayed its name around the town in these giant letters; it showed a pride and confidence in itself.

There was a beautiful view down to the sea from here, and then they started the steep climb down.

They passed through a metal gate and climbed down some steps before taking some narrower muddy paths where you could see and hear the sea as you walked. Either side was bracken, hedges with their remaining berries, small trees with their remaining gold autumn leaves. Down some wooden steps to Flower Brook. Susan loved this little park, with two springs running into it from the downs above and home to scores of interesting wildflowers and creatures, the gentle sound of water trickling contrasting with the sound of the waves below.

Having walked in single file up until this point, they now broke into small groups as they crossed the park. Nikki walked next to the man who was now her fiancé, Nathan. He had the fair good looks of an archetypal surfer and wore his blond hair up in a 'man-bun'. Torri walked with her partner, the chef, Trystan, an older, much more serious man, with greying hair and a beard. Colette walked alone, while Robert fell in naturally next to Susan and she started to ask him about his visit to the mainland.

'Good. I went to my son's and helped him build him a shed, so a productive day away.'

'Your children are lucky to have you.'

'You spoil your daughter when you see her.'

'I suppose I do. Mind you, she would never ask me, or her dad for that matter, to do any DIY! Now, what did you make of the news about Nathan and Nikki?'

'I was surprised when Nathan sent me a text,' said Robert. 'I never thought Nikki would agree to getting married.'

'I got the impression she was doing it for Nathan.'

'Maybe she has decided it's time to settle down, fully commit to Nathan.' He raised an eyebrow in a knowing way.

'Now what do you mean by that?'

Robert looked around and grinned. 'I'll tell you a bit of gossip. Pete, my mate who's still in the police force, is a member of the drama group Nikki is in. Now, he tells me that she seems to be very friendly with one of the members, they have a tendency to "disappear" during breaks in rehearsals.'

'Oh, honestly. I can't imagine Nikki having a relationship with anyone else. Nathan is always off surfing, and I've seen the girls who go down there with him. No one ever comments on that, do they? No, and that's because he's a man and he's allowed to go off and be "one of the lads".'

Robert laughed. 'Okay, you've made your point. Anyway, they are engaged now.'

'They are, and they make a good team up there. They have certainly transformed The Glanville since they took it over. If Trystan could get this Michelin star, it would be the making of the place and put Ventnor on the map.'

'Yes. Mind you, the town is changing slowly anyway, isn't it? For the better, I mean. Still crime, drugs and the like, but it's getting a good reputation as a place to come for a day out or for somewhere to eat in the evening. I've even seen it featured in the Sunday supplements as a new cool place to stay, or even buy.'

'I've seen that. Well, as long as it doesn't prevent locals buying somewhere to live. I'd hate to see Ventnor spoiled.' She laughed. 'I want it both ways, don't I? The tourists' and incomers' money, but nothing to change.'

They were now taking the steep descent to the sea. Susan held Rocco on a tight lead, so he didn't pull her over. The sound of the waves became louder as they descended to a concrete path that would lead them all the way to Steephill Cove.

Down here, the sea roared and crashed on to the artificial boulders, part of an enormous coastal protection scheme. This section of the walk took them through Castle Cove, which years ago was a private bathing place for the castle estate. The castle had gone and now the pathway along the front made the cove accessible to everyone. Susan loved how, even in the summer, she could walk here and not meet a soul.

Between the boulders was a long concrete jetty reaching down into the sea. Susan and Zoe used to stand on it, skimming stones.

Robert looked ahead to Colette, who was walking now with Trystan and Nikki.

'How has the so-called lodger been behaving then?'

'That's all going fine.'

'I bet she's still not paying you.'

'I don't want money. I know you had your reservations about me taking her in but, honestly, she's good company and she's working hard. I just hope she doesn't spoil things—' Susan paused.

'In what way?'

'I'm not sure I should say anything. I had a difficult conversation with Colette last night. I'm quite worried about her, actually.'

Robert checked around. 'No one is too close, tell me, what's up?'

Susan hesitated but then decided to share her concerns.

'It's to do with her gran, who was in the nursing home here, and her locket.'

'Colette told us about it last Thursday.'

'That's right. Well, the home contacted Colette yesterday morning. They found her gran's locket,' Susan explained.

Robert eyebrows shot up. 'After all this time? That was lucky.'

'Colette doesn't believe it had anything to do with luck.'

'What do you mean?'

Susan had found him good at keeping confidences and slowly she told him everything Colette had told her.

'So, she believes that either Nikki, Nathan, Torri or Trystan stole her gran's things?' said Robert, clearly unconvinced.

'Exactly, or possibly Beatrice as well.'

'Her evidence sounds extremely flimsy to me.' He grimaced. 'I know you like to support her, but be careful. Colette could be the kind of girl who would make things up for attention. What if this story was concocted for a bit of drama?'

'But we know her gran was at the nursing home and the locket has been found.'

'But she could have had the locket all the time and taken it up to the nursing home on Thursday night herself.'

Susan shook her head. 'No, she wouldn't do that. I saw how upset she'd been by it, and I don't believe she is making things up. However, that's not to say I agree that anyone here stole anything from her grandmother.'

'She will upset a lot of people if she starts throwing accusations around.'

'That's what I told her. I have a bad feeling about all this, but apparently, she's going to confront them all this afternoon.'

Robert smiled in a reassuring way. 'I wouldn't be surprised if she didn't back out when she sees them all down there. I, for one, wouldn't want to take that lot on. Can you honestly imagine accusing Beatrice of theft to her face?'

Susan managed a faint smile. 'Well, we've arrived now, let's hope you are right.'

They reached the corner, still unable to see Steephill Cove. To their right was a holiday home with the appearance of a lighthouse. Passing this and turning into the cove, they reached the wooden gate with the notice 'Steephill Cove' on it. No matter how many times Susan came here, the first sight of Steephill Cove with its pretty thatched cottages and brightly painted beach huts took her breath away. The fact that it was inaccessible to cars gave it a feeling of a place frozen in time. The presence of the fishermen reminded you it was still a place of work, as it had been for hundreds of years.

At this time of year, with the wind blowing and the waves crashing, there were few visitors, and the cafés were closed. The dogs had to be kept on leads, and Susan was happy with this on a blustery day. They walked along to the top of the beach and as they gathered, Susan saw Beatrice arrive at the bottom of the steps and come over to them.

As Beatrice clambered down onto the beach, Nathan turned to them all. 'Great, we are all here, the party can start.'

He took plastic glasses out of his backpack and Nikki handed them around and then he produced a large bottle of champagne. He opened it expertly, without spilling a drop, and started to fill people's glasses. He smiled with the easy confidence of a good-looking man. With his sun-bleached shoulder-length hair and fashionable short rough beard, and wooden bead necklace, he looked like a model from a surfing magazine.

Once everyone had their drinks, Nathan made a short speech. 'I'm not going to rabbit on, it's too cold for that, but thanks so much for coming and for all your support over the past three years. As you know, Nikki has at last agreed to be my wife.' He smiled sheepishly over at her, and she grinned in return. 'And so today is a double celebration. So, drink up and tuck into the snacks Trystan and Torri have made and here's to the next three years.'

Everyone raised their glasses and Trystan and Torri handed around dainty nibbles and pastries.

Trystan was his usual crumpled, serious-looking self. Although he appeared initially unremarkable, there was passion in his eyes that drew you to him. His life was cooking, and every dish he prepared had to be as near to perfection as he could make it. Today, each delicate morsel was carefully served on a small china plate. He watched each of them as they ate, as if awaiting some life-changing test result at the hospital. Susan wondered what it must it be like to constantly care so much about how something you had created was received. Here they were, standing on a windy beach, with a pretty undiscerning audience, and yet even here it mattered. Finally, Torri handed around her Portuguese tarts, but Colette turned one down.

'Is that all you're eating?' asked Torri, looking down at Colette, who was squeezing cream cheese onto her bread.

'I've my special marshmallows for my film night later' – she glanced over at Nathan – 'and these are safe for me to eat, not like the ones you sell at the hotel.'

Nathan shrugged. 'I'll sort it sometime.' Then he lifted up the tart he was eating and shouted over to Trystan, 'Torri's cooking is amazing. You need to watch your back, mate.'

Trystan simply scowled in return. Torri blushed and turned back to Colette. 'You shouldn't be staying down here on your own, it's not safe.'

'Well, you run up the top in the pitch black every Sunday, that's even crazier,' replied Colette.

'We keep well in from the cliff. In fact, we usually run up on the main road.'

They all sat together, wrapping their coats around themselves as the wind picked up, their dogs sitting quietly next to them. It should have been an easy gathering, and yet there was an uneasiness, reflected in the grey clouds gathering on the horizon.

Colette sat close to Torri and Trystan, nibbling at some of the snacks she had brought for herself. Susan could see one of her feet tapping, and she was biting her lip, clearly on edge.

Torri didn't look any more at ease. She opened her bag and tutted. 'I've forgotten my cigarette papers, have you any spare, Colette?'

Colette handed over the packet of papers and Torri started to roll her cigarette. Trystan leant over her to reach something but as he did, he spilt his drink over her bag and the small packet of cigarette papers resting on top.

'Oh, no, I'm so sorry,' Torri apologised to Colette. 'I'll bring you some more.' She turned to Trystan, spoke softly. 'You need to be more careful.'

Trystan frowned. Not known as someone who smiled easily, Susan thought that even for him, he was looking grumpier than usual. Her thoughts were interrupted by Colette, who gave a loud, theatrical cough and everyone turn towards her.

'I'm sorry to spoil the party, but there is something I need to talk to you about.'

No one appeared too bothered. They continued to eat and drink, looking casually in Colette's direction until she reached into her bag and took out a small box. Slowly, she got their attention as she held up the locket, dangling it from her fingers, the gold locket swinging gently in the breeze.

'This is my gran's locket, the one I told you all last Thursday had gone missing. The nursing home rang me, it was found in the garden on Friday.'

'That's lucky,' remarked Nikki. 'I'm glad you have it back.'

'It wasn't luck,' snapped Colette. 'It's mad to think the locket would just turn up the day after I'd mentioned it to you. No, this locket was taken up to the nursing home after I mentioned it and left somewhere for the gardener to find the next day.'

'This is absurd,' protested Nikki. 'I can't imagine why one of us would have had your gran's locket, but if we had, we'd have simply returned it to you.'

'You would if you had an innocent explanation, but not if you'd stolen it with a valuable brooch and a children's book, all of which were hidden in my grandmother's jewellery box.'

'What are you talking about?' asked Torri.

'I visited my gran, and she showed me her hidden valuables. She'd never told the home about them. There were three items, as I said, the locket, the brooch, and a book. Gran died a week after I visited her. When my uncle collected her things, all three things were missing. My uncle asked the home about them, they had no idea they existed or what had happened to them. My uncle decided to leave the matter. I, on the other hand, am determined to find out where they are.'

'But what has this got to do with any of us?' pleaded Torri.

'My gran told me she saw one of the "hotel bunch", that is you lot, looking at her jewellery box and she seriously suspected that person was planning to steal the contents. When I came over to find what had happened to Gran's things this year, I decided to start my investigation here, at the hotel. It was a gamble, but it paid off.'

'You got a job with us, just to spy on us?' asked Nathan.

'That's right. I searched your rooms, including Beatrice's, but I found nothing and so I laid the trap. I told you all I was looking for Gran's stolen valuables, but if I could only find the locket, I'd stop digging. One of you was pathetic enough to believe me and went up to the home and left the locket for the gardener to find.'

Nathan interrupted. 'Colette, you have got your locket and that's great. You need to drop this now. This has nothing to do with anyone here, and you shouldn't be suggesting it has.'

There was a rumble of approval. Nikki held her glass up. 'Well said, Nathan, how about a top-up, everyone?'

'No!' screamed Colette. 'We are not just moving on, Nikki. Someone here stole from my gran. I want to know who it was. I want to know what happened to her brooch and the book she read to me as a child.' She held up the locket. 'If you assume giving me this will silence me, then you don't know me.'

A wave crashed against the rocks. Susan stared at Colette, who suddenly seemed to hold them all in a spell. No one dared move, even breathe.

'Now is your chance to come clean, confess to what you did.'

She waited, but no one spoke.

'If you don't come forward of your own accord, I will force you out into the open. It's been very handy being the cleaner, I've been in all your rooms. It gave me the chance to search for my gran's things. Unfortunately, I didn't find them, but I did find other things. I discovered that each of you have some pretty nasty secrets closeted away. Not one of you are quite the nice respectable people you pretend to be, are you?' She glanced over around the group. 'Some of you already know I'm not bluffing. My uncle passed on my grandmother's jewellery box to me and I have collected evidence of these secrets and put them in the hidden drawer. If you don't confess to me in the next day, then I shall make sure all these secrets are revealed, no one will escape. It's not fair you should all pay the price, but life's not fair, tough, deal with it. I have had to all my life, it's your turn now.' She glared at them defiantly, the wind from the sea whistled around the cove, the sky was grey and threatening, and yet still no one moved, no one spoke.

Susan was horrified. This was different to simply searching through a few drawers, looking for her gran's valuables. This was prying, rummaging among people's most private belongings. Had she done the same in Susan's home? Or maybe she was simply fantasising, like Robert said. She glanced around, everyone there seemed to be taking Colette very seriously, no one was brushing this off. There was something very frightening in the air now, they looked like a pack ready to attack.

5

Susan stepped forward. 'That's enough, Colette.'

'You don't understand, this is the only way people like them are going to listen to me. None of them take me seriously, to them, people like me don't count, you should know that from all the kids you fostered. No one cares about me, I walk out of a room, and I'm forgotten. I have to fight for myself and now for Gran, no one else is going to.'

'That's not true, I care about you, lots of people do.'

Colette's face softened. 'I know you do, Susan, and I promise you I've not been looking among your things. You never deserved that.'

Beatrice stepped forward. 'It is getting very cold now, the evening is drawing in, and I for one would like to go home.'

Susan saw Nikki turn away and silently start to pack up, and the others took their cue and started to get their things together.

Colette spoke directly to Susan. 'Will you take this home for me?' She held out the locket. 'I wouldn't want to lose it down here. Could you keep it safe for me?'

Susan took the locket from her. 'Of course, but I think you should come home now.'

'No, I want to stay and go round to Castle Cove later. But could you also take Libs with you? She's had enough. It's getting too cold for her.'

'Of course.'

Colette was about to hand Susan the lead when her phone rang in her bag. 'Sorry, I need to check my phone—'

She opened her bag, and unzipped the compartment inside. Susan spotted the small red velvet pouch tucked next to her phone.

Just as Colette was reaching for the phone, the ringing stopped.

'I'll check that when you've gone,' she said and zipped up the compartment and closed her handbag. 'I'll see you later.'

Robert came over to Susan. 'Are you all right? Shall we walk back now?'

Beatrice interrupted. 'You look exhausted, Susan, why don't you come in the car with me?'

'I'd like that, but I have two dogs. Can you fit us all in?'

'Plenty of room.'

'That's great.' Susan turned to Robert. 'I'll take the lift, okay?'

'Of course.' Robert gave her a reassuring smile and went to join the others who were walking back.

Susan and Beatrice left the beach. She saw the others walking ahead of them and pass through the wooden gate and then disappear around the bend on their way to Ventnor via Castle Cove and the cliff path.

Susan and Beatrice's route took them up a steep path just before the gate.

Susan glanced back at Colette and then started to walk up the steps with Beatrice.

At the top, they turned right and soon started another muddy path. There were more steps. 'Mind this,' shouted Beatrice as she pointed to a large log across the path. 'It took me by surprise coming down today, I nearly took a tumble, it wasn't there yesterday when Biddy and I came.'

They paused and looked out at the grey seas. Beatrice looked out wistfully. 'My sister is off on a cruise in the Mediterranean at the moment, lucky thing.'

'She's gone with family?'

'Her husband. They invited me to go with them, but I didn't want to. Still, it was a nice thought, being just the two sisters made us close. I'll miss our Sunday chats, but the signal will be awful. We'll have lots to catch up when she comes back.'

Susan looked again at the beach. 'I hope Colette doesn't hang around too long.'

'Young people like some time to themselves. She'll be all right.'

'I hope so.'

They arrived at the car park and settled the three dogs in the back of the car and drove off. Beatrice switched on the radio and seemed content to travel home in silence. Susan wondered if she should go back to Colette, but Colette was an adult, she couldn't force her to leave.

Once she was at home, Susan fed and settled down the dogs. Libs looked slightly bemused. 'It's okay, Colette will be back later,' she reassured her and Libs slowly made her way over to her bed and settled down to sleep. Susan sensed, though, that the dog wasn't completely relaxed and was waiting for Colette to return.

Susan walked around the room, unable to settle. She was so confused now about Colette. She felt she'd seen a different side to her, a side that frightened her.

Susan went over to the piano, lifted the lid. Since Steve had left, she had been playing more. She had had lessons all through her childhood and kept practising. Sometimes she played on a Saturday evening at The Glanville, light, easy pieces providing gentle background music. She was also a stand-in pianist for the local amateur musical society. Nikki again had dragged her into that. This year, they were performing *The Sound of Music*, and Susan was enjoying learning the music.

As she played, she was aware of listening out for Colette, becoming more anxious as the time passed and the skies darkened. The threatened storm had not arrived, but the air was thick, heavy, too still, and she wished Colette would come home.

As the clock struck eight, Susan left the piano, made herself a drink and toast, removed a pile of books from the chair, and curled up close to the wood burner, with Rocco on her feet. Looking back, she realised that Steve finally conceding to getting a rescue dog two and a half years ago was one of the things he'd been doing to prepare her for life without him. Glancing around, she noticed again the mess she'd allowed the house to fall into since he'd left. One day, she'd have to move, and it was going to be an enormous task if she let it continue to accumulate clutter like this.

Time ticked by but still no Colette. Susan admonished herself, this was stupid. Colette was an adult, she had to lead her own life.

She heard a roll of thunder. It was coming up to quarter past eight. It was no good, she had to phone Colette. There was no reply to text or call and, looking for reassurance, she rang Robert and told him about her concerns.

'I know it sounds stupid, I'm very concerned about her, but there's nothing I can do—'

Robert interrupted her. 'Look, I don't mean to worry you, but I've just had a call from my friend Pete, we were going to go out for a drink, but he had been warned that someone had been found down the cove and he might be needed.'

'Oh, god, I need to go down there.'

'It might be better to wait until we hear more.'

'No, I have to go.'

'Well, you're not going on your own, I'll come and pick you up.'

'Be quick then.'

Susan settled Rocco and Libs down and ran to answer the door as soon as Robert arrived.

'We could park at the top of Steephill Cove and walk along,' Susan suggested.

The streets were deserted, and they soon arrived at the car park.

'Come on,' urged Robert. 'I've got a torch, keep close to me.'

'Watch out, there's a log across one of the steps,' she shouted, remembering the clamber up here earlier in the day.

'I've got it, hang on.' He passed her the torch and heaved the log to the side.

Susan returned the torch, and they slowly descended the steps. She was relieved to get to the bottom. Steephill Cove appeared deserted; there was a surprising amount of light from the moon, which shone on the sea and rocks.

They passed through the gate, passed the lighthouse holiday home and turned the corner. In contrast to the still emptiness of Steephill Cove, Castle Cove, which they could now see ahead of them, was buzzing with activity.

They could see a large group of people, torches flashing, and a static floodlight lit up the area. Susan could see the flash of the reflective strips on tabards and uniforms, the front lights of a four-wheel drive vehicle, and then she heard the whirling sound of a helicopter heading their way.

As they walked along the concrete pathway, the waves were crashing into the boulders – Susan could feel the spray wetting her face. Her heart raced, thumping against her ribcage. She saw a man, alone with his dog, staring ahead and ran towards him. 'What is it?' she screamed. 'What's happened?'

6

'I found this girl, oh, god—' replied the man.

Susan asked the question she already knew the answer to. 'Do you know who she is?'

'I recognise her from the bar at The Glanville – pretty girl.'

Susan clutched her stomach, it was her, it had to be. She pushed past the man, she had to get to Colette, she couldn't lie there surrounded by strangers.

As she walked over to the group, a man with the words 'Operational Commander' on his bright yellow tabard approached her.

'Can I help you?'

'I think the girl you are looking after is Colette, I know her, she lives with me.'

The man nodded. 'We found her name in her purse, you say Colette lives with you? Could you give me a few details so we can get her NHS details up?'

'I want to talk to her.'

'I'm sorry, it's best you stay here. The paramedics are trying to help her, but she is very poorly, and is being taken to hospital by helicopter now. It would be a huge help if you could answer some questions for me. So, let's start with date of birth, and any medication she is on.'

Susan took a deep breath, tried to steady her voice 'She is twenty-three, her birthday was on 2 September.'

'Good, and medication?'

'She has an EpiPen, she is allergic to shellfish.'

'Thank you, that's helpful. I need to go and pass that on. Stay here, please.'

As he left, Susan heard a rumbling. She looked up as the noise got louder, and the lights of the helicopter came into view.

Susan and Robert stood transfixed, watching the helicopter getting into position. In the darkness, only parts of the helicopter were lit up, and it looked like an alien spacecraft. Finally, Susan saw a stretcher being lowered and then slowly hoisted back up.

'Hang on, I can see Pete, my friend in the police. I'll go and see if I can find out more about what is happening.'

However, as Robert walked towards the team, the operational commander came over to them.

'It would be best to stay here,' he advised firmly.

'How is Colette?' asked Susan.

'As I told you, she is very poorly. Are you able to tell us any family we can contact?'

'There is no one on the island, and she has no living parents. She does have an uncle, but I don't know his address. Colette works at The Glanville, they may have his details? Sorry, she is a bit of a loner.'

'You've been very helpful. Do you have any idea why she was down here on her own?'

'She liked to come down to watch films on her phone. I didn't like the idea of her being down here on her own, though.' Susan's voice broke, she took a deep breath to steady herself. 'Shall I make my way to the hospital now?'

The man grimaced and glanced at Robert, who was standing just behind Susan. 'We need to let the paramedics do their job now, they are taking very good care of Colette. I suggest you go home for the time being. Give me your contact details and I promise you we will be in touch as soon as we know how things stand.'

Robert stepped forward. 'I see the police are involved?'

'Yes, we informed them. I suggest you both leave now, and as I say, we will be in contact as soon as we can.'

Robert put his arm around Susan's shoulder. 'It's best we go. I'll take you home. They need to get on with their job. Come on, they will tell us any news as soon as they can.'

Reluctantly Susan turned away and started to walk back along the path. Before they turned the corner, she glanced back.

There was nothing magical about the place this evening, it was dark and menacing.

Susan was exhausted when they got home. Robert offered to stay but she wanted to be on her own. She made herself coffee, looked around the empty house.

It was then that the storm really started. A roll of thunder shook the house; lightning split the room. Both Rocco and Libs sat, heads up, ears pricked, and looked at her. She gave a quick, reassuring smile. Fortunately, storms had never bothered Rocco too much, and Libs took her cue from him. However, clearly sensing her upset, Rocco went running to her. 'Rocco, what are we going to do?'

Slowly Libs approached her. Susan saw the lost look in the little dog's eyes and held her arms out to her. 'Oh, Libs, how am I going to explain this to you? Rocco and I will look after you.'

Susan had no idea how long she sat holding her mug, cuddling the dogs on the sofa, but soon after midnight, she heard the doorbell ring.

Susan opened the door to find two uniformed police officers, who after showing their ID followed Susan into the house.

One of the police officers, clearly taking the lead, introduced them. 'I am Detective Constable Alison Stubbs, and this is Constable Chris Pierce. Please call me Alison.'

Susan held her breath, knowing before they spoke the words what they were going to say.

'We are so sorry to tell you that Colette died a few hours ago.'

Susan felt her head spin, her eyes burned, she felt very sick.

'Colette's dead?' she whispered.

'I am so sorry,' replied the detective.

'But how?' She blinked, looked again at the officer. 'You're not the paramedic – he said he'd come.'

'The paramedic asked me to speak to you. The point is, Susan, we have taken over the case now.' The officer might have spoken gently but the word 'case' seemed to shout out.

'What do you mean case? What's happened?'

'I'm sorry, I can't discuss any details yet. I understand Colette has an uncle; we have his number on Colette's phone, but he's not answering our calls. I wonder if you know of any friends or close acquaintances she has on the island?'

'She didn't have many friends. She only came over in August, I met her dog walking, got to know her, and asked her if she would like to come and live with me as my guest.'

'Even though you didn't know her?'

'I felt sorry for her, she seemed vulnerable. She was easy to have here, and she was out at work a lot. She worked at The Glanville as a cleaner—'

'Ah, thank you, we will go up and talk to them. Now, we need to get a clear idea of the hours leading up to Colette's accident. I wonder if you could tell us anything you know about them.'

Susan started by telling them about the previous day, starting with the preparations for going to Steephill Cove and mentioning Colette's allergies.

'Ah, right, we noticed the EpiPen loose in her bag.'

'Loose? She usually kept it in a small red velvet pouch in the zipped compartment of her handbag, although she did show me the zip on the pouch itself was broken, she used a rubber band to keep it together. I suppose it could have fallen out.'

'Did she seem well informed about her allergy? Had she ever had to use her EpiPen as far as you know?'

'She'd only been diagnosed about a year ago. I know she'd been reading up about it, and she was very careful what she ate, checked packets and things and took her own food for the picnic. We joined the others for a walk first and then had the picnic at Steephill Cove.'

'A strange time of year to all be meeting outside like that?'

Susan explained about the double celebration.

'And so, who was at the picnic?'

'People from our dog-walking group. There was me and Colette. Then Nikki and Nathan who own The Glanville, the picnic was their idea, and then Trystan, the chef at the hotel, with his partner Torri, who is the pastry chef. There was also Beatrice, a friend who lives close by, and Robert Moore. He's an ex-police officer, I guess you might know him.'

'He is a fair bit older than me, but yes, I know of him.' The detective looked down at her notebook. 'So I can contact most of these people easily at the hotel, could you give me Beatrice and Robert's addresses?'

Susan did this and then, at the detective's prompting, started to tell her more about the celebration at the cove that afternoon. It was difficult to know how much detail to give of the discussions about the locket, but she did feel she should mention the accusation that someone there had stolen it, and the detective took careful note.

'And did anyone own up to this or claim to know anything about it?'

Susan shook her head.

'Okay, thank you. So, what happened after this?'

'We started to tidy up and we all left apart from Colette.'

'You left Colette on the beach?'

Susan cringed. 'I did. She insisted on staying down there.'

'That seems odd, it would have been dark early, the weather looked threatening.'

'I know, I didn't want her to stay on her own, but she was very insistent. She told me she was going to watch films on her phone, she'd done it before.'

'Was she meeting someone?'

'She didn't mention anyone.'

'Maybe she was intending meeting a boyfriend but didn't want to tell you?'

'Of course, it's possible.'

The detective sat back. 'Well, thank you. You've been very helpful. I'm very sorry for all you have been through. It does look as if it might not be that easy to track down family. If we don't manage to get hold of her uncle this morning, I wonder if you would be prepared to come and formally identify Colette's body for us? I know it's a difficult thing to do, but it would help us—'

'Oh, god... um, well, yes, I suppose I could.'

'Thank you, it would be this afternoon. I could come and pick you up, but we'll sort that out later. Now, did Colette have a laptop or tablet of any kind?'

'She had a tablet, but she mainly used her phone. I can go and find the tablet for you.'

'Thank you, I'll come up with you.'

They went to Colette's room. Colette kept her room very tidy, but it looked empty and abandoned now. The detective had a quick look through her wardrobe and drawers and found the tablet easily enough on the side of the bed.

'Thank you, that will be all for now.'

Susan closed Colette's bedroom door and they went back downstairs.

The detective put her notebook away. 'Thank you, you have been very helpful. Now, do you have any questions for us?'

Susan felt she should have a hundred, but her mind went blank. As if understanding, the Detective Constable said, 'It's a lot to take in, isn't it? Do get in touch if you have any questions or if there is anything else you think we should know.' She glanced at the other officer and, in silence, they stood up.

The detective looked around. 'Are you on your own? Would you like us to contact anyone for you?'

'No, thank you. I have plenty of friends close by if I need someone.' Susan stepped closer to the detective. 'They will investigate this properly, won't they? I know Colette wasn't part of the community here and didn't really have any family, but if she was attacked, you have to find out who did this.'

The detective nodded. 'Of course, this will be treated with the utmost seriousness. It doesn't matter who someone is, an unexplained death is going to be the top of our priority list, I promise you.'

When the police officers had left, Susan collapsed onto the sofa. Libs came running over and she cuddled her, she looked so lost. 'Don't be scared, I'll take care of you now. You're safe here.' Her voice broke, and the guilt crept around her like a cold chill, she'd failed Colette, she'd not kept her safe.

Susan changed into her night clothes but couldn't face sleeping upstairs on her own and so she went back downstairs to sleep on the sofa with the dogs.

She woke, stiff with a headache, and stumbled to let the dogs out into the garden. It was a dark, foggy, cold morning, but it seemed right that the sun shouldn't shine today.

Susan felt lost and disorientated, so she decided that she would go down to the beach. The dogs needed walking and she desperately needed to do something 'normal'. However, she was nervous about seeing the other dog walkers and wondered how much they would know about what had happened to Colette.

After dressing, she got her things together and left the house. Libs looked up at her, the same lost look in her eyes, but followed Rocco's example and walked with them down the hill.

The fog had lifted slightly, the sea still and grey. Everyone was gathered on the beach, no one was missing today. They were all huddled together, talking to Robert.

Most of the dogs, however, were off playing as usual. Neither of Robert's dogs liked the sea, and his pointer Gem Gem was mooching among a pile of seaweed, Dougie, the cocker spaniel, was burying some old rope he'd found, and Max was just loving digging a deep hole the sand. Only Duke stayed with the group chatting together.

Nikki came running over and hugged her. 'Oh, god, Susan, how are you? Robert has told us everything about Colette's accident, I can't believe she's died. How awful. We are all in shock.'

Susan looked over at Robert, who looked pale, older, the sparkle in his eyes dimmed. 'Pete rang me to confirm Colette had died,' he said quietly.

Nikki leant down and stroked Libs. 'Oh, darling, what will happen to you?'

'She's coming to live with Rocco and me,' Susan answered firmly.

'Do you have any idea what family Colette has?' asked Torri.

'She was alone in the world apart from an uncle, the police will be contacting him.'

'So, tell us what happened.' Nikki's eyes were bright with something too close to excitement.

'I was at home last night, waiting for Colette to return, when I rang Robert. He told me that he'd heard there was an emergency down at the cove and so he drove me to the spot where you parked, Beatrice. It was so dark but luckily Robert had a torch. He moved this log out of the way—'

'Well done, it was so dangerous,' Beatrice said.

Nikki agreed and then asked, 'What was it like when you got down there?'

'There was no one at Steephill Cove, but even from there we could hear a helicopter, so we rushed around to Castle Cove.'

Suddenly she was there, it was too real, and she started to shake.

Robert took over and told them what had happened on the beach, and then Susan spoke again.

'Once I was home, I just waited. I thought there would be a phone call, but instead the police came.'

'Oh, god, never a good sign,' Nathan groaned. 'What do they reckon happened?'

Susan shrugged. 'They won't say anything yet.'

'But they must have some idea.' Torri looked questioningly at Robert.

He shook his head. 'I know no more than you.'

'I wonder if it could have been her heart, Susan?' Torri continued. 'You hear about that even with young people, don't you?'

'I have no idea, but she appeared to be perfectly healthy to me.'

'Maybe she was attacked. You must get some odd people down there at night,' insisted Nathan. 'Something is up if they've involved the police.'

'That is routine in an unexplained death,' Robert pointed out.

'I suppose she could have fallen, those rocks are lethal,' continued Nathan.

'I don't think we should speculate,' Robert warned.

'What time did you two go down there?' Nathan asked Robert.

'Just after half eight.'

'And she was dead then?'

'They only told us she was in a bad way at that point,' Susan replied. 'They wouldn't let me anywhere near her. We spoke to the man who found her, it must have been terrible for him. They asked me if Colette had been meeting someone. I don't suppose any of you were going back to see her, were you? Or maybe she mentioned she was meeting someone?'

They all looked at her and shook their heads.

'I can't see any of us hanging about down there. I was at drama anyway,' said Nikki. 'I'm always at rehearsals on a Sunday night.'

'Did you go surfing, Nathan?' asked Torri.

He shook his head. 'No, I thought there was a storm brewing, so I didn't go in. I was working on my own in the shed on my next board.'

'We don't mind a bit of wet weather, so Trystan and I were out running,' said Torri.

'Did you see anyone?' Nathan asked.

'When it's dark, we run up along the top, along Steephill Road, we can't see the coves from there,' Torri replied.

'I was on a phone call, chatting to my sister,' Beatrice answered. 'I certainly wouldn't have been arranging to meet someone down there in the dark, far too treacherous. If anyone had been thinking of going down there, they'd have put it off, there was clearly a storm on the way.'

'They will be checking Colette's phone. We'll get answers soon enough,' Robert explained.

Nikki turned to Beatrice. 'Funnily enough, I rang you from rehearsals, and didn't get an answer. They wanted to know if you would help with costumes on the next production.'

'I'm sorry you couldn't get hold of me, but yes, I would be pleased to help.'

'It's *The Sound of Music*, isn't it?' asked Torri. 'I'd like to come.'

To Susan's surprise, talk turned to the production. People seemed full of questions, which Nikki seemed keen to answer, even adding some amusing anecdotes from rehearsals. To Susan, it seemed everyone was anxious to change the subject from Colette. A young girl they'd all known had died in tragic circumstances and yet no one seemed too shocked or upset, it was strange.

Nikki glanced over at Susan and brought the story she was telling to an abrupt close. 'Sorry, we must seem a bit disrespectful, it's so hard to know what to say. I am sorry, though, that our last time together was so tense, all that silliness over the locket, but what does that matter any more?'

Nathan put his arm around Nikki. 'Of course it doesn't, but it was only natural that we were put out by some of the things she said.'

'You're quite right,' Beatrice agreed. 'You were perfectly entitled to feel annoyed at the accusations Colette made.'

'She said some very offensive things,' Trystan grumbled.

'But she was young and vulnerable,' Nikki argued. 'She was a loner, the kind of person who drifts in and out of your life.'

'And is then forgotten,' interrupted Susan. They all looked her way. 'Colette's words, "No one cares about the likes of me, I walk out of a room, and I'm forgotten." But the point is, Colette was not some oddity who wandered into our lives. She was a young girl who lived with me, worked for you all. What's happened is a tragedy and she's not going to just be forgotten.'

'You're right, Susan,' Nikki agreed. 'Of course you are.'

Susan suddenly felt exhausted, she needed to leave. 'I'm sorry, I need to go home now, I'll see you all tomorrow.' Susan called Rocco and Libs and left.

'I'll walk up with you,' said Robert.

'No, thanks, I need some time on my own,' she replied and left.

Back home, Susan fed the dogs, and then collapsed on the sofa, closed her eyes and finally allowed herself to helplessly weep and sob. It was all so unfair; Colette was finally allowing herself to dream. How cruel that her life had been snatched away, as if someone had crashed down the piano lid on her fingers, silenced her for ever.

Slowly the storm of emotions began to ease, and Susan began to focus on the day ahead. She should tell Zoe what had happened, not that she needed to talk, but it was part of the deal she'd made with Zoe that, now she was on her own, she would always tell her if something important happened.

She sent a text and Zoe was able to snatch a moment in school to phone her back. They talked briefly, but she promised she would still go over on the weekend, and they would talk more then.

As she finished talking to Zoe, Susan received a call from Detective Constable Alison Stubbs, arranging for her to go that afternoon to the hospital to identify Colette's body. As she ended the call, Susan decided that she needed a friend to accompany her, and Robert seemed just the right person to ask. Robert readily agreed to going with her and drove her to the hospital.

Once in the mortuary, Susan stood with him, looking through the glass at Colette, who lay, eyes closed, as if sculpted from marble, no marks on her face, no sign of trauma

Although Susan had confirmed to the police officer that it was indeed Colette, it all seemed so unreal. Had they really just been chatting in the kitchen yesterday morning?

It was hard not being allowed into the room with Colette, Susan so wanted to hold her hand, tell her she wasn't alone, because she'd spent too much time in her life on her own, feeling forgotten and uncared for.

An anger burned in Susan. 'I won't forget you, Colette,' she promised. Her hand went to the locket around her neck, she felt it cold, hard in the palm of her hand, no, she wouldn't forget.

Eventually, she was ready to leave, and Robert drove her home.

'Have you any brandy in the house?' he asked. 'You look like you could do with one.'

'Maybe at the back of the cupboard, Steve had some there.'

Robert found some and poured her a measure. 'You stay there, and I will take the dogs out, you need to rest now, this has been a terrible shock.'

Too tired to protest, Susan lay back in the chair. It was while he was out that Susan heard from Beatrice. She was so insistent that Susan go round for a meal that she reluctantly agreed.

Robert returned with the dogs, and then left.

It was early evening when Susan finally left and made her way to Beatrice's house.

It felt very odd outside. The evening was cold and calm, the sea in the distance still. It felt wrong, as if nature wasn't reacting to the tragedy.

Slowly she walked down the hill until she finally reached Beatrice's house. She was aware Beatrice had been much quieter than the others. She didn't quite understand Beatrice's relationship with Colette, maybe she would learn more this evening.

7

Beatrice lived in a large detached modern house. To the side of the house stood a neat double garage, and in front of the house were manicured lawns maintained by a gardener.

Susan rang the doorbell. Beatrice answered and ushered her in. 'Come in, come in, you must be exhausted.'

The front door led into a white hallway with an old-fashioned wooden coat and umbrella stand. On the hooks were a collection of coats, and at the bottom were a few umbrellas and a number of ornate wooden walking sticks.

The house felt very modern and light. The hallway led to a large open-plan room, with dining area one end, and sofa with TV at the other. Susan wondered how Beatrice kept the white marble floor and leather sofas so pristine when she had a large dog in the house.

Biddy got up off what appeared to be a new large grey bed, stretched and lolloped over to Susan, who stroked her head.

'Something smells good,' Susan said to Beatrice, who was stirring something in a pot on the stove.

'It's my signature beef in oyster sauce – I get so many compliments, but the star of the dish is Trystan's fish stock. I've made a double lot as I have Nikki and Nathan coming round this week, every few weeks they come and we eat, drink and talk business.'

Beatrice left the hob and went to pour two a large glasses of red wine. As she handed one to Susan, she suggested she go and relax on the sofa while she finished preparing the meal.

Susan was relieved to sink back into the sofa with Biddy lying at her feet. As she sipped her wine, she was suddenly glad she'd come, it was lovely to be looked after like this.

She looked around the room. There was an eclectic mixture of ornaments and fine porcelain on some shelves and a large wooden glass-fronted bookcase in one corner. In the opposite corner sat a small table with a sewing machine and a set of shelves, with all Beatrice's sewing things arranged neatly. Susan wandered over and saw the stacks of clear plastic boxes neatly arranged on shelves and labelled. There were a number of small boxes, each containing neatly cut out squares of material and, next to the sewing machine, a partially completed patchwork bag.

Beatrice came to join Susan and glanced over at the sewing materials. 'I enjoy making these simple tote bags. Nothing fancy.'

From the drawer she took a pretty blue tote, made of differently patterned flowered squares. 'This is for one of the residents at the home, she wanted a new knitting bag.'

'I don't know how you have the patience.'

'I find it relaxing. I can't sew clothes like Nikki, though. I did offer to make her one of these once, but she very politely refused.' Beatrice laughed.

'What a talented lot you are. I've seen some of the clothes Nikki has made, they are amazing. That skirt she wore at the summer barbecue was fabulous.'

'I'll let you into a secret, Nathan made that. He's very good, you know, not at Nikki's standard, perhaps, but he's made a few things.

He doesn't let on; it doesn't go with the surfer image. Right, let's sit down, it's time to eat.'

They sat at the table, set with a crisp white lace cloth, silver cutlery and a candle.

Appreciating the effort Beatrice had been to, Susan said, 'This is lovely, thank you so much.'

Beatrice smiled. 'I always sit up at the table like this, even when I'm on my own.'

'Really? I suppose I always sat up with Steve and the children, but I don't bother much now.'

'But you should. You can't just spend all your time looking after everyone else, fighting their battles.'

Susan looked around, looking for a change of subject, and saw a painting on the wall. 'I'd not really noticed that before, I'm afraid I don't know much about art but it's lovely.'

'Thank you. Nikki and Nathan bought a job lot of old prints before they moved into the hotel, this one was spare, and Nikki offered it to me the other day. It's called *Woman with a Mirror* by Titian. Torri was telling me about it. I'd not realised she knew so much about art, but then I forget she has quite an academic background.'

'I know, she's so quiet and unassuming, it's easy to forget.' Susan looked down at the shelf below the painting. 'You have so many interesting pictures and ornaments. I've always admired that vase.'

Beatrice followed her gaze. 'It's not a vase, it's an urn.'

'Oh, I'm so sorry,' stammered Susan. 'I didn't realise.'

'It's okay, I chose an attractive urn for my husband's ashes so that people would mistake it for a vase.'

'I see, you didn't want to scatter his ashes then?'

'No. Because we've lived all over the place, there was no particular place that was important to us. I like having him here, close to me.'

Susan glanced around the room. 'You don't have any photographs of him?'

'No, I'd rather not.'

Susan waited for Beatrice to explain, but instead she served out the beef. As she did, Susan was surprised to realise how hungry she was.

'Thank you so much.'

'I knew you'd not have eaten properly, especially after all that has happened.'

'No, last night and today seem like some kind of blur.'

'You've had a terrible time, haven't you? It was so sudden, we are all in shock, but you were the one who took Colette under your wing.'

'I tried to.'

Susan began to eat, the food was warm, and the wine was slowly warming her. The day was starting to drift away from her until Beatrice brought her back to the present.

'I wonder where Colette's family are. They will need to find someone to formally identify the body, won't they?'

Suddenly her mouth felt very dry, the food hard to swallow, and she started to cough.

'Are you okay? Have some water,' Beatrice offered.

Susan sipped from the glass and once she'd stopped coughing, she explained. 'There is only her uncle that I know of, and he is somewhere on the mainland. The police asked me to go and identify the body this afternoon.'

'Oh, Susan, how awful. You should have phoned me; I'd have come with you.'

'Actually, Robert came. He seemed the natural person to turn to.'

'Of course. And so, did the police give you any more idea of why Colette died when you went there?'

'They haven't told me anything else.'

'Hopefully we will know more soon. It is such a shame we had such an unpleasant afternoon with all that business with the locket and her gran. I don't suppose we'll ever know the truth of it now.'

'Maybe not.'

Beatrice took a sip of her wine. 'Do you believe Colette was serious about collecting people's secrets?'

'I have no idea. I've not given it a lot of thought.' She looked away, the notion of Colette prying in that way still upset her. However, Beatrice hadn't finished.

'I'm not saying for a minute that Colette would have found out anything of any weight, but I think it's important to dispose of anything she might have squirrelled away in her grandmother's jewellery box.'

Susan was shocked by the intensity in Beatrice's voice.

'I suppose I could check in the jewellery box. I was just going to pack it up with all Colette's things to return to her uncle. I can remember how she said to open that secret drawer, if there is anything, I could return it.'

'That would be best, or as I suggested, you could simply throw it all away. After all, if you started reading through whatever it is, in a way, you would be as culpable of invading someone's privacy as Colette.'

Susan took a deep breath. 'Goodness, you have given this a lot more thought than me. To be honest, I wouldn't expect to find anything, but now you've mentioned it, I'll check and get rid of things.'

'Good, yes, that is the right thing to do.'

Susan picked up her fork and continued her meal. 'I suppose there will be all kinds of things I've not thought of. A death brings so many unlikely consequences. Colette may not have been a close relative to any of us, but her death will affect us all in different ways.'

'I agree, and it's particularly hard for you, and poor little Libs. How is she?'

'She's doing very well; Rocco is lovely with her. They sleep downstairs together. I see Biddy has a new bed, where is that from?'

They easily slipped into talking about the merits of various types of beds and then onto the myriad subjects that dog lovers love to discuss.

When they finished eating, they had coffee sitting on the sofa. Susan was aware time was moving on.

'I ought to get back to Rocco and Libs. Thank you so much for the meal, it's been wonderful.'

'You know you can come down here any time you like, it's going to be a strange few days for you now.'

They walked into the hallway and for the first time, Susan noticed the sound of rain pattering on the windows.

'Oh, goodness, I've only got this thin jacket.'

'I have a few spare umbrellas here. Take your pick.'

Susan looked at the assortment of walking sticks and umbrellas.

'You have some really interesting walking sticks; I've not seen you use some of them.'

Beatrice picked up one with a carved horse's head. She pulled at the head, and to Susan's astonishment, she revealed a short, sharp dagger.

She grinned at Susan. 'I'm not sure it would be legal to take this one out. I've a few like it, I collect them at auctions. They are not all as lethal as this one!' She removed the round metal top from the next one. 'See, this one has an empty bottle inside it. People would keep perfume in them to dab on themselves when going through the poorer areas of the city, I find them fascinating.'

'They are very unusual,' replied Susan. 'I'll stick with a plain red umbrella, thank you.'

'You can borrow a coat as well.' Beatrice took down an old mac with brown cord on the collar. 'I keep this even though it's a bit scruffy now, it's huge and just right for a muddy walk in the woods.'

'I'm fine with my jacket and this umbrella, and thank you again so much for looking after me, I feel a lot better.'

Susan walked home as quickly as she could, but the rain became heavier, and she was walking against the wind.

By the time she'd returned home, she was exhausted, the rain had soaked through her shoes and her feet were sodden. The dogs came rushing to greet her and she made a fuss of them both.

'Now, don't you imagine I'll be going out again in that,' she told them firmly. 'It's a quick visit to the garden tonight.'

After she'd changed, she let them out. Neither dog was inclined to stay out long, and after wiping them down, they seemed glad to return to lie down by the log burner.

'Right, I'm off to bed now. Tomorrow has to be better, doesn't it?'

Susan went upstairs and was about to go to bed when she paused outside Colette's room. A voice was urging her to go in, look for the jewellery box, but she hesitated. Did she really want to find out Colette had been keeping secrets about people? It wasn't something she liked to imagine. But then, she had told Beatrice she would check, she had to be brave and go in.

Her hand trembled as she pushed open the door and reached to switch on the light. Susan glanced around the room, but the jewellery box didn't seem to be on display.

She looked through the drawers and Susan noticed more personal belongings. She found a few souvenirs from Colette's travels. In the bottom drawer of her chest, she found a teddy bear wrapped up in a blanket. She wondered where it had come from, maybe a treasured present from her mother, or possibly one from a foster home. Whatever its origin, there was something deeply moving about it. Susan hugged it gently and then carefully replaced it in the drawer.

She continued to search the room, and finally she looked under the bed, and there, right at the back, well hidden, was the jewellery box.

Susan pulled it out, sat up on the bed and tried to remember how to open it. She fiddled with the drawer and finally it slid open.

She sat staring at the contents. So, Colette had been speaking the truth, she really had been collecting things. Beatrice had told her not to read them, but she was too curious about them, how could she possibly not check them out? There couldn't be anything too serious, her friends weren't that sort of people. No, she'd have a quick look through and then throw it all away.

It appeared to be a neat collection of assorted letters, photos and objects.

Susan picked up the page carefully torn from a magazine. It was a list of contents with an article about attracting wildlife into your garden circled. The date at the top of the page was February 2010. It meant nothing to Susan and so she picked up the newspaper cutting lying next to it. This was from the local paper, dated Saturday 13 October 2012 and showed Nikki, Nathan and a group of people posing in a photograph. Susan recognised a few local dignitaries and noticed a very tall man with a moustache standing rather self-consciously at the back. The headline was 'Exciting New Venture in Ventnor' and was clearly taken the night of the opening of the hotel.

Next, Susan picked up a rather startling torn fragment from a letter saying, 'LEAVE NOW'. The words were clearly cut out from the pages of a book. Had someone sent this to Colette, threatening her?

Susan then picked up a smart green textured envelope. On the outside was written the title of a Welsh love song, 'Myfanwy'. Susan carefully opened the envelope and inside she found a tiny hand-made bunch of yellow roses. They were very delicate, and Susan was sure this had to be some kind of romantic gesture. Looking back at the envelope, she saw that someone had drawn a heart. There was a word that had been smudged, but she could make out the first two letters, 'Co...' This must mean this had been sent to Colette, but who had been her secret admirer?

The final item was a photograph and Susan recognised that it was a picture of the urn and other ornaments in Beatrice's living room.

She looked at the small pile – the magazine page, the newspaper cutting, the letter fragment, the roses and song and the photograph of Beatrice's room.

Colette had claimed these things were clues to secrets people in the group were hiding. But what did any of them really mean and which clue connected to which member of the group?

She knew she'd intended to throw them away but somehow, it felt too soon to do that. In a way, it was as if Colette was entrusting them to her, telling her to keep them safe. She would hold on to them a little longer.

8

After a fitful sleep, Susan let the dogs out, then went and showered. She decided she would mention what she'd found in Colette's jewellery box to Robert, it would be good to see what he thought about them.

When she arrived at the beach, Susan met Beatrice, Nikki, Torri, and Robert. Once the dogs were running free, she found herself walking with Nikki.

'I heard you went for a meal with Beatrice last night.'

'I did, now how did you know I went there?'

Nikki grinned and tapped the side of her nose. 'It's my business to know everything that goes on.' And then she laughed. 'Actually, Beatrice was just telling us. I'm glad you had company and Beatrice is a good cook.'

'It was very cosy round there, I must admit. It's so hard to think about anything other than Colette at the moment.'

'I can't imagine what happened to her. Is it possible she took drugs or something?'

Susan blinked. 'That hadn't crossed my mind. Colette smoked

roll-ups. I know the smell of cannabis but never smelt that around her.'

'No, I agree. For someone of her age, she seemed unusually sober.'

'Did you ever hear mention of a boyfriend or anything? Was there any gossip at the hotel, which must have been the most likely place for her to meet someone?'

Nikki shrugged. 'Not that I heard. What gave you the idea there could have been someone?'

Susan paused and then answered, 'I was sorting a few things out in her room, and I found this envelope, it had the title of a Welsh love song written on the outside and inside there was a tiny bunch of handmade paper roses.'

Nikki blushed. 'Hang on, you believe these things were sent to Colette by some lover?'

'Yes, that is what I thought.'

Nikki nodded. 'I see, well, we all know Trystan is crazy about Welsh music, but I don't think he would ever cheat on Torri, would he? Of course, Torri did say she got worried about Colette sometimes, Trystan often went out in the gardens to smoke with her. But Torri is jealous of everyone, it doesn't mean anything. No, I expect it's some young boy who's been in for a drink or something.'

Nikki's dog Duke was, as always, walking close to her. Today she'd brought a frisbee to throw for him, but he seemed to be fetching and returning it more out of duty than for fun.

'I thought my Rocco was easy-going, but Duke beats him.'

'I know, he should run about more, he loves his food, and I am always watching his weight.'

Nikki threw the frisbee again and asked, 'By the way, was it you who told the police we all had a "row" with Colette at Steephill Cove the day she died?'

The question was asked with the force of an accusation.

'I told them she'd been upset about her grandmother's locket, yes. Why?'

'They came and interviewed us all yesterday afternoon. Asked us about our relationship with Colette, that kind of thing.'

'Beatrice didn't mention it when I saw her last night.'

'Maybe she was trying not to talk too much about Colette. I am sure, though, you telling them about the argument at Steephill Cove meant they felt they had to check up on us all. I know Colette worked for us, so they were bound to want to talk to us about her, but it shows you have to be careful what you say to them.'

'I'm sorry, I didn't mean to accuse anyone of anything.'

'Just be careful, that's all.'

Susan could sense Nikki's annoyance, but then they were both distracted by a cold, strong gust of wind.

'God, what a morning,' complained Nikki and reached into her handbag. She took out a bright red lip gloss. 'I keep plastering on this stuff, Beatrice gave it to me, it's very expensive, all the rage in China apparently. She gave one to Torri as well. Beatrice had bought a few but found them too bright for her.'

She turned and smiled at Susan, apparently having moved on from her earlier irritation. 'Does it feel very odd, being in the house on your own again?'

'I miss Colette, but it's just over two years now since Steve left. I should be getting used to living alone.'

'But you lived with him for a long time, didn't you?'

'We were married for forty years. I was always quite independent, but it was a shock all the same. We always got on well, we were good friends, in fact, he had been my best friend for a long time.'

'I'm not surprised you looked so lost when we first met you that April, he'd only been gone a month or so.'

'I'd not realised I looked quite so bereft.'

'Oh, yes, it's why I invited you to walk with us.'

'That was very kind of you. Through you, I learnt that an unexpected but welcome upside of owning a dog was that it was a great way to make friends, like parents meet through their children at the school gates.'

Nikki threw the frisbee again. 'My dad had an affair. Mum took him back, but they were miserable.' The bitter words shot out. 'The trouble was she was totally dependent on him, both financially and practically. It was a huge mistake; I shall never get myself in that situation.'

Nikki looked over at Beatrice. 'Now, I'd love to know what her marriage was like, but she always changes the subject when I bring it up. Does she talk to you about her husband?'

'No, maybe it hurts too much.'

'It doesn't feel like that, though, does it? I saw something odd when I was round there having a meal with her. She took her glasses off to take something out of the oven – you know the way your glasses steam up – well, she put them on the side, and I was admiring them. I am going to need reading glasses soon, and I love her frames. The strange thing was, when I picked them up, I saw they were plain glass. I asked her why she always wore them, and do you know what she said?'

Susan waited.

'She told me she liked hiding behind them, that they were like her barrier against the world.'

Susan shrugged. 'Well, she has her reasons. Personally, I find glasses a real nuisance.'

'Well, Beatrice is a real mystery to me.'

They were coming to the end of the walk, and Torri, Beatrice and Robert came over to them.

To Susan's surprise, Nikki suddenly blurted out, 'It was Susan who told the police about the argument on Sunday afternoon.'

'It was the right thing to do,' Robert insisted, and Susan appreciated his support.

'But it made me very uncomfortable,' mumbled Torri.

'The police would have been to see you all anyway,' Robert replied. 'They need to get as full a picture of Colette's life as possible.'

'But they have to be careful how they use their time now. Nathan told me someone said the police are up to their eyes with this people-smuggling business. A police officer came in for a drink at the hotel and told him they'd had instructions to keep arrests to a minimum, all their efforts have to be focused on that,' she laughed. 'Not a good idea wasting time talking to the likes of us.'

Robert frowned. 'The officer shouldn't have been talking like that, the police will always make time for serious incidents.'

'I'm just saying they don't need to be wasting their time interrogating the likes of us,' argued Nikki.

'Well, if it helps with their enquiries into Colette's death, then being interviewed is fine by me,' said Beatrice. 'I am sure you did the right thing, Susan.'

They all called their dogs and started to leave the beach. However, Susan reached out to Robert and asked him if she could speak to him privately.

'Of course, I'll walk up the road with you. Do me good to do some hills, I don't get as much exercise as you do, living down here.'

As they walked, Susan told him about the jewellery box. 'I opened it and there was this strange collection of things – remember Colette told us on the beach about collecting secrets about people?'

'Oh, what had she found?'

'There was a magazine page, a newspaper cutting about the opening of the hotel, a bunch of roses and mention of a song, a photo of Beatrice's living room, oh, and a fragment of a letter which

I have to say looked threatening. I don't know what any of it means, do you think it's anything important?'

'Tell me more about them.'

As Susan explained the items in more detail, it was the letter that Robert seemed to pick up on.

'I could mention that to Pete, if you like, he can see if it is something they need to follow up on.'

'Thank you.'

'It might take a few days. I know I was defending the police just now with Nikki, but Pete told me it is a bit of a nightmare, all leave has been cancelled.'

'It really is that bad?'

'Yes. I didn't say anything back there, but they are sure that what they have discovered so far is just the tip of the iceberg, although they won't release much to the press yet. The investigation is involving police forces all over Hampshire and unfortunately the island seems to be a major player in it all.'

'That's terrible, how could people do such a thing?' She paused. 'This won't mean they will cut corners on Colette's investigation, will it?'

'Of course not, they will look into everything, I am sure. By the way, Pete told me that the post-mortem was today. He also mentioned they'd got hold of the uncle, so he is meant to be coming over tomorrow.'

'I guess I should sort out Colette's things for him.'

'I expect he'll come round to see you.'

Susan sighed. 'It's so weird to find myself doing any of this.'

Robert smiled kindly. 'I can understand that, it's not as if Colette was family or anything. You don't have to do it on your own, you know; I can come round and help.'

'No, it's all right, but thanks.'

'Did you know Nathan is doing his yearly foraging guide this afternoon, do you fancy coming?'

'Oh, I don't know—'

'You must come, it will do you good. I'll pick you up.'

Susan felt herself back away, she hated feeling pushed into something.

'I'll decide later and make my own way there if I decide to go,' she replied stiffly.

He grinned. 'Of course. We meet at Firestone Copse at two.'

They had arrived at Susan's and Robert turned to leave. 'Hopefully see you later.'

Feeling she'd been a bit harsh, she added, 'Thank you for the chat, I do appreciate being able to talk to you. I might see you later then.'

She watched him leave and went into the house.

As she was giving the dogs their breakfast, she realised she needed to get on with sorting through Colette's room.

Susan took some large bags for life up and began sorting through clothes and the items in the drawers. She found the jewellery box, emptied it of the contents in the hidden compartment, and put them in a small cardboard file. The jewellery box itself, of course, should be returned to Colette's uncle. She piled the bags for life into the antique wardrobe, and locked it, as this was the only way the door stayed shut.

The final task was to strip the bed. It was relatively quick to do but seeing it laid bare at the end was very moving. Colette would never come back, never sleep in the bed again, this was the end.

Wiping away a tear, Susan left the room and went back downstairs.

The morning went quickly and after lunch, as the sun had broken through, she decided it would be a good thing to get out and join the foraging group. She left Rocco and Libs at home but when she arrived, she saw Robert had brought his dogs.

'I should have brought mine, but I'm still getting used to walking two dogs at the same time and was worried about keeping track of them while I was listening to Nathan,' she explained.

Robert smiled. 'I don't blame you. I will keep Gem Gem by me as there are a lot of pheasants around at the moment, but Dougie won't go far, he's always checking I am close by.'

Nathan stood in front, very much the person in charge. 'Now, a few rules. Only pick what you will use, remember the foods we pick are also vital nourishment for the wildlife in the winter. And carefully pick at the leaves, don't disturb the roots of plants. Right, off we go.'

As they walked along, Nathan told them what to look out for. 'Ah, you see these beautiful little wild plums. You can use them for jams and preserves. They are not quite ready for picking, though.'

They stopped to watch some red squirrels, and then Nathan pointed out one of the trees, with purple leaves. 'Come over here, feel the rippled bark. Use all your senses in the woods. Smell, touch, look, listen, and of course, when it's safe, taste. Now, these lovely little nuts are beech nuts. Again, we are a bit early. I love to roast these. Ah, but over here we have some hazelnuts, these are cob nuts, and these are ready to pick.'

They moved on to berries. 'Now, we obviously have to be careful.' He paused. 'Ah, here are some, no, don't touch,' he warned and pointed to some shiny round black berries. 'They will taste sweet but two of these innocuous-looking berries could kill a child. They are of course belladonna – deadly nightshade. We will keep well away from them. Ah this is better, rosehip... top up your Vitamin C before all the winter colds are doing the rounds. Also over here, prunus spinosa, sloes for your gin.'

The group scattered for a while until Nathan called them back together. 'Now we move onto fungi. Again, remember the rules, don't over pick, and also pick carefully. My golden rule is, if in doubt, leave it. October is the best month to see fungi of all shapes and sizes.

'Now, this here is a field mushroom – but as with all mushrooms there are others that look remarkably like this and are very poisonous. These, though, I can assure you, you can pick. I shall pick some for the manager at the nursing home, she loves them. Now, we have all picked a few, so let's move on to the woodland flora, and Nikki is the expert in that.'

Nikki smiled and started to explore the forest floor with them. Susan was entranced by the names such as harebells, also known as witches' thimbles, fairy bells and cuckoo's shoe. Nikki proved as knowledgeable about flowers as Nathan was about the other plants.

* * *

Susan had really enjoyed the walk. She had learnt a lot and returned home much refreshed.

After taking the dogs for a quick walk, she put a ready meal of lasagne in the microwave and opened her laptop. She read a long article about the conservation in Brazil and was setting about writing a response when a message arrived.

Hello, Susan. I am Colette's uncle, Keith The police officer gave me your mobile number. I wonder if I could come and visit you tomorrow at midday? Please let me know if this is a problem in any way.

Just as she'd finished replying, Susan received another text, this one from Robert asking her to send him a photo of the threatening letter to pass on to Pete. Susan went upstairs, took the photo, and sent it.

She realised at this point how exhausted she was and that she still hadn't eaten her tea. Finding the meal standing in the microwave, she took it out, ate it hungrily and finally went up to bed.

However, once in bed, she found it hard to settle, and picked up her latest read, Shakespeare's *Anthony and Cleopatra*. Zoe thought it was crazy that she found such books relaxing, but she loved to get lost in the beautiful language and poetry of the words. Reading soothed her and eventually she fell asleep. It was annoying, therefore, to be woken up only a few hours later by the sound of a distant creak. She told herself to ignore it and turned over to go back to sleep but then she heard a louder creaking sound and felt a creeping sense of unease.

Was that a noise in the hallway? She frowned, it was an old house, there were often odd sounds, but no, she heard it again.

She gripped her duvet cover, listening intently. Another creak, someone was definitely out there. Susan shook herself – of course, it had to be one of the dogs. Rocco never came upstairs, but it might be Libs feeling lonely, maybe even looking for Colette.

Susan got up, put on her dressing gown, and opened her bedroom door. She was right, Libs was sitting outside looking up at her. However, as she leant down to stroke her, she heard a creak on the bottom stair. Suddenly alert, she turned on the landing light. As she did, she heard footsteps in the hallway, and froze. Someone was down there; she was sure of it. She held her breath listened, there was a click, the front door opening and then... silence.

9

Susan started to run down the stairs, ignoring the voice of her daughter in her head – 'Don't ever try to see anyone off in the house, barricade yourself in the room.'

Libs followed her into the kitchen, where Rocco was still asleep in his bed. As she switched on the light, he wagged his tail in anticipation of a midnight walk.

'No, we're not going anywhere,' she explained. 'Did you hear someone down here... why didn't you bark?' She looked over and saw the back door was firmly locked and then returned to the hallway. She went straight to the front door, checked the locks. Nothing had been forced, how could someone have simply let themselves in? Streetlights lit up the empty pavements, there was no one out there. Had she imagined it all?

She went into the living room, turned on the light, quickly scanned the room. The silver cups, the laptop and TV were untouched. It didn't appear as if anyone had been in there.

She sat down on the edge of the chair. It had been a terrible few days, her mind was all over the place, she needed to calm down.

Susan went into the kitchen, made herself a drink, and gave the dogs a treat. It must have been her imagination and, as upsetting as it had been, that was a relief. Anything was better than the reality of having a stranger in her house at night.

However, as often as she told herself all was safe, Susan wasn't comfortable about returning to her bed. Instead, she settled down on the sofa in the living room, pulling the blanket she used as a cover over herself. The dogs quickly got the idea that they were not being taken out and jumped up onto the sofa to join her.

The few hours' sleep proved to be surprisingly refreshing. In the morning, Susan got up, showered, and went down to the beach to meet the other dog walkers. As they went down onto the beach, she let the dogs off and watched Rocco and Libs run over to their friends. The owners all greeted them as well, leaning down and making a fuss of them. Susan decided not to mention the scare of the night before, preferring to join in with more general gossip and news.

It wasn't until she was returning up the hill after the walk that she suddenly remembered the key safe on the wall at the side of the house. She'd had it installed when Steve left. It was useful for her when she locked herself out or if she went away. Nikki and Beatrice had watered her plants, Trystan came to pick herbs, most people knew about it. She cringed when she remembered telling Robert the code was 12345 and he told her to change it, but she was scared of forgetting a new number so never had.

When Colette had moved in, she'd given her a set of keys, but Susan had been glad of the spare herself last week when yet again she'd locked herself out. She went and examined the box, where the number of the code was showing. That seemed odd to her as she always moved the numbers around so that at least a stranger would have to make some kind of effort to open the safe. Today it opened easily, and another thing struck her as odd. The key was there, but it was on the base of the safe, not hanging on its hook.

Slowly the fear that someone could have been in the house the night before started to return. Maybe she hadn't imagined it.

The dogs were pulling to go around the back of the house, she looked down at them, and remembered watching them greeting everyone on the beach earlier. There had been plenty of tail wagging, but no barking. Her mind went to the night before; of course, if someone they knew had broken in, they would not have barked.

Susan pushed the safe door closed and went down the side of the house.

Once the dogs had been fed, she went upstairs to Colette's room. She pushed open the door, and immediately she saw the wardrobe door hanging open, the key lying on the floor. She gasped, clamped her hand over her mouth. Oh, god, surely that had been closed before? Her hands shook and she held herself tight, had someone really been in here last night?

She sat on the edge of the bare mattress, trying to calm herself down. She could be mistaken about the key safe and now this wardrobe door, and she was only guessing about the dogs not barking because they recognised the person who'd broken in. Maybe they'd not barked simply because there had been no one there.

It crossed her mind to ring Zoe or Robert but she knew they would insist on her going to the police and she was sure that would achieve very little. Nothing had been taken, there were no signs of a break-in, they would see her as a woman under a huge amount of strain imagining things.

There was nothing to be done but to carry on, allow for the possibility that maybe she had imagined it all. For good measure, she would take extra care locking up at night and someday soon get the locks changed.

Colette's uncle would be here soon, she had to get herself together.

* * *

Susan was relieved when she heard the doorbell ring at twelve, Colette's uncle, Keith, had arrived.

As she led him into the kitchen, she saw he was tall and had the same fair good looks that Colette and her gran had, as well as her reserved way of speaking. There was a watchfulness in his eyes that reminded her of Colette.

'Are you okay with dogs?' she asked him.

'Fine, isn't this Colette's little dog?'

'Yes, this is Libs, she is living with me now.'

'That's very kind of you.'

'Have you come far?' she asked him.

'From Manchester. I travelled down last night and stayed overnight in a Premier Inn in Southampton. And then got the car ferry over – the journey wasn't too bad.' He paused, he seemed distracted. 'I'm sorry, I can't get my head around it all. What a tragic way for Colette to die, what a terrible accident.'

Susan sat up. 'Do you have any information about how Colette died then?'

'Oh, yes – I thought they'd have told you.'

'No, nothing—'

'The police said she died from anaphylaxis. You know she had a very serious allergy to shellfish?'

'I did, but she was very careful, and she always had her EpiPen with her.'

'All I know is that they say she ate something with shellfish in it and, as she is allergic, she had a very bad reaction and it killed her.'

Susan felt her stomach muscles clench. What an agonising death it must have been.

'The police believe the coroner will allow for the release of her body fairly soon. There isn't any other family to invite to a funeral, but I shall attend the cremation.'

Susan was shocked they'd moved so quickly on to talking about the funeral.

'Um, yes, sorry, so the police are sure her death was some terrible accident?'

'Yes, that is what they told me.'

'Is that it then? The end of the investigation?'

'I assume so.'

'But why on earth did Colette eat anything with shellfish in? She was so careful. And in any case, she had her EpiPen – why didn't she use it?'

'I didn't ask a lot of questions. I am sure they will give you more details if you want them.'

Susan frowned, it seemed sad that he wasn't more interested, but she was not satisfied, she would have to find out more.

She found some biscuits and put them on a plate, trying to think of a tactful way of finding out more about Colette.

'I really enjoyed having Colette living here but I never felt I really got to know her that well. I got the impression life at home had been difficult for her?'

'Oh, yes. Her mum, my sister, had a lot of problems. I'm afraid our father left us both very scarred, inside and out. I struggled with a drink problem for years.'

'I'm sorry.'

'It's why I saw so little of my mother, Colette's grandmother, over here. I know none of it was her fault, but she had so much to deal with herself, she never took enough time to look after my sister and me. Still, I'm glad Colette was fond of her.'

'Colette told me that during her visit to her grandmother at the nursing home, her gran told her about some valuables in a jewellery box, there was a locket, a brooch and a children's book. And that they had gone missing after her gran died.'

'Ah, Mum's "valuables".' He made inverted commas with his fingers.

'You knew about them?'

'Oh, yes. Mum showed me the so-called valuables she kept in that secret drawer in her jewellery box. The locket she'd bought for herself, second hand, but the brooch and book were given to her by a lady she'd worked for.'

'Colette told me you didn't believe the stones in the brooch to be real.'

Keith screwed up his face. 'It looked very pretty, but, yes, I was sure it wasn't worth much. I offered to get it checked for Mum. I mean, if it was valuable, it should be put in the safe, but she wouldn't let me take it away or tell the staff about it.'

'I see, but all the valuables she hid in that drawer disappeared after she died?'

'They did. I came over the day she died. She'd had a tummy upset but it was her heart that gave way. Mum didn't have a lot of stuff. When I got home, I checked the jewellery box, and the hidden compartment was empty. I rang the nursing home, but of course they had no written records and I couldn't prove anything. It was upsetting, though. The locket had meant a lot to her, and I always felt Colette should have it.'

'What did you decide happened to them?'

'At first, I wondered if she'd given anything away and the manager did check, but no one appeared to have been given any of the items by Mum. They also checked her room and the store cupboard they'd kept all Mum's possessions in, but there was no sign of anything. I came to the conclusion that they must have been stolen.'

'That is pretty serious, were the police involved?'

The uncle sat back. 'The home told me I had a right to go to them but to be honest, I didn't, I had no happy memories to keep. I paid for the funeral and as far as I was concerned, that was the end of it. Despite what Mum maintained, I didn't believe the brooch was worth a lot, I mean, would an employer really give away valuable jewels? No, I decided to leave it.'

'But Colette didn't?'

'No. She came to see me in January out of the blue. She'd been off for a few years but seemed to have calmed down and wanted to know about the locket, brooch and book her gran had shown her. When I told her they'd gone missing, I was surprised at how determined she seemed to find out what had happened. I told her the brooch was probably fake and there was nothing of value there, but she didn't agree. She told me she was coming over to find out what had happened.'

'She had more luck than you anticipated.' Susan told him the story of the locket.

He whistled. 'Well, I never, good for Colette. Where did she find it?'

Susan explained what had happened and Colette's suspicions.

'Did your mum ever express any worries about any member of staff?'

Keith smiled. 'Colette told me in January what Mum had told her. That was why she got work in the hotel.'

'Had you met any of the people who went to set up the hotel when you were visiting your mother?'

'She mentioned Nikki. Mum told me she had a boyfriend who went in, and what a nice young man he was.' He looked at her searchingly. 'You seem very interested in all this.'

Susan nodded. 'I guess I am.' She told him about the scene at Steephill Cove.

'My god, so she accused your friends of stealing from Mum? I bet that went down well!'

'Well, they were angry, understandably.'

'I guess they would be... still, it all sounds a bit fishy, maybe Colette was onto something.'

'Maybe.'

'Listen, Susan, I am not going to pursue this. I've told you I have to leave the past where it is.' He looked at his watch. 'I think I should be making a move soon, I guess Colette has a fair bit of stuff here?'

'Let me take you up to her room.'

They went upstairs and she took the bags for life out of the wardrobe. 'Colette didn't have a lot. Just what was in these bags. It should all fit in your car.'

'I suppose it could.'

Susan could sense a reluctance in his voice. 'I don't mind sorting it, taking any clothes to the charity shop, if that would help.'

'That's kind, thank you. I'm sorry, I'm finding this all so hard to cope with.' She saw his hands were trembling, his eyes brimming with years of unshed tears.

'That's quite all right,' she said gently. 'One more thing. What about the jewellery box and locket? They both belonged to your mum.'

'I don't want them. I am sure Colette would like them to go to you.'

They left the room and although Susan invited him to have lunch, he seemed eager to get away.

'Thank you for giving Colette a home, I am sure she was happy here. At least she was looked after for the last few months of her life.'

Keith shook his head sadly and then left.

It had been an emotional meeting, and Susan felt desperately sad for him. She went upstairs to Colette's room and piled the bags for life into the wardrobe. She couldn't face sorting things out at the moment, but she did pick up the locket. It was a beautiful piece of jewellery and loaded with meaning for Colette and her gran. It was awful that Colette had had to battle to find it.

Susan opened the locket, looked at the photo of Colette, a wide grin, an innocence that was taken away from her too young. She closed it, put it around her neck and held the locket in her hand.

'I understand why your uncle has to walk away, Colette,' she whispered. 'But I'm not going to forget you. I'm going to find out the answers you were looking for and I'm going to find out exactly what happened to you at the cove the night you died. Why did you eat something you knew would harm you, and why didn't you use your EpiPen?'

Susan decided that she would go and see Robert, maybe he would have some answers about Colette's death. However, he couldn't help her with the mystery of the grandmother's stolen valuables. She paused and then decided what she could do. She would visit the nursing home herself, maybe talk to a few staff and residents. Yes, that friend of Colette's grandmother, what was her name... Alice. That was it, she would see if she had anything to say that would help.

Of course, it would be better if she had an excuse to go there, it would look very odd to just go asking about the locket. Fortunately, Susan knew she had the answer. She was pretty sure the manager would be open to the idea of her visiting to play the piano for the residents, maybe play some songs they could sing along to. She went straight to ring the nursing home and her offer was enthusiastically accepted. They arranged for her to go that Friday afternoon.

10

Susan made her way down to Robert's that evening. He lived close to the beach in a messy but homely house. One end of his kitchen was clearly his workshop and once he'd offered her a glass of red wine, he showed her his latest project, a doll's house for his grand-daughter. She found it a surprising project.

'It's so beautiful, I love all the little details, the pictures on the wall, flowers in the vase and look at the tiny cooking utensils, it's fabulous. I could never have imagined you making something like this.'

He held up his large, muscular hands. 'I don't find all the fiddly bits that easy with these, but I find it really satisfying. There is something fascinating about dolls' houses, creating this world you can control. I can see why my kids liked them. Colette was abso-lutely enthralled with this, I don't think she'd had one when she was young.

Susan put down her mug. 'I never knew Colette came here.'

He blushed. 'Just the once, she had a few things she needed to say.'

'Her uncle, Keith, told me it was definitely anaphylaxis.'

'Yes, the police are sure of that. She was found unconscious by the dog walker around eight that evening. The pathologist estimates Colette had ingested the shellfish and gone into anaphylaxis sometime between seven and eight. When you and I arrived at the cove, soon after half eight, Colette was being transferred to the hospital and her time of death was recorded there.'

'That is so terrible and so quick. I don't understand how she came to eat the shellfish or why she didn't use her EpiPen.'

'They have concluded the shellfish was in some marshmallows she'd eaten.'

'No, the marshmallows she ate were safe. They were quite expensive and in a special cardboard box.'

'Yes, they found a few left in the box, but she also had the remainder of a pink packet of marshmallows in her pocket, and these unfortunately contained fish gelatine made from shellfish.'

'But what were they doing on her?'

'No one discussed that as far as I know, but the pathologist knows she ate them. There were traces in her mouth and on her lips.'

'I don't understand it at all... they are sure these marshmallows were what caused the reaction?'

'It's not quite as exact as that. Because of the way the chemicals had broken down, it's not possible to say the allergen was in this particular thing she ate. However, they can tell she had a severe allergic reaction to shellfish, and the only thing that she had eaten appeared to be these marshmallows.'

Susan nodded. 'I don't understand it. Look, can you get back in touch with Pete and tell him Colette knew about different kind of marshmallows? I'm sure she wouldn't have eaten them.'

'Okay, I'll tell him that.'

'Thank you, and can you also ask about the EpiPen... why didn't she use it and why was it loose in her handbag? It should have been in that red velvet pouch.'

Robert put his head to one side, looked at her with gentle eyes. 'I will mention those things, I promise, but remember, the police will be very thorough, you can be sure of that.'

Susan felt her lips trembling. 'I know, but I need to have a clear picture of what happened to her. I remember her telling me how frightening it had been in the restaurant when she had anaphylaxis, the feeling of not being able to breathe, the panic, and she went through that on her own. I feel I should have looked after her, made her come back with us.'

Robert placed his hand on hers. 'Colette wasn't a child, she was a young woman who had the right to make her own choices. You couldn't have made her leave the beach, none of this is your fault. Accidents happen, you know.'

'You don't suppose the police will close the investigation yet, do you?'

'They won't do it until they are completely satisfied.'

'But you told me they were stretched; they must be tempted to accept the most obvious here so that they can move on.'

Robert frowned. 'However busy they are, they will not cut corners in the investigation of a young girl's death.'

'I hope not, because I'm not happy with this. I know Colette hasn't any family over here, but I will fight for her.'

Robert smiled gently. 'I know you mean well, Susan, but you have to trust them to do their job.'

Susan nodded, but she wasn't satisfied. She left Robert soon after and walked slowly home.

As she climbed the hill, she mulled over her conversation with Robert. He might accept the explanation of Colette's death, but she

was far from satisfied. She was determined to get to the truth of
exactly what happened to Colette down at the cove that night.

* * *

Next morning, Susan felt in need of a solitary walk. She'd not slept
well the night before, with the events of the day buzzing around in
her head. Also, when she did start to drift off, she found herself
imagining noises in the house, creaks on the stairs. In the end,
she'd slept fitfully with the light on, and it had been a relief when
day broke, and she was able to get up.

She took the dogs up to the downs. It was cold and windy, and
she could see the white tips of the waves on the sea. There was
something about the wildness of nature that morning that echoed
the tumult she felt inside.

Susan returned home exhausted but feeling calmer. She spent
the day baking, playing the piano, and gardening.

In the evening, she was about to settle to some reading, when
she was surprised to receive a visit from Pete, Robert's friend on the
police force.

As they sat together in the kitchen, he explained, 'I spoke to
Robert last night; he told me you were worried, so I came round to
see if I could put your mind at rest. I know there were a few things
you were particularly worried about, and I put these things to the
team this morning.'

'Thank you so much.'

Pete nodded sympathetically. 'Robert told me your concerns
about the marshmallows, and I brought it up at the team meeting.
The problem is we know she ate a lot of sweets, bought them in
town and from the vending machine, it's not unlikely she picked up
a packet by mistake.

'It could be that, despite what she said to you, she was hungry down at the beach and decided a few wouldn't hurt. In fact, we know she ate some and now we know how she came to be in possession of them.'

Susan sighed. 'I just can't see her taking that chance.'

'People don't always act logically, you know, and she was a young girl. She ate them of her own accord, she was alone and so no one could have forced her to eat them.'

He might have meant this as a throwaway line, but Susan grabbed it. 'Hang on. How can you be so sure about that? I'd not really considered someone else being down there with her, but of course, that would make all the difference.'

'Of course, one of the first questions we would always ask in a case of unexplained, sudden death has to be – were there any signs of foul play? However, we are satisfied Colette was down there alone. Firstly, there were no signs at all that anyone else had been down with Colette, no empty cans, no cigarette butts, or debris. Added to this, Colette didn't mention she was meeting anyone, and no one has come forward to say they were down there.'

He took a breath and continued. 'Of course, someone going down with the intention of harming her would be anxious to remove any sign they'd been there. But then we look at Colette herself. The pathologist found no evidence of a struggle, no attack, nothing like that. In particular there was no unexplained bruising around her mouth, no signs of gagging or marks on her face. We found no suspicious circumstances surrounding her death. Nothing at all. We questioned anyone who was close to her, no one had any kind of motive for wanting to hurt her. She'd not been here long, didn't know that many people, and her life seemed to revolve around her work. I know you mentioned about her grandmother, but there was no record of the incident or of anything going missing, nothing was reported. We really don't think that has any relation to this incident.'

Susan listened, trying to take in all he was telling her. They certainly had been a lot more thorough than she had given them credit for. However, she still had questions.

'But why didn't she use her EpiPen? Did you find the red velvet pouch which she kept it in, by the way?'

'Robert mentioned that. No, there was no sign of a velvet bag, but I understand the zip was broken, she must have thrown it away.'

'No, she wouldn't have done that, it was very special pouch, she told me she would always keep it.'

Pete screwed up his eyes. 'It will never be possible to explain every detail. The explanation for her not using her EpiPen must be that she simply left it too late. All the advice is to use your EpiPen sooner rather than later, but she failed to do this. She was alone, she panicked and I'm afraid she failed to take the medication in time.'

Susan listened. Maybe that was how it happened. It all sounded so plausible.

'I'm so sorry, Susan, but I'm afraid this was a terrible accident. No one else was involved, we are sure of that. There is no obvious motive, there is no physical evidence at the scene or on Colette's body.'

'You sound like the case is closed, isn't that rather soon? I know you have this big case with the people smuggling and all that—'

Pete interrupted her. 'I know we are short-staffed and very stretched, but we would never cut corners on an investigation like this. We will be presenting our findings to the coroner, and there will be an inquest. If any new evidence comes to light, it will of course be investigated.'

'I'm sorry, I didn't mean to offend you, but I feel responsible for Colette. She only has her uncle and he's not interested in fighting for her, someone has to look out for her.'

'I can understand how you feel, but you need to trust us to do our job. I know it's hard, but it would be better for you to accept this now.'

He stood up. 'I have brought you the details of how to contact someone from victim support. This has been such a shock for you. They will provide specialist help on how to cope and recover and get your life back on track.'

Susan accepted the leaflet, stood up and walked with him to the front door.

'Thank you so much for taking the time to come.'

Pete smiled. 'I hope I've helped set your mind at ease.'

She watched him walk back to his car and then went back into the house.

Maybe she had got it all wrong. The police had worked hard, and this was their job, they knew what to look for.

However, she had questions about why Colette had eaten the marshmallows, not used her EpiPen and lost the red velvet pouch. The police had answered these questions, concluded Colette's death had been an accident.

Susan shook her head, it was no good, the answers did not satisfy her; however, what was the alternative? What if someone really had been down there with Colette? Had someone accidentally given her something to eat and panicked, run off? No, she could still have used her EpiPen. Of course, someone could have wanted to frighten her for some reason. No, none of this made sense.

Susan knew where her mind was taking her – what if someone had gone down there with the sole purpose of harming Colette? She had no idea how, but could they have forced her to eat shellfish, hidden the EpiPen, watched her die and somehow mislaid the red pouch on the way?

Susan swallowed hard; this was too distressing to even contemplate. Who would do such a thing?

Her mind went to the group sitting at Steephill Cove that cold
Sunday afternoon, watching Colette accuse them of theft, talking
about collecting their secrets... would one of them really have gone
down to silence Colette? They all knew she would be there alone;
they knew about her allergy.

Susan paused. Was she really allowing herself to imagine one of
her friends doing something so wicked?

11

When Susan left the house early the next morning with the dogs, she saw that mist had come in from the sea, thick and damp. She could hardly see the houses on the other side of the street, let alone the sea in the distance. There was an eerie silence, and she was only aware of a car coming her way when she saw the headlights close to.

Pushing past dripping hedges, she kept the dogs on short leads as she headed down the hill. It wasn't until she was clambering down onto the beach that she saw everyone was down there apart from Robert.

'How are you doing?' Nikki asked. 'We missed you yesterday.'

'I went up on the downs, life has been a bit hectic. Colette's uncle came to see me on Wednesday. Have you heard the results of the post-mortem?'

'No, Robert didn't come down yesterday either, he usually knows what is going on. We've been kept in the dark. What do you know?' Everyone turned, their eyes trained on her. The mist seemed to wrap her words in cotton wool, and if felt as if even the waves had paused.

'They are saying Colette died of anaphylaxis; as a result of eating shellfish.'

'My god, how awful. What the hell had she eaten?' Nikki turned to Trystan. 'What was in the food you brought to Steephill Cove then?'

Trystan scowled. 'That's not remotely funny. Anyway, Colette didn't have any of my food.'

Nikki held up his hands in mock surrender. 'Sorry, only joking.'

'That wasn't possible in any case,' Susan explained. 'The reaction would be very quick, if Colette had eaten anything she was allergic to on the beach with us, we'd have seen her being very ill. The police found a packet of the marshmallows that contain fish gelatine in her pocket and believe she ate them.'

'But why did Colette even have them on her? She knew she couldn't eat them,' said Torri.

'The police are assuming she'd picked up a packet by mistake and then either ate some, again by mistake, or decided a few wouldn't hurt. I find that hard to imagine, but it seems to be the only explanation.'

'Wow, eating a few of the wrong marshmallows killed her!' Nathan exclaimed.

'But she had one of those EpiPens – why didn't she use it?' asked Nikki.

'The police believe she panicked and left it too late. I'm surprised about that. And also, the EpiPen was loose in her bag when I know she kept it in this special velvet pouch, and that was nowhere to be found.'

'How are the police explaining all this?' asked Beatrice.

Susan shared everything Pete had told her.

'That all makes sense,' said Beatrice and then looked more closely at Susan. 'You don't look happy, though.'

'I'm not. Even if she'd bought those marshmallows by mistake, I don't think Colette would have eaten them, and I want to know where the velvet pouch is. I am sure she would never have thrown it away.'

'But the police have to be right,' said Nathan.

Susan glanced around the group. 'Unless, of course, someone else was down there with her.'

She watched them, no one flinched, in fact it felt as if, for a moment, the whole group froze. It was Trystan who spoke first.

'Do the police think that is possible?'

Susan shook her head. 'No, not at all. They have looked into it and are convinced no one was down there, but I'm not so sure.'

Beatrice frowned. 'It sounds to me as if the police have thought this through, Susan. I think we have to accept what they have found.'

The others nodded in agreement and Susan decided not to say any more.

'Let's give the dogs a quick run,' Beatrice suggested and they let the dogs off their leads. They began to walk along but stayed as a group.

'So, what was Colette's uncle like?' asked Nikki.

'Seemed a nice enough man. He told me about his upbringing with Colette's gran, which wasn't very happy. His sister, Colette's mum, married a man as abusive to her as her own dad had been to her mum. So sad. Poor Colette had a hard time in and out of care.'

'She hid it well,' commented Torri. 'She seemed very together to me, older than her years if anything.'

'I think she had to be like that. By the way, her uncle knew about the missing items from Colette's gran's jewellery box.' She looked at each of them with a challenge in her eye and only Nikki held her gaze.

'But the home confirmed they knew nothing about the valuables?' Nikki asked.

'They did, but they must have been concerned when Colette's uncle told them things had gone missing. Are you sure they never asked you about them?'

Nikki blinked fast. 'I was thinking about it, and they did give me a ring about a week after I'd left, but I didn't know anything. Her uncle isn't going to dig it all up again, is he?' This time, there was no mistaking the shake in Nikki's voice.

'No, he's not inclined to.'

'So, the mystery dies with Colette,' said Trystan.

The words came out hard like a boulder hitting a brick wall. They shocked Susan and she looked carefully at him. 'It could do, unless of course anyone else wanted to pursue it.'

'But who would want to do that?' asked Nathan.

Susan was aware of them all staring at her through the mist. 'I don't know, but I am going to talk to Alice, a friend of Colette's grandmother at the nursing home, and see if she remembers anything.'

'But why?' demanded Trystan. 'There is no point now.'

Again, Susan felt them all watching her, waiting to see what she would say.

'I feel I owe it to Colette to at least check a few things out.'

'But you don't suspect any of us of stealing, do you?' asked Torri.

'Of course not,' replied Susan automatically.

'What happened to Colette's possessions?' asked Beatrice.

Susan caught her eye and remembered their conversation about throwing away the contents of the jewellery box.

'I am going to sort them out. Colette's uncle told me to keep the jewellery box and locket, I shall deal with them.' She looked over at Beatrice, who gave her a swift nod, and Susan hoped she took this to mean she had disposed of the contents of the box.

'And I hope that will be an end to all this,' insisted Trystan. 'No good can come from digging over the past.'

'That's what I said to Colette when she told me she was seeing a psychic,' said Beatrice.

Susan blinked. 'Did you say she was seeing a psychic?'

'Yes. A medium called Lauren over in St Hilda's. Colette had been asking her about her grandmother. I told her they would say anything for money, but she wouldn't listen to me.'

'Now, enough of all this, it's so depressing,' said Nikki, breaking the silence. 'Have any of you got tickets for the next production yet? It's not long.'

No one seemed inclined to pick up the conversation, however, and they continued to walk along quietly, with only the odd comment. Everyone seemed preoccupied and they quickly agreed the weather was not that pleasant for walking and to go home.

Once home, Susan went and found her laptop. She remembered the psychic was called Lauren and lived in St Hilda's. Susan found her phone number easily.

Susan rang her up and was fortunate to catch her. She wasn't sure quite what she was expecting but the woman was refreshingly frank and business-like. She remembered Colette and had been very concerned when she'd read in the paper what had happened. Susan asked if she could go and see her, explaining that although she didn't want a reading, she would like to book a formal consultation as she had something she wanted to show her. They booked for an hour's consultation the following Tuesday.

Susan had a sense of relief at having organised something. Also, of course, she would be seeing Alice, the lady who had been a friend of Colette's gran at the nursing home that afternoon. Hopefully she would get some answers there to the mystery of the locket, even a hint as to who had taken it. It sounded as though, if Colette's gran had confided in anyone, it would be Alice.

Susan set off for the nursing home after lunch. It was set high up in the town and had a wonderful view down to the sea. The reception area was very bright and cheerful, and Susan was welcomed by one of the senior health care workers, who took her through to the lounge. Susan found about ten residents waiting for her and she introduced herself to them all.

The session went well, and Susan enjoyed it as much as the residents. When she'd finished, one of the nursing staff, a middle-aged woman with very short black hair and bright red glasses, whose name badge read 'Kathy', offered her a cup of tea. They began chatting about life in Ventnor, and it wasn't difficult to introduce the subject of Colette. As expected, the news about the terrible accident was widely known now, and Kathy seemed quite excited to be talking to the person Colette had lived with.

'Poor Colette. I heard it was something to do with an allergy she had?'

'I believe so,' Susan said guardedly.

'I know Nikki, she runs the hotel where Colette worked. Nikki and I became good friends when she worked here, she even invited me to the opening of the hotel. Of course, I'd met Colette myself, she came here a few times. Her grandmother was a resident here, she liked talking to Alice, who had known her.'

'Colette was so pleased the home found her gran's locket. Who'd have thought it after three years? I think a few other things went missing, didn't they?'

Kathy stepped back, the easy friendliness on her face melting away. 'I don't remember anything about that. Now, I can't stand here chatting. Maybe you would like to meet Alice? That's her sitting over there. I'm sure she'd enjoy chatting to you.'

Susan walked over to Alice and, seeing her, thought Colette's estimation of her being around ninety was probably correct. Her hair was fine, straight, and white, her complexion papery thin, with gentle wrinkles on her pretty heart-shaped face.

Alice looked up as she saw Susan approach, her thin lips spread into a smile and behind her neat glasses, sparkling clear grey eyes. She was holding an iPad, her hands slightly shaky and curled in a way that suggested arthritic fingers.

'I so enjoyed your playing,' said Alice. 'It was very kind of you to play the old songs for us. The piano could do with a good tune, I have mentioned it to them before.' There was a slightly tight, tremulous quality to her voice, but her manner was clear and precise.

Susan sat down. 'Thank you. So do you play?'

'Not very well, my mother did, though.'

Susan paused. She'd come with every intention of asking Alice about Colette but now she was here, it dawned on her that, of course, this elderly woman might have no notion of what had happened to Colette and if she didn't, was she the right person to be breaking this news?

Susan thought she would open gently. 'Have you always lived in Ventnor?'

'Oh, no, I ran the village shop over in Bishopstone for years. My daughter still lives over there.'

'I lived over in Freshwater when I was still a baby, but we went over to Compton and Brook beaches a lot. Apparently, my dad's side of the family originally came from Bishopstone, but that was a long time ago. I love the village. If my husband hadn't been offered a partnership in the surgery over in Ventnor, we might even have moved there.'

'Well, what a small world it is.'

'It's a small island, anyway. There's a lovely nursing home over there, why did you come all the way over here?' asked Susan.

'I was worried my daughter would feel obliged to keep popping in, they have their own lives to live.' Alice paused. 'Now, I was told Colette used to live with you. She used to come and chat to me; I am wondering if that is really why you have come today? Did you want to talk to me about her?'

Susan was taken aback but also relieved by the directness of the older woman.

'Do you know about what has happened to Colette?'

'One of the nurses here told me she died of a nasty accident, had eaten some shellfish. All they kept telling me was that it had been very quick and that she'd not suffered. I know they were trying to save my feelings, but I explained to them they had no idea how Colette was feeling when she died. The problem is when you get to my age, people assume any little thing will upset you, when in fact there is very little left that can shock someone who has lived for ninety years. So, I am very glad you are here, and I would be very grateful if you would tell me everything that has happened to poor Colette.'

12

Susan nodded. 'Of course, and you are right, I have come to speak to you about Colette. I am so shocked and, to be honest, rather confused about what has happened. Colette used to talk to you?'

'She did. I had been great friends with her grandmother, Pam, as she was to me. She liked hearing about her, but she was also worried about what happened to some of her things after Pam died.'

'She told you about that? Do you remember them going missing?'

'Nobody said anything to me at the time, but I heard on the grapevine there had been questions about something going missing. It was interesting to meet Colette, she reminded me a lot of her grandmother, but she had more fight in her than Pam. Such a bright girl and so pretty, what a waste.'

'I agree, it was tragic for her to die so young. She was just starting to dare to have dreams and make plans for her life.'

Alice nodded. 'You're right. I am glad she was able to talk to you, there were so few people she trusted. She used to talk about the other people in your dog-walking group, but she wasn't that close to them, was she?'

'You know about them as well?'

'Oh, yes.' Alice smiled. 'I do love hearing all the gossip, I miss that from my days in the shop. Colette told me all about them. Of course, I'd met most of them when they worked here. I've been here five years now. I got the impression that Nikki and you were the only ones in that group that Colette particularly liked. Now, before we move on, tell me what is happening about her little dog Libs? Colette was so fond of her.'

'She is staying with me. I have a dog of my own, Rocco; they have quickly become friends.'

'Good, I'm glad. Now for Colette. The last time I saw her was the Saturday before she died, she came up here and was told they'd found Pam's locket. Colette came in and showed me, she was very worried about it all, I know she suspected someone from the group of stealing it.'

'Colette told you a lot.'

'There was to be some meet-up at Steephill Cove the next day, I know Colette was planning to confront them all. I warned her not to, but I had a feeling she was determined to go through with it.'

'Oh, yes. In fact, it was a really difficult afternoon.'

'Ah, I wondered, tell me what happened.'

'Colette showed them the locket, she told them she was convinced one of them had stolen it from her grandmother. It was very awkward—'

'But I don't suppose anyone owned up, I told Colette no one was going to admit to such a thing in front of everyone. Did she say anything else?'

Susan wondered about telling Alice about the secrets Colette had threatened the group with but was reluctant to do so. In the same way she had been uneasy about Colette's methods of searching for secrets, and then using them, she was pretty sure Alice would not approve either and why spoil her memory of Colette?

'I can't think of anything else.'

'I see. Now, the nurse told me Colette had eaten something that set off her allergy, is that right?'

'Yes, apparently she ate some marshmallows with fish gelatine in them.'

'You don't look convinced?'

Susan told her the story of the packets of marshmallows.

'So, they believe she bought a packet with fish gelatine in by mistake, and then ate them on the beach?'

'That's right. But then why she didn't use her EpiPen? I'm sorry, I don't mean to worry you.'

'No, it's fine. I had a feeling something didn't sound right. I knew how careful she was, and she showed me that pen thing. I couldn't understand why she'd not used it either.'

Susan felt relieved that at last someone else was asking the same questions as her.

'Yes, and there is another mystery. Colette kept the EpiPen in a velvet pouch and that is missing.'

'But the police must be asking all the same questions as us, aren't they? Although I know they are very busy at the moment, a terrible thing, bringing people over here and treating them as slaves.'

Susan blinked. 'You know about that?'

'Oh, yes, I am very lucky. The nurse who looks after me tells me a lot of the gossip, although as I say, she tends to miss out anything she thinks might upset me. So, with Colette, do you think they are being as thorough as they should?'

'I have been reassured several times now that they have been very thorough, and everything has been checked up on. You see,

they don't suspect anyone else being involved, and they have
grounds for that, and so they are prepared to accept she died accidentally.'

'Yes, I can see that. Why are they so sure no one else was down
there with her?'

Susan told her about the lack of physical evidence and the fact
Colette had not talked about meeting anyone.

'I see, but someone could have decided to go down there
without warning Colette, presumably everyone in the group at least
knew she would be down there.'

'They did, but they are not admitting to it if they did. Why
would they go down there anyway? They could talk to her back at
the hotel if they needed to say something.'

'That is assuming all they wanted to do was talk.'

Susan took a deep breath, moved closer to Alice. 'Are you
suggesting someone wanted to hurt Colette?'

Alice pushed her glasses back, held her chin up. 'I am sure it's
what is in the back of your mind.'

Susan frowned. 'It is, I admit that, but why do you think anyone
want to harm her?'

Alice tapped held out a crooked, shaking finger. 'We know that
she had accused someone in that group of stealing from her
grandmother.'

'I thought about that but then, is that really a motive for hurting
her? Even if someone in the group had stolen the locket from
Colette's gran, they would know there is no proof, and it was three
years ago, would anyone care now?'

'But it wasn't just the locket, was it... there was also the book and
the brooch, which Colette's uncle might have been mistaken about.
If the brooch had been real, it would have been worth a lot of
money. A big temptation if someone had seen it.'

'Who here knew about the jewellery box?'

'The only resident Pam told was me. However, she did show the brooch to Beatrice, asked her to value it.'

'Did she?'

'About two weeks before she died. Beatrice told her it was fake, but Pam didn't believe her. She was going to ask someone else. So, Beatrice and I knew and, of course, Pam did find someone actually handling the jewellery box one day.'

Susan sat up. 'She told Colette that as well. Do you know who it was?'

'No. It was later on the day Colette visited. Pam told me she'd seen one of "the hotel bunch" holding her jewellery box and they looked very guilty.'

'She then said she thought she should get a second opinion about the brooch. If it was worth something, she agreed it would be wiser to have it locked away. She was going to ask a man who visited here, a jeweller from the town.'

'And what did he say?'

'I never got to ask Pam. I think he must have looked at it a few days before she died. I don't know what he said.'

'But she never had the brooch put away?'

'No, unfortunately she died and there was no time to sort it out, she died so suddenly.'

'Colette's uncle told me she died after a tummy upset and then her heart failed. Is that right?'

Alice nodded. 'Yes, in fact we had an outbreak of food poisoning, she wasn't the only one to be unwell, but it hit her worse than the rest of us and then her heart just couldn't take it. Anyway,' continued Alice, 'I'm glad Pam had the locket right up until the end, she told me it was one of the few things that reminded her of when she was truly happy.'

'Colette said very much the same thing to me about the locket.'

'Yes, she'd had it hard, hadn't she? It's why I worry about all this so much. It's not as if she has family to fight for her.'

'And you really believe someone needs to be fighting?'

Alice nodded. 'Yes, I've had my concerns since I was told about Colette's death. What with the locket and the confrontation that day, it all seemed too much of a coincidence. Now, talking to you, I am even more convinced. Colette was clearly getting closer to knowing who the thief was, they had to have realised that.'

'You seriously think someone would hurt Colette because they were frightened she would reveal they were a thief?'

Alice placed one hand over the other, and spoke sternly. 'Susan, it would be better to speak frankly here. I know you may be more comfortable with the word "hurt", but what we are really talking about is murder. The question we are discussing is did someone in your dog-walking group murder Colette to stop her revealing them to be a thief?'

Susan gasped. The words were too hard, too raw. The gentleness she'd seen in Alice had melted away and been replaced by white-hot anger. Susan was suddenly scared of Alice, she wanted to run away, forget the conversation had ever happened.

Alice met her eye and spoke more softly. 'I'm sorry, but that is the truth of it, and you know it deep down. Now, there is also something you are not telling me. When I asked you if anything else had happened on the beach, you hesitated.'

Susan fiddled with her rings. 'I didn't want to spoil your memory of Colette, she did something and I'm still not sure how I feel about it.'

Alice nodded. 'I thought as much. It would be much better if you told me, you never know, I might understand it better than you imagine.'

Susan took a breath and proceeded to tell Alice about Colette's collection of secrets.

'I see. She found out things about each of the people in the group, kept evidence and was planning to blackmail someone into confessing to being the thief?'

'I don't know about blackmail.'

'Again, it's important to use the correct word. Colette was using damaging information she had found out about people to demand something in return. If you face up to the word, you will see why you are so uncomfortable about admitting to Colette doing it and also, we can try to unpack why she did it.'

'She sounded desperate, claimed it was the only way people would take any notice of her.'

'And she was probably right. The other way hadn't worked, had it? You have to remember Colette had a very different upbringing to me or you. She was raised in a jungle, she had to learn how to survive. I don't like the fact she did it, but I can understand why.'

Susan breathed out slowly. 'That is it exactly. However, I have no idea what any of the things she did collect mean.'

'Ah, so you looked, tell me what you found.'

'There was a mixture of things. A newspaper cutting; a letter; some photograph she'd taken at Beatrice's house; a page of contents from a magazine; and some tiny yellow roses and a mention of a love song.'

'Tell me more exactly about each one.'

Susan went through each one in detail.

'I see. Well, the rose and song indicate some kind of love interest.'

'Yes, but she never mentioned anything to me about a boyfriend or anyone like that.'

'No, but the fact she'd kept the flower and song among her collection of secrets suggests the man was someone in the dog-walking group.'

'That would be Trystan or Nathan, but both are in relationships with other people. Although, funnily enough, when I mentioned this to Nikki this morning, she suggested Trystan might have been interested in Colette.'

Alice smiled. 'Did she now? Oh, but there is another man in your group, isn't there? He was a policeman.'

'That's Robert, he had nothing to do with the nursing home and I am sure he wasn't in any kind of relationship with Colette, he is much older than her.'

Alice gave a sly grin. 'You defend him well.' She sat in silence for a moment and then said, 'This photo of Beatrice's room sounds interesting.'

'I think she had some doubts about Beatrice's husband. Do you know Beatrice at all?'

'A bit. Pam loved that dog, Biddy. I'm not so fussed on them. There is a hardness in Beatrice, isn't there – I wonder what had happened or what she's done. There is something there. I don't suppose there was anything else in the photo?'

'Not that I can recall.'

Alice sighed. 'It's all very confusing, isn't it? If someone killed Colette, in a way we can't figure out yet, then we have two lots of motives. There is the revelation about the theft or the revelation of these secrets.'

'Or, of course, it could have been someone else entirely.'

'No, I don't believe so,' said Alice. 'This was no stranger. It was someone who knew Colette well, that she'd be down at the cove. Also, they knew about her allergies and where she kept her EpiPen. There had to be some connection with what occurred on the beach and that would be one of the people in that group.'

'But it had to be someone desperate, didn't it? I mean it was a horrible way to kill someone. And here we are suggesting it was someone I see most days, chat to on the beach – I can't imagine any of them doing such a terrible thing.'

'No, of course not, but then we never really know people, do we? I'm not saying everyone is hiding a side that could do something quite so wicked – well, I don't think so.' Alice paused as if considering this. 'No, on balance, a person who commits premeditated murder has to have something about them that sets them apart from most people, a darkness, a coldness, a selfishness even. Fortunately, most people do not turn to murder as a way of solving their problems and for that we must be grateful.'

Susan smiled. 'You speak so matter-of-factly. I came in and saw a sweet little old lady, I had no idea what went in your head.'

Alice smiled back. 'For some reason, people assume that as you get older, you get soft, you see everyone as an angel, but that is ridiculous. We have lived a long time; we have seen the best but also the worst of people. However, just because I can speak so calmly about such terrible things, doesn't mean I am not angry and shocked by what this person has done. But that won't help Colette, will it? No, we need to think coolly and carefully if we are to solve this.'

'It's such an awful thing to contemplate.'

Alice sat up. 'I know, but unfortunately people can be a lot more wicked than we realise.'

'Colette used the word "wicked" as well. She told me that I'd not thought carefully enough about the kind of person who would have stolen from her grandmother.'

'Yes, I believe she was only just starting to realise that. Now, I don't suppose you know what any of them were doing when Colette was killed?'

Susan blinked, thought back to the discussion on the beach. 'Nikki was at drama. Nathan, um, yes, he didn't go surfing, he was in his shed. Torri and Trystan went running and Beatrice was talking to her sister on the phone.'

'I see, well, it would be worth checking up, people do tell a lot of lies, you know. And then there is motive. We have the clues among these treasures, but I can't help feeling we are missing something. However carefully you plan a murder, it's risky, and there has to be a decent motive and we need to find that.'

Susan sighed. 'I will try to find out what I can, Alice, but I can't promise anything.'

'No, but you are a very bright woman, I have every faith in you. You do need to be very careful, though. Remember, if we are right, this person has already killed someone and believes they have got away with it. They are not going to take kindly to you interfering.'

'Yes, I can see that. Now, I am guessing you would like me to return sometime and keep you up to date.'

'Of course.' Alice looked around. 'I suppose you've heard about our tenth tea party do coming up?'

'No, nothing.'

'It's two weeks tomorrow. They are trying to get everyone together who has worked here during that time. You come along to that; we can chat then.'

'I'm not sure I quite qualify.'

Alice grinned. 'Come as my guest.'

Susan smiled back. 'Okay, I'll come, thank you.'

'Good,' said Alice and then her face became more serious. 'And remember the last two people who wore that locket are dead.'

'I shall watch my back, don't you worry.' Susan got up to leave.

'I shall look forward to seeing you again and don't forget to bring me those items Colette had been collecting, I'd like to see them for myself.'

'Of course, I will try to come back soon.'

Susan made her way out of the nursing home and began her walk home.

She was feeling rather stunned by the conversation. She had just admitted to believing someone in her group was a killer, a murderer. This person was someone very close to her, someone she saw every day. Which one of them was it?

And then she remembered the break-in that night. What if the person who killed Colette had been the same person who'd broken in? If so, she had been lying in her bed, sleeping, totally unaware that a killer was in her home, close enough to hear her breathe, close enough to take that final breath away from her.

13

It wasn't often that Susan felt the need to get off the island, but as she gathered things together for herself and the dogs that Saturday morning, she was glad to be leaving, if only for the day. She was tired, grieving and she needed a break.

Instead of going to the beach, she took Rocco and Libs up on the downs early to have a good run around. She had never taken two dogs away in the car or on the ferry and she had no idea how Libs would travel.

Packing up to leave with the dogs reminded Susan of taking Zoe and the foster children away when they were little, when there was far more stuff for them than herself. For herself, she just needed her bag, phone, keys, and money. For the dogs, she needed food, blankets, water, leads, poo bags, treats, the list went on.

However, just as she was finally ready to leave the house, she heard the postman at the door. With no sense of what he might be delivering, she opened the door with a smile and took the letters.

But then she saw the official letter in her hand. The day she had been dreading had come.

She closed the door, walked into the kitchen, and made herself open the letter. Scanning it, her heart sank as she read the words: *made final and absolute and that the said marriage was thereby dissolved.*

She reread the words – the odd ancient words like 'thereby' added to the seriousness of the document, and then the word 'dissolve', not a word most people used to describe the end of their marriage, but in a way, a good one. When you dissolve salt in water, it disappears, but of course the tiny particles are still there, affecting every drop of water in the glass, and that was how it felt to her.

All those years she had been with Steve, all those memories were still part of her. She had loved him and felt loved most of those forty years, but this piece of paper told her that had officially ended.

It wasn't the fact that she wasn't a 'married woman' any more that upset her, she had always held the notion of being married quite lightly. No, it was as if someone had taken away a beautiful book she'd spent years compiling, full of stories and adventures, and replaced it with one of those fancy but rather scary blank journals and told her to start again. It wasn't exciting, it was terrifying.

As so often with huge, life-changing moments, Susan did not collapse into tears. Her body was protecting her and instead of a vast outpouring of emotion, she was wrapped up in cotton wool, anaesthetised against the hurt.

Susan checked her watch, it was getting late, she needed to leave if she was to catch the ferry.

She took the bags to the car and then settled the dogs securely in the back. Forcing herself to concentrate on the road, she drew away from the house.

Once on the ferry, she bought coffee, asking for a double shot, and sat sipping her drink. Fortunately, Libs was proving to be a good traveller and for that Susan knew she had to be grateful to Rocco. He had always loved going in the car, and the ferry, and had been doing it since he was little. Libs simply took her cues from him.

Her mind went back to that awful final evening with her husband, no, her ex-husband, Steve. Everyone says you see it coming, or at least in retrospect you see signs you missed. But Susan had seen none. Life had been exactly as normal until the evening he sat down and quietly told her he was leaving her for someone else. Not only that, but he was taking early retirement with her, and they were going off sailing.

Before she could speak, he told her he'd seen a solicitor, the house was now in her name, she was well provided for.

Looking back, Susan couldn't believe she hadn't rowed and fought with him, but she had been in shock, totally numb.

The following evening, she had still been in denial as she'd watched Steve pack his things and load up the car to take to Hester's house. Was this real?

It was only as the days went by and Steve didn't return from work, as she found herself looking for shirts to wash and throwing away half the rice she'd cooked for tea, that she really started to believe he was never coming back.

The island gently held her, wrapped her up, and Rocco's love of finding everything new seemed to hold out a tiny glimmer of hope. They walked miles together, going to isolated hidden beaches or up on St Boniface downs, the highest point on the island where she could look down, like the buzzards, on the sea or on tiny villages among the carpet of fields and woodland.

Over time she'd started to heal, or at least she thought she had, until events like this morning tore the plaster off to reveal a gaping sore.

The drive the other side was not too long, as Zoe and Fay lived in a small village outside of Portsmouth. The small newbuild seemed to suit their lifestyle well. As Susan approached, she saw

Zoe look out of the bedroom window. She came running down to meet her and gave her a huge hug.

'Mum, it's so lovely to see you – it's just you and me today, Fay is off at a meeting.'

The dogs were given an enthusiastic welcome too and they went straight out into the garden.

'We'll go for a good walk in the woods later, shall we?' suggested Zoe.

Susan thought her daughter looked well, and yet there was an underlying tension in her manner, a slight edge to her words, a restlessness.

She turned to Susan. 'How are you, Mum? What a time you've had, you look exhausted. I am so sorry about Colette.'

Susan began to tell Zoe the latest updates from the police.

'It's awful, Mum. It was a terrible thing to happen to Colette. You have to try and put it behind you.'

'The problem is I have questions about her death that are not being answered. I know the police don't believe anyone else is involved, but I'm not so sure.'

'Why is that?'

Susan tried to explain as briefly as she could what she and Alice had been talking about. Zoe's eyes grew wider and wider.

'Good god, Mum, you are thinking one of your dog-walking friends could have killed Colette? If one of them had been involved, the police would have found out about it.'

'But I knew Colette, things don't add up.'

'Listen, Mum. You've been through such a hard time, maybe this accident has got a bit out of perspective. You have let this lady Alice wind you up; remember she is sitting around in that nursing home with hours to mull things over. She's probably let her imagination run wild.'

'She seemed pretty together to me.'

'Even if she is, the police are the people who should be handling this. Listen, all this digging around you are doing, don't you think you are really simply trying to appease some misplaced sense of responsibility for Colette's death? You have always been the person who looks after everyone and for some reason you feel you failed Colette.'

Susan squirmed in her seat. 'I suppose there is an element of that.'

'Then stop. You gave Colette a home, you took good care of her. You don't need to be doing any more. The police are the experts. These people are your friends, it was all right for Colette to go throwing accusations around, but you live with them. Now, how about lunch and then a walk in the woods?'

The walk did Susan good, and she finally felt able to tell Zoe about the letter that had arrived that morning.

'Now the divorce is final, it's rather thrown me.' Susan felt her lip tremble but she mustn't cry in front of Zoe. Even at thirty, she was still her child to be protected. 'I'm okay, I just need it to sink in.'

'This is so much harder for you than Dad, isn't it?'

Susan took a deep breath. 'I don't want him to take all the blame—'

'You are very generous, Mum, but I do hold him responsible for all this. However, I am trying to get on better with him, we have had a few good chats.'

'Good, I'm glad.'

'The thing is, Mum, I have my reasons now for wanting us all to get on better.'

'Why is that? What's going on?'

They had reached a clearing in the woods and sat on a small bench.

'I'm not sure how you are going to take this, Mum, but, well, Fay and I are having a baby.'

Susan gasped, the news couldn't have more of a surprise.

'Sorry. What?'

Zoe laughed. 'Fay and I are having a baby. You are going to be a granny.'

Susan quickly tried to gather her thoughts. 'Darling, I am thrilled for you, tell me all about it.'

Zoe let out a long sigh of relief. 'Well, we decided about a year ago to look into our options and decided to go for sperm donation, using a clinic. We had one or two friends we could have asked but we were worried about, well, the future, we really want this to be our baby.'

'So, um—'

Zoe laughed. 'I'll explain. We had to decide whose eggs we were going to use, and who was going to carry the baby.'

'And—'

'Fay has never wanted to be pregnant; it terrifies her, to be honest, and so we are using my eggs and I am carrying the baby.'

Susan stared at her.

'And now I'm three months pregnant.'

Susan felt a flood of emotions well up inside her, she was close to tears.

'That is so wonderful, how have you been keeping?'

'Really sick, actually.'

'Oh, you poor thing. I was too, it's awful.'

'I know if one more man tells me they have heard being sick is a good sign, I will hit them. Still—' she laid her hand protectively over her stomach '—it feels wonderful at the same time.'

Susan grinned. 'It's fantastic news, I am so pleased for you both.'

'Thank you.'

'We will get all the legal things sorted out so that we are both equal guardians. I want Fay to feel this is as much her baby as mine, and in fact she has been asking at work about taking a year or two out to stay at home and look after the baby.'

'And you would go back?'

'Yes, I know I moan about work, but I'd go crazy without it – a headship is coming up in a very good school, I am thinking of applying.'

'You have thought things through very well. Have you told Dad yet?'

'No, I wanted to tell you first, but I'll ring him later. I expect he'll fuss about what I should and shouldn't be eating. He doesn't trust anyone medically, does he, but I think he's going to be pleased, isn't he?'

'Of course he will, we sometimes talked about having grandchildren. I've still got some of your toddler toys at home, your Duplo and a doll's house. I was going to give them away, but Dad said to hold onto them.'

Susan bit her lip hard to stop herself crying. This was a moment she'd always dreamed of sharing with Steve. They had both cared so much about children, and they had always been totally in sync about how they felt children should be raised. She was sure they would have been great grandparents, but now it would be something they would do separately.

Susan was aware of Zoe watching her, and suddenly Zoe put her arm around her.

'Oh, Mum. It's a lot to take in, isn't it?'

'It is, but I am so pleased for you and Fay.'

'Thank you, I knew you would be. Now, I did have a favour to ask. I was wondering if you would be happy to come over again next weekend, bring the dogs, stay the night.'

'When you have Dad and Hester coming?'

'Yes. They are coming for a walk on Sunday morning and then they are taking Fay and me out for Sunday lunch. Us three could have Saturday together, and then on Sunday, I was thinking we could all have coffee and a nice walk together. You could, of course, come out for lunch as well, I could tell Dad to book for five, what do you think?'

Susan saw that heart-wrenching hope in Zoe's eyes. She had to try for her sake.

'Look, I've not met Hester yet or seen your dad for a long time, it's not going to be easy. How about I come over Saturday, stay the night and join in with coffee and the walk the next morning. I think I'll skip lunch, that will be enough for now, I think.'

Zoe have her a big hug. 'Thank you so much, Mum. Hester is a bit – oh, never mind, you'll cope, I'm sure.'

'It's probably time I met her.'

'That's great. Now, Mum, there is something else I need to ask you, it might take a bit more thinking over, though.'

Susan listened to Zoe, her mind racing as her daughter spoke. What was she going to do?

They returned to the house, and later she drove away, her head full of all the news. It was dark by the time Susan drove onto the returning ferry. The feeling of returning to the island was always the same, one of going home. The adventure completed and now all she wanted was for the sailing to end and to be back on the island.

Her mind drifted to that final part of the conversation with Zoe. Her daughter had asked if she would think about moving over to live with her, Fay and the baby. They had apparently been looking at a larger property and it had a bungalow in the grounds. Susan grimaced at the thought of a 'granny flat' but Zoe quickly explained it was very self-contained. However, it would be great to have her close by to help with the baby...'

Sensing her reluctance, Zoe had gone on to reason that her mum was going to have to think about moving soon in any case, the house was too big, the hills too much for her to clamber up each day.

Susan had answered as tactfully as she could, but she would need time to think about it. She could see Zoe was disappointed. Zoe liked to act once she decided something, and Susan guessed she wanted to go home and put an offer on the house immediately, but she explained to Zoe that this was a huge decision, and she couldn't rush. Zoe was honest enough to admit that Fay had warned her that Susan might feel like this and had backed off.

Susan felt torn. She knew she'd been hiding from the idea of moving house but guessed sometimes she was going to have to face it. She hadn't really thought about leaving the island. However, if Zoe and Fay needed her, maybe she should go. And to be so close to her grandchildren would be wonderful, wouldn't it? However, would it really work, her being so close to Zoe and Fay? They needed to make this life together. Fay's parents lived away in Scotland, and Susan was sure they had no intention of moving. It crossed her mind that Zoe and Fay might think of moving there if she said no to being close to them. Susan shook her head, no, she couldn't go making decisions on that basis.

She sighed, closed her eyes, and tried to unwind, recognising she was far too tired to make a sensible decision about this tonight.

The announcement to disembark came over the tannoy, and so Susan took the dogs down to the car, settled them in their beds and drove off the ferry.

She drove through all the familiar villages, Whippenham, Wootton, Arreton, until she finally arrived at Worrall... nearly home. The darkness was comforting, the dogs quietly snoring in the back.

Finally, she arrived at the outskirts of Ventnor, felt herself relax as she drove through the town and into her road. Home.

She parked outside the house, windows pitch black, eyes shut.

The dogs were sitting up now, but she took out the bags first, climbed the flight of steps and opened the front door. Dumping the bags in the hallway, she returned for the dogs.

However, as soon as she closed the front door, she was aware that something was badly wrong. The dogs, sensing her panic, ran back to her, and she stood frozen, numb with fear.

14

Susan could see that some of the pictures down the hallway were slightly skewed, and she knew for certain someone had been in her home. Maybe they were still there. She walked slowly and quietly down the tiled hallway, listening all the while, but the house was silent. She pushed the kitchen door fully open and saw that a packet of oats that had been sitting on the kitchen worksurface had toppled over and spilled all over the floor. Walking around the room, the surfaces were cluttered and untidy, but nothing had been disturbed.

She went into the living room. The room was a mess, that was its usual state, but some cushions had been pulled off the sofa, they had definitely been moved. It confirmed her fear, someone had broken in while she'd been away. Susan froze, of course, they could still be here. She stood very still and listened. No, she couldn't hear anything.

The dogs were still busy sniffing for the remaining few oats on the floor and she crept upstairs.

The bedroom doors were open. Glancing in, her own room seemed hardly touched, but there were signs of greater disruption in Colette's room. Drawers had been pulled out, the wardrobe door was flung open, and bags emptied onto the floor. However, the only thing that appeared broken was the beautiful old wooden box which lay on the carpet in pieces.

Susan ran back downstairs to ring the police.

The first thing they expressed was concern for her safety and when they learnt she was alone, they told her she should leave the house immediately. Susan replied that she was sure the intruder had left, and they told her they would send someone round as soon as possible.

Susan waited nervously, the dogs by her side, and she realised they had not been out since they returned. She went to the back door, noticed it was secure and locked and let them out into the garden. While she was watching them, the doorbell rang and Susan welcomed in a young police officer. He seemed alarmingly young but was very calm and matter of fact, which was just what Susan needed.

He went around the house with her, checking the windows and doors, there was no sign of a forced entry. Looking at the state of the rooms, he tried to ask tactfully how much had been disturbed and Susan was able to tell him exactly what had been moved. It was then Susan remembered the key safe and she took the officer out to check it. To Susan's horror, she saw the door swinging open and the key missing.

'My god, they used my key, that's how they got in.'

'It certainly appears that way. Let's go back inside and see if you can tell me if anything is missing. Do you have anywhere you keep cash, jewellery, expensive laptops, that kind of thing?'

'Not really, none of my jewellery is that special, my laptop is an old one of my daughter's and I think most people would think my TV far too small now. The piano is the most expensive thing we have ever bought and that's not that easy to pop into the back of a van.' She gave a hollow laugh.

'Um, no, exactly, well, let's check around again.'

They walked around the house again, nothing appeared to be missing, and only the jewellery box in Colette's room had been damaged.

The officer didn't seem unduly surprised. 'You do not appear to have the kind of items a burglar might be looking for.'

Susan smiled weakly. 'The benefits of living simply, eh?'

'I guess it is. Now, you may want to claim on your insurance for the broken box, I will leave you to sort that out. We will provide you with a crime reference number, take photos before you tidy things away.'

'Will anyone one else will be coming round?'

'As nothing is stolen, I doubt it.'

'So, no one is coming to take fingerprints?'

'No, they won't do that. You can tidy up now. I would get a locksmith around, sort out your keys and change the code on your key safe. If you have any further worries, though, do call us. Now it might be a good idea to call a friend, have them come round?'

Suddenly the doorbell rang and Susan opened the door to Nikki. 'I saw the police car, are you okay?' she asked in a rush.

Susan blinked back tears. 'Someone broke in, but nothing appears to be missing. Come in.'

The young police officer gave a gentle cough, 'I'll be on my way now. As I said, we won't be calling again, but don't hesitate to get in contact if you think there is anything else we need to know, or if you are concerned in any way.'

He smiled at Nikki and quickly left. The dogs came running to meet Nikki, and while she made a fuss of them, Susan explained.

'I think they must have used the key in the key safe. I've been stupid, I should have put a decent code on there, in fact, I shall get rid of the thing all together.'

They went into the kitchen and Susan went to put the kettle on. However, Nikki noticed an unopened bottle of wine on the work surface. 'I think you need something stronger.' Susan found two glasses and Nikki poured the wine.

Before they sat down, Susan asked, 'I wonder if you'd come upstairs with me? I have to take photos of Colette's room and I feel a bit nervous about going up there.'

'Of course, come on. Let's do it now. I can help you clear up then, if you like.'

They walked upstairs and went into Colette's room.

'Wow, the little bastards made a right mess in here,' commented Nikki. 'Is that the jewellery box Colette told us about?'

'Yes, it's been pretty thoroughly destroyed.'

'It certainly has.'

Susan put down the untouched glass of wine and took some photos with her phone and then went to the wardrobe. She knelt down, picked up the teddy, lying among the mess, and held it to her. The stress and emotion of the past week tore at her, her whole body shook as she sobbed.

'Oh, no, oh, Susan, you poor thing,' said Nikki and she put her arm around her.

'I'm sorry,' sobbed Susan. 'It's all too much. Talking to Alice and then the news from Zoe, I'm so confused. My marriage has ended officially today, you know, it's finished. It feels like everything is ending, and I've failed. I've failed at saving Colette, I can't even keep this house safe.'

Nikki sat next to her, put her arm around her and finally spoke.

'None of this is your fault. You didn't fail Colette. Susan, you are exhausted. Why don't you come to the hotel tonight? I've plenty of spare rooms made up. We can take Rocco and Libs, they can settle with Duke, what do you think?'

Susan looked up miserably, glanced at her watch. It was only nine o'clock; the thought of a whole night here alone was unbearable.

'I don't know.' She was so shaken, it was hard to think straight.

'Come on, Susan, all of this will be a lot easier to face in the morning.'

Susan smiled weakly. 'That's really kind, thank you. Yes, I think I might take you up on that. I'll pay, of course—'

'No way, come on, you only need a nightie, everything else is provided for you.' Nikki smiled. 'We are a very boutique hotel, you know. Mind you, if we take the dog beds, they will probably settle better.'

They put a few things in a bag for her, picked up the dogs' beds, and shut up the house. The dogs seemed excited to be going out again, although they only had a short distance to walk.

The hotel was a large, neat, detached Victorian house, painted white and grey, and smart tiled steps with neatly manicured potted shrubs to the side led to an immaculate white front door. Warm lights welcomed you in.

Inside, Nikki and Nathan had worked hard to keep the 'bones' of the Victorian building, with stunning bay windows and high ceilings, and Susan knew Robert had spent hours carefully restoring the elaborate plaster mouldings and ceiling roses.

On the walls were paintings and photographs of the rare Glanville fritillary butterfly, a butterfly found in secret chalky places on the island and almost nowhere else in Britain. Susan had not seen the butterfly often but when she had managed to, she was in awe of its beautiful orange and brown chequered patterning.

To the left of the reception area were the restaurant and bar.

This evening, Susan followed Nikki to the office behind the reception area.

This was a large room, and Duke was curled up asleep in his bed at one end. He opened one eye and, seeing Rocco and Libs, he slowly got up and wandered over to greet them.

'Your friends have come for a sleepover,' said Nikki and arranged the other dog beds next to his.

Susan led Rocco and Libs over to their beds and they sniffed them before getting into them, watching her all the while.

'It's okay, Duke will look after you,' she assured them.

'They will be fine, there is a big bowl of water over there, and Duke is so easy-going, he'll not bother them,' explained Nikki. 'I'll take you to your room and then come back and check on this lot. Nathan or I will make sure they go out for a final pee later on.'

They walked back to reception and then up the carpeted stairs to the first floor. Nikki took Susan straight to her room. 'I don't suppose you feel like nattering. Would you like something to eat or drink?'

'No, thank you.'

Nikki turned on the lights. The room was decorated in white and blue with comfortable chairs and a huge bed. A large bay window looked out into blackness and Nikki pulled the curtains.

'I'll leave you now, but phone down if you need anything.'

'Thank you again, Nikki, you've been so kind.'

'It's only what you would do for any of us, try and sleep now.'

Once Nikki had left her, Susan went over to look out of the window. She opened it slightly. A cold blast of air pushed its way in, and in the distance, she could hear the waves breaking on the shore.

Back in her room, she saw the minibar, with bottles of water, a coffee maker, and a small smart TV. All she wanted was to have a shower and go to bed.

She undressed and went into the white marble en suite. There she found a range of smart products and she lingered in the hot shower as if trying to wash away the day.

Back in her room, she put on her nightie and climbed into the fresh white cotton sheets. It crossed her mind to ring Zoe but she decided she really couldn't face raking up the events of the evening just yet.

As she lay back, exhaustion took hold, she closed her eyes and very soon she was fast asleep.

15

Susan woke briefly a few times but still felt refreshed and stronger in the morning. After showering again, she knew she needed to get home. Checking her phone, she saw it was seven.

Downstairs, she found Nathan in reception, and the hotel was buzzing with activity. Staff were busy in the dining room, greeting early guests and arranging the buffet area, and the delicious smells of hot pastries and freshly cooked bacon filled reception.

Nathan came straight over to her. 'I'm sorry to hear about the break-in. How are you? Did you sleep well?'

'I slept really well. I can't thank you and Nikki enough for taking me in, your rooms are just gorgeous, it's a fabulous place to stay.'

He smiled smugly. 'We are rather proud of it, I have to say.'

Suddenly the phone rang and Nikki appeared from the office. Seeing Susan, she asked Nathan to answer the phone so that she could chat to Susan.

'How are you?' she asked.

'I have just been thanking Nathan. I feel so much better now. I should get to the dogs.'

'They're fine. Come and have some breakfast. I can get Trystan to make you some of his wonderful eggs benedict and Torri's pastries are all freshly made.'

'That sounds wonderful, but I must get home, and I need to get the dogs out for a walk.'

'Nathan has already taken them out for a quick walk.'

'That's a relief, thank you, but I really would like to get home now.'

'Of course. Now, look, I know this is the last thing you are going to want to hear, about, but we have a problem. Our pianist at the production has sprained her wrist. Honestly, she was out in the woods picking chestnuts when she fell... I mean, she should be more careful at her age.'

Susan smiled as she knew the woman was younger than her. 'You need someone for rehearsals tonight?' she interrupted Nikki.

'Only if you feel up to it, and it should be just tonight. The pianist assures us she will be fit for next week.'

'Of course, I can't just sit in the house all day. What time are you meeting?'

'I pick you up about quarter to six? Sorry, it's an early start, as we have so many children involved. She tries to do as much as she can in the first hour and a quarter and then we have a break for about half an hour, some of the adults are not needed until then. I tend to go for the whole thing, I like seeing it all.'

'Fine, it will do me good to do something normal.'

Nikki walked with her towards the back of the hotel. 'Oh, and when you were so upset last evening, you mentioned your divorce – has something happened?'

'I got my decree absolute through yesterday. I guess I was shocked, silly, I know.'

'Not at all, it's very hard process. No one I know has found it easy and you have had so much to deal with.' Nikki paused and then added, 'You mentioned you'd been to see Alice?'

'I went up there to play some familiar songs, and then got chatting to Alice, the resident who Colette used to visit.'

'Did she know what had happened to Colette?'

'She'd been told Colette had died in an accident, but she wanted to know more and so I told her what had happened.'

'I hope she wasn't too upset, I expect the staff had been trying to play it down.'

Susan heard a hint of criticism and defended herself. 'I think it was helpful for Alice to know the whole story. Colette had talked to her a lot more than I realised. She'd told her all about looking for the contents of her gran's jewellery box, and showed her the locket after it turned up at the nursing home.'

'You certainly had quite a chat, but you need to be careful with the residents, they tend to dwell on things more than they should.'

Again, Susan heard the harshness in Nikki's tone and replied, 'Well, I think she was glad to talk. In fact, she invited me to the tenth tea party the weekend after next. '

'Oh, right, a few of us will be going, of course. Torri and Trystan are doing the catering, Trystan is leaving everything here in the capable hands of his sous chef. Torri is making desserts in advance. It all takes planning.'

'I'm sure it does. Oh, I didn't tell you, I did have one piece of good news yesterday, Zoe is having a baby. They are so excited.'

'That's wonderful. So you are going to become a gran, that's great, something to look forward to.'

They had arrived at the office, where Nathan was now working at the desk. Rocco and Libs came running towards Susan.

'Good morning, you two, I hope you have been behaving,' said Susan, fussing them.

Nathan looked over at Nikki. 'I've a guest who wants his wallet back. Apparently you'd put it in the safe for him?'

'That's right, it's in the safe. He didn't want to carry too much around, I think he thought he was going to get mugged in Ventnor High Street.'

Nathan went over to the safe. 'What's the code?'

'For god's sake, Nathan, it's your birthday – 140175.'

He grinned and opened the safe.

Nikki looked over at Susan. 'Now, Nathan is taking Duke down to the beach later, would you like him to take your two as well?'

'Don't worry, I'll take them on the downs later. They can have a run in the garden until then.'

Nikki opened the patio doors. The fresh sea air caressed Susan's face and she breathed in deeply.

'You can go out this way if you want,' suggested Nikki. 'You go out into the courtyard and down the right side of the hotel. There is a huge metal gate down the side, it's to put people off just wandering into the courtyard but it's never locked.'

'Well, thank you again, and I'll see you later, Nikki.'

With both dogs on leads, Susan left.

The courtyard, which Susan knew was a lovely place to sit with a drink in the summer, had a sad, neglected air now. The sunshades had been taken down, the chairs were resting against the tables to allow the rain to drain off them.

At the side of the courtyard was a small lodge where Torri and Trystan lived. Next to the lodge was a small cultivated area, well fenced off. As she glanced over, she saw Trystan come out of the lodge in his chef's whites. He turned to watch a blackbird rummaging in the leaves and she called over to him.

When he didn't reply, she walked over and tapped him on the shoulder.

'Morning!' She felt him flinch and he spun around.

'What are you doing here?' he asked crossly.

Susan explained and his face softened. 'God, that's awful, I'm sorry. Nothing taken, you say?'

'No, nothing. The young police officer who attended suggested I didn't have anything worth stealing!'

'Charming! Still, it's a terrible feeling to know a stranger has been in your house, it should be a place you feel safe.'

He spoke so passionately that she asked, 'Has something like this happened to you?'

He pursed his lips angrily. 'I've been receiving these bloody anonymous letters. They started coming way back in the hotel I worked in before I was a chef at the nursing home.'

'How awful.' Susan paused. 'I don't suppose the words in the letters had been cut out?'

Trystan nodded. 'Yes, that's exactly what they are like. Why do you say that?'

'Because I am pretty sure I found a fragment of one of those letters among Colette's things.'

'Oh, god, I told her to throw it away. She found it in our bin when she was cleaning and asked me about it. I told her it was none of her business, I didn't realise she'd kept it.'

'I didn't know it was anything to do with you obviously and so when I found it, I sent a photograph to the police. I was worried someone had been threatening Colette.'

'Oh, god, the police? I don't need them getting involved.'

'But they may be able to track down who is sending them.'

'I don't need them to do that, I know who it is. He'd love the publicity. He's out to ruin me.'

'But who is it?'

'It's Ben, a chef at the hotel where Torri and I worked before going to the nursing home. He was just jealous of me. A nasty review appeared on TripAdvisor, I am sure he was the one who posted it, and then the anonymous letters started. He just wanted me out of the hotel, preferably off the island, I think.'

'Where was the hotel?'

He shrugged. 'Just somewhere over the west side of the island. Anyway, I'd had enough, we decided to move on. They were advertising at the nursing home for a chef and kitchen staff. Although it certainly wasn't the kind of kitchen I was hoping for, it gave us both a job, at least in the short term, and gave us time to decide what we were going to do next. Torri, of course, wanted to go to Portugal, and maybe we would have gone out there once we had some savings, but then the opportunity at the hotel cropped up. It was too good an opportunity to turn down.'

'But you are still receiving the letters?'

'I am, but listen, I will sort this out in my way. I will talk to the police, explain they were nothing to do with Colette.' His heavy eyebrows drew over his eyes. 'I'd better go and get back to the breakfasts. Sunday is a nice quiet start as the guests tend to have a lie-in, but they will all be down soon.'

Susan watched Trystan as he walked over to the kitchen door. The conversation had been pretty intense and she allowed her attention to be drawn to the garden. She knew Torri and Nathan shared a love of wildlife gardening and had both worked on this area. They had succeed in creating something quite beautiful, and it seemed to merge effortlessly into the woods behind. A robin was singing on the branch of a hawthorn bush, and below, the blackbird Trystan had been watching was still frantically turning over the dead leaves. Susan knew that in the spring and summer, there would be a carpet of wildflowers. Now the hedges were full of berries, and at this time in the morning, intricate webs that had been spun by the spiders overnight. To the right she noticed a new addition, a small pond.

'We had our first frogs this spring.'

Susan turned to see Torri with her terrier on a lead. He wagged his tail when he saw Rocco and Libs, and Susan leant down to fuss him. 'I love your garden, it's wonderful, I recognise a few things from the foraging trip with Nathan.'

'He spent ages helping me choosing plants for this area. Nikki is interested as well; she's been borrowing my wildlife magazines for years.'

'Yes, he told us about those black berries, and are those called harebells?'

'That's right, fairy bells, so pretty.'

'Oh, are those the mushrooms he warned us about?'

'They could be. There are a few pretty poisonous things here, it's why I have a fence. I've put a little gate for myself, I was tired of struggling over the last one. This wooden box is for my tools – I'm lucky I don't need a lawn mower, just the essentials.'

She lifted the lid and Susan saw a neat array of garden implements. 'I have my kneeler there and this is my new garden knife, it's very sharp, so I keep it in here in the sheath.' Closing the lid, she added, 'I've also put a small feeder for the squirrels. Of course, one day when we go to Portugal, I'll have a proper piece of land, and I'll keep chickens and grow all the produce we will cook with—' Torri suddenly looked at Susan. 'Hang on, what are you doing here so early?'

Susan explained about the break-in and Nikki's kindness in offering her a bed for the night.

'How awful for you. I am so glad you came here; you could never have slept there on your own last night. You say nothing was taken?'

'No, which I know is a good thing, but it feels a bit odd.'

'Did the police take fingerprints? Do they think they will catch whoever did this?'

'No, they are not that interested as nothing was taken.'

'That's not right, is it?'

'I suppose they have to rationalise their work now.' She hesitated and then added, 'I just saw Trystan going, he seems very stressed.'

'Even off season, being a chef means long hours, and when he isn't cooking for the restaurant, he is working at perfecting his recipes.'

'It doesn't help then that he is receiving the letters—'

Before Susan could finish the sentence, Torri interrupted her.

'He told you about the letters? I didn't think he would tell anyone about them. It's nonsense.'

'Trystan seems worried.'

'I know, but I keep telling him to ignore them.' Torri looked around. 'The person sending them will get bored and they will tail off. Now I need to get on and help Trystan.'

Torri rushed across the courtyard and into the hotel.

As Susan left, she could hear the strains of a CD of Welsh songs coming from the kitchen, and strains of Trystan singing along. As she walked home, she breathed in the crisp autumnal morning and looked over at the sea, grey-blue in the distance.

Once she arrived at the house, aware of how nervous she felt, she opened the front door and went slowly into the house. The dogs rushed ahead of her, at least they were glad to be home.

Breathing more easily when she saw the house was undisturbed, she went and fed the dogs, and then rang the locksmith. He replied he would be round as soon as he could and she went upstairs and changed, deciding she needed to face Colette's room again.

She looked around it more calmly now, this was definitely the room that had been the most disturbed. Noticing the broken jewellery box again, she knelt down and started to pick up the pieces. Slowly it dawned on her what might have been happening here.

As this room was the only one seriously searched, it had to

suggest that the aim of the break-in was to find this jewellery box, or in particular its contents. The mild disruption in the rest of the house must have just been an attempt to disguise the main purpose of their visit.

Her mind flashed back to the night when she'd woken, suspecting someone had been in the house while she was in bed. There were striking similarities – the use of the key safe, the fact it was Colette's room that had been the only room disturbed.

Susan started to breathe more heavily, she could feel her face grow hot, her mouth was dry as the full impact of what she'd discovered sank in. The same person had broken into her house twice now looking for the jewellery box and if she and Alice were right, this person was someone in her dog-walking group and a killer. A murderer had been in her house twice, walked around the rooms, had access to her most private possessions.

But of course the reason they'd been here was that they were desperate to find the contents of that jewellery box. She looked at the smashed box on the floor, imagining the frustration and fury of the person as they struggled to open it and then found it empty.

Susan rushed into her room and opened a drawer under her bed. From the back, she pulled out a small file containing Colette's collection of secrets. They were all still there.

She was relieved to find them but also aware that the person who had broken in would still be frantic to find them, and a person this reckless was not going to give up.

16

Susan tipped out the contents of the file. The letter, she now knew, was from this chef Ben to Trystan. Susan had no idea how much Colette had found out about Ben and the hotel, maybe she thought threatening to show people the letter would be enough to blackmail Trystan.

Susan did wonder if there was more to the letter than Trystan or Torri had told her. Their reaction to her informing the police about it seemed a bit odd.

Susan picked up the beautiful yellow paper roses, and that song, and remembered Nikki's hints about Trystan and hearing the Welsh music coming from the kitchen. It could be that Trystan had fallen for Colette, even had a relationship with her. She glanced at the other objects, she'd learnt nothing new about any of them, they all remained a mystery.

Susan was startled by the sound of the doorbell and ran downstairs, assuming it was the locksmith. However, she opened the door to find Robert with Gem Gem and Dougie.

'Oh, it's you.'

He smiled. 'Sorry to disappoint.'

Susan explained she was waiting for the locksmith and invited him in.

'Torri just told me what happened, I wanted to see if you were all right.'

'A bit shocked.' She looked down at the dogs. 'Do let them off so they can join the others, I'll open the back door.'

They went into the kitchen and after a few sniffs, Rocco and Libs were happy for Gem Gem and Dougie to join them in the garden.

'So, nothing was stolen?'

'No. The jewellery box that belonged to Colette's gran was broken, that was all.'

'It didn't have any jewellery in it?'

'No, but remember Colette talked about keeping her collection of secrets in it. I am thinking, as this was the only thing disturbed, that someone must have broken in to find them. In fact, and I haven't told you, I am pretty sure this is the second time they'd broken in looking for them.'

Robert's face creased into a more serious expression than she'd ever seen. 'Tell me what happened last time.'

She told him about the break-in while she'd been in bed.

'Why on earth didn't you tell me about it? I don't like the sound of it at all.'

'You believe me then?' Susan swallowed, it was actually more frightening that Robert was taking her suspicions so seriously and she realised she had wanted him to brush them off.

'Of course, I wish you'd told me when it happened.'

'I didn't want to think about it too much, I guess.'

'You said the locksmith is coming to change all the locks?'

'Yes.'

'Good. And this was all to get to these supposed secrets Colette was collecting? Did they find anything, by the way?'

'No. I'd moved them, the box was empty.'

'I see, well, let's hope this person will presume Colette was bluffing when they found the box empty. At least that means they won't be coming back.'

'You think so? I'd not looked at it like that.'

'I am guessing you suspect someone from our dog-walking group?'

'I can't see who else would be doing this.'

'No, I agree with you.'

'I went to see Alice at the nursing home, she has the same reservations about Colette's death as me, she suspects someone from the group of being involved.'

Robert shook his head. 'That is such a wild accusation. Granted, from the break-ins, someone is pretty worried about whatever it was Colette had been hiding away, but murder? The police are not fools, Susan, if they say it was an accident, then I believe them. They will have investigated a lot more thoroughly than you know.'

'But at the end of the day they have to weigh up what is most likely, and I can see why they are opting for accidental death. But they have not answered my questions about why she ate marshmallows, why she didn't use her EpiPen and where was the velvet pouch?'

Again, he shook his head. 'But why would anyone want to murder Colette? These secrets are obviously worrying someone, but is that enough to commit murder? And then there is the theft of Colette's grandmother's valuables. Just say it was someone in our group, they must know it would be very hard to prove after all this time.'

'I can understand your reservations but that doesn't mean I am going to stop looking into this.'

'But what will you do?'

'I can talk to people, see what people tell me. That's how I have to start, I think. I'm going with Nikki to drama this evening, it will be interesting to see what goes on there after your friend Pete's insinuations.'

'Don't take them too seriously, he's a bit of a gossip.'

'I'll be tactful, just look around. I also want to find out a bit more about Beatrice if I can. Everyone agrees she's a bit of an enigma.'

Robert smiled and then sighed. 'I'm not going to stop you, am I, but be careful. You should have told me about that break-in.'

Susan could feel herself getting irritated. 'I am very good at looking after myself, you know.'

'I'm sure, but this person who has been breaking in worries me. It's not something I would have imagined anyone in our group doing, which means I have misread one of them badly, and usually I have a good nose for someone a bit crooked. Look, how about I help out a bit, I am pretty good at finding out about people, after all, it was a large part of my job.'

'Why do I get the feeling this is an excuse to keep an eye on me?'

He grinned. 'Ah, you guessed. Yes, maybe that is partly it. Now, to prove to you I'm serious, I'll go off and see what I can dig up about Beatrice, how about that?'

She put her head to one side. 'Okay, thank you, I'll let you do that.'

'Good, right, I'd better go and find those dogs, but remember, you be careful now.'

'You are as bad as Alice.'

'What did she say?'

Susan shrugged and gave a quick laugh. 'Oh, some nonsense about the last two people who wore this locket were dead.'

'Well, she's right, isn't she? This isn't something you should laugh off, you know.'

'Okay, I'll be careful.'

'Maybe I should take away Colette's collection of secrets. I could make sure everyone knows I have them.'

Susan shook her head. 'No, definitely not. In a way, I feel Colette has entrusted them to me, I won't let go of them.'

'I am only saying all this because I care about you, Susan, you know that.'

Robert was close to her now, their eyes met and she could feel her heart race, her cheeks were burning.

Susan stepped back. 'I will be fine, I can look after myself.'

'I know you think that but promise me you will call on me at the first sign of trouble.'

'Okay, and thank you.'

Robert went and called Gem Gem and Dougie. As he was leaving, she saw the locksmith arriving.

'I'll be perfectly safe now,' she called to Robert. 'I'll see you in the morning on the beach.'

Susan showed the locksmith the key safe and the front door locks. He was an older man who greeted her with the gloomy air of a man who always feared the worst. His thick eyebrows were drawn together and the creases in the corners of his mouth looked set in a state of despondency.

'Another break-in, then,' he moaned. 'What's the island coming to? Time was no one ever even locked their front doors.'

'No, well, times change.'

'For the worse. Terrible feeling, isn't it, a stranger breaking into your home, your sanctuary, I mean, how do you ever feel safe again?'

Susan wasn't sure what to reply but the question was clearly rhetorical as the man continued, 'Of course, the police don't want to know now, do they, and yet the crimes are escalating and getting worse. These youngsters breaking in think nothing of carrying a knife or even a gun, yes, there are guns over here now. You can change the locks but that's not going to stop anyone getting in if they really want to, is it?'

'Um, no, right, I'll leave you to it then.'

She ran into the house, into the kitchen, and slammed the door. Anger welled up, how dare this man frighten her in this way? She had to live here, sleep here alone tonight and now all she could hear were those words echoing around her head, 'How do you ever feel safe again?'

17

Nikki picked Susan up at quarter to six.

'How are you? Have you managed to get everything back to normal?' Nikki asked.

'I've tidied up, but I had the most awful man come to change the locks. He quite scared me.'

'I should take no notice, some people love a bit of bad news.'

'I guess they do.'

'Look, nothing was taken. I am sure it was just kids.'

Susan took a breath. 'I'm not so sure. The only room really touched was Colette's and the only damage was that broken jewellery box. It did cross my mind that someone might have been after the contents, it looked like it had been thrown on the ground in frustration.'

Susan saw Nikki's grip tighten on the steering wheel.

'But why would someone be after that?'

'Colette told everyone she had been collecting evidence of people's secrets, didn't she? Maybe she got someone worried.'

'But that would mean it was one of us. That's ridiculous, none of us would do such a thing. In any case, I am sure Colette was bluffing. We all know each other pretty well, no one is likely to be hiding some great secret.'

'But you said you thought Beatrice might have a past.'

Nikki laughed. 'I wasn't being serious. No, I'd forget all that.'

Susan decided to move the conversation on, there was something she realised Nikki might be able to help her with. 'I had quite a long chat with Trystan earlier, he was telling me about how he moved from some big hotel to the nursing home. I wondered where it was.'

'Um, over where that new gift shop is, along the coast on the way to Alum Bay. Seashells, I think it's called, it's a bit run down now, it's a fair way away.'

Susan loved the way islanders talked about the distances between places. Some argued that if you were here long enough, you adjusted to a different scale, others that the lack of main roads meant that relatively short distances, particularly in the summer, took a disproportionate length of time.

Susan had her own theory. She felt the island was like a whole country packed into a little island. It had such variety, downland, woodland, towns, the coast, it was all here, and the west was so different to the east, the north to the south. It might be small, but as you travelled around the island, you experienced so many different places, it felt you'd gone on a much longer journey.

'Why are you asking about Trystan's previous places of work?' asked Nikki.

'I've always thought it was a bit odd that he went to the nursing home when he's obviously a very talented chef, why didn't he go onto somewhere more prestigious?'

'Nathan knows more about it than I do. He tells me some chef Trystan worked with was really jealous and spreading rumours about him. He chose the nursing home as it was low profile, kept his head down for a bit.'

'And Torri followed him?'

'Of course.'

Susan could see the theatre ahead.

'Right, here we are.' Nikki pulled into the car park.

'It's only a short drive but I don't like walking home in the dark. We are so lucky to have our own theatre, not having to rehearse in some village hall, not having to pack everything away and build sets on site. It's only small but it's perfect for us. Colette was impressed when she came to help out with make-up, that kind of thing.'

They got out of the car, but before they went in, Nikki looked up at the sky, which was scattered this evening with thousands of tiny pinprick stars.

Nikki took out a pocket telescope. 'Here, use this, it's amazing.'

Susan held it to her eye. 'That's fabulous, thank you. I didn't know you were interested in the stars.'

'Oh, yes, I always carry this with me and share it. I lent it to Colette once, she couldn't believe how much she could see with it.'

Susan returned the telescope, and they went into the theatre.

She had been to the theatre to see various productions Nikki had been in before. Steve usually made an excuse not to come but Susan enjoyed them. It was a lot of effort and expense to go to the mainland to see productions and so the amateur productions on the island were generally very good and well supported.

Susan went down the front of the theatre and headed for the piano.

The director, Vera, a woman she'd worked with before, came and greeted her.

'Thank you so much for standing in. This is the list of scenes we are going through this week. I'll do the young children first so they can get off and then we'll rehearse the scenes in the convent. After that, I need to sort out Liesl and Rolf, who have had some huge falling out. Last week was a nightmare, Nikki did her best to try and sort them out but the scenes they did together were dreadful. Honestly, I could do without this with the production only a month away.'

Susan smiled sympathetically. 'You always swing it around. I have my ticket.'

'Great, sales are pretty good, but I'd love to sell out, looks good in the paper. By the way, I was sorry to hear about that girl, Colette. I met her a few times, I'd have liked to rope her in, I think she'd have been good on stage. That age group is never easy to find on the island. I train them up and off they go to university, and I never see them again.' Vera paused. 'Sorry, that's not quite the point, is it? I am truly sorry for what happened.' She looked around and saw the cast she'd got together had broken up and were in smaller groups, dotted around the theatre.

She walked to the centre of the stage. 'Right, everyone, let's get started. I want the youngest children up here to go through "Do Re Mi" with Maria, and then we will do the convent scene, so, nuns, don't disappear.'

Susan could see some of the backstage team busy painting scenery. One of the men was very tall and looked familiar. Suddenly she realised it was the man she'd seen in the newspaper cutting among Colette's collection of secrets. His height and that moustache made him easy to recognise. She also saw Pete, the police officer, looking quite different in jeans and a sweatshirt, helping out. He caught her eye and gave her a quick wave.

The rehearsal began and soon Susan found herself totally wrapped up in the production. It was good to put everything else out of her mind.

At ten past seven, the director announced a break. 'As usual, children and the nuns can leave, but everyone else, please stay on. Liesl and Rolf, I will be working with you two first, so make sure you are ready. I've brought some cupcakes to keep us all going, please help yourselves.' She turned to Susan.

Susan saw some of the nuns gathering up their bags and bidding their friends good night, although others took a cake and went to sit in the stalls, clearly intending to stay on. She could understand it. In the theatre, it felt like you'd entered another little world, why rush back to demanding families, or work?

Nikki came over. 'I'm going to help backstage, so I'll catch you at the end.' Susan went to use the cloakroom and then went back into the theatre. She realised she had no idea when they were meant to finish and decided to ask Nikki to get an idea of how much longer they would be there.

She made her way up onto the stage and into the wings, but Nikki was nowhere to be seen. 'Has anyone seen Nikki?' she asked.

Pete, who was painting scenery, looked up. 'Her and Phil are probably working on the website, they work on it most weeks.' He quickly returned to his work.

The response seemed a bit strained, and Susan wondered why. She went downstairs to the bar area to look for her, but the room was in darkness. However, as she started to climb back up the stairs, she heard a noise from a small side room and could see a light shining under the door.

She went over, knocked on the door and opened it.

She found Nikki and the tall man she guessed was called Phil, but they were not working at a computer. Instead, Nikki was lying down on a therapist's couch, half undressed, and Phil was now wearing a white coat.

'Oh, god, we didn't lock the door,' exclaimed Nikki.

'I'm sorry,' Susan stammered and was about to run out when Nikki called, 'No, Susan, wait.'

Nikki turned to Phil. 'I think we'd better stop now. I need to explain what is going on to Susan.'

He nodded, gathered his possessions and left, while Nikki jumped up, grabbed her clothes.

Once she was dressed, Nikki gave a nervous smile. 'Phil is a physiotherapist who used to come into the nursing home, and he even helped us with some of the building work at the hotel, he is multi-talented. He also happens to have a qualification in acupuncture and he's been treating me for the past few months on a Sunday evening.'

'For a bad back?'

'Arthritis. It started when I was working in the nursing home, I used to just take painkillers but it's getting really bad now. I have medication from the doctor, but the acupuncture helps a lot, in fact after the session last Sunday, he told me he could see a big improvement.'

'That's great.'

'It is, but no one else knows about this, please keep it to yourself.'

'Why the secret?'

'Who wants the world to know you are getting old? And I don't want Nathan thinking he is in business with some kind of invalid.'

'Nathan loves you, he would want to support you.'

'I'll have to come out and tell everyone one day, but not yet.'

Susan bit her lip. 'Um, did you realise that some people are not convinced you two are off working somewhere on the website? I'm pretty sure Pete upstairs thinks there is something going on between you.'

Nikki laughed. 'I'm not surprised. While I'm having the treatment, Phil posts something on the website, we have got away with it pretty well. Mind you, I remember when Colette came down here, caught us on our way out. I saw her face then, wondered what she thought was going on. Well, they're all wrong, it doesn't bother me what they gossip about.'

'But if Nathan was to hear?'

Nikki shook her head. 'He'd never believe anything like that. It's not like I'm taking secret calls, slinking off to meet Phil somewhere, no, he'd know it was rubbish.'

Susan wasn't so convinced but didn't reply.

Nikki stood up. 'Right, they will be calling us back to rehearsals, we'd better make a move. And remember now, no telling anyone.'

'Of course,' replied Susan and they left the room and returned to the rehearsals.

Later, at the end of the session, they walked out to the car together. Nikki talked about one of the songs in the production, and Susan was pretty sure she was avoiding continuing the earlier conversation. As they drove home, she asked Nikki if they had a busy week ahead at the hotel.

'Actually, we do. We are fully booked, partly due to a group of older people all coming for someone's sixtieth birthday. It's lovely to have the custom but a bit of a pain when I am short of cleaning staff until Wednesday. Nathan and I will have to cover it between us. The place has to look good and the staff who live in work such long hours, it's a perk I like to provide.'

This gave Susan an idea. 'Why don't I come in tomorrow and help out?'

'No, no way.'

'Seriously, I'd be happy to, and it would be my way of thanking you for having me to stay last night.'

'Are you sure?'

'Of course.' And so it was agreed Susan would go in the following morning.

Susan got out of the car and as she listened to Nikki drive away, she looked up at the house. It was in complete darkness, and she wished now she'd left some lights on. She told herself firmly that the locks had been changed, no one could have broken in again.

And yet, a voice nagged away, they don't need a front door key. There were doors and windows around the back, think of all those people on TV dramas breaking in by miraculously sliding a credit card down the lock.

She shook herself, this was stupid, the dogs were waiting, she needed to go in.

She found it hard to use the new lock with her hands shaking but eventually was inside. She immediately turned on the hall lights, and Rocco and Libs came running to greet her. She then switched on all the lights downstairs and took a deep breath.

Susan glanced over at the back door, reassured herself it was locked and then opened it to let the dogs out.

She found the bottle of red wine Nikki had opened and poured herself a drink and decided to check that newspaper cutting about the hotel opening. She let the dogs back in, locked the door and then went upstairs. Her nerves returned and she quickly turned on the lights and checked Colette's room. To her relief, it was as neat and tidy as when she'd left it, and she went into her own bedroom.

She took out the file with the collection in and found the newspaper cutting. Yes, the tall man was definitely the person she'd seen with Nikki. She guessed Colette had suspected her of having an affair. Presumably that was why this picture was here. From the way Nikki had reacted to people gossiping about her and Phil, however, Susan didn't think Colette would have got very far blackmailing her with that information.

Of course, she had learnt one important thing without realising it. Vera had confirmed Nikki was at the rehearsal the week before and as Nikki had talked about her treatment that week, there was no way she would have had time to nip out of the theatre. This meant Nikki had to have an alibi for last Sunday when Colette died.

18

Susan woke to a wet Monday morning, but she knew that, whatever the weather, the dogs needed a walk.

As there was a strong wind, she dug out Rocco's coat and a spare for Libs. Today was going to need full wet weather gear.

As she left the house, she saw the streets were deserted apart from a few other dog walkers and she guessed most of those were sticking to the streets today. One of the good things about meeting up with a group, however, was that it made her walk a bit further than she might do otherwise.

They headed down the hill. The sea was grey and white, barely distinguishable from the sky. The weather didn't seem to bother the dogs, who pulled ahead. Libs seemed to have settled down and Susan was pleased to see the little dog thriving.

Ahead on the beach she saw Robert, Beatrice, Torri and Nikki. Their dogs were already running around the beach.

Once she joined everyone, Susan let Libs and Rocco off and they joined the other dogs. The wind and rain buffeted her face and that, combined with the crashing of waves, made conversation difficult.

Nikki managed to shout a thank you for helping the night before and check she was still able to go and clean at the hotel.

They didn't walk far, and Torri was the first to put her dog back on a lead. 'That's quite enough of that, he's covered in sand! I'll be off,' she said and left the beach.

Nikki laughed. 'Torri can't cope with the cold, can she, she's not into exercise.'

'But she goes running every Sunday with Trystan.'

'That's what she wants everyone to think. I know she goes off with Trystan every Sunday in her joggers and trainers, drives up to the Falaise Hall car park, but I can't see her keeping up with Trystan, can you? I could imagine her just running a short way and then stopping, Trystan is very good, he never lets on.'

'But that's silly, why bother? She could stay at home, let him go off running.'

'It's daft, isn't it, I don't think she even trusts him to go off running on his own. Bit pathetic, really.'

Susan's mind started racing. Torri's alibi for the night Colette died was that she was running with Trystan, but now it seemed she probably wasn't.

The wind was finally starting to drop, the rain easing off, so the rest of the group decided to stay.

Nikki started talking to Robert about a possible decoration at the hotel and they walked off together, leaving Susan walking with Beatrice.

'How are you, then, after this break-in?' asked Beatrice. 'Have you thought of getting an alarm? I've got one, I can give you the contacts.'

'I'll think about it, thanks. I must admit, when I returned to the house last night after going to rehearsals with Nikki, I was very nervous. I'm going to have to get used to it again, though.'

'You will, us women who live alone have to dig deep sometimes.

My sister always tells me she couldn't live on her own, but I answer that I have no choice and I'm proud of the way I cope. Oh, I finally heard from her last night, by the way. She is back from her cruise, it sounded like she had a superb holiday.'

Susan could see Nikki was leaving the beach and waving to them. Robert hung back and joined them.

'Nikki is full of plans,' he laughed. 'I wish I had half her energy.'

Beatrice turned to Susan. 'I wondered if you would like to come over to Ryde with me tomorrow?'

Susan sighed. 'I'm so sorry, I have an appointment at eleven.'

'Oh, you are busy?'

'I've arranged to go and see this medium that Colette was seeing.'

Beatrice stared. 'Why in the world are you doing that?'

'I'm not going for a consultation, I just want to chat about Colette. I thought I'd take the locket, see if that meant anything to her.'

'You're not still trying to find out about those things Colette claimed were stolen, are you? You remember she was implicating one of us, I'd have thought you'd have known that was ridiculous idea.'

'Look, I just need to check this out, that is all.'

'I should come with you,' said Robert.

Susan blinked; she'd not even considered him going with her.

'No, I'd rather go on my own,' she stammered.

He shrugged but looked a little hurt and then called Gem Gem and Dougie. 'I'd better be off, I think.'

Susan realised the rain was starting to come down heavier again and, turning to Beatrice, they decided they would also leave.

The climb back up the hill seemed even harder today and after wiping down the dogs and feeding them, Susan would have loved to curl up with a hot drink and rest. A part of her regretted her offer to help out at the hotel, but of course she knew she would go.

After showering and putting on dry clothes, she felt better and set off down the road.

Susan was greeted by Nikki in the reception area of the hotel. 'Thank you so much for this, filthy weather, isn't it? I'll show you where the cleaning materials are and give you an overall to protect your clothes. If you could start with reception and then go on to the restaurant? Finally, there are the staff rooms. It's pretty straightforward. Today, with the staff areas, just dust and Hoover around, they can do their own bathrooms.'

Susan looked over at a pair of beautifully carved wooden chairs. 'These are lovely.'

'They are one of Nathan's purchases. He loves looking online and going to auctions. Nathan gets these toys still boxed in immaculate condition, he says they will appreciate in value, but I'm not convinced. I like a bargain, better to get what you like and who knows, maybe one day hit the jackpot.'

'Well, I shall be careful when I'm cleaning in your flat,' said Susan.

'Oh, leave that till last. If you don't have time, don't worry.'

'Where are the rooms for the staff?'

'There's Trystan and Torri's lodge, two small rooms along from the office used by kitchen staff, and then our flat. But remember, only a quick dust and Hoover in each. Now, here's where the cleaners' supplies are kept, it's quite small.' Nikki opened the door of a small windowless room and turned on the light. There were shelves and shelves of cleaning products, hooks with overalls and boxes of tissues and toilet rolls. Susan also noticed a small area of unmarked boxes. Following her gaze, Nikki laughed. 'Those are Beatrice's. They've been there since the day we opened, I guess she will take them one day. Now, we have two key safes, this is the safe we keep the keys to the staff rooms in – it's an easy code, 4321. I have the code for the other, it has all the spares in.'

Nikki opened the safe and passed the keys to Susan and then handed her some overalls. 'Just put them back in here when you've finished.'

Susan was not particularly fond of housework, but cleaning in someone else's property was far more satisfying than cleaning at home. As she dusted surfaces, she noticed, for the first time, a vending machine tucked into an alcove. She wiped over the glass front and noticed they were still selling the marshmallows in the pink packet Colette had complained about.

Susan went into the bar area, where a young girl was stocking the bar.

'Is it okay if I Hoover in here?' Susan asked.

'Of course, carry on.'

The girl leant over the bar. 'I'm Penny, you're the lady Colette stayed with, aren't you? We were all so sorry to hear what happened.'

'Thank you, it was a shock. Did you know Colette well?'

'She tended to keep herself to herself, but she was friendly enough and very pretty. All the men used to make passes at her.'

'I can imagine. She never mentioned a particular boy, though, maybe she didn't want to tell me. Colette did talk about the chef here... I think he's called Trystan?'

Penny laughed. 'She didn't fancy him! We're all a bit scared of him, to be honest.'

'I hear Nikki and Nathan are engaged now, that's exciting.'

'Yes, Nikki's a lucky woman, grabbed one of the few decent-looking men around.'

'The staff like Nathan, then?'

'Oh, yes, he's great. So good-looking but not full of himself.

Nikki's done well there. Mind you, she nearly let him slip through her fingers.'

'You think he might have been tempted elsewhere?'

Penny paused, looked over at Susan as if registering for the first time who she was.

'Hang on, you usually play the piano, don't you?'

'I'm just helping out today, Nikki is short-staffed.'

'Of course, because of Colette. She was such a hard worker, her and Nikki got on well. Colette was always being given extra hours. Some of the staff who've been working here a long time got a bit miffed, thought Colette was getting above herself, but she was obviously bright and going to get on. Nikki was always very careful how she handled her, too scared of her walking out. She'd never have had a row with her like Nathan did.'

This last remark caught Susan's attention. 'You say there was a row, what was that about then?'

'It was the Saturday Nikki and Nathan announced their engagement. Colette came to work in the bar at lunchtime, and at the end of her shift, she asked me where Nathan was because she wanted to talk to him. She looked cross, I could tell something was up. Anyway, I told her I thought Nathan was on his own in the office and she went off.'

'I see, I wonder what was up?'

Penny leant forward. 'I had to take something to reception and I heard a bit of what was going on.'

Susan didn't think the girl would have heard much from reception and wondered if she'd gone to listen at the office door.

'I heard Colette say something about roses? I couldn't make out the next bit, but he did say she was not to say anything to anyone. I was wondering if she was criticising the gardener, then he had a point. It was all very intriguing but then someone shouted in the bar and I had to go and deal with them.' The girl sighed and then looked at the clock. 'I suppose life goes on, as my mum would say. It's time for my break and I guess you need to get on. See you around.'

Susan stood watching Penny leave the bar. She'd learnt a few things from the conversation. There had been gossip about Nathan and someone, had it been Colette? That row, had it been about that yellow paper rose? Had Colette been threatening to tell Nikki?

Susan shook her head, she couldn't be sure about this, she needed to find out more.

She went back to her cleaning, and once she'd cleaned the area, she set off to Trystan and Torri's lodge. She was relieved to find the rain had stopped and glanced at Torri's garden as she pushed open the door to their lodge. A robin was drinking water from the pond, a blue tit hung acrobatically from a feeder, and a blackbird was pulling dark blue berries off a bush.

Susan had been inside the lodge before and as she pushed open the door, she saw it was as tidy as usual. It did seem different being in there on her own, and she had to shake the feeling of being an intruder. Today, as she Hoovered and dusted, she looked more closely. She noticed how many books they had. One shelf was devoted to some beautiful copies of classics, and some old children's books. Another to books about Portugal, Portuguese cuisine, and a Portuguese dictionary, as well as books on music and Renaissance art.

Standing in a row below a bottom shelf was a neat collection of wildlife magazines. The publication date of each was printed on the spine and she could see they were arranged chronologically and went back to 2009. Susan took one off the shelf and realised that the magazine page in Colette's collection had been torn from magazines like these. It was interesting but she couldn't understand why Colette had done it.

She didn't notice anything else of significance in the room and when she'd finished cleaning, she returned to the main building and went to work in the two smaller bedrooms along from the office. They didn't take long, and she realised she had enough time to go up to Nikki and Nathan's rooms.

Susan went upstairs and let herself into the flat. It was large and had been built as an extension over the garage. It consisted of a living room, two bedrooms and kitchen. It was at the front of the house and was light, with wonderful views over to the sea. Nikki had good taste and the apartment was decorated in white and blues, similar to the guest rooms.

Susan made her way round, dusting and Hoovering, and checked around as she did it. She noticed a shelf of ornaments, old books, eggcups, thimbles and guessed these were the 'bargains' Nikki picked up at jumble sales. In the bedroom, she found a large dressing table, clearly Nikki's domain and covered in cosmetics and perfumes. There was also a large jewellery box consisting of three large trays sitting on top of each other. Susan slid them open and saw drawer stuffed with brightly coloured glass and crystal dress jewellery. Susan thought how much Beatrice would hate it all.

One area of the room was a sewing area. A tailor's dummy stood wearing the top half of a red taffeta dress. She had a few shelves next to the table and on this were boxes of various sizes containing spare cotton and patterns, and a range of lengths of materials were folded neatly besides them.

On one bedside table tottered a pile of thick romance novels, bowls and a half-drunk glass of water. On the other, presumably Nathan's side, sat a solitary surfing magazine, and a small framed photograph of him and Nikki down on the beach. Above this, on the wall, he had a few wooden shelves with the collectable cars, buses and trains.

She didn't feel she was learning anything new about Nathan, however, until she opened the top drawer of his bedside cabinet.

Inside, she found a packet of envelopes, made of a very distinctive textured green material. These were identical to the one in Colette's collection. Susan rummaged further down in the drawer and found a scrap of notepaper with a labelled sketch of a surfboard. What really grabbed Susan's attention here was Nathan's handwriting. The 'M' was written with a flourish and was exactly the same as the 'M' on the envelope. She was sure that Nathan had written the word 'Myfanwy', and therefore the song and the rose must have been sent by him.

Susan sat back on the floor. So this was proof that Colette and Nathan had had a relationship. As the reality of it sunk in, she felt an anger growing inside her. How dare he use Colette like that, a vulnerable young girl who was employed by him?

Susan paused, she needed to think about this. Nathan had asked Nikki to marry him on the Friday night and the following day, Colette had rowed with him about the rose and whatever she'd said, maybe threatened to tell Nikki, Nathan had been angry. How upset and threatened did he feel? He didn't have an alibi for the Sunday night, it had to be possible that he'd been down to the cove.

She glanced at her watch, her two hours were up, and she was about to leave the room when she recalled Nikki saying something about catching Colette looking in her wardrobe. Susan went over and started to rummage among the usual boxes of shoes and clothes that had fallen off hangers. At the back, she found a smart cardboard box with a lid, and she pulled it out.

There was the usual collection of photographs, snaps from holidays and birthdays, and some older memorabilia such as school report. However, further down, she found a newspaper cutting, similar to the one Colette had among her collection. It was clearly taken on the same evening, the opening of the hotel, but this time you could see Nikki more clearly. You could make out her beautiful evening dress, and Susan wondered if she had made it herself. She had just started to look for Phil in the photograph and anyone else she might recognise when she became aware of a creak on the landing outside the room.

She quickly hid the cutting in the pocket of the large apron she'd been given, gathered her cleaning things and left the room. Downstairs, she put the cleaning things away, quickly concealed the cutting in her handbag and went into the reception area.

Here she found Nathan chatting loudly to guests at the desk. Susan glanced over at him, seeing how the guests were being swept along by his easy charm. She was about to make her way to the door when Nathan called out, 'Thank you so much, how did you find it?'

Susan turned around but found it impossible to return his smile. 'Fine, I've put everything away in the cupboard.'

She saw him register the change in her manner towards him and he went over to her. 'I do hope we haven't worn you out. I don't know what we'd have done without you. Has Nikki, um, settled up?'

'I don't want any money,' she stated firmly. 'It was the least I could do to thank Nikki for giving me a refuge on Saturday evening. Cleaning someone else's place is always so much more enjoyable than cleaning your own.'

Nathan grinned. 'Well, any time you want to come and work for nothing, please feel free.'

She nearly returned the smile but instead turned to go.

Clearly confused by her cold manner, he added more seriously, 'It was very kind of you. I hope you are okay after the break-in, it must have been a terrible shock. Nikki told me you thought they'd gone looking for the jewellery box in Colette's room.'

'Yes, I did. You remember she told us she'd collected some interesting things.'

'So, what was it, what was she hiding?'

He was close to her now, but she refused to back away.

'There were some little yellow roses, there was reference to a "Myfanwy", a Welsh love song.' Susan watched him carefully, saw the colour rise in his face. 'I wondered who might have sent them to Colette.'

He stepped back quickly, bumped into a guest who was walking past. He apologised, and then turned back to Susan, clearly flustered. 'I'd better get back to work,' he stammered. 'Thank you again.'

'Um, yes, well, right, I'd better get on.'

She left, feeling his eyes burning into her back as she walked away.

Susan was glad to return home, and let the dogs out while she made a sandwich for her lunch.

Exhausting as it had been, she had learnt a lot that morning. Most significantly, she'd found out about the relationship between Nathan and Colette. She'd also found out where the magazine page came from and discovered another newspaper cutting.

At that moment, her phone rang. Picking it up, she saw it was Robert. She wondered if he was going to ask again about going with her to see the medium, but he seemed to have moved on from that.

'Hiya, well, I hope you are impressed, this has taken me hours online. I've been trying to track down Beatrice's husband. I started by tracking down various jewellers that were in Sussex five years ago. To cut a long story short, I discovered Beatrice had reverted to using her maiden name and was married to a jeweller called Rowson Mart.'

'Gosh, well done. Rowson Mart, you say, that's an odd name.'

'Well, it's the name over the door of their jewellers – "Rowson Mart – Family Jewellers" in Brighton.'

'Wow, that's great, thank you. We should now be able to find out more about him.'

'Indeed, but that's as far as I've got today, I need a drink now!'

'You deserve it, and thank you. And by the way, I've also been doing a bit of investigating, in fact, I've found out quite a lot.'

She told him all she'd found out about Nikki at drama, the letters to Trystan and the affair between Nathan and Colette.

'Gosh, you have been busy, you're the one who deserves the drink. I'm really sorry to hear about Nathan, I always thought he was completely devoted to Nikki and I don't like the idea of him hurting Colette.'

'No, I don't either. He's not quite the charmer we thought.'

'Obviously not. However, remember, Susan, that doesn't make him a killer. This letter business is interesting, some chef over in Freshwater, you say, is sending them?'

'That's right. In fact, I was thinking, do you fancy going over there one night for a meal, see if we can meet this Ben?'

'Of course, I'd like that.'

'I'll book it, and text you. Could you make this Wednesday?'

'Yup, I'm free, but I don't hold out a lot of hope. This chef isn't going to talk to us, is he?'

'Maybe not, but I'd like to try.'

'Great, well, it's a date, tell me the time and I'll pick you up.'

Susan put down her phone and was about to relax back into her chair when she sat upright. Robert had used the word 'date'. She panicked, what had she done?

19

Susan woke exhausted the next day and stumbled down the stairs.

Instead of going to the beach, she headed for the downs. Above her, buzzards made their mournful cry, but in the bushes a robin sang, and just watching Rocco and Libs chasing across the wet grass was enough to lighten her mood. The sea was grey, but there was a glimmer of sun pushing through the clouds that reflected on its surface.

Once home, Susan settled the dogs down, had breakfast and then prepared for her trip to St Hilda's.

She was looking forward to it now. As a child, her parents had brought her over to St Hilda's beach. She also had a friend who'd taken over the running of a bookshop in the village and decided it would be a good opportunity to visit her as well.

Susan enjoyed the journey as it took her through places that brought back some wonderful memories. There was Shanklin with its amazing chine, which felt almost prehistoric with its enormous wet ferns and hidden birdsong. And then along Sandown, where they would have so much fun on the beach and the pier. Susan drove inland from there, passing the Roman villa at Brading, where she'd spent many a wet afternoon helping children complete the worksheet and the waxworks she'd mistakenly taken Zoe to and had given her nightmares for weeks after.

Eventually, Susan arrived at St Hilda's. It was a pretty village with a large green, surrounded by cosy restaurants and pubs and her friend's bookshop.

Checking out the medium's address, she decided to park close by on the green and walk down to the house.

Realising she had a few minutes to spare, Susan decided to pop over and see her friend. As she opened the door, an old-fashioned bell tinkled, and she breathed in the wonderful smell of old books and paper.

Unaware of her entrance, a woman continued to sort out books on one of the shelves and Susan went over to her, touched her shoulder.

'Morning, Wendy.'

The woman swung round and grinned. Wendy's long hair was grey now and she wore a long denim skirt and baggy jumper.

'How wonderful to see you,' Wendy exclaimed and engulfed Susan in a hug. 'What are you doing over this way?'

Susan simply replied, 'I have an appointment over this way. I've literally popped in to say hello, I could do with seeing a friendly face.'

'Where's Rocco?'

'I took him out earlier, I've come on my own.'

Wendy scrutinised her more closely. 'Are you okay?'

Susan could feel tears and blinked them away. 'A lot has happened, including the fact I am now officially divorced.'

Wendy put her arms around her again. 'Oh, love, I'm sorry. You and Steve were like two halves of a whole, he was a fool to leave you. He should have talked to you before, he should have been kinder, less selfish.'

'But—'

'No buts. If he was that unhappy, he had the right to go, but the bastard did it in such a cruel way. If I ever see him, I shall make sure he knows that.'

Susan smiled. 'You're always on my side.'

'Of course I am, you are one of the loveliest people I know.' She hugged Susan again. 'Let's have coffee.'

'I can't, not today. By the way, Zoe is having a baby.'

'Wow, that's fantastic. My Julie is expecting as well, look at us, both grans.'

The doorbell rang and an older man in a raincoat entered. 'Goodness, this is rush hour for us,' Wendy said laughing.

'I'll leave you to it and I'll be in touch again soon.'

'Make sure you do. Ring me, okay, we'll go for a drink.'

Susan smiled and left the shop.

The route to the medium's house took her down a street off the green with rows of old terraced cottages on either side. Susan rang the doorbell, and a woman about Zoe's age answered the door.

'You must be Susan, I'm Lauren, come in.'

Susan was not exactly expecting an old woman wearing purple floaty clothes, but she was completely thrown by this young woman in jeans and trainers, who looked like she should be running a playgroup.

Susan was taken into a bright dining room and Lauren brought in a cafetiere and biscuits. They sat at a pine table, on comfy dining chairs.

Lauren smiled. 'I know you came to talk about Colette, but maybe it would help if I told you a bit about what I do. I facilitate conversations between those in the physical world and those in the spiritual world. I call myself a psychic medium as there are times when I do get strong feelings of foreboding, and the like, but not always.'

'I see.'

'Now, why have you come to me about Colette?'

It was a very direct question, and Susan wasn't too sure where to start.

'Colette lived with me for about three months. We became quite close; I don't know how much she told you about her grandmother?'

'I know she was concerned about her; she came to me to contact her.'

'And did she talk to her?'

'Yes, her gran was able to reassure her that she was well and safe.'

'I'm glad. I'm not sure if she told you, but Colette was concerned about some of her gran's things that went missing after she died.'

Lauren didn't reply, but she seemed to be waiting for Susan to explain further. Taking a sip of coffee, Susan told her the whole story.

'Yes, that is exactly what Colette told me. I'm not sure how I can help you—'

Susan could sense Lauren's reluctance to continue.

'I know it seems like I am just being nosy coming here, but it's not that. I have a feeling something is very wrong, and I am searching for ways to find out the truth.'

'I see, well, I know from Colette you are very caring. She told me how kind you had been to her.'

'I enjoyed having her living with me.'

Lauren smiled. 'Colette was very grateful; I don't think a lot of people had shown her kindness in this world. It's why her gran meant so much to her.'

'You're right and I was sorry that she felt so, well, unappreciated. She said something to me which just won't go away. "No one cares about the likes of me, I walk out of a room, and I'm forgotten" – that seems so wrong to me.'

'And do you feel that is what has happened? Colette has walked away, and she is now being forgotten?'

'Yes, that is exactly how I feel.' Susan hesitated and then added, 'Part of my worry is how she walked away.'

Lauren sat forward, her face serious now. 'You think maybe she was forced to leave this world?'

Before she could answer, Lauren closed her eyes. Susan waited, not sure what to do.

Suddenly, Lauren opened her eyes. 'I thought so, Colette's grandmother is here.'

Susan sat up, not sure what to say.

Lauren smiled at her reassuringly. 'It's all right, you don't need to be scared. She is pleased to see you and wants to thank you for everything you did for Colette.'

Susan swallowed hard, she'd not expected this. 'I see. Um, can you tell her I was very fond of Colette, and you can also maybe show her something.'

Gently Susan pulled the locket from under the neck of her jumper. 'It's her locket, I have it now. Tell her it's safe and I am trying to find out what happened to her other valuables, the brooch and the book.'

Lauren closed her eyes for a moment and then spoke again. 'Ah, she is saying not to keep looking for them. She was warning you it could be dangerous.'

'But does she have any idea where they are or who might have taken them?'

Lauren again sat very still, listening, and finally turned to Susan. 'I'm sorry, I think I am losing her. She did say something about happier days and then rabbits. I think she was remembering her childhood, but sorry, she has gone now.'

Susan held up the locket. 'Colette had intended to bring this to show you, she only found it a few days before she died.'

Lauren frowned. 'That is interesting, would you mind terribly if I held the locket? I can feel a kind of heat coming off it, it's very significant, for some reason.'

Susan undid the locket and handed it to her. Lauren closed her eyes and cupped it in her hands.

Susan saw Lauren's face slowly change, she nodded quickly and suddenly looked older, deadly serious, and completely engrossed. The mood had changed now, they were no longer just two women having coffee together.

Finally, Lauren opened her eyes and Susan saw her shoulders relax as she exhaled deeply.

'That was Colette.'

'She's here?'

'Yes, she is, and she was very intense. She is so excited to see you, and so grateful to you, but she is also terribly worried about you. She is telling you to stop looking for her grandmother's valuables. Your safety is much more important.'

'But I'm not just worried about her grandmother's valuables, I am also concerned about how she died, I don't believe it was an accident. Can you ask her, please, about that pink packet of marshmallows, and why she didn't use her EpiPen?'

Lauren nodded and closed her eyes. Susan waited, holding her breath. Lauren seemed to be less intense this time and it wasn't long before she reopened her eyes. 'I'm sorry, Colette was quite distressed. She didn't know anything about the marshmallows but after that, she just kept repeating that you were to leave this alone. She is safe now, and that is all that matters. You must look after yourself, those were her final words, and then she left.'

Lauren handed the locket back to Susan and then put her hands flat on the table. 'Are you okay? Listen, Susan, I don't know the full story, obviously, but I promise you I don't often get warnings like this coming through. Whatever is going on, you need to take them seriously.'

'Thank you. I feel quite shaken up, to be honest.'

'I can understand that. Is there anything else you want to ask me?'

'Oh, there is one more thing, if you wouldn't mind taking a look at this.'

From her handbag, she took the photograph of the urn in Beatrice's room.

'It was among Colette's things. It is the urn containing the ashes of the husband of Beatrice in our group. His name was Rowson Mart. I wondered if he would talk to you, be able to tell us what happened to him?'

Lauren scrutinised the photograph. 'Colette showed me the same picture.'

'Really? What did she say about it?'

'She told me she cleaned for a woman, and this urn was meant to contain her dead husband's ashes. She didn't know his name, but she did say she thought he'd been in some kind of trouble.'

'And did you communicate with him?'

'No, no one came to me.'

'You didn't get anything from him?'

Lauren looked puzzled. 'No, nothing. All I can say is that I got a very bad feeling when I saw the photo.'

Susan put the photo away. 'Thank you.'

She sipped her cold coffee, trying to hide the frustration. If Colette really had just been here in the room, why hadn't she answered her questions?

Lauren smiled. 'I think you are disappointed, and I know you'd love me to have given you answers. But if Colette and her grand-mother think you are better not knowing things, they must have their reasons. I am sure they were very concerned about you, you have to listen to what they said.'

Susan smiled but didn't reply and Lauren frowned. 'I think you are planning to ignore them. Susan, why are you doing this?'

'Because someone has to fight for Colette.'

'You do that a lot, don't you, fight for the underdog?'

'Someone has to, and anyway, I thought I was offering Colette a place of safety and yet I failed her.'

She was about to get up when Lauren said, 'You are not a failure, and you need to stop telling yourself you have failed.'

Susan looked at Lauren, their eyes met, and the words slowly sank in.

'Thank you.'

'Don't do this out of guilt, you took good care of Colette, it was others who didn't, and you can't be responsible for that. You have to keep yourself safe.'

'I understand what you are saying, but I need to find out the truth. If someone harmed Colette, then it is not right that they are walking free.'

'You are a good woman, Susan. I can see why Colette was so fond of you, but don't ignore the warnings.'

'I promise to be careful, and thank you.'

Susan paid Lauren, and quietly left.

She walked back to the car and drove down to the Duver. She started to walk along the beach and breathed in the air as if breathing in hope. The island always did this, took enormous, overwhelming events and slotted them into a bigger picture, put them in their place.

It had been very moving to imagine Colette there in the room. She wasn't at all sure what happened, but Lauren was certainly an intuitive woman and she had helped her.

Beatrice's husband remained a mystery. Susan tried to

remember what Beatrice had said she was doing on the night Colette died.

That was right. Beatrice had claimed she'd been talking to her sister on the telephone.

Susan paused. She'd been accepting this as Beatrice's alibi, but something felt wrong.

And then it came to her. Of course, on the Sunday afternoon of Colette's death, Beatrice had told her about how much she would miss talking to her sister later that evening, as she was on a cruise and the signal was poor. Recently, Beatrice had confirmed she'd been unable to speak to her sister, when she'd mentioned what a relief it had been that the cruise had ended, and they'd finally been able to catch up

Susan took a deep breath. The day after Colette's death Beatrice had emphatically stated she'd been on the phone to her sister during the hours Colette died, but Susan now realised that she'd been lying.

Beatrice's alibi for the night Colette died didn't stand up, but why had she lied? And most importantly, where had Beatrice been the night Colette died?

20

Susan prepared to go out on the Wednesday evening with Robert with trepidation. She kept telling herself it wasn't really a date. The most important thing was to try to find out about Ben the chef who had worked with Trystan.

However, she had couldn't ignore the fact she was going out on her own with a man who wasn't Steve for the first time in a very long time. She was also pretty sure this meant something to Robert, she'd seen the way he was with her. But how did she feel about him?

Susan shook her head, she couldn't even go there at the moment. She certainly wasn't ready for a new relationship, maybe she would never commit herself to one person in the way she had with Steve.

She moved the pile of clothes that had been thrown onto the dressing table and looked in the mirror. She could do with a trip to the hairdresser, but it was too late for that now and so instead she brushed her hair and gave herself a reassuring smile. She put on her comfortable jersey empire-line dress, and her favourite necklace. It had officially been a present from Steve but of course she would still wear it. She'd actually gone out to buy it herself because Steve was too busy, and she was pretty sure Steve, if asked, would have no idea what it looked like.

She went downstairs, checked on the dogs and left. Robert was, as always, on time and they drove to the hotel. Conversation was a little forced as Robert told her in minute detail about the football practice he'd led the night before and she was relieved when they saw the sign for the Seashells Hotel.

They pulled into the car park up on the clifftops and Susan had to battle against the wind to get out of the car. The view this late in the day was minimal, and the stiff breeze from the sea buffeted the door as Susan tried to get out.

As she stood up, she was aware her hair was flying everywhere, and she was going to arrive at the hotel looking pretty wild. She bent her head down, walking quickly to the entrance, where Robert stood, opening the door for her.

'Here we are then.' She could hear the forced jollity in his voice and guessed he felt the same nerves as her. They went inside and were shown to their table. There were very few people, and she wondered if the reason it was so empty here was not solely down to the time of year.

Susan quickly read through the menu, which was safe, if a bit basic.

'Nothing wrong with simple food if it's cooked well, what matters is what it tastes like and if it fills me up,' said Robert, smiling.

The waiter came over to them. Robert, as the driver, was strictly non-alcoholic and so ordered a lemonade to go with his rare rump steak, but Susan ordered a large glass of wine to go with her vegetarian lasagne.

They settled back into something like normal chat when their drinks arrived.

'So, tell me, am I right in thinking you did a degree in history, not music?' asked Robert.

'That's right. My dad lectured in chemistry, Mum worked in the hospital in the labs. I think they were secretly disappointed I didn't go into one of the sciences, but did well at hiding it. Dad was pretty conforming, but my mum was a really active member of what was then called the women's liberation movement. She was so excited when I joined the peace camp at Greenham Common. If she'd not been unwell, she'd have been there as well.'

'Wouldn't that have been when you were married?'

'It was a few years before I had Zoe, but Steve knew it was something I had to do.'

'That was pretty extreme.'

Susan grinned. 'I believed it was the right thing to do then, I'd do it again even now. I still have the same fire deep inside.'

Robert smiled. 'Good for you.'

Susan grinned. 'What about you? Were your parents in the police force?'

'Oh, no, Dad was a builder, Mum worked in the local shop. They were very proud when I joined the force.'

At that moment, the waiter brought their meals and they paused to start eating. Soon, however, they resumed the conversation.

'I can imagine you were very good at your job,' commented Susan.

'I hope so, I missed it when I had to leave, but I had to look after my wife Carol, and then I was so lost when she died. It seemed so sudden.'

'I'd not realised.'

'It certainly felt it. It was five years ago, but sometimes feels like yesterday. I feel fortunate to get on so well with the kids.' She saw the pain in his eyes.

'I'm sorry, that is very hard. Do you ever think about moving over to live by your kids?'

'They ask, but I don't think I shall. I like it here. What about you?'

Susan told him about Zoe and the baby, and the invitation to move. 'I feel in a state of flux. I need to think about moving house, but I don't know whether I should go over to be with Zoe or stay here. I finally got my divorce through on Saturday, I feel it's a sign that somehow, I should be moving on, but I've no idea where to go.'

'Then do nothing would be my advice. You've not been on your own long, take your time.' He took a sip of wine, adding carefully, 'You don't think getting involved in all this to do with Colette is a kind of distraction for you, do you? I mean, you are quite obsessed with it.'

'I don't think so, no. Granted, if it was back when I had Steve and the children living with me, I might not have had the time to think so much about it all. But I'm glad I have the time now.' She paused and smiled. 'God knows what Steve would make of me going to see a medium.'

'Oh, right, how did it go?'

Susan told him what had happened, and Robert screwed his face up, unimpressed.

'You didn't learn anything much then.'

'I got Lauren's impressions of Colette, found out she'd been asking about Beatrice's husband, it was interesting to talk to her.'

'I suppose that is something.'

They chatted more generally until their main meals were finished and the waiter came over to collect their plates.

'Everything okay with your meals?' he asked.

Although Susan's hadn't been that good, she replied it had been fine. However, Robert replied, 'Unfortunately, my steak was well done, not rare, and the potatoes were hard.'

Susan cringed but the waiter seemed to take it in his stride. 'I'm sorry, if you'd mentioned it, I'd have asked the chef to cook you another steak.'

'I don't believe in throwing away good food. It won't kill me, just thought the chef might like some feedback.'

Looking quite unperturbed, Robert suggested they order pudding.

'How is the doll's house coming on, then?'

Robert took out his phone. 'I've been taking more up-to-date pictures to show my daughter, checking I'm going in the right direction.'

He handed his phone over to her and she started to scroll through them. She was about to go on to the next picture when her hand hovered over the phone. She stared at the picture.

'What's wrong?' asked Robert.

'Nothing,' she answered quickly and handed him back the phone.

However, what she'd seen had shocked her. There, on the miniature dresser, was a tiny bunch of paper flowers. Apart from being red, the bunch of flowers were identical to the flowers she'd seen among Colette's collection of secrets. Why hadn't Robert told her that he'd made those yellow roses? What if the roses had been sent to Colette separately to the envelope? Susan remembered Robert's blush when he let slip Colette's visit to him. Had he made a pass at her? Did she keep the roses as witness to some kind of infatuation he'd had?

She glanced over at Robert, who was tucking into his pudding. Was it possible that he had killed Colette in some kind of angry response to either being rejected by her or by some threat to expose him and make him look a fool?

'Don't you like your soufflé?' Robert asked. 'You've not touched it.'

Susan tried to steady her voice. 'I'm not hungry, I'm full.'

'Well, if you're sure, I'll eat it.'

Susann watched him eat the pudding, feeling increasingly sick. All she wanted to do was get away from him, but if she refused to have a lift, it would look crazy.

Oblivious to her panic, Robert grinned. 'I've had a great idea.'

He lifted his hand to the waiter, who came over.

'That pudding was excellent, I wonder if the chef has a moment? After my previous complaint, I'd like to thank him personally for this.'

He glanced around the room. 'We're not exactly rushed off our feet this evening, I'll go and have a word.'

Soon a man in chef's whites came into the room and was directed over to them.

He was younger than Trystan, but he walked in a dejected way, without purpose.

'That pudding was fabulous,' declared Robert. 'Thank you very much. Actually, I was wondering if you are Ben who used to work with a friend of ours, Trystan over at The Glanville Hotel. I think he worked here at one point.'

There was no mistaking the look of horror on the man's face. 'Oh, yeah, I'm Ben. That was a long time ago now.'

'He's doing well at The Glanville.'

Ben looked at Robert warily. 'So I heard.'

Robert raised his hand, and the waiter came over.

'Please let me buy you a drink. I saw you had a twenty-five-year-old whisky on the menu?'

Ben looked around and then shrugged. 'We're finished for the night, so why not?'

'Great, make it a double,' Robert ordered, adding, 'and please bring the bill.'

Ben sat down, and the drink arrived. He took a long sip.

'That's better, I've been working since lunchtime. People just get more and more demanding, see all this fancy stuff on TV. Have you any idea the overheads for somewhere like this? They want to pay McDonald's prices and dine as if they are in the Dorchester.'

The waiter brought the bill, which Robert paid with his card, giving a shake of the head to Susan who gestured to share it.

'Trystan must be lucky, his restaurant is pretty full most nights,' Robert remarked. 'There is talk of him being considered for a Michelin star, which would be brilliant, wouldn't it?'

Ben turned a dark, ugly red. 'I'd not heard that. But then he always did know the right people to suck up to.'

Susan spoke quietly in confidential tones. 'I did hear something about Trystan having to leave here, someone had left a fake review? Talking to people, it seems some of them think you may have had something to do with it.'

Ben's eyes burned now. 'What the hell?'

Robert sat forward. 'Trystan has always suspected you. Why did you do it?'

Ben threw his hands up. 'You can't prove anything, but I'll admit to it here, I'm glad I told the world what an arrogant bastard he is.'

'And what about the letters? Wasn't it enough that he'd left you? Why keep sending them?'

'What?' Ben was shouting now. 'I never sent any letters, for god's sake, what are you talking about?'

'I don't believe you,' Susan insisted.

Ben threw back his head and laughed. 'You're raving mad.' He stood up. 'I'll not stay and listen to any more of this crap.'

Other diners were looking in their direction, so Robert pushed back his chair and stood up too. 'I think it's time we went now.'

'And don't come back,' screamed Ben.

They left quickly, but as they pushed open the main door, an older woman in a smart grey suit and name badge saying Yvonne came over to them.

She spoke in a quiet voice. 'I don't want to interfere, but I overheard some of the conversation.' She looked around nervously. 'Look, I can't talk now, but I want you to know the truth.' Yvonne took a small card from her pocket and scribbled a number on it. 'Text me, and I'll reply, we can talk but not here.'

Susan slipped it into her handbag, and they left.

'Are you okay?' asked Robert as they walked to the car. 'That became more heated than I expected.'

'I'm fine. Do you think he sent the letters?'

Robert paused. 'I honestly don't know. I would like to hear what this Yvonne has to say.'

'Yes, I agree.'

They had reached the car, the fracas with Ben had pushed some of Susan's fears about Robert to the back of her mind. However, as she heard the clunk of the doors unlocking, she found herself frightened to get into the car.

'Get in, come on, it's cold,' Robert shouted over the sound of the wind.

She took a deep breath and got in.

'Are you okay? You went very quiet at the end of the meal,' he asked.

'I just need time to think, sorry, I'm rather tired.'

Robert accepted her explanation and put some music on. It seemed a long time until they finally drew up outside her house. She undid her seat belt, and then realised Robert had undone his. Her heart started racing as he leant over towards her.

She pulled back, fumbled with the door. 'I have to go, then, thank you for the meal,' she stammered and dashed out of the car. Not looking back, she ran up the steps to her front door and then, with a trembling hand, opened the door and slammed it behind her.

The dogs came running to meet her and she fell down and cuddled them.

She sat still, slowing her breathing, it was embarrassing to have run off like that, but she was so confused. She felt calmer after making a drink, took the card Yvonne from the hotel had written on and picked up her phone. It would be best to get back to her now before she had time to change her mind.

When would you like to meet? I can come over any time.

She waited for a reply, but none came. Maybe Yvonne had already decided it was too much of a risk. Susan hoped not, she really wanted to know what this woman had to say.

However, it wasn't Yvonne she was thinking about when she went to bed, it was Robert. Had she just been letting her mind run away, or was she right? Had she got someone so wrong? Was the one person in the group she'd been trusting a killer?

21

Susan avoided the dog walkers for the following few days, choosing to walk Rocco and Libs up on the downs again.

On the Friday morning, she received a call from Colette's uncle, Keith. He didn't seem inclined to chat, but had clearly felt he should ring to inform her about Colette's funeral.

'It is to be next Tuesday,' he explained. 'Just a quiet service at the chapel in the crematorium. I will be the only person from the family coming over, but I thought I should let you know in case you wanted to attend.'

'I would, thank you. What time will it be?'

'Eleven in the morning. A local chaplain will take it. As there will be so few people there, I didn't really see the point of organising a wake after.'

Susan realised there would probably be very few people there, but this felt stark and rather cold.

'I could find a reading or say a few words of eulogy, if you would like,' she offered.

'No, I'm sorry, I need to keep this short. The chaplain will be the only person speaking. I shall arrange a small flower arrangement for the coffin, I thought white roses as Colette had mentioned them to me as something she liked. Otherwise, I don't think we will have flowers. If anyone wants to make a donation, I would suggest a children's counselling service. I will give you details on the day.'

'Okay, I will pass that on, and I shall definitely be there.'

'That's good, and about the ashes...' Keith paused '...I was going to leave them at the crematorium, unless of course you would like to scatter them?'

'Yes, I'd like to do that.'

'I will let them know then and ask when you can collect them. I won't be taking part in any other services, though.'

'I understand.'

'Thank you, well, I need to get on. Hopefully I will see you next week,' and with that, he was gone.

Susan immediately sent a text to anyone she thought had known Colette, including asking Nikki to let the staff at the hotel know the time and place of the funeral. At least she could try to ensure there were a few more people at the funeral apart from her and Colette's uncle.

Robert was the first to reply. He thanked her for letting him know and added a vague enquiry about how she was. She replied briefly that all was well and left it at that. There would be time enough to talk to him after the weekend, as it was, she needed to concentrate on that.

She was dreading meeting Steve and his partner at the weekend, although she had some interesting plans for the Saturday, which were providing something of distraction.

Susan travelled over early on Saturday morning. The ferry was busy, the main groups making their presence felt were the teams of school-age children going over to compete in games. Their voices were high, excited, like chattering hedge sparrows. Libs was well in routine now and settled at her feet with Rocco.

Fortunately, the roads were quite quiet for her drive to Zoe's, and she arrived in good time.

As she hugged her daughter, she stood back. 'Look at your bump, it's starting to show now.'

'My jeans are getting too tight already.'

'You are a lot neater than I ever was. How are you feeling?'

'Not too bad, sickness is finally abating.'

Fay came down the stairs, and ran to give her a big hug. 'I'm sorry I missed you last time. It seems ages since I last saw you. This must be Libs.' She leant down and greeted both the dogs.

They had drinks and then Zoe, always one to get to the point, asked, 'So, any more thoughts about moving over here?'

Fay grimaced but her tone was gentle. 'Don't nag, Zoe, it's a big decision.'

Susan smiled at her gratefully. 'I still need time to think about it, I'm sorry. I know you had somewhere in mind, but I can't rush this.'

'Exactly,' commented Fay and she went over to Zoe and put her arm around her. 'Doesn't she look beautiful pregnant? I am so proud of her.'

However, Zoe was not to be deflected. 'But it would be good for you, Mum, a fresh start and, as you get older, I want you closer to us. You know how it can be with the ferries, there can be times when it's impossible to get over. If you were to fall or be ill, I want you near so I can look after you.'

'I'm sixty-two, not eighty-two!'

'But that house and those hills—'

Fay sighed. 'Leave it now, Zoe, Susan can make up her own mind. Now, how about we take these dogs out? Where shall we go?'

Susan grinned. 'I have an idea. There is a large village outside Chichester I'd love to visit. There are a few pubs there we could have lunch—'

'What's this about?' asked Zoe.

'It's somewhere I'd like to visit, that's all.'

'Come on, Mum, what's going on?'

'Well, okay, I do want to check up on something Beatrice, one of the dog walkers, told me. She used to own the jewellers there and I am trying to find out about her husband. She says he is dead but I'm not so sure – the medium couldn't find anything.'

'The medium? Good god, Mum, what have you been doing?' Zoe screwed her eyes up sceptically. 'Is this to do with Colette? I thought you'd decided to leave all that to the police.'

'You suggested that, but I decided to keep digging around.'

'Oh, Mum!'

'Please, I'd like to go to this place, just humour me.'

'I fancy a pub lunch,' said Fay. 'It sounds fun.'

Zoe drove them to the village, and once there, they took the dogs over to the park. There was a small café in the park, and they had coffee and cake before heading to the shops.

They found the jewellers quite easily, but it was at this point that Susan panicked about what she was going to say when she went in.

'I know, I could come in and ask to look at earrings, and that will leave you free to chat away to the assistants,' Fay suggested. 'Come on, let's try it.'

Before she could change her mind, Fay had propelled Susan into the shop.

Inside was the genteel atmosphere of all old-fashioned jewellers. Clocks provided a comforting background noise, and subdued lights shone on glittering stones.

'Hiya,' Fay greeted the woman, her voice echoing around the shop. 'I'm looking for silver earrings, plain drops. I saw some in the window, could I look at them, please?'

The assistant walked slowly, as if she was going through some religious ritual, and returned with a tray.

Fay started to pick out various pairs, held them up to her ears while looking in the mirror.

'Mum used to come here years ago, didn't you?' Fay looked over at Susan, clearly giving her a cue to join the conversation.

Susan walked over to them. 'I knew one of the owners, Beatrice. I wondered how she was doing?'

'Oh, right, hang on, I'll get Elaine, she's the owner now.'

The assistant returned with an older woman, tall, with a tidy brown bob and glasses resting on her head.

'You wanted to know about Beatrice Mart? I'm afraid I didn't know her that well, our dealings were pretty much restricted to the business. I think she was moving up north somewhere. She needed to get away, you can't blame her, can you?'

Susan decided to take a gamble. 'Do you mean because of her husband?'

'Of course.' Elaine lowered her voice. 'At least he's away for a long time.'

'Away?'

'Prison – you must have known—'

'Um, yes, so... Beatrice?'

'As I say, I think she moved up north, she might even have changed her name. I wouldn't blame her if she did. Sorry I can't be much help.'

'That's okay, thank you.' Susan turned to Fay. 'How are you getting on?'

'I've found the perfect pair.' Fay held up the earrings, and then handed them to the assistant and paid for them.

As they left the shop, Susan called out, 'Thanks again,' and closed the door behind them.

Zoe was waiting outside with the dogs.

'Well? How did it go?'

'Your mum was brilliant, and look, I've bought myself some really expensive silver earrings!' said Fay, laughing.

They walked up the road towards the pub.

'Fancy your friend's husband being in prison!' said Fay. 'You had no idea?'

'No. It's a complete surprise.'

'I suppose people go over to the island and they can be whoever they want,' Fay remarked. 'I rather like that idea.'

As they sat waiting for their meals in the pub, Zoe picked up her phone. 'If Beatrice's husband really is in prison, we might be able to find him online – hang on.'

She took out her phone and frantically typed away until she finally looked up. 'Got him. God, he was a nasty man.'

She read out loud from the article she had found. 'Today, Rowson Mart was sentenced to life in prison for carrying out an armed robbery which ended in murder. Rowson Mart admitted shooting Mr Laurent during a robbery of a jeweller's in Manchester.'

Zoe sat back and whistled. 'You never know who you are going to meet dog walking, do you? Mum, you've been walking with a woman whose husband is in prison for killing someone and you had no idea? That's scary!' She paused then added, 'I met Beatrice. She appeared to be so posh, I'd assumed she was very well off and respectable, imagined her and her husband being members of things like the local Rotarians, that kind of thing.'

'I know, it's hard to believe. You know, I'm sure Colette had at least an inkling about this.'

Fay leant forward. 'Zoe told me you had suspicions about Colette's death. I know Zoe is pretty sceptical, but it sounds to me like you could be onto something. The police aren't going to have time to look at everything, are they?'

'They have been pretty good,' admitted Susan. 'However, I knew

Colette and can't agree with some of the things they are prepared to accept.'

'You're not suspecting Beatrice of killing Colette, are you?'

Susan shrugged. 'I'm not sure yet. I keep finding out surprising things about them all.'

'Didn't Zoe say Colette had some kind of allergy?' asked Fay.

'She did. She was allergic to shellfish. One of my problems is that they say she ate some marshmallows they found in her pocket containing fish gelatine, but I don't think she'd have eaten them, she was very careful. However, everything else she ate was fine, so how else could she have ingested shellfish?'

'Hang on.' Zoe picked up her phone again. 'I've just thought of something.'

Susan waited while Zoe quickly searched on her phone. After a few minutes, she looked up excitedly. 'Yes, I was right. Listen to this – some lip balms and lip glosses contain things called chitosan and chitin, which, according to this, are natural polymers found in many crustaceans. Some manufacturers also use crayfish to make the lips look redder – it's popular in China at the moment.'

'That sounds familiar,' Susan commented, trying to think where she'd heard about it. 'How interesting, well done.'

'I was the designated first-aider on a school trip. We had a few children allergic to things, I had to check sun cream and all sorts.'

'I see, well, thank you, I will have a think about that. The lip gloss rings a bell for some reason.'

At that point, their meals arrived, and Susan moved the conversation on to talk about Fay and Zoe, and then after the meal they went for a long walk on a local common. By the time they returned to Zoe's, they were all ready for a quiet night watching a film.

At about ten, Susan took the dogs out for a quick walk, settled them down in the kitchen on their beds for the night, and said good night.

Before she went up the stairs, Zoe gave her a hug. 'I hope you sleep well, Mum, try not to dwell too much on this business with Colette. I know it can be kind of intriguing, but I wouldn't want you to get obsessed with it. At the end of the day, I'm sure the police know what they are doing.'

Susan smiled. 'I know, I just need to be sure of a few things, don't worry about me. Now you enjoy as many good nights' sleep as you can before that little one comes into the world.'

As exhausted as she felt, sleep evaded Susan when she got into bed. She turned over in bed, tried to stop her mind running on, she would never sleep if she carried on like this and she needed to be alert tomorrow for seeing Steve again.

Through a gap in the curtains, she could see the lights of houses stretching into the distance, but of course there was no sea. All she wanted at that moment was to go home, sit on the seat at the top of her garden and be as far away from meeting Steve and his new partner as possible.

22

Susan woke with a start the next morning, her thoughts immediately full of Steve's visit that day. She showered, dressed and went downstairs. Zoe was already up eating breakfast, and had let the dogs out into the garden.

'I'll take them for a quick walk just around the streets,' said Susan.

Zoe smiled tightly, and Susan could sense she was also pretty nervous.

When she returned, Susan couldn't face eating but drank a strong cup of coffee. Fay tried to keep the chat light but when the doorbell rang promptly at half nine, they all seemed to freeze in panic. It was Zoe who recovered first and she jumped up and ran to the door. Fay gave Susan a reassuring smile and they went to join Zoe.

As Zoe opened the front door, Susan could only initially see Steve. Their eyes didn't meet, instead he looked down at the two dogs who were racing to see him, particularly Rocco, who was barking and jumping up in excitement.

Susan scowled. She knew it might be illogical but she'd have preferred it if Rocco had shown at least a modicum of restraint. However, Libs was also looking for a fuss now.

'Hello, you must be Libs,' he said. 'Zoe has told me all about you.'

Again, Susan found it annoying he knew about Libs, she was nothing to do with him.

Susan could feel a hard rock lodge in her throat and she blinked hard to stop tears. He was tanned, and had new glasses, although he'd lost a bit more hair.

Finally, he looked up and their eyes met and she saw the slight twitching of his right eyelid that always happened when he was stressed.

'Nice to see you, Susan.' The formality in his voice hurt. He then turned to the woman next to him. 'This is Hester.'

Susan's heart raced as she looked more closely at the woman behind him. She'd expected some slim, short grey-haired, fit doctor, with little make-up but a pleasant, sympathetic face. Hester, however, was none of those things. She was quite short, blonde curly hair, well made-up and very smiley, and Susan guessed had retired young, maybe in her late fifties. She stepped in front of Steve and thrust a beautiful bouquet of flowers towards Zoe.

'For the mother-to-be, many congratulations to you both.' She turned to Susan. 'And how wonderful to meet you at last.' Before she could escape, Susan found herself engulfed in a bear hug.

Susan swallowed and stepped back and stared at Steve, who had that frozen smile on she knew so well. It was the kind of incident they would have both laughed about, but of course, it was different now.

'Let's have coffee,' Zoe suggested in her best bright teacher voice, and ushered them all into the living room.

Zoe and Hester led the conversation. They talked babies and children, Hester had two children, both now in their twenties. Steve was quite quiet until they started to talk about their travels, when Hester fed him questions in an attempt to make him join in. Susan guessed he was trying to downplay his excitement at the places he'd visited for her sake, but there was no mistaking the fact he was having a wonderful time.

At one point, they were talking about somewhere Zoe and Fay had also visited, but was completely unknown to Susan. It wasn't easy watching two couples sharing memories like that.

It was Fay who seemed to pick up on her discomfort and suggested they drive to some local woods for a walk.

Susan travelled in the car with Zoe and Fay.

'Are you okay, Mum?' Zoe asked

'It's bound to be difficult, but, yes, I'm okay,' she replied.

Once at the car park, Susan put both dogs on leads. Zoe took Rocco, while she walked Libs. It was a beautiful autumn day, and Susan felt better for being out in the woods.

Steve came to walk with her. 'So how are you?' he asked. 'I was sorry to hear about the girl who was living with you, Zoe mentioned she'd had an accident. That must have been really difficult.'

'It was awful. Colette was quite complicated, but I liked her.'

'I'm sure you were very kind to her.'

'I tried to be.'

'How are you feeling now?'

Susan took a breath. It would be such a relief to talk to Steve as she had before, but she stopped herself. No, those days were gone.

'I'm coping,' was all she replied.

She could see he picked up on the coldness of her voice. 'I'm sure. How are things more generally on the island? I expect having two dogs keeps you busy.'

'I walk with a group most mornings, the couple who run the hotel and others who work there. Oh, and Robert Moore walks with us. His wife was a patient of yours. He's an ex-policeman, his wife died suddenly five years ago. He was saying how much you helped him.'

Steve frowned. 'Oh, yes, Robert, I remember, he was very distraught about it all. His wife had been unwell for a while, I tried to prepare him, but he was in complete denial.'

'So, his wife's death wasn't that sudden?'

'No, she'd been seriously ill for some time, but Robert didn't want to face it. How is he now?'

'He's doing well. He's got two dogs, Gem Gem and Dougie, and so I see him most days when we are out walking. He's been a good friend. I had a break-in, I don't know if Zoe told you.'

'Briefly. She said they'd not taken anything, but it must have been a shock.'

'It was. Nikki from the hotel invited me to stay the night it happened, and Robert came round. I was fortunate to have good support.'

'You're seeing a lot of Robert, then?'

There was no mistaking the jealousy in his voice and it angered Susan.

'I need new friends. A lot of people I assumed were friends with us both have taken your side.'

'I'm sure that's not true, I think most people think of me as the bad guy in all this.' She heard a mixture of bitterness and self-pity in his voice.

'Look, I'm not saying it was all your fault, but it was cruel the way you simply laid out everything as a done deal,' she snapped.

'I thought it would be less stressful for you that way.'

'Of course it wasn't. I was in shock for weeks after.'

He blinked, looking genuinely surprised. 'In shock? I thought you knew the way things were going. I'd been talking about going sailing, and it was clear it wasn't something you'd want to do.'

'I don't think I'd realised quite how serious you were about it all. And in any case, that is not the reason you left, you left me for Hester.'

He frowned. 'It wasn't as simple as that.'

'That's how it felt to me.'

'You've always been so independent, I assumed you'd settle into a new routine without me very well.'

She stared at him. 'Did you really think that? I loved you, Steve, we'd been together for forty years, you were my closest friend—' Her voice broke.

'I'm sorry,' he mumbled. 'I probably should have handled things better. I was so tired, exhausted, I had to get away.'

'Yes, I can see that now. But I deserved better.'

They walked along in silence, hearing only the crunching of the leaves underfoot.

'How is the island then?' asked Steve. 'I miss it.'

'You are having a far more glamorous life now.'

'I know, but I don't have Hester's energy, I sometimes miss our evenings by the log burner reading.'

Susan felt herself being drawn back, but she couldn't do that, she couldn't put herself back to square one. 'That part of your life is over. You and Hester must find your own way now.'

Steve kicked the leaves on the path, sunk his hands further into his pockets. 'I didn't come today to argue, I want us to be friends again.'

'I think you will have to wait for that one.'

'I see, well, I shall be patient. I still care for you and want you to be happy.' He paused and then added, 'And talking of that, be careful with Robert. He's not the sort of man who copes well on his own. I worry he might be the type who would be a bit desperate to find someone else.'

Susan glared at him. 'Desperate enough to settle for someone like me, you mean?'

'God, I don't mean that, you are so over-sensitive.'

'Don't you dare minimise my feelings.'

He gave a faint smile. 'You've not changed, have you? Look, I'm sorry. You don't need to go rushing into anything, that's all. If he is the reason you are reluctant to come over and live by Zoe, then think again.'

'You know about that?'

'Zoe told me about inviting you over, and I think you should come. She really could do with your support, you know. You can't stay in that house for much longer, and we both know what hell all those hills are in Ventnor, I had old people become housebound because of them.'

Susan bristled. 'I wish everyone would stop making me out to be some helpless old woman. Zoe and Fay can go ahead with this house purchase if they want, but my move is something I won't be rushed into.'

'Zoe hasn't told you the whole story about this house. It is her dream house, but they can only afford to buy it if you sell up and put some of your money into the project.'

'Why can't you and Hester help Zoe out?'

'Look, giving you the house was a very generous settlement which the solicitor tried to talk me out of. As comfortable as Hester and I are, we have to watch our savings. She has more expensive tastes than you, it's not always been easy.'

Susan sighed. 'That is your problem, Steve. I won't be cajoled into leaving my home.'

Fortunately, they'd caught up with the others, and the conversation came to an abrupt halt.

Zoe suggested they go home, and Susan was relieved to go back. She was feeling very shaken up and emotional, words and feelings she'd been storing up had come pouring out and she was exhausted.

Once back at the house, Zoe went to the kitchen to make coffee and Susan went to find her.

'Love, I'd like to get off now.'

'Oh, Mum, please stay and come for lunch. How was your conversation with Dad? You both looked so serious.'

'It was bound to be like that, but I hope it cleared the air.'

'Are you okay?'

'Yes, in fact, I think I worked a few things out as we were talking. Your father and I are pretty strong, you know, you are not to worry about us.'

'At least stay for lunch, Mum—'

'No, honestly, you'll have a far more relaxed time without me, and I would much rather get going. I should be home soon after lunch, I might take the dogs down to the beach.'

Zoe smiled. 'You and your island, you can't wait to get back, can you?'

Susan grinned. 'You know me too well. Now, I'll go upstairs and get my things together.'

'Fine, take a coffee up with you.'

Susan quickly packed her bags, and despite it being rather hot, she quickly downed her coffee before heading back downstairs to find everyone in the living room.

'Zoe tells us you are leaving now,' said Steve. 'Are you sure you won't come for lunch? I'd mentioned we might be five.'

'No, no, I'll be off now.' Susan looked over at Steve and Hester, who had stood up.

'No!' The word came out too loud and too hard, but she'd panicked as she saw Hester looming towards her. She quickly stepped back. 'Don't come out to the car, bye, then.'

Although both the dogs had been curled up on the rug, seeing

Susan in her coat, they had run over to her. She had their leads ready and put them on.

Zoe went over to her. 'I'll come out with you.' And together they went to the car.

Once they'd settled the dogs, Zoe gave Susan a hug, saying, 'Thanks so much for coming.'

'You take care, love, look after yourself and your little one.'

'I will.' She kissed her mum on the cheek and then returned to the front door.

Susan was about to put the keys in the ignition when she saw Fay running down the path clutching something.

Susan opened the window and Fay passed through the small parcel. 'I packed some cake for the journey.'

'That's so kind, thank you.'

'And one thing,' added Fay, 'don't fret too much about the move, of course it would be lovely to have you close to us, but do it in your time.'

'Thank you. You and Zoe are going to make great parents, this baby is going to have a wonderful life.'

'I quite agree, this is going to be one very spoilt little baby,' she replied, and walked back to Zoe at the front door.

Susan waved and drove away. Only once she was well away from the house did she feel able to let out a long sigh and try to relax. Thank god that was over! She drove to the ferry and was lucky enough to catch an earlier one than she'd planned and was back on the island at two o'clock. As she drove off the ferry, that feeling of being able to breathe more easily returned, she was where she truly belonged.

She drove along from Ryde to Ventnor, taking the inland route through Wotton and over Arreton Down. From up there, she looked down on the patchwork of fields and saw the sea twinkling in the distance.

Parking outside the house, Susan felt a momentary shudder of those nerves she'd had since the break-in. She took the dogs up the steps, opened the front door and relaxed, all was well. The house seemed very quiet after all the turmoil of the day, and today that stillness gave her a sense of peace and calm.

She let the dogs into the garden and they ran around sniffing, and, in their own way, showing they were equally pleased to be back. After emptying the car, and having a coffee, she wondered what to do with the rest of the day.

Part of her was tempted to curl up in front of the TV, work her way through some box sets. However, the dogs could do with another walk, and she herself felt in need of blowing away the tension of the day. She also knew that, as autumn moved on, there would be fewer bright days like this and she needed to savour them while they were still here.

She didn't want to walk down on the beach here and so she decided to head for Steephill Cove. The tide would be out, the dogs could have a good run, and she was unlikely to meet anyone she knew.

Susan prepared Rocco and Libs, took them down to the car and drove to the car park at the top of Steephill Cove.

They walked down the rough path and she was relieved to find the beach empty, apart from one other dog walker.

They walked along the esplanade to Castle Cove. Susan stood watching the waves creeping over the concrete jetty where Colette had been found that awful night. How many times the tide must have come and gone since that night, washing the jetty. It seemed odd that everything looked normal, there was no outward sign of the tragedy that had occurred here. Maybe sometime she would think of a fitting memorial to be placed down here.

She turned away, walked further along and then finally returned to Steephill Cove and took the dogs down onto the beach and let them off their leads. They ran wildly about, sniffing and digging, and Susan sat, perched on a large boulder, facing the sea, letting the sounds and smells wash over her.

After some time, she realised the light was fading, and the brilliance of the blue sky had turned grey. The shards of warmth had gone, night was creeping in, it was time to leave.

Susan called the dogs and left the beach. She was about to return to the car when she saw someone she knew slumped against the concrete wall, looking down at his phone.

She walked over to him. 'I'm surprised to meet you down here.'

'I came for my run a bit earlier this evening. Torri is back up at the car park, she's a bit tired tonight.'

'Of course, your Sunday run. I didn't realise you actually came down onto the beach, I thought you said you ran at the top.'

He shrugged. 'It depends.'

'I don't suppose you saw anything of Colette that Sunday night then?'

'I've already said I didn't, and I wasn't down here that night.'

She decided to take a chance. 'But Torri wasn't with you. I am sure of that. She can't keep up with you, can she?'

She saw him wince. 'Not always. I leave her back in the park, but please don't tell anyone, she'd be embarrassed.'

'If you were on your own, no one can vouch that you didn't come down here, can they?'

'I don't know what you are implying, but there is someone who can verify that.' He looked around and stepped forward. 'This is between you and me. I have a friend up on the main road, I visit her sometimes on a Sunday. There is nothing going on, she's been unwell.'

'Does Torri know?'

'Yes, but we don't go on about it. The point is, if someone official ever needed to know where I was, I could tell them.'

The sea crashed against the boulders; the spray sparkled in the moonlight.

'Have you had any more of those anonymous letters?' Susan asked gently.

'Nothing since I spoke to you last.'

'I went and saw Ben over at the hotel, I asked him about the letters.'

Trystan stared, she could see the fury in his eyes. 'Why the hell did you do that? This is nothing to do with you.'

'But it is. Colette had a fragment of the letter, I need to find out why she was keeping it.'

'Why? Oh, Susan, I wish to god you'd not interfered like this.' He hesitated. 'What did Ben say?'

'He admitted to writing the bad review.'

'I knew it! The bastard!'

'But he denies sending the letters.'

'God, that man is such a liar.' Trystan ran his hand through his hair. 'I hope this doesn't encourage him to post even more stuff. How did you leave it?'

'Actually, he chucked Robert and me out.'

To her relief, Trystan grinned. 'Now there is one chef who never tries to maintain the customer is always right. I bet he got into trouble for that.'

He picked up some small pebbles, started to throw them in front of him. 'So why all this interest, Susan? Why all the questions about where I was the night Colette died? And why are you bothering with those bit and pieces she collected? The case is closed now.'

'But I'm still worried about some aspects, I'm not convinced yet that Colette's death was a tragic accident.'

'You think someone else was involved?'

'Yes, that is what I believe.'

She held her breath, how was he going to react?

However, rather than anger, she saw a look of astonishment on his face. 'And if you are looking at where we all were and trying to unravel those things in the jewellery box, you must think it was one of us. Good god, Susan, you think one of us is a killer? That's crazy and, well, awful.'

'I know it sounds like that and I don't like doing this, but I have to fight for Colette. I have to find the truth.'

He nodded. 'But just say you were right. Doesn't that frighten you? I mean, if they killed once, they could do it again.'

He moved very close to her, she noticed the pebble in his hand this time was more the size of small rock.

'I think it's time I left,' she stammered, stumbling back.

'Yes, it's late, I need to get back to Torri. You be careful now.'

She nodded, turned and, without looking back, walked with the dogs back up the slope. The pathway was very dark now, the light from her phone seemed faint. When she was about halfway up, she paused to listen to see if Trystan had followed her, but it was deathly quiet. She scrambled up the last part, out of breath now, and dashed to her car. Her hands were shaking as she tried to open the door, but once she put the dogs in, she quickly got in the driver's seat and immediately locked all the doors.

23

The next morning, Susan arrived at the beach to be greeted by Nikki.

'How are you doing?' asked Nikki.

'Settling back in, thank you. Has your new cleaner arrived?'

'She has, but she's not nearly as good as Colette... or you, for that matter. Still, she is all we can get at the moment.' Nikki pulled her coat closer around herself and then reached into her patchwork bag for a tissue. 'It's freezing, I hope I'm not going down with a cold.'

'Is that a new bag?

'Yes, I finally agreed to letting Beatrice make me one, it's a bit different to her normal style. I like reds and oranges, not pastel colours. Now tell me, how was your weekend?'

Susan chatted about her time at Zoe's and Nikki told her how things had been at the hotel. Eventually, Susan noticed the other group coming their way.

'We're all leaving now,' called Robert.

'Good idea,' replied Nikki. 'I need to get on this morning. Oh, I'll be going to Colette's funeral, and I shall try to arrange the shifts so that any members of staff who wish to be there can also attend.' She looked over at Susan. 'Should we send flowers, do you think? Some of the staff had mentioned doing some kind of collection—'

'Colette's uncle suggested donations to the children's charity, he's going to give details at the funeral.'

'That's a nice idea, we'll do that. Bye then, see you later.'

As Nikki left the beach, Susan found herself walking beside Beatrice. It occurred to her that it would be good to somehow engineer an invite to her home.

'I could really do with a proper coffee this morning,' she said. 'The trouble is, I don't think I have any decent coffee in the house. Never mind.'

'Oh, come to me, I've got plenty.'

'That's kind, thank you.'

They left the beach and walked back, chatting about the usual topics of dogs and the weather until they reached Beatrice's house.

'I'll put our coffee on and it can brew while I feed the dogs. I'm guessing Libs is okay with the same food as Rocco and Biddy?'

'She is, thank you.'

'Great, go and sit down, I won't be long.'

Susan sank back into the comfy sofa and soon the rich smell of freshly ground coffee filled the room. The dogs noisily ate their breakfast and then lay down to rest.

Beatrice was about to pour the coffee when the doorbell rang. 'Oh, sorry, I have someone coming to sort out the pond in the garden, I'd forgotten. I'll be a few minutes, then I can leave them to it.'

Susan noticed Beatrice stopped at the hall mirror, brushed her hair, used a lipstick to touch up her lips and then went to answer the door. She greeted the man and then pulled the front door behind her and Susan heard them go round the back of the house.

Susan looked over at the urn. How odd to live with this,

pretending your husband was dead. Susan looked around the room and now understood the lack of photos, anything personal.

She heard the back door opening, Beatrice was returning and so she quickly went to sit down.

'All sorted,' said Beatrice. 'Good luck to them, it's a really messy job. I'll need to keep Biddy inside.'

Beatrice poured their coffee and sat opposite Susan. 'Tell me about the weekend.'

Susan coughed and took a deep breath. 'Well, we had an interesting time on Saturday.' She went on to tell Beatrice about her visit to the jewellers.

She watched the look of horror spread across Beatrice's face and was tempted to back down. However, she knew she had to keep going, even telling Beatrice what Zoe had found online.

'I can't believe you did this,' said Beatrice, her voice shaking.

'I'm sorry. I had to know why Colette had that photograph of the urn. She had taken it to the medium, you know, I am pretty sure she knew the truth of the matter. Maybe that is what you were talking about when you had that serious conversation on the beach the day before she died?'

Susan held her breath, bracing herself for the reaction.

'Why did you think any of this was anything to do with you? I thought we were friends and yet you go spying on me, digging around. It's a horrible thing to do, Susan, I didn't think you were like that.'

'I'm sorry, Beatrice, but I needed to know.'

'Who in the group have you told?'

'I've not told any of them.' She paused, better not to mention Robert. 'And anyway, no one is going to hold you responsible for what your husband did.'

'That's rubbish. Of course I'm judged on what my husband's

done. There are people out there who hate me, wish I was dead. Can you imagine that?'

Susan shook her head.

'No, of course not. And how do you think people over here would react if they knew? The moment they found out my husband was in prison for killing someone, they would completely change towards me. I know, it's happened before. People see me living in a nice house and start wondering how much I knew, what I got away with.'

Breathing heavily, Beatrice walked over to the sideboard and poured herself a drink of gin and knocked it back.

'When I walked out of the court the day my husband was sentenced, the wife of the man he killed came over to me. She was young, pretty, and pregnant. "You have destroyed my life; you have killed me. My life is futile now, I wish I was dead. Every Sunday evening at mass, I will pray that you rot in hell." They took her away from me screaming and crying, I shall never forget it.' Beatrice poured another drink. 'I came here to escape but of course that is impossible.'

'But you didn't kill her husband, she was angry, upset, that is natural. You can't blame yourself for what happened.'

'Can't I? I knew he was getting in with the wrong people.' She sat down, her voice calmer now. 'I thought, when we bought the jewellery shop, he wanted to settle down, but that was stupid. It was a cover for him. I don't know how he got involved in the last job in Manchester. He was always the go-between, never actually got his hands dirty with the robberies. I'd learnt not to ask questions. He could be violent, but that was no excuse, was it? If I'd stood up to him, that woman's husband, a good man, would still be alive.' Beatrice sat down, and the years of unhappiness spread across her face, etched themselves into every crease.

'I'm so sorry. Do you ever see your husband now?'

Beatrice shook her head. 'No, I don't want anything to do with him.' She lifted up the heavy fringe, took off the thick-rimmed glasses and Susan shuddered as she now saw the long red scar showing through the make-up. 'He did this, told me if I ever betrayed him, he would do a lot worse. I was very scared of him, still am.'

'Can you divorce him now?'

'He'd never accept it. My best chance is to hide away over here.'

'But you can't lead you whole life like this.'

'You have no idea, Susan.' Beatrice waved her hands around the room. 'Anyway, I've seen worse prisons.'

'Colette knew, didn't she?'

'Yes, she'd worked it out. You know how dogs can smell out illness, Colette was like that, she had a second sense for lies. I think she'd looked in the urn, checked online, it's not difficult, as you know. You're right, the day before she died, she told me she'd found out about my husband and what he'd done.' Beatrice's voice broke. 'She told me she was sorry for me, but when she said all that about the jewellery box the next day, I guessed she would have told people if she'd been desperate enough.'

Beatrice narrowed her eyes and then replaced her glasses. 'I didn't kill her to shut her up, if that is what you are thinking.'

Susan looked down.

'Come on, all the questions,' continued Beatrice. 'You don't think Colette's death was accidental, do you? So what is it? You think someone went and pushed those marshmallows into her mouth? It could have happened, I suppose, but it wasn't me. No, I was here.' Beatrice continued but her voice was softer. 'To be honest, if she had told people about my past, well, I'd have had to decide whether to stay or move on. I know it's only a matter of time, look how easily you found out.' She gave Susan a piercing stare. 'I can't go around killing everyone who knows about my past now, can I?'

'But I know you didn't tell the truth about what you were doing at the time Colette died, you can't have been talking to your sister, she was on her cruise and you said the signal was too bad.'

Beatrice raised an eyebrow. 'You don't miss much, do you? No, I wasn't talking to my sister, it was a stupid lie, I panicked. What I was doing is my business, but you can be sure I wasn't down at Castle Cove killing Colette.'

Susan could see she wasn't going to get any further and stood up. 'I'd better go. I'm sorry, I really am, for everything that has happened to you.'

Beatrice walked with Susan and the dogs to the door. 'It's a bit of a relief someone knowing, I hate living like this, hiding away. But keep this to yourself.'

As she walked home, Susan thought about the conversation. Did she believe Beatrice when she said she'd have coped if Colette had told everyone about her past?

Once she was home, she was surprised to receive a text from Yvonne at the hotel, asking if they could meet that evening.

Susan replied that she would like to and they arranged to meet at the Spyglass Inn on Ventnor seafront.

Before she got on with some housework, Susan decided to ring the nursing home to ask them to let Alice know about Colette's funeral and to offer to take her if she would like to go.

The nurse who answered the phone asked her for the details, and then suggested she talk to Alice and the manager and would get back to her as quickly as she could.

Susan went into the kitchen and was busy cleaning out the fridge when her phone rang. It was the nurse from the nursing home. Alice would like to go to the funeral, and as she had mobility problems, someone from the home would take her.

Susan was very grateful and asked them to pass on the message that she would see Alice at the funeral. She was about to return to her cleaning when she received another text.

This time it was from Robert.

Would you be free to chat sometime today?

Susan swallowed hard and knew it was time to talk.

Yes, of course, when would suit you?

I'm over at Borthwood Copse with the dogs, I could call in after.

Susan paused before replying. She'd not been over to the copse this autumn and would enjoy the walk.

I could come over there. I'd be about half an hour?

Great, see you in the car park.

She called the dogs, who wagged their tails enthusiastically at the thought of another walk. She was nervous. She had already confronted Beatrice that day, and now she was going to have to do the same with Robert. What on earth was going to happen this time?

24

Susan put some calming harp music on in the car and tried to relax on the drive. When she arrived, she saw Robert's car, but there was no sign of him. Guessing he was making his way back out of the woods, she started to get the dogs ready and waited at the gate. It was only then she really noticed the full magnificence of the woods and the riot of orange and red leaves. Autumn might officially go on for a few months, but the window for the real riot of colour was small. Today was one of those special days, when she could fully immerse herself in the depth and intensity of the colours.

Suddenly she was aware of Robert calling her name and waving to her. She opened the gate and let Rocco and Libs off their leads. They ran to greet Gem Gem and Dougie.

'It's a beautiful day,' said Robert.

Although he was smiling, she could see lines of tension in his face

'Last time I was here, it was spring, and the woods were covered in bluebells. I used to come over a lot with Zoe and the foster children. It's easier to see the red squirrels here than Parkhurst. I also love the feel of the history here, with the oaks and hazel, you can imagine its days as a medieval hunting ground.' Susan paused, aware she was talking very quickly, avoiding silence.

They'd reached a clearing in the woods now; the dogs were sniffing around. As so often when she stopped walking in woods, Susan was struck by the stillness. As you walk, you generate so much noise, the rubbing of trousers and coats, the crunching of your feet on the leaves. When you stop, all that 'white noise' ceases and it can seem very quiet.

'I didn't mean to upset you when I dropped you home. I, um, judged things wrong, that is all,' stammered Robert.

'It wasn't what happened then that upset me,' she said quietly. 'Look, there is no easy way to say this. I need to know why you didn't tell me that you had made these paper flowers that were among Colette's collection in the jewellery box. Why did you give them to her?' Susan held her breath as she waited for his response.

Robert shook his head. 'I didn't know those were the roses you were talking about.'

'But you must have recognised them.'

'No, you've never physically shown me the collection, I had no idea these were there.'

Suddenly she realised he was right about not seeing them. 'I'm sorry. I saw the photograph of the doll's house when we were having the meal and recognised them.'

'Then why didn't you ask me then?'

She could feel her cheeks burning but she was determined not to back down now. 'Because I remembered your confusion when you appeared to accidentally mention that Colette had been down to see you. I'd not realised she'd been to your house, and you were clearly uncomfortable talking about it.'

He stood back. 'Let me think. If this was with Colette's things, then you thought she was holding the flowers to use one day to blackmail me. Now, how would she do that? Yes, you must think I had some kind of obsession with her, maybe made a pass at her, badgered her with gifts, something like that?'

Susan couldn't answer, she swallowed hard, waited to see what he was going to say next. He frowned. 'That's a pretty horrible thought, isn't it? She was so young and clearly vulnerable. You thought I could do that and... my god... do you think I killed her to stop her telling anyone?'

Susan stood very still; she was frightened now. Suddenly a blackbird screeched in front of them, shouting its alarm call.

Robert shook his head. 'It's very hurtful that you should have been thinking all this. Listen, on the evening Colette died, I was helping at football training for the youngsters at the church hall. I never left the main room from seven until I left to collect you at about a quarter past eight. Plenty of people saw me, there were parents and, of course, the kids. Pete phoned me while I was there and I was thinking about phoning you when I got in, but you beat me to it.'

'I'm sorry,' she said quietly.

'As for this rose, I can't see why Colette had one.' He paused and then his eyes lit up. 'Gosh, I know who did ask me for a bunch of these, though—'

Susan could feel her heart racing. 'Who?'

'It was Nathan. I didn't connect it when you told me what you'd found out about him and Colette. He came round and was admiring the doll's house; you know he loves making things and he appreciated the work involved. When he saw the flowers, he asked me if he could have a bunch, he said he was going to use them on a card he was making for Nikki, but I can see now he intended to give them to Colette.'

'The roses were with the envelope,' admitted Susan. 'I'm so sorry, Robert, I got a lot of things wrong.'

He kicked the trunk of a tree with the toe of his boot. 'And I guess you want an explanation for the confusion around Colette's visit to me. I was embarrassed to tell you about it because it was, well, delicate, shall we say. Colette came round to check out my intentions towards you. It was quite sweet, really. She was very fond of you, and she told me to treat you well as you'd been hurt badly by Steve.' He gave a shy smile. 'She was looking out for you.'

Susan blinked and felt a tear trickle down her face. 'She really said that?'

'She did, and it took a lot of nerve.'

'That's so lovely, bless her, she was trying to look after me.' Susan shook her head. 'But I didn't look after her, did I?'

Robert came close, his face creased in concern. 'You looked after her very well. Her coming to see me just shows how fond she was of you.' He reached out, gently wiped the tear off her cheek.

'I'm very sorry, Robert, I should never have had those dreadful thoughts about you. And about the lift home from the hotel—'

He held up his hand. 'It's okay. That was a mistake.'

'But Robert, I would still like to be friends. I am truly sorry for the accusations I made—'

'You are forgiven.' He smiled. 'And I would like to carry on being friends as well.'

A cold wind was starting to rustle among the leaves, the darkness drawing in early.

'We should start making our way back,' said Robert.

They turned around and then he asked, 'Did you hear anything from the woman at the restaurant?'

Susan told him she was meeting her that evening, asking if he would like to join her. Although she felt Yvonne would feel more able to speak with just her, she felt it was important to offer the olive branch.

'I think you would handle this better without me,' he replied.

'Fine, oh, goodness, I have other things to catch you up on as well. Firstly, there is Beatrice.'

She told Robert all about her visit to the jewellers and about Beatrice's husband. When she'd finished, Robert whistled. 'I had a feeling something was up, but never suspected that. You did well to discover all that.'

'I talked to Beatrice about it as well.'

His eyebrows shot up. 'Now that was brave, I'm impressed. How did she react?'

'It was all rather sad in the end. I don't know, the idea of stealing jewels and passing them on sounds quite exciting, romantic even, but the reality of it isn't nice at all.'

'No, it never is.'

'He sounds a terrible man who abused her, and made her life hell. It shows you never know what is going on in someone's life, doesn't it?'

'And have you discovered anything else?'

Susan told him about talking to Trystan about their visit including the fear she'd felt at the end of their conversation on the beach.

'He was bound to have been upset by your insinuations. Goodness, Susan, you are offending a lot of people, aren't you? Remember not everyone is as nice as me.'

'But look at everything I've found out, you have to admit, everyone has secrets they would have liked kept under wraps.'

'Yes, but you have no proof anyone was down in the cove, no proof anyone killed Colette.'

'But I will find it, I'm sure.'

'Tomorrow is the funeral, it can provide a time of closure, you know.'

'It might for some people, but not for me, there will be no closure until I know for certain what happened to Colette the night she died.'

25

As she walked along the esplanade that evening, Susan could see the lights from the Spyglass Inn ahead. To her left lay the dark mass of the sea, and she could imagine, years ago, the smugglers coming into the deserted bay with their contraband from the French coast only a few hours' sail away. She knew there were caves hidden away and the pub she was going to was named after the inn Long John Silver frequented in *Treasure Island*.

Once inside the pub, Susan took a few seconds to find Yvonne, as it was very busy that evening. However, she found her eventually, sitting in a quieter well-lit area at the back. She was bundled up in a woollen coat, one hand clutching a full glass of orange juice.

'Sorry, I took a minute to find you,' Susan said, approaching Yvonne.

'It's quieter here, I'm sorry, I have problems hearing otherwise.'

Yvonne lifted her hair to show her hearing aids. 'These help a lot, but I still have problems in very noisy places.'

'I understand. I'll get myself a drink, do you want anything else?'

'No, I'm fine, but leave the dogs with me if you want.'

'Thanks, it's a bit of a struggle with two.'

She went to the bar, ordered a drink and returned to sit opposite Yvonne. 'Thanks so much for coming to meet me. By the way, if I don't speak clearly enough, let me know.' She looked down at the dogs, both lying under the table. 'I'm glad you like dogs, these two should settle quickly.'

'It's nice having them there.' Yvonne sipped her drink. 'Now, I wanted to explain to you about Ben. He's a nice enough chap, believe it or not, but he's not got that extra spark Trystan has and he knows it. Instead of learning from Trystan, he just got jealous, and it ate him up inside. I always suspected him of posting that review, but it was impossible to prove.'

'He told me he found Trystan to be arrogant and a bully. Do you think others saw him like that?'

Yvonne shook her head. 'No, he was a perfectionist but never a bully. I thought once the fuss over the review died down, Ben would back off. I was very surprised when Trystan showed me the letters.'

'So, you think he sent the letters?'

Yvonne sighed. 'Oh, yes, although it seemed a lot of hassle for him. It was terrible that he drove Trystan away from the hotel, the place has gone down since we lost him. I didn't expect him to move to work in the nursing home. I thought he'd have gone to another hotel or restaurant, or even moved abroad, I know that's what Torri was keen to do.'

'Yes, Torri has always wanted to go to Portugal.'

Yvonne nodded. 'Yes, she told me. I could understand that. It's warmer than here! She really loves Trystan, doesn't she, a nice woman. Yes, I was very sorry when they both left. I am so pleased Trystan has kept in touch, though. Of course, he needs the help, but I appreciate him coming round on a Sunday sometimes, especially since I've been unwell.'

Susan sat forward. 'He comes to see you?'

'Yes, and Torri knows. She says she is okay with it but between you and me, I know she hangs about outside the house while he is with me. I can see her arrive, just after him, and then she leaves as soon as I open the door. Trystan hasn't twigged yet. I don't want to interfere. He should reassure her more, but he's not very good at showing the softer side of himself. Now, I saw it when we worked together. He was so considerate of my hearing loss, always made sure I understood him. I suppose it's partly because he understood but it was still kind of him.'

'That's a side of Trystan I don't see so much. Everyone speaks very highly of him as a chef, but people have complained about him being a bit difficult to work with lately.'

Yvonne bit her lips. 'He has his reasons, you know.'

'You mean because of this business with Ben?"

'It's not just that. It's the frustration, the fear, it can get under your skin, I know all about that.'

'What is going on?'

Yvonne screwed up her mouth, tapped the side of her glass. 'I can't really tell you, that's for him to say, it's personal, but all I can say it's a difficult time for him.'

'I see. That's okay. Look, I did want to ask you one more thing, though. It's about the girl who used to live with me who died down at the cove last month, her name was Colette.'

'I remember, she had some kind allergic reaction, didn't she?'

'That's right. I think Trystan sometimes comes to see you on Sunday evenings, I was wondering if he was with you the night she died?'

Yvonne frowned. 'Yes, he was, definitely. I remember hearing about Colette the following day. I found it hard to reflect on the lesson, knowing what had been happening so close by.'

'You used the word "lesson" and earlier you told me you helped him when he came round. Are you his teacher?'

'You could say that. I'm just trying to give him the tools to cope with some changes that are going on, that is all.'

Susan screwed up her eyes in concentration and then she saw it. The reason Yvonne understood Trystan so well, and how she was helping him. 'Does Trystan have a problem with his hearing? I know when I called over to him one day he didn't look up and when I tapped him on the shoulder, he was ever so startled.'

Yvonne slowly nodded. 'You're right, but please don't tell anyone. Trystan is very upset and needs time to take this in. He's not even had a proper hearing test yet, he's so scared. I have been talking to him, teaching him some lip-reading, but he needs to get professional help. He's not even told Torri yet.'

'But why not? Everyone would support him.'

'He thinks people will change in the way they treat him; he's scared Torri will go off to Portugal without him—'

'That's not going to happen, is it?'

'You never can tell, can you? But his biggest fear is that it will ruin his career. That people will not want to employ him if they think he can't cope in a busy kitchen.'

'I'm so sorry he feels like that, it's good he has you to talk to.'

'I enjoy seeing him. He comes to me for general advice but also to work through some lessons on lip-reading and basic sign language. We usually video the sessions, I can look over them, spot weaknesses. It's strange, though, I didn't like reviewing the session we recorded the night Colette died, like I said, it seems so wrong to be engrossed in something else when that was happening so close by.'

'So, the time and date would be recorded on the video?'

'Oh, yes. That one was an hour, between seven and eight. I remember thinking it was a particularly long one.'

'That's really helpful, thank you. So, Torri sometimes follows him? Did you see her that night?'

Yvonne nodded. 'I only noticed her when we were finishing. I looked out when Trystan was leaving and saw her disappearing, but I don't know how long she'd been there.'

'I see, well, that's great, thank you. It's been lovely to meet you, Yvonne.'

They finished their drinks and left together. Well, she knew now that Trystan had an alibi for the night Colette died, although she couldn't be sure about Torri. Imagining her standing around opposite the house seemed so desperate. Susan knew now that the person who had been interested in Colette was Nathan. However, Nikki thought Torri suspected Trystan and maybe Torri herself had got it wrong. Would that desperation to hold on to Trystan give her a motive for killing Colette?

* * *

The next day was Colette's funeral. Susan drove to the crematorium the next morning with a heavy heart. As she entered the chapel, she was relieved to see it was not quite as sparsely attended as she had feared. Alice was sitting at the back with a nurse and smiled over to her. Nikki and a number of staff from the hotel were there and Colette's uncle, Keith, sat at the front alone. Susan made her way down to sit next to him.

She noticed a small wreath of white roses on the coffin, they looked beautiful. It was very quiet in the chapel, with gentle music playing in the background. Susan had attended large funerals where there was a buzz of talking before the funeral started as friends and family who had not seen each other for some time reunited. However, it was not like that today and it did seem particularly poignant that so few people were at the funeral of such a young girl.

The vicar who took the service gave a brief eulogy. He had taken the time to learn as much as he could about Colette from Keith and spoke warmly of her love of travel and art. It was thoughtful and Susan knew that having never met or known Colette, he was doing the best he could. However, it had the feel of an obituary written by a stranger and as he spoke, Susan felt herself falling into despair. 'No one cares about the likes of me, I walk out of a room, and I'm forgotten,' Colette had said. Susan saw no heartbreak, heard no stifled tears. Would they all just walk out of here and forget Colette?

And then she heard a change of tone in the vicar's voice. There was a sudden passion and conviction in his voice. 'I would like to read this verse from Matthew 10:29–31. "Are not two sparrows sold for a penny? Yet not one of them will fall to the ground outside your father's care. And even the very hairs of your head are all numbered. So don't be afraid; you are worth more than many sparrows."'

Susan thought of Colette, her fine blonde hair, her pale face, the description of a sparrow seemed fitting, and the words comforted her.

'Every person, every living thing matters. A mayfly's flying life is less than a day and yet they are special. They are the oldest living group of winged insects, dating back to the Carboniferous Period, about 300 million years ago. Their life above the surface may be brief and yet they are an important part of the food chain in rivers, streams, ponds and lakes. A fossil of mayfly larvae that was 120 million years old has been found, so tiny but never forgotten. Every living thing matters. Colette will have affected every person she knew, every person and animal she loved. Fossils show us nature never forgets and neither must we.'

Susan was so grateful for those words, and they gave her some kind of comfort.

After the funeral, Susan turned to Keith and asked, 'As there isn't a wake, I wondered if you would like to have a drink back at my house?'

He accepted, and she went to the back of the chapel to speak to Alice. She was sensibly wrapped up in a smart blue woollen coat and black trousers.

'How are you?' she asked.

'It's so terribly sad. I have been to too many funerals of people my age, but to come to one for such a young girl is very upsetting.'

'I'm sorry, I hope it hasn't been too much for you.'

'No, I'm glad I came.' Alice sighed and then tapped Susan's hand. 'Don't forget the party, and bring that collection of Colette's.'

'Of course, yes. I shall see you on Saturday.'

Susan left Alice and made her way across the courtyard to the ladies' cloakroom. She was washing her hands when Nikki came in.

'Just need to freshen up.' Nikki stood next to Susan, looking into the mirror, and shivered. 'I hate these places. All those plaques to the dead outside, it's like graveyards, spooks me out, anything about dead people does. Was Beatrice right when she told me you went to see some medium?'

'Yes, I went to the woman Colette had been seeing.'

'You shouldn't do things like that, seriously, Susan. You don't need to go looking for the dead, they'll find you easily enough.'

Nikki returned to looking in the mirror. From a bulging make-up bag, she took out a lip gloss that she applied over her thick red lipstick. She smiled via the mirror at Susan. 'You've never bothered much with make-up, have you?'

'My mum always hated make-up, said it was a stain on women's rights. I think feminism has moved on from that, you know, your body, your choice and all that, but, well, at the end of the day, I just don't think I can be bothered.'

Nikki laughed. 'I think it's a matter of habit for me. I started wearing make-up in my teens and just carried on. I dread even Nathan seeing me without it now.'

'I'm sure he'd think you were just as beautiful.'

'Maybe, but I enjoy wearing it. I'm going to have to save up to buy this lip gloss Beatrice gave me, I'm getting through this so quickly.'

Suddenly Susan remembered why Zoe mentioning lip gloss had rung a bell.

'Can I look at it?' she asked.

'If you want.' Nikki handed it to her.

'It looks nice, can I take a photo of it? Zoe likes this kind of thing.'

'Of course, carry on.'

Susan took the photo and then handed the lip gloss back to Nikki, her mind racing.

'I don't suppose you know if Beatrice gave any of this to Colette?'

Nikki shook her head. 'No idea – why?'

'Oh, nothing, just thinking.'

As soon as Nikki left the room, Susan Googled Nikki's lip gloss. Yes, it had been made in China and the product proudly boasted it contained crayfish to 'lacquer your lips with a fishy sheen'.

Susan stared at her phone. The police had looked into the food-stuffs consumed by Colette, in particular the marshmallows, but what if Colette had ingested shellfish some other way? Robert had told her that they could directly state what foodstuffs the fish oil had been in, that had been pieced together. But what if it wasn't food at all, what if it was lip gloss?

Her hands shook as she put her phone away. There were two possibilities: one was that Colette had used the lip gloss by mistake, the other was that someone had gone down to the cove and offered her the lip gloss, knowing the dangers, but assuring Colette it was safe to use.

Maybe, for some reason, Colette had been prepared to accept the reassurance and allowed herself to be talked into trying the lip gloss.

Susan knew that Beatrice and Nikki had this lip gloss, and she was pretty sure Nikki had said Torri did as well. She needed to find out if there were any signs of that lip gloss being on Colette.

Susan rushed out of the cloakroom and quickly found Robert. She grabbed his arm. 'I need to speak to you now, quick.'

She guided him to a quiet corner in the courtyard and told him everything she'd been thinking.

'You need to ask Pete, find out if Colette had this lip gloss.'

He took a deep breath. 'Okay, hang on, I can see where you're going. The thing is they found traces of the fish gelatine marshmallows in her mouth.'

Susan frowned. 'Ah, I'd forgotten... but wait. If someone else was involved, they could have wiped a marshmallow around the inside of her mouth to confuse the investigation, to distract from the lip gloss, worried that it would be easy to trace.'

Robert shook his head. 'I don't know, but I'll ask Pete, see what he can come up with.'

'Great, now I'd better go and find Colette's uncle, he's coming back for coffee.'

Susan found Keith easily and he followed her back to her house in his car. She noticed how exhausted he looked as he walked into the house.

'It's been a difficult morning,' she said.

'It has. Poor Colette, such a sad end.'

He looked around in a kind of daze. 'Seems a long time since I was last here.'

'A lot can happen in a few weeks, let's sit in the living room.'

They went in and she brought them both coffee and biscuits.

'Do you know when the inquest is likely to be?'

He shook his head. 'No, it could be a while, they are behind, apparently. I think the police are pretty satisfied with it being an accidental death and don't expect any surprises at it.'

Susan sipped her drink and then asked, 'I wonder if you'd mind looking through something for me. Colette collected a few items which she said were significant. I wonder if you could take a look and see if you can tell why they were important to her.'

Before he could comment, she went and found the file containing Colette's collection of secrets.

She laid them out on the coffee table. Keith looked quite baffled. 'I don't see how any of these things could be of any significance.' He picked up the photo of the urn, the flowers, the magazine page but then paused as he picked up the newspaper cutting of the opening of the hotel.

'Some of those people were at the funeral today, weren't they? I recognise her—'

He pointed at Nikki. 'I've just made the connection. She worked with Mum at the nursing home, I remember meeting her, she's done well for herself, hasn't she?'

'She has. Wait, I have another newspaper cutting.'

Susan picked out the second picture she'd found.

Keith took it from her, looked at it casually, and then held it closer, and studied it more carefully. 'God, yes, I'm right, look at that.'

He pointed to Nikki's lapel.

'I'd swear that was Mum's brooch. Yes, look, I'm sure of it. How the heck—'

Susan's heart was racing. 'Do you mean the special brooch?'

'Yes, the ruby and diamond one. I'll be damned, do you think Mum gave it to her after all? But why didn't Nikki say when I was asking about it?'

'Nikki had left by then, but I think she'd have been asked by the manager.'

'It looks very suspect to me.' He looked up. 'I suppose I could go to the police with this.'

Susan could feel herself shaking. 'You could.'

'But what if I'm wrong?' He put his head in his hands. 'No, I told you I can't get involved.'

He looked up, pale, his eyes red. 'I don't know how to explain this, but I don't want anything to do with it. I have tried to do the right thing by Colette, but she's gone now. I can't handle this.'

'But your mother's things have been stolen and it looks as if you now know who took them. Don't you want to do anything about it?'

His whole body seemed to be shaking. 'No, no, I can't. Anyway, what's the point? This Nikki has her life now, why ruin it over what is probably a worthless trinket?'

Susan was taken aback. 'You really don't want to know?'

'No.' He stood up. 'I've finished here, I shan't be coming back to the island. The crematorium said you can collect the ashes any time after next Tuesday. I have arranged for them to be placed in a wooden casket.'

He spoke fast, sounding very business-like, but she could hear the hurt and pain in his voice. Susan longed to hug and comfort him, but she could tell it was the last thing he wanted.

'Thank you,' she said calmly. 'I understand why you feel like you do. Please keep in touch if you want to.'

He gave a sad smile. 'You are very kind. Forget this brooch business, don't say anything to the lady involved. It doesn't matter any more, and to be honest, if the police or anyone in authority were to ask me again if I recognised the brooch, I would deny it.'

'I see, well, that's your decision and I shall respect it.'

Susan walked with him to the door.

He stood on the doorstep looking over at the sea and breathed in the air. It seemed to calm him. 'Have you always lived here?'

'Not in Ventnor, but I have always lived on the island.'

'You've never wanted to leave?'

'Not really.'

'You're very lucky. Not to feel you have to get away, try to escape bad memories. I have spent my life moving on, trying to forget.'

She gave him a gentle smile. 'I am very fortunate. One thing I've never asked you was why did your mum choose to come to live on the island?'

'She'd been here on holiday as a child, had always wanted to come back, and so she moved here once my sister and I left home. I was angry when she came here at first, I felt she'd purposely made it harder for us to see her. But when I visited her in the nursing home, she tried to explain that the island made her feel safe. She liked that strip of water. Funnily enough, winter was her favourite time here, there were fewer people, she loved walking on empty beaches and up on the downs with only the birds for company. It was a very healing place for her.'

'I'm so glad and I am sure Colette felt the same about it.'

He sighed. 'Well, I'd better be getting on or I will miss my ferry. Take care, Susan.'

After he'd driven away, Susan went back into the house, and sat down, looking again at the newspaper cutting.

What was she going to do next? The obvious thing would be to ask Nikki, but if she'd really stolen this brooch, she was never going to tell the truth, was she? Susan idly picked up the anonymous letter. She read through it again, and then it struck her. My god, why hadn't she seen it before! She remembered the conversation with Ben at the hotel, of course, now it all made sense. She would see someone tomorrow, she was going to solve this part of the puzzle once and for all.

26

FRIDAY

Susan woke to the thud of rain on the windows and groaned. She opened the curtains to see a dark, grey, wet day. It was certainly not a day that would tempt you out for a stroll along the beach, but she could already hear the dogs moving about, alert to her getting out of bed.

She threw on old clothes and went downstairs. Libs and Rocco came bounding towards her and she couldn't help smiling. 'I can't believe you are so keen to go out in this.'

Susan put on her waterproofs, got the dogs into their coats and set off.

The rain was so hard, she had to keep her head down. The strands of hair that escaped her hood were now plastered to her face, the sound of the rain was deafening.

They walked down the hill and today she only saw one member of the group on the beach. It would be interesting to talk to her, but how on earth were they going to hold a serious conversation in this weather?

Torri looked paler than ever and didn't even attempt to smile.

They both kept their dogs on leads, this was not a day for dogs to roll in seaweed or wet sand, and they walked briskly.

A gust of wind threatened to blow Susan's hood off, and it was impossible to hold onto it with two dogs on leads.

'Can we walk with our backs to the wind?' she shouted.

They turned and it was slightly easier walking with the wind behind them.

Suddenly Torri stopped walking, looked at Susan. 'I would like to talk to you sometime.'

'We could chat now back at my house if you have time?'

'Thanks, yes, that would be great, if you can cope with a wet me and a soaking dog.'

They pushed their way through the rain and wind and left the beach. The walk up the hill was hard work, and they were relieved to get back to the house. They took off all the wet layers and laid them on the airer Susan had stood up in readiness, while boots were placed on newspaper. Susan took off the dogs' coats and used towels to wipe down their fur before pouring kibble into the bowls.

'I'll put the kettle on. We can go and sit in the living room, hopefully escape the wet dog smell. The dogs can crash out in here in front of the wood burner.'

Eventually they both sat with steaming hot drinks and biscuits. Max had refused to leave Torri and was lying on an old towel by her feet.

Torri carefully put down her mug. 'Trystan told me you went to the hotel we used to work in. He also told me you suspected one of us of, well, killing Colette. Is that true?'

'I'm not sure – um—' replied Susan, not daring to look Torri in the eye.

'At first, I was naturally horrified and couldn't even contemplate the idea,' continued Torri. 'But then I started to think about it.'

Susan sat up. 'Really?'

'Yes, I've been thinking I can understand your question about that small velvet pouch, I mean, it has to be somewhere, doesn't it? It's definitely odd.'

'Yes, it is.'

'And like you said, why would she eat those marshmallows when she was so careful?'

'Exactly, that still worries me. So tell me, have you any ideas about it yourself?'

'Well, I know this is almost too awful to think about, but my first thought was Beatrice. Let's face it, none of us know anything about her. She's turned up on the island, she could tell us anything, couldn't she? Maybe Colette found out something about her, something serious enough for her to kill Colette to silence her.'

Susan couldn't help thinking that for someone who'd found the whole thing so horrendous, Torri gave every appearance of enjoying sharing her suspicion.

'I suppose it's possible.'

'I could be wrong, of course, but all I'm saying is that I don't think your suggestion that someone else was down there with Colette is complete crazy. I mean, when she threatened everyone with those secrets at the cove, she was baiting people a bit, wasn't she?' Torri sipped her drink and then added with slightly forced casualness, 'I am guessing you still have all those items Colette collected?'

'Yes, I have kept them.'

'I know you have part of one of the letters sent to Trystan, what else is there?'

Susan sat forward. 'One of the items is a page carefully torn out of a wildlife magazine. It is the contents page, with a circle around a particular article. I have to say, I've not been able to make out why Colette would have saved that.'

She was watching Torri carefully, but there was little response and so she continued, 'And then last night I looked at it again, and suddenly everything fell into place. I saw the date at the top of that page, February 2010. Now, I am guessing you and Trystan were working at the hotel then, it wasn't long before you left and went to work at the nursing home.'

'Yes, that's right.'

'And it was about that time Trystan started to receive those anonymous letters? The print from the magazines, the ones you take, is identical to the print in the letters.'

Torri stared, her eyes wide, her face deep red. 'You know?'

Susan nodded. 'You are the person who has been sending the anonymous letters to Trystan, aren't you?'

Torri covered her face with her hands. 'But I didn't know what else to do.'

'Tell me about it,' said Susan gently.

Torri sat back. 'I know people think I'm mad, that I'm obsessed with Trystan, but I have always been petrified of losing him too.'

'What has that got to do with the letters?'

'When we were in the hotel, I was sure he was falling for one of the women who worked there. She was older than us but the two of them had a kind of bond.'

'You mean Yvonne?'

Torri looked up clearly surprised Susan knew the name. However, she continued, 'Yes, that's her. I know Trystan sometimes still sees her. He tells me they are just friends, but how can I be sure?' She sounded so desperate that Susan's heart went out to her.

'I am sure he loves you.'

'Are you? I'm never sure. I get so down about it all, I make mistakes.'

'What do you mean?'

'I don't know, I just think why would any man choose me, and I love him so much. When that chef, Ben, posted the fake review, I thought it was my chance to make Trystan want to leave the hotel and we could go to Portugal, live my dream. Well, I succeeded in making him want to get out of the hotel, but then Trystan decided we needed to save to go to Portugal and so I went with him to the nursing home. Then, of course, the job at The Glanville came up—'

'And so you started the letters again.'

'I thought it would be the spur he needed to finally get away from the island, but it hasn't worked, has it? We're still here and I'm always worried about losing him, frightened he'll find someone else.'

Susan noticed Rocco and Libs had come in and were curled up on the floor close by.

'But would you feel any more sure of him if you went to Portugal?'

'I know this sounds terrible, but you see, I speak fluent Portuguese and Trystan doesn't speak a word. I'll have more control over there.'

'Oh, Torri, this isn't right. Your self-esteem can't be so low that you honestly believe you could lose Trystan so easily. You need to start believing in yourself. You're a bright, beautiful, talented woman and if Trystan doesn't love you with all his heart, well, he's not worth fighting for, is he?'

Torri looked up and smiled. 'You make it sound so easy.'

'I'm not saying relationships are straightforward, look at me, I'm divorced now. But I do know you have to work at believing in yourself.'

Torri put her head to one side. 'You don't seem to be judging me for what I did.'

Susan shook her head. 'Look, writing those letters wasn't a good thing to do. It put Trystan under a lot of stress, and it was bad for you as well. You must have felt miserable.'

'I hated it.'

Susan took a long drink from her mug. 'I was wondering, do you think Colette knew what you were doing?'

Torri looked away, didn't answer.

'Yes, I think we both know she did,' said Susan. 'I am guessing that if I looked up the circled article, I would find a page with words cut out. You could have thrown that magazine away, but I think you were loath to break up your collection.'

Torri nodded. 'I am sure she did. One day, I found her looking through the magazines and when she saw me, she quickly put them back on the shelf. A look passed between us, I had a feeling she knew.'

Torri clasped both her hands and looked directly at Susan. 'The one thing you have to believe is that I certainly did not go down to the cove to stop Colette telling Trystan, I wasn't that desperate. We'd have sorted it out somehow, I knew that.'

Suddenly she stood up. 'I will talk to Trystan, please leave this to me.' Max stood next to her, clearly taking the cue that it was time to leave.

'Right, I'll see if your coat is dry.'

Torri's clothes were still very damp, but she insisted on putting them on and was clearly eager to leave. 'I can see you have found out a lot more than I realised. That is clever but also quite dangerous. You need to watch yourself.'

Susan watched Torri leave, wondering if that passing shot to be careful had been one of consideration or a threat.

27

The following day Susan left the house at dusk to go to the tea party at the nursing home. She found this time of day unnerving, ominous, and it would almost be a relief when night-time arrived.

As she walked down the driveway of the nursing home, she saw Nikki and Nathan were also arriving.

'It's strange to be back,' said Nikki. 'I've not been here for ages. I've been invited to the odd Christmas do but I'm always so tied up with the hotel.'

Susan noticed she had a large bunch of flowers. 'Those are pretty.'

'Yes, I always like to bring some. Nathan brings mushrooms, I bring them flowers,' she said, laughing.

Nathan held up a brown paper bag to illustrate her point.

'I remember when we were foraging, you told us you bring them up for the manager here. Have you done any of your handyman jobs since opening the hotel?'

'When we first left, I did pop up for the odd job, but they have a good handyman to replace me now. Oh, here come Torri and Trystan, I see Torri has her contribution.'

They waited for them to catch up and Nathan looked down at the box Torri was carrying. 'It has to be the famous tarts.'

Torri smiled. 'It is.'

They entered the nursing home together.

The reception area was decorated with bunting and balloons, as was the main sitting room where the party was being held.

The nurse she'd met before, called Kathy, was greeting and showing people the way to go and she seemed surprised when she saw Susan.

'Hello, it's Susan, isn't it? How lovely to see you again.' Her words were friendly enough, but the smile didn't reach her eyes, and Susan had a feeling she wasn't entirely welcome.

'Alice has invited me; I hope it was okay to come.'

'Of course, I know you both had a long chat, do come this way.'

Susan wasn't too sure why Kathy had seemed on edge, but maybe they had more guests at the party than they expected.

The residents were sitting in chairs spread around the room, and children from a local school were stationed to hand out cakes and sandwiches.

The manager of the home clapped her hands with an air, Susan imagined, very similar to Zoe at school, and everyone turned to face her.

'Thank you so much to everyone for coming to celebrate our first ten years together. I have to admit I'd not expected such a great turnout. Now, I'd sure you'd much rather be eating some of this fabulous spread than listening to me, so I'll just thank you so much for coming and I'd encourage you all to mingle and chat to as many people as possible.'

Susan looked around. She saw Trystan and Torri were already engaged talking to someone, and Nikki was with one of the residents. There weren't many people there she recognised, although she did spot Phil, the physiotherapist, and remembered Nikki had told her he treated some of the residents here.

Susan was looking around for Alice when a nurse came over to her. 'Alice is still in her room. She wondered if you would mind popping down there and then joining the party in a minute.'

'Of course, is she okay?'

'Oh, yes, she wanted to show you something and then she will walk back here. I'll take you to her room, it's not far along this corridor.'

They found the room easily and Susan knocked on the door and went in.

Alice was sitting in her armchair, holding a small frame, but once the nurse left, she said, 'I don't suppose you want to see this picture of my daughter and grandchildren, but it seemed a good reason to get you in here.'

'Actually, I'd love to see a photograph of your family,' said Susan and she looked down at the photograph. 'Your daughter looks very like you, and so does your granddaughter, for that matter.'

Alice smiled proudly. 'Peas in a pod, my mum would have said. My daughter's husband is away a lot, he works on ships that do geological surveys. She is a clever girl, went to university, she's a teacher at the high school, head of department.'

She carefully put the frame down on the bedside table next to her chair.

'Now, did you bring that collection of Colette's?'

'I did, and I know a lot more than when I last saw you. I must show you the most significant find first.'

Susan explained about the newspaper cuttings, and what Colette's uncle had told her about the one she herself had found.

Alice took the cutting and inspected the photograph and when she handed it back to Susan, her face was stern. 'I'd put money on it that Nikki is wearing Pam's brooch. It seems incredibly brazen to be wearing it out in the open like that. Have you talked to her about it?'

'Not yet. I would guess she will either deny it's Pam's or say Pam gave it to her.'

'But if Pam had given it to her, why not own up to Colette?' Alice shook her head. 'But if she had stolen it, why wear it so openly only a few days after? I wonder where the brooch is now?'

'I don't know. Colette couldn't find it, and it wasn't among her jewellery when I looked in her room.'

'If it was genuine and worth a lot, she may have sold it. That's not as easy as it sounds, mind you, unless she knew someone with connections – someone maybe who'd been in the jewellery business, I was thinking of Beatrice? What do you think?'

Susan sat up. 'Oh, goodness, Beatrice. I need to tell you what I found out about her first.'

Susan went on to explain and added, 'So, if Beatrice's husband had been involved in illegal activity with jewellery, then Beatrice may know some of those connections. If Nikki had confided in Beatrice about the brooch, then maybe Beatrice would have known who to sell it on to.'

'Yes, that's a possibility. Can I see that photograph of her husband's urn?' asked Alice.

Susan handed it to her. 'At least we know why Colette had that now.'

Alice, however, gave the photograph closer inspection than she expected. 'Above the urn, I can see a print of a painting I recognise. It's Titian's *Woman with a Mirror*. You'd not mentioned that before.'

'I didn't think it was important. I don't think it meant anything to Colette.'

Alice dropped her hands, the photograph resting in her lap, and she looked ahead at the wall, clearly deep in thought. Finally, she looked back at Susan, frowning.

'Do you know when Beatrice bought it?'

'It was given to her a few years ago by Nikki or Nathan, I think. Why?'

'It's given me an idea, which is all. I agree, I don't think Colette would have seen its significance, but maybe fate led her to include this in the photograph.'

'I'm sorry, I don't know anything about this painting. Now if it was a bit of Shakespeare, I could help. I'm working my way through the tragedies; I am about to start *Macbeth*.'

Alice frowned seriously. 'Yes, that would do, read that carefully... of course, I could be wrong.' She paused again and then seemed to shake herself back to the present. 'Right, is there anything else?'

Susan told Alice about the acupuncturist before finally telling her about Nathan and Colette.

Alice frowned. 'What a foolish thing for Nathan to do. It sounds like he was feeling neglected by Nikki but all the same, to use Colette like that was wrong. She felt things deeply. I would guess he'd be pretty keen for their romance to be kept a secret from Nikki. Does he have an alibi for that evening?'

'No, he was in his shed on his own.'

'What was Nikki up to?'

'I told you she is seeing this chap for acupuncture during her drama rehearsals.'

'I see, and she definitely saw him that night?'

Susan frowned. 'I assumed she did, maybe I need to check that. I saw he was here, I'll try to nab him later.'

Alice looked down at the collection. 'So we have explained the rose and the song, and we have started to understand the urn in the photo. The newspaper cutting Colette found was not actually what she thought, there was no affair, but we know now about the brooch. That leaves the magazine page and this letter.'

She picked up the anonymous letter. 'Do you know anything about this letter?'

'Oh, yes, quite a lot,' replied Susan and went on to explain.

'So this man, Ben, was it? He maintains he left the review but that he didn't send the letters? Do you believe him?'

'I do, because I have discovered the other half to this story. You see that magazine page, well, that holds the answer.' Susan explained about Torri sending the letters.

'Fancy it being Torri all this time,' exclaimed Alice. 'It's so easy to underestimate quiet people, isn't it, you forget all the time they are not speaking, they are thinking and planning. It makes them far more dangerous in a way. And you say she knew that Colette had guessed what she was doing?'

'Yes, she did, but she told me she wasn't that desperate about Colette telling Trystan.'

'I find that hard to believe. I can't imagine Trystan would be too happy.'

'No, I agree. I've found out a bit more about him as well.'

Susan told her about Yvonne.

'So he has an alibi for when Colette died? That's interesting.' Alice sat back. 'You really have found out a lot.'

'Yes, but I'm no closer to knowing who killed Colette.'

'No, but you are finding out more about the people in the group and possible motives and that is vital.' Alice sighed. 'Now, I think we ought to go and join this party, don't you? Pass me my Zimmer, it's a horrible old thing, but it gets me from A to B.'

They walked slowly back into the main room, where there was a gentle hubbub of conversation and clattering of plates. Susan found them two spare seats and they sat down. Alice looked around.

'They've arranged it very like it was for the leaving do for Nikki, Trystan and Torri. It's hard to imagine I sat next to Pam, not knowing it was the last meal we would share.'

'Didn't you mention an outbreak of food poisoning? Did they find out what caused it?'

Alice looked directly at her. 'The nursing home told us it was something to do with the uncooked fruit punch.'

'You'd not have thought a fruit punch would make anyone ill, would you?'

'I agree, but that is what they told us. Most people were only mildly affected, stomach cramps, a few were a bit sick, that was all. Apart, of course, from Pam.' Alice was still holding her gaze and Susan had a feeling she was meant to be picking up on something.

'You are being mysterious today, Alice. I thought you were all for plain speaking. First there was all that business about the painting and now Pam.'

Alice smiled. 'You're quite right, it's not fair of me. But I am unsure of so many things and I don't want to mislead you.'

'I'd still rather you were straight with me.'

Alice looked around. Fortunately, the other people on the table were all completely engrossed in conversation.

'I will tell you what I've been thinking, then. I had accepted the fact Pam died suddenly after the food poisoning – when you get older, these things happen. But then I heard about the missing brooch and it got me thinking. There were a lot of people around the night of the party, anyone could have gone into Pam's room. However, Pam would have noticed pretty quickly that it was missing. The answer would have been to make sure she didn't live long enough to discover its loss. But, you see, I had no idea who had done it or how, it was more a feeling that something wasn't right.'

'Are you seriously telling me you think someone murdered Pam?'

Alice grabbed her arm. 'Keep your voice down.'

'Do you think Colette had these suspicions?'

Alice shook her head. 'Definitely not. I certainly never

suggested it to her. How could I even suggest to her that her grandmother had been murdered when I had no proof?'

Susan stared at Alice. 'But you think that it's possible?'

'Yes, but I have no idea how anyone did it. We all ate and drank the same thing. People's reaction to the fruit punch was pretty quick and very similar, everyone else was fine. Pam had a bit of a stomach ache similar to the others who'd had the punch. She didn't want to take any medication for it, she said she would rest and went to bed. By the morning, she was dead. The doctor saw her, though, and he was convinced it was her heart that gave way, and maybe he was right.'

'I can understand why you didn't say anything to Colette.'

'Yes, but it did cross my mind that if someone had killed Pam, they would be very worried if Colette started asking questions about the events around the time of her death.'

'Yes, it gives a new motive to consider in Colette's death. I don't suppose you remember which doctor was seeing Pam at the time? It might be useful to talk to them.'

'Of course, it's the same doctor we have now, he's over there.'

Susan looked over at a harassed-looking man standing up, sipping tea.

'That's John, he worked with my husband. I think he's been nabbed by one of the relatives, I'll have to catch him later.'

'That's a good idea. Now, I didn't ask you about the retired policeman,' said Alice, grinning.

'I had a few qualms about him, to be honest, but he's in the clear, he has an alibi.'

Alice smile grew wider. 'I'm very glad about that.'

At that moment, Beatrice came over to them. 'Hello, Alice, lovely to see you again. I see you and Susan have got to know each other.' She held out a plate of small eclairs and they both took one.

'Thank you. Have you brought Biddy with you?' asked Alice.

'I thought he was better left behind today; he'd be begging for food from everyone.'

Susan laughed and then spotted someone sitting on his own. 'I recognise him, that's Phil. He was at drama, I'll just go and say hello.'

She went over to him. 'Fancy seeing you here.'

'I have seen a few residents here for more traditional physio-therapy, it's how I first met Nikki.'

'Of course. I'm sorry again about walking in on you and Nikki. Your work sounds very interesting. I don't know a lot about acupuncture.'

He placed his cup in the saucer and smiled. 'There are a lot of strange ideas about it, but it has a very good scientific basis and I've had a lot of success with it.'

'Nikki explained to me why she was having it. Do you have to have a lot of sessions for it to be effective?'

'That varies from patient to patient.'

'And would it matter if they missed a week or two?'

'Not necessarily. Nikki takes the odd Sunday off, which isn't ideal. In fact, it was a bit annoying when you interrupted us the other Sunday as we'd had to cancel the Sunday before as well.'

'Nikki didn't have treatment on the eleventh?'

'That's right. She came to drama but then insisted she had to dash to the shops in the break. She wanted to get some chocolates for someone at work, their mum was unwell or something.'

'And she went to the shops?'

'Yes, I saw her leave, I had to move my car for her to get out.'

'It's pushing it to get to the shops and back in the time you have a break, isn't it?'

'I suppose it is. She was late back; told me she'd not been able to park.'

'So how long was she gone for?'

He looked at her and frowned. 'About an hour. Why all the questions?'

Susan was frantically trying to think of an excuse. 'Look, this is a bit delicate but her fiancé, Nathan, asked me to find out what she was doing that evening. He'd tried to phone her and not got an answer and he'd, well, he'd heard rumours about her seeing someone.'

Phil sighed. 'Oh dear, I told Nikki we should tell people what we were doing.'

'Yes, I will have a word with her, maybe she should tell Nathan.'

'Yes, I think you are right.' He rested his cup and saucer on a small table close by. 'Right, I think I shall be off now. Nice to meet you again.'

As he left, Susan stood watching him. Nikki had left the theatre the night Colette died; she'd been away for about an hour. That gave her time to drive to the car park at Steephill Cove, go down to Colette and return to the theatre.

Susan's heart was racing. She now knew Nikki had been wearing that brooch after Colette's grandmother died and she knew about the lip gloss.

She needed to get out and get some fresh air and made her way out into the front garden of the nursing home. As she walked along beside the neatly kept borders, she wondered which one Colette had found the locket in. Her eyes wandered over to the immaculate lawn and the red-orange leaves scattered over the surface. She spotted some mushrooms growing up through the grass and wondered if these were safe to eat and remembered how confusing it was.

Susan looked down at them again, remembered Nathan carrying that bag into the nursing home. Her mind raced on to the food poisoning, maybe she'd hit on something here. At that moment, she saw her former husband's ex-colleague, John, coming out of the nursing home.

28

John was walking quickly, looking straight ahead, a man leaving the building with purpose.

Susan called his name and he waved to her as she went over to meet him.

'Susan, how lovely to see you. How are you?' he asked, smiling.

She grinned back. 'You don't really want me to answer that, do you?'

He laughed. 'You can tell you've lived with a doctor.'

'You look like a man escaping.'

'Honestly, I've had these relatives on my back the whole time. I wouldn't mind so much if they ever bothered to visit their dad, but they just like to cause trouble and complain.' He let out a deep breath. 'Sorry, you don't need to listen to me moaning. Seriously, how are you keeping?'

'I'm doing well, thank you.'

He paused and she noticed that awkwardness people felt when they first met her after Steve had left her. It was like they were meeting someone bereaved and were not sure what to say.

'I heard that you and Steve had separated, I'm sorry. He is off sailing now?'

'He is. I saw him last weekend, he looks well. So, are you the doctor assigned to the home?'

'Yes, I've been attached to the home for five years now, which is nice. I've really got to know the residents and some of their families.'

'I don't suppose you remember someone called Pam, do you? I had her granddaughter living with me for a few months. Colette, you might have heard of her, the girl who died down the cove?'

'What a tragedy. Anaphylaxis, I understand.'

'That's right. I wonder if you could help me with something. I know Colette came to visit Pam when she was a little and then once again about a week before Pam died.'

'I think I remember Pam saying something about that. She didn't see her family much, although there was a brother?'

'You have a good memory.'

'It's not that long ago and I saw Pam quite a lot.'

'Yes, you saw her the night she died, I think. It was food poisoning?'

'Well, it was her heart that gave in.'

'Yes, but she'd had food poisoning, they thought it was the fruit punch?'

'That was it.'

'How would that make them ill?'

'Uncooked fruit and vegetables cause a lot more food poisoning than most people realise. Poor food preparation can lead to produce being contaminated with harmful bacteria, such as E. coli and salmonella. Fortunately there was some of the punch left and I asked for it to be tested.'

'Even though no one had been that ill?'

'Yes, because of Pam. She was so unwell, I wanted to be sure what food poisoning she'd had. I was able to be sure this way there hadn't been any real nasties in the fruit punch.'

'Was it possible Pam had something else as well that had upset her... maybe mushrooms?'

He frowned. 'Mushrooms? What on earth would make you think that? No, I'd remember if there had been mushrooms on the menu, it goes with the usual suspects for food poisoning like seafood and chicken. The home keeps a meticulous record of all the food and drink the residents are offered and I saw the list. It was an afternoon tea, cakes and cucumber sandwiches. The only thing we found that the sick residents had in common was the uncooked fruit punch.'

'But Pam reacted very badly to it?'

'No worse than anyone else, but when you get old, it can be something fairly minor like a fall or a tummy upset that can set off a whole chain of events in a frail body. Poor Pam. They called me during the early hours of the morning, and I could see she was in a very bad way. She was having hallucinations, on top of being terribly sick, but it was her heart that really concerned me. It was racing and I knew it wasn't coping with this upset. Her heart had been in a bad way for some time, and unfortunately this was the thing that finally made it give way. I stayed with her, but there was little I could do.'

He looked over his shoulder. 'I'd better get back. I've a load of paperwork back at the surgery and I don't want to get caught again.' He put his hand on her arm. 'You've been through a lot, if you ever need to talk, you can always make an appointment. To be frank, I was rather shocked at the way Steve treated you, I think we all were. You can come to me any time.'

Susan smiled. 'That's so kind, I'll bear that in mind.'

She watched him walk away. He'd sounded so sure about the

fruit punch, and no one had eaten mushrooms, she'd gone off at a tangent. Maybe there really wasn't anything suspicious here.

When she returned to the dining hall, the party was breaking up. Tables were being cleared and residents were starting to make their way back to their rooms. Alice sat alone, staring at the table.

As Susan approached, she noticed a change in Alice. She saw the deep lines on Alice's face, she looked old and weary for the first time.

'Are you all right, Alice?'

Alice looked up at her. 'Sit down a minute. I've been thinking.' She looked around nervously. 'You have to stop this, Susan; you must stop it now.'

'Why on earth are you suddenly saying this? You said how well it's going—'

'Nathan came over to chat and he told me about your break-in, you hadn't mention that.'

'It's okay, I've changed the locks. I'm safe now.'

'Are you? Someone was in your home.' Alice looked over at Nikki and Nathan talking to Torri, Trystan and Beatrice. 'Seeing them all here makes me realise how close to home this all is. These are people you see every day; they know where you are, what you are doing a lot of the time. I don't want to make the mistake I made with Colette and underestimate the danger you are in.'

'I can look after myself, and I've just talked to the doctor. I'm not sure there was anything suspicious about Pam's death.'

'We don't know that for certain. Listen, I have to go into hospital for an operation on my wrist and after that I am going to stay with my daughter in Bishopstone for a few weeks. I don't like to think of you carrying on while I am away.'

Susan smiled. 'I will be fine, and you take care with this operation.'

'I will, thank you.' Alice sighed. 'I think I will go back to my room now, I'm very tired. Just be careful, won't you?'

Susan gave Alice a light kiss on her forehead. 'I promise I will, and next time we see each other, we must talk about happier things.'

She left the home, thanking the nurse on the desk. As she went out of the door, she could hear Torri and Trystan behind her. Susan walked out quickly; she didn't feel like chatting any more.

As she walked down the road, she was reminded that it was of course Halloween. Small groups of children in fancy dress wandered the streets, trick or treating. She used to take Zoe out and find it good fun but tonight she felt uneasy seeing the masks and children dressed up. She veered off the main pathway and took the lower path close to the cliff. It was darker and quieter down here, and she could hear the sea below. She looked down at the sea, it wasn't that far from where Colette had been.

Suddenly she felt a hard shove on her back, and she fell forward. She lost her footing and immediately was plunged forward towards the cliff edge.

29

Susan grabbed hold of the thin rail. Catching her breath, she spun round. There was no one in sight but she heard footsteps running away.

'I'm not scared of you – come back,' she screamed, but she was shaking.

Only waves crashing below answered her. Checking around, Susan quickly walked uphill and joined the upper path with the streetlights.

Once home, she realised that, yet again, she'd forgotten to leave any lights on. Her hands trembled as she opened the front door and reached for the switch. The dogs came racing to greet her and she slumped down on the floor. 'I'm home, thank god, I'm home.'

She wondered about phoning Robert but decided that he might want to drag her down to the police station, which she was sure would be a waste of time. Someone had pushed her, but who?

Of course, it could be someone from the group – apart from Robert, they had all been at the tea party. They might have been worried seeing her talking to Alice. It brought home to her the importance of taking better care of herself, no more lonely walks along the cliff tops at night.

Susan spent the evening staring mindlessly at the television, and finally crawled to bed. She was so exhausted, she fell asleep and didn't wake until eight the next morning.

Going downstairs, she quickly let the dogs out into the garden and made coffee. She spent the day quietly reading, taking the dogs for gentle walks. That push from the day before kept coming back. It had shaken her up more than she realised.

It was early evening when she took the dogs out for their final walk. She decided to walk up into a different part of town, up by the church. There was no service that evening, and the church was in darkness apart from the security light that shone over the porch.

As her eyes became accustomed to the light, she realised she could make out a figure, someone was sitting on a bench close to the porch. The reason she knew who it was because she saw the large dalmatian sitting next to her. She looked deep in thought and Susan was sure she wanted to be alone, but it seemed so strange. What was Beatrice doing sitting up there alone on a Sunday evening?

* * *

The next day, Susan had arranged for everyone to meet down at Castle Cove to scatter Colette's ashes at ten that morning, after she'd collected them from the crematorium.

Fortunately, it was a cold, bright day.

Susan parked in Steephill Cove car park next to Nikki and Nathan, and Beatrice, and they started the walk down the path.

'Robert moved the log, the path is clear now,' said Susan.

'Good man,' said Beatrice.

'Thank god, I nearly broke my neck before,' added Nikki.

They reached the bottom, walked along, went through the gate and then turned the corner to approach Castle Cove. Susan saw Torri, Trystan and Robert waiting for them.

As she approached them, Susan's mind was racing. She had just realised something hugely significant, and she needed to find the courage to confront them all about it. Holding the urn closer to her, she spoke silently to Colette. 'I will do this for you. I am scared now, but I will see this through.'

They stood together at the foot of the concrete slipway where Colette had been found.

Susan had prepared a few words and some simple poems to read. She ended with the words, 'Colette, your life was short, and at times so sad. But you also had warm sunny days, and you had dreams. Your life was unique and precious. I promise you, like the fossil of the mayfly proves, you will never be forgotten. You will always be loved and so you will always be with us.'

Susan carried the urn to the end of the slipway and scattered the ashes on the surface of the sea. She remained watching as the ashes slowly disappeared, the sea accepting them, taking Colette into its care.

When she returned to the beach, the friends gathered around her.

'Well done,' said Nikki. 'It was good to do this. Nathan has a hot toddy for us all.'

They each took a glass, and as Beatrice raised a toast, they chinked their glasses together and sipped their drinks.

The tension started to recede, and they finished their drinks. Susan stood, summoning up the courage she needed. It would be so easy to walk away, but she couldn't do that. She let them have a few moments of chatting, then coughed and spoke in a slightly louder voice to get their attention.

'Just now, I said to Colette that she would never be forgotten.

Part of remembering and honouring her memory for me has been trying to find out exactly what happened to her that night when she died down here.'

'Now is not the time, Susan,' said Torri.

'But now is exactly the right time. You all know I've been unhappy about the police's conclusion that Colette's death was accidental. I just couldn't work out why she would have eaten those marshmallows, why she didn't use her EpiPen and what had happened to her red velvet pouch. None of those questions have been answered.'

'There will never be answers to everything,' said Nathan.

'I knew Colette. I knew she wouldn't eat marshmallows she wasn't sure were safe, I knew she would use her EpiPen, and I knew she wouldn't throw that velvet pouch away. I have been forced to face the fact that it was highly likely that someone in our group was down here with Colette that night, and today I have received solid proof, evidence I'd missed, as to who that person was.'

They stared at her and then at each other.

'This is crazy,' protested Trystan. 'I'm not listening to this. I need to get back to work.'

'No, wait,' said Susan. 'Nikki, you need to explain to me and to everyone else how you came to know there had been a log on the top of that path we just came down. The log was not there on the Saturday before Colette died, Beatrice knows that, it was only there on the Sunday, until Robert moved it. So how come you, as you just said, nearly broke your neck on it? I remember you agreeing with Beatrice when we were talking the day after Colette died that the log was dangerous. And yet you walked along the lower path to Steephill Cove with everyone to the celebration that afternoon, and returned that way. How do you explain how you know there was a log on that path?'

Nikki stood with her mouth open for a second and then stammered, 'I don't know what you are talking about.'

'But you do. You also need to explain how you came to be wearing Colette's grandmother's brooch less than a week after she died at the hotel's opening night.'

Nikki put her hand to her mouth, her eyes wide with fear now. 'But I didn't—' She turned to Nathan. 'We have to go now.'

'But I know you were wearing it, so when did you steal it from Colette's grandmother?' persisted Susan. 'I know it was her brooch, there is a newspaper cutting of you wearing it at the opening of the hotel.'

'Not on the cutting Colette had.'

'So, you noticed she'd taken that from the box at the bottom of your wardrobe?'

'Well, yes, but it didn't matter, I wasn't going to sack her for that.'

'No, because it didn't mean anything, did it? But Colette wasn't the only person who snooped when cleaning your room. I found the other cutting and it is far more damning, isn't it?'

'How dare you? I trusted you.' Nikki looked away. 'Anyway, you can't tell what I'm wearing from an old picture.'

'Oh, yes, the brooch was very distinctive, Colette's uncle and Alice are sure of it.'

'That's a lie!' screamed Nikki. She turned to Nathan. 'Tell her it's a lie.'

'This is a terrible thing to accuse Nikki of,' said Nathan. 'You have to stop this, Susan. Nikki was at drama the night Colette died.'

'Not the whole time. I understand she left to, what was it, pop to the shops. She was about an hour?'

'I went to the shops. If I'd come down here, I'd have told the police,' said Nikki.

'That depends on what you were doing down here.'

'How dare you.' Nikki burst into tears.

Nathan stepped forward, his face dark with fury. 'Leave her alone,' he shouted. 'If you don't—'

'What would you do, Nathan? Push me off a cliff?'

He glared at her but didn't reply.

Susan turned back to Nikki. 'You were here, weren't you, Nikki?'

'If I had been here, it would have been to talk to Colette. There were private things I needed to talk to her about.' Nikki was looking straight at Susan, as if pleading with her to understand. 'I'd never have hurt Colette. Maybe if I'd come down as far as the gate, stood and looked over, I might have seen someone going towards Colette, and decided to leave.'

She turned to Nathan. 'We have to go.' He put his arm around her.

'I will come with you,' said Beatrice and the three of them left the cove.

'You can't go around saying these things,' Torri cried. 'There will be some explanation for everything, I'm sure of it.'

'I've had enough of this,' said Trystan.

He shot an accusatory look at Susan and the two of them left.

Robert blinked. 'My goodness, Susan, I wasn't expecting that. Do you really think that Nikki stole the brooch and then came down here to kill Colette?'

'I wasn't aiming to confront Nikki about the brooch today, but when she said that about the log, I couldn't ignore it. She had to have been down here and she as much as admitted it.'

'I'll concede she appeared to admit to coming down here the night Colette died. I'm very surprised she'd not owned up to that before. However, she did also intimate she'd come to talk to Colette, and that could have happened. There is no proof whatsoever that she came down here to harm Colette. Are you sure about the brooch? You need some kind of motive here.'

'Colette's uncle and Alice are both sure of it.'

'If she stole it, then why would she risk wearing it the following week? Is this a black and white photo?'

'Well, yes—'

'I'm not sure that will convince anyone then, and this log business is pretty iffy. How do you know she was talking about the same step, the same log?'

'She had to be. Don't you want me to be right?'

'I don't want Nikki getting accused of something she didn't do. I think you need to talk to her properly, get the whole story.'

'There is the lip gloss as well,' Susan added.

'Ah, I meant to tell you, Pete has confirmed that there was no lip gloss on Colette. She wasn't wearing any and there was nothing in her handbag.'

Susan stepped back. 'Oh, no, I was so sure. So we are back to the marshmallows. Well, Nikki could have taken them down. Nikki has to be the prime suspect. You saw the way she reacted. I'm sure she was down here that evening.'

He nodded. 'I have to agree with you there, but as I said, there could be a lot of explanations for that. Now, I'm guessing you're up at the car park? I'll come up with you but then I'm going to walk back, I could do with clearing my head after all that.'

'I'll be fine to walk up on my own. You go on, I'll be in touch.'

'Okay, but—'

She held up her hand. 'Don't say "be careful" – I've had enough of that.'

He smiled. 'Okay, well, I'll see you around.'

* * *

Later that evening, Susan relaxed in front of the wood burner with a glass of wine, reflecting on the day.

Generally, she was pleased with the progress she'd made. She'd found evidence that Nikki had been down the cove the night Colette died and also that Nikki had been wearing the brooch that had belonged to Colette's grandmother. Susan sipped her wine and smiled, she was finally getting somewhere. She raised her glass to Rocco and Libs. 'You two have a very clever mum.'

Susan had just stood up ready to go to bed, when her phone rang. She glanced down, saw the call was from Steve and groaned. No, she wasn't talking to him at this time, he could wait. Resolutely, Susan switched off her phone, turned off the lights, and went to bed.

30

Susan was woken early the next morning by someone hammering on her front door. She grabbed her dressing gown and ran downstairs.

She opened the door to find Nathan, ashen faced, breathing hard.

'What's happened?'

'It's Nikki, she fell. Oh, god, what if she dies?'

'What on earth has happened?'

'She had a fall, up on the cliff walk – she's in the hospital.'

He started to sob and staggered into the house and slumped into a chair in the kitchen.

Without asking, he took out his tobacco and papers, and began to make a cigarette. Susan could see his hands shaking and yet the act seemed to calm him. He licked carefully along the paper, and then took out his lighter, flicked it several times and finally lit the cigarette. He took a long drag, sat back and breathed more slowly.

'Why did you have to say those things to her?' he asked, his voice desperate. 'She was in such a state, that's why she fell. It was all your fault.'

'I'm sorry this happened, but I only spoke the truth. Nikki had the brooch and she gave away that she'd been at the cove, it wasn't just guesswork, I had proof.'

Nathan shook his head. 'Well, you had it all wrong. No one stole the brooch, certainly not Nikki. The brooch was given to me by Colette's grandmother.'

Susan gave him a sceptical look. 'Really?'

'Yes, I promise you. She gave it to me on the Saturday morning before she died. She'd been told again that it wasn't worth a lot, but she thought it would make a lovely gift for me to give to Nikki. She knew how fond I was of Nikki but I was always skint. In the end, I accepted it and gave it to Nikki. Nikki had been a bit worried about me accepting a gift like that, but she understood the thought that went behind it. I even checked with Beatrice. She told me it wasn't worth anything and she saw no harm in accepting the gift.'

'And so Nikki thought it was okay to wear it at the hotel's opening night?'

'Yes. She'd been so upset to hear about Pam's death, it was her way of remembering her. Of course, when all the fuss about Pam's things blew up, she stopped wearing it.'

'Why on earth didn't you both explain to everyone what had happened?'

'I know we should have but I was scared no one would believe us. What if they thought Nikki had really stolen the brooch? You know how rumours spread and we were just starting at the hotel, it wouldn't have done our reputation any good.'

'What did Nikki do with the brooch?' asked Susan.

He took a long drag on his cigarette. 'She made it into a bracelet.'

'You say you love Nikki, but I know you had a relationship with Colette.'

'No—'

'I have proof. I have the paper rose, the envelope and your writing. Robert told me you asked him for one of the roses he'd made, and I found the envelope in your drawer. I also recognised your handwriting and I read the start of her name in the heart.'

He shook his head slowly. 'No. When you told me that day that you'd found the rose, I had a feeling you thought I'd sent it to Colette, but you've got it all wrong.'

'Have I?'

He swallowed hard. 'I never had an affair with Colette, she must have found those things somewhere else.'

'Where would she have found them?'

He took a deep breath. 'Colette found the rose and that envelope in Torri's room.'

Susan blinked hard. 'I don't understand, why would she find it there?'

'It was a fling, nothing more. I'd listened to too many people warning me that Nikki was seeing someone at drama. I knew the chap, he's handsome, clever, it ate away at me. I felt sorry for Torri, being led on by Trystan. Then it dawned on me that maybe Torri and I would make a perfect match. We get on so well, she was easier going than Nikki, wanted to settle down and have a family like me. I would happily given up everything to go off to Portugal with her, it was my dream. Sun and surfing, instead of all the responsibility of a hotel.'

'What about the name in the heart?'

'That wasn't the start of Colette. You read the first two letters of the Portuguese word for heart... *coração*. I just looked that up online, I don't know if it's right, but I certainly wasn't writing Colette.'

'I can't believe this! Torri is devoted to Trystan, and you have just become engaged to Nikki.'

He held up his hand. 'I know, it was madness, we both soon

realised that. Torri should have thrown away the damn rose, but she'd buried it in a drawer. When Colette said all that business about secrets at Steephill Cove, Torri remembered, went back to the lodge and found they were missing. She sent me a text, frantic that Colette had found and taken them. Neither of us need Trystan or Nikki seeing those things, I hope you will destroy them.' He put his head in his hands. 'Not that it might matter any more for me. Oh, god, why did you have to interfere? You've ruined everything and for what? You know Beatrice has said she's leaving the island?'

'No. When did she say that?'

'Yesterday evening. We were all having a drink at the hotel. Beatrice blurted out she was moving on; she'd already spoken to an estate agent. She's going as soon as she can. And then Torri piped up that she and Trystan were planning to as well. This is all your fault, stirring things up.'

Nathan stood up, pushing back his chair, shouting now. 'I'm in danger of losing everything, my fiancée, my hotel. Why do you hate us all?'

Susan swallowed, close to tears herself. 'I don't hate you. I need to find out what happened to Colette. Nikki was down there, I know she was.'

'She told me she'd gone to talk to Colette about the brooch to put her mind at rest, but then she saw someone. You see, Susan, you've got everything wrong. You think you know better than the police. You think you're clever, but you're not. You are a sad, lonely woman meddling in other people's lives to make up for the fact your husband doesn't love you any more. I'm going back to my fiancée. If she dies, I will hold you responsible, her blood will be on your hands.'

Nathan stumped the remains of his cigarette out on a stone coaster, then got up and stumbled out of the house.

Susan sat in shock; a tornado had torn through her. What had she done? Nikki was lying in a hospital bed, because of her. Last night she'd felt so clever and now she felt a fool, and a dangerous fool at that.

Her phone rang and, not thinking, she answered it before she realised to her horror that it was Steve. 'Susan, I tried ringing you last night.' He sounded in a real panic.

'Yes, um, sorry, I was tired – what's up?'

'Zoe had a phone call last night from the people selling the house they want to buy. They have had a higher offer on the house but if Zoe and Fay can match it, the house is theirs. They need an answer immediately. Zoe is frightened to put pressure on you, but I think it's pretty obvious what you need to do.'

'Sorry. What are you saying?'

'You need to phone Zoe before school and tell her you are going to sell up and buy this house with her.'

'Hang on, you can't just ring up and take over like this.'

'Is this about Robert? Are you staying over there because of him?'

'It's nothing to do with him or you, for that matter.'

She ended the call; the dogs came running to her.

'I have to get out, come on.' She ran upstairs, got dressed and then left the house with the dogs and drove to the downs, parking today up at the old radar station.

There was a thick fog this morning, and she kept the dogs on their leads. Up here, you were immersed in history. Behind her, hidden under gorse, was the bronze age burial site, and further over, she knew where to find the remains of the ammunition store looking like a cave. As she walked, she could feel her breathing slowing down. She had heard it said that life hurts you, but nature heals, and the island healed her in a unique way each season. Now it was the time of the prickly gorse, the sea mists and crisp autumn days. In winter nature rested, in spring it woke and the larks sung sweetly in the skies above. Finally, in the summer, you would find the fresh early morning breeze even on the hottest days, and see the flashes of blue from the Adonis butterflies among the heather.

Susan stared into the mist, and her mind went back to that first time she'd met Colette up here, a young, pale girl, her white-blonde hair flying in the wind. She felt her presence today.

'Oh, Colette, I've made such a mess of everything,' she whispered. 'So many people's lives have been turned upside down because of me, Nikki might even lose her life. I'm so sorry, but I am going to have to leave now. Zoe needs me, I have to put her first and anyway, you warned me to leave this alone, didn't you? I should have listened before.'

Susan drove home, heavy hearted but determined. She fed the dogs and then rang Zoe.

'Hiya, love, sorry to ring so early.'

'It's okay, I'm at school, are you all right?'

'I'm fine. Listen, I've heard about the house and the offer, and I wanted to tell you to accept. I shall put my house on the market today and move over as soon as I can.'

The line went silent. 'Hello, Zoe, are you there?' she called.

'Yes, Mum, I'm here. I am guessing Dad has spoken to you?'

'He has, but this is my decision.'

'And you're sure about this, you want to leave the island?'

'It's the right thing to do.'

'That's not what I asked. The thing is, Mum, we have decided not to take this house. I don't like being pressurised like this, I don't believe all this stuff about another offer, I just panicked when I spoke to Dad, that is all.'

'Oh, I see. Well, the offer still stands, if you and Fay want to look for a bigger place, I am very happy to come in with you. I don't have to live with you, of course, but I could move nearby to help look after the baby if that is what you want.'

Suddenly she heard a burst of laughter from Zoe. 'Oh, Mum, you sound so sad. Listen, one of the main reasons I was asking you over here was because I was worried about you. I've seen how things have been since Dad left, you don't eat properly, the house is a mess—'

'I know, but I'll put that right. Well, a bit, anyway. I was always messy before I lived with your dad, and I'm not a very good cook, but I will try harder now. I've been in some kind of bubble, but I'm coming out now. I do need to get out of this house, I am sure of that.'

'But I don't think you need to leave the island, do you, Mum?'

Susan sighed. 'I would find it hard.'

'Well, stay there, it will be a lovely place to bring the grandchildren. Who knows, we may even move back there one day, the island is in my DNA, as well you know.'

They ended the call amicably, and Susan gave a sigh of relief. With fresh resolve to at least start eating better, she made coffee and poured some granola and milk in a bowl and sat down at the table. The chair where Nathan had been sitting was still pushed out at an angle, and she wondered how Nikki was. Later she would ring the hospital or Torri – the nurses had enough to do.

Susan looked over and saw the shrivelled remains of the cigarette Nathan had left on her coaster. Colette had talked about sharing different flavoured papers with Nathan. What had she been using that night? Liquorice, that was it.

Susan placed her mug on the table with a thud, spilling some of the contents. 'Of course, why didn't I see it before?' she said, loud enough that both dogs looked over at her, alarmed.

She'd made mistakes but she was also stumbling towards the truth. She got up with fresh determination, she knew exactly where she needed to go now.

31

Susan walked along the high street, loving the chaotic, eclectic mix of shops. There were an increasing number of cafés and restaurants, but in many of the small shops there were reminders that this was a holiday town, with a tower of postcards on a stand, buckets and spades stuffed into boxes.

There were two places Susan was heading to this morning, and she had arrived at the first.

The bell tinkled as she entered.

'Good morning,' said a man, coming out from behind a glass cabinet.

'Hiya, I was hoping to speak to someone who used to visit a relative at the nursing home here about three years ago? It's about a brooch they were asked to value by one of the residents.'

The man nodded seriously. 'I think I am the person you are looking for. I'm afraid I don't go up there now, my father sadly passed on.'

'I am so sorry for your loss.'

'Thank you. Now, how can I help you? You say it's about a brooch?'

'Yes. I had a girl living with me called Colette. It was her grand-mother's brooch that was valued. The brooch was very pretty, possibly ruby and diamonds? Unfortunately the gran, called Pam, died not long after you'd seen her. Colette is the girl who sadly died down at Castle Cove recently.'

'Ah, yes, so sorry. What a terrible accident that was. And yes, I do remember the brooch. I'd not realised it was her grandmother that I saw. It was very difficult. People have such expectations, it's hard letting them down. I get people coming in here with family heirlooms, and things they have picked up at car boot sales, hoping they're worth millions, people who watch too much *Antiques Roadshow*.'

'Are you saying the brooch was not valuable?'

'It was a nice piece, pretty, but none of the stones were diamonds or rubies, I'm afraid.'

'I see, and was Pam very upset?'

'She was disappointed, definitely. She really had thought it was genuine, and was hoping to leave it to her granddaughter. Anyway, there we are. May I ask why you're so interested in all this? It was a few years back now.'

'Colette told me about seeing a brooch with her grandmother and she had been under the impression it had disappeared after her gran died. Do you remember any fuss?'

The man shook his head. 'No, nothing. No one came here asking about it.'

'Well, thank you, you've been very helpful.'

Susan was about to leave when she paused. 'I don't suppose you'd have time to look at one thing for me, wouldn't you?'

He smiled, looked out of the window. 'Well, the customers aren't queueing up this morning! How can I help you?'

Susan took the locket from around her neck. 'I just need to be sure of something. Is this locket worth a lot of money, do you think? Please don't worry, I'm not expecting it to be.'

The jeweller took the locket in his hand, took out his eyeglass and studied it carefully.

'It's a very nice piece, I love the old photographs in it. It is silver and has been gilded with gold. It's worn and quite damaged, so no, I don't think it's worth a lot. A very nice piece, though.'

Susan smiled. 'Thank you, I'm quite relieved.'

'That's not what people usually say.'

'No, but this was given to me as a gift and I'd feel guilty keeping it if it was very valuable. Now I can wear it freely. Thank you so much for your help.'

'It's nice to have a chat, to be honest, pretty quiet here in the week during the winter, people prefer to buy things online.'

'It's a difficult time,' said Susan sympathetically. She thanked the jeweller again and left.

Susan began the long walk up the hill to her next destination. That confirmed the brooch was worthless, and made Nathan's story all the more credible.

However, she did want to check on one more thing.

She was approaching the home now and hoping to see one of the care workers. Fortunately, she saw Kathy as she walked into the nursing home.

'Ah, hello, I was hoping to see you.'

Kathy looked surprised. 'Really? How can I help?'

'I'd like to speak to you, somewhere private would be handy.'

'Um, okay, come in here.'

They went into a tidy side room.

'I wanted to ask you about one of the valuables that went missing after Colette's grandmother, Pam, died.'

'I don't see how I can help you, you need to speak to the manager,' said Kathy. Susan noticed her eyes glance at the door as if she was preparing her escape.

'I think you can answer my question. This is important, I'm not going to get you into trouble. This is to help clear someone's name. You see, I have seen a photograph of Nikki wearing the brooch that went missing. Nathan claims he was given it by Pam. You were friends with Nikki, I think she may have talked to you about it?'

Kathy edged forward on her seat, her eyes went to the door, again.

'Please don't rush off,' said Susan. 'I know the brooch wasn't worth anything. All I need to be sure of is that Nathan was given the brooch by Pam.'

'Um, I don't know what to say.'

'Please, just tell me what happened.'

Kathy sighed. 'Okay, Nathan told me on the Saturday morning of the do that Pam was very keen to give him the brooch. She liked him and knew he was desperate to settle down with Nikki. She thought it would make a nice gift for her.'

'What was your advice?'

'It was difficult – officially, of course, we are not meant to accept anything from the residents. Nathan knew that, and he had tried to turn it down, but Pam was quite upset. I told him it had to be his decision and left it at that.'

'And so he accepted it and gave it to Nikki?'

'Yes. Sadly, Pam died the next day and then her son came over the weekend after and noticed some things were missing. I'd seen Nikki wearing the brooch at the hotel opening, I knew she had it, but I didn't want to get her into trouble.'

'You didn't tell her about Nathan and the gift.'

'No, I thought it best not to.'

'Did you talk to Nikki about it?'

'I did, and we agreed it was best forgotten. I'd thought that was the end of it, and then, of course, Colette came up here, asking questions about her gran's things. I wasn't sure whether to say anything to her, but decided it was best left.'

Kathy looked at Susan, her eyes pleading to be let off the hook.

'To be honest, Kathy, I think it would have been good for her to know the truth about this.'

'It's too late now, though, no point in raking it all up.' Kathy looked at her watch. 'I ought to be getting back. Nikki and Nathan aren't going to get into trouble, are they? I'm sorry, but I shall deny any knowledge of it, I can't go losing my job.'

'I'm not going to tell anyone, but I'm glad to know that what Nathan said was true. Did you know Nikki is in hospital?'

Kathy looked alarmed. 'No, what happened?'

Susan explained about the fall.

'My god, I'll ring Nathan later.'

Susan left, satisfied that Nathan had been telling the truth about the brooch, at least she knew that was out of the picture now.

That evening was bonfire night, a stressful evening for pet owners, and she knew the bangs and explosions would go on all weekend. She would be staying in, looking after Libs and Rocco.

Susan was about to open her laptop when she glanced over at the TV and she remembered the cosy evening watching programmes with Colette. It was something she'd never done with Steve or her parents. Somehow, even their spare time had to be spent doing something worthwhile, reading something meaningful or writing emails.

She went over to the TV and found the station Colette had shown her, and a whole series of *Sewing Bee*. To appease her conscience, she found some knitting, to continue making blankets for the local animal shelter, and then settled down.

She loved the gentle pace of this programme, the concentration as the different task were undertaken, taking all those sperate pieces of material and making a beautiful garment out of them. If only she could do that with all the pieces of information she'd learnt about Colette and the people in the dog walking group. She knew so much and yet nothing seemed to fit.

She knew someone had been down in the cove with Colette, she knew a lot about the secrets people were hiding, but were any of them so desperate to hide them that they would kill? Now she knew the brooch was worthless, there couldn't be a motive connected to the valuables hidden in Colette's grandmother's jewellery box. The locket wasn't worth a lot either and that only left the book.

Suddenly, like a flash of lightning illuminating the whole room, she saw it. She put down her knitting and stared at the wall. The one piece of this whole pattern she'd been ignoring from the start. Tomorrow, she would go and see the expert, but she was sure she was right.

Susan had planned an early expedition the next morning, she was anxious to check out her new theory. However, she had just found the dogs' leads when her phone rang.

To her amazement, it was Nikki, her voice shaky and quieter than usual.

'Hi, Susan, I wanted to speak to you.'

'How are you? Nathan told me about your accident, I'm very surprised you are well enough to be able to ring me.'

'It's just cuts and bruises, he's massively overreacted, although it was a miracle he turned up like that. He seemed to be there in a flash after I fell and called an ambulance. They were most worried about my head, nasty gash on that, but I was very lucky. I managed to grab a tree that stopped me falling any further.'

'He was very worried about you.'

'I know, but there was no need to take it out on you. He told me he's explained about the brooch. I'm glad it's out in the open now, to be honest. I'll go to the manager and explain, I don't think they will want to do anything, I mean it's not the kind of publicity they want, is it, and you said the uncle isn't interested. Nathan told me he'd explained why I was down the cove.'

'He said you were going to tell Colette about the brooch.'

'I did, I felt it was the right thing to do.'

'But why go down to the cove at night?'

'I knew she was there on her own and you know how this place is, someone would have seen me talking to her, and I had a feeling it was going to get emotional, if they'd seen her crying, or me crying for that matter, it would have been everywhere. It was better to see her somewhere quiet. However, when I stood at that gate and saw someone else going to see Colette, I panicked, I didn't have long and so I left. That was it.'

Suddenly the enormity of what Nikki had just said sunk in. Why hadn't she registered it before?

'Of course, you saw someone else down there! Did you see who it was?'

Susan waited, not daring to breathe.

'No, I'm so sorry. I saw a light, I guess from someone's phone being used as a torch. I didn't even see if they went to Colette, but I shall tell the police what I saw.'

'Why on earth haven't you told the police before?'

'Partly because I was scared they might start digging around and find out about the brooch and think I stole it, but even more, I was terrified that if that person knew I'd seen them, whatever they were doing down there, well, they might have come after me. You know how quickly word gets round, and people get up to all sorts in the quiet corners of this island. They could have been down there selling drugs or all sorts. I wanted to keep out of it. It felt safer to stay quiet. It was wrong, I can see that now, and I shall talk to the police today.'

Susan paused and then asked. 'This fall you had... did you sense anyone had been following you?'

'God, no – but why—' Nikki hesitated. 'Oh, you're not thinking someone could have pushed me, are you? That's ridiculous, although I do remember looking around, thinking someone was there, but that was just stupid. No, no one would want to hurt me.'

'Maybe it was the person you saw down the cove and they were frightened you'd recognised them.'

'Oh, god, you don't think so, do you? Stop, Susan, you're frightening me. I'll go to the police and tell them I was down at the cove, that I saw someone but didn't recognise them. That will be the end of it.'

'I think you could be right, make sure you see the police today,' said Susan and rang off.

It might be the end of the matter for Nikki, but it certainly wasn't for her.

Susan looked down and realised the dogs were waiting to leave. She put their leads on but took them to the car.

She listened to the news as she drove and decided that before she went to the place she was heading for, she'd give the dogs a run on the nearest beach.

It was good to walk along the Duver beach, for the dogs to run in and out of the beach pools, to clamber over the rocks. The sea air was invigorating, and it cleared her head.

When she was coming to the end of the walk, she phoned her friend Wendy up at the bookshop and as she drove back up to the green, she saw her waiting outside the shop.

'Morning,' Wendy greeted her, smiling. 'Great to see you again, you can bring the dogs in.'

'Thanks, I'll wipe their paws, they're a bit wet.'

After Wendy had made her a drink, she looked over at Susan. 'So, is there anything in particular you needed to see me about?'

'There is. I need to ask you about second-hand books, I mean rare children's ones.'

'Were you thinking of collecting them or do you want something valued?'

'No, I'm trying to solve a bit of a mystery. I've never seen the book in question, but I know it was old, and it was about animals, oh, and it must have been quite small as it was kept in a secret compartment of a large wooden jewellery box.'

Wendy grimaced. 'If it was valuable, that was hardly the right way to be storing it. They need special covers to protect them at the very least.'

'I don't think the person who owned it had any idea it was worth a lot of money. I know this is a long shot, but can you think of any rare children's books about animals?'

Wendy laughed. 'There must be quite a few.'

'I should have thought this through before coming here, all I remembered was Colette telling me she loved animal stories.' Susan paused and then her eyes lit up. 'Of course, that is who I should phone.'

She took out her phone and rang Colette's uncle, Keith.

'Sorry to call out of the blue, but it's important. Do you know the title of the book your mum kept in her jewellery box?'

'Yes, it was an old copy of one of the Peter Rabbit books.'

Susan turned to Wendy. 'It was a Peter Rabbit book by Beatrix Potter.'

Wendy sat forward, her eyes wide with excitement.

'Really? Ask him what it looked like. I need every detail he can remember. What colour was the cover, were there coloured illustrations... anything.'

Susan asked Keith.

'Let me think.' He hesitated and then replied, 'That's it, if I close my eyes, I can still smell it, feel it. It was a dull, faded beige kind of colour cardboard cover with some line drawings of bunnies on the outside and there was only one coloured picture in it, I think of

Peter's mother feeding him chamomile tea in bed. The rest were plain line drawings. I remember my mum read it to me a few times, but I was disappointed with the lack of pictures. Even way back when I was little, most of our books had coloured pictures, I was taking comics then.'

Susan related this to Wendy.

'This could be very exciting,' she replied. 'Anything else he can tell you? Does he know what the spine was like, was it flat or rounded?'

'I think it was flat, funny the things you remember, but I can almost imagine holding it. I do remember Mum telling me to be careful as it was very old, it was written the same year Queen Victoria died. She said you could tell because the person who wrote it had signed it. I think it said, "*For Mr Price, from Beatrix Potter with kind regards and best wishes for Christmas 1901*".' He paused. 'I'd not thought about it for years, it really was very old, wasn't it?'

Wendy had heard everything on speaker phone and was now looking it up on her laptop.

'You remember a lot about it.'

'My mum didn't spend that much time with us and I knew it was special to her because she wouldn't let me keep it in my bedroom. The woman from the house who gave it to her had said she'd read it to her own children and hoped it would give Mum the same pleasure.'

'And yet you've not talked about being upset about the book going missing, even though it was as important to you as it was to Colette.'

'The problem is the good memories can hurt more than the bad ones when they are so rare. It's like life gives you a quick snapshot of how things could have been and takes it away, it would almost have been better if you'd never seen it.'

'I see, I can understand that,' said Susan.

'Why are you asking about it? Has it turned up?'

'No, not yet, but I have established the brooch wasn't worth a lot, I'm afraid.'

'Ah, I thought not.'

'But it might be the book was worth quite a lot of money. I am in a bookshop with the owner at the moment and she is looking very excited.'

She heard Keith hesitate. 'I'd like to know, of course, but if we do ever find it, we will have to think of a good cause to donate the money to, I'm sure you can understand.'

'I do, I'll be in touch, thanks.'

Susan finished the call and went over to Wendy, who looked up, her eyes bright, her voice shaking with excitement. 'Susan, there were only two private printings before the first commercial edition in 1901, and the editions are really rare. The first private print run Beatrix Potter did was only 250 copies, and it sounds like it could be signed by her. If all the things he remembers are true, then this book could be worth upwards of £20,000.'

'Wow. I really don't think Colette's gran had any idea how valuable it was, nor did her children, or even Colette. Would many people know it was worth anything like that?'

'Collectors are getting more and more well informed. Rare books are being stolen to order, and if you know the right people, you can get a lot for them. So, tell me, why all this interest? I want to know everything.'

Susan sat down and related the whole story. Wendy sat very still, a look of astonishment spreading over her face. 'You honestly think one of your mates you go dog walking with stole this book?'

'I do, but I have no idea what they have done with it.'

'Do any of them know about antiques?'

'Beatrice says she only knows about jewellery, but perhaps she knows about other things as well. Nathan goes to auctions. Torri loves old books, and Nikki had some children's books, although they were modern books on the whole.'

'That doesn't exactly narrow it down!' Wendy screwed her eyes up. 'It would be wonderful to know where that book is now, but no one is going to just come out into the open and tell you, are they? In fact, they will not be at all happy with you poking your nose in.'

'No, I realised this.' Susan stood up. 'Thanks so much. I'll let you know how it goes.'

Susan put the dogs in the car, and drove home. Who would have known about the value of the Peter Rabbit book? As Wendy had said, people were better informed about these things nowadays. Any of the group, if they'd seen that book, could have known.

Her gut feeling was that the book was still somewhere around. It would not be an easy object to sell on, but the more time they put between the theft and the sale, the better. It was only going to become more sought after, more valuable, it was worth holding on to until someone was desperate enough to try and sell it.

Later that evening, Susan went upstairs, but before she went to bed, she looked again through Colette's collection of secrets. Picking up the photo of the urn, she was reminded of the painting.

Alice had said that although Colette hadn't known the significance of it, it was 'interesting'. Why had she said that?

Susan turned on her laptop, what was the painting called? That was it, *Woman with a Mirror* by Titian. She Googled the painting, and after finding out the usual background notes, one paragraph leapt out at her.

Woman with a Mirror is by the Renaissance painter, Titian. It hangs in the Louvre Museum and depicts a young, beautiful Venetian 'belladonna' who may have used atropine drops to dilate the pupils of her eyes to enhance their beauty. Atropine drops come from the plant deadly nightshade.

Susan gasped and quickly typed in 'deadly nightshade'.

Atropa belladonna is more commonly known as deadly nightshade, and is a perennial woody shrub. The berries are beautiful
but deadly. Purple-brown flowers appear before the berries. After
the flowers fade, berries develop from late August to October.
They are shiny black and very attractive with a sweet taste. As
few as two berries is enough to kill a child. Symptoms of
poisoning include rapid heartbeat, vomiting, hallucinations, and
finally death. Deadly nightshade has a long and violent history;
it's thought to have been used by Shakespeare's Macbeth to
poison Duncan's troops.

The more she read, the more Susan was gripped. Alice had
mentioned Macbeth, yes, this had to be what she was referring to.

Alice had said this in connection with the death of Colette's
grandmother. The doctor had talked of a raised heartbeat, hallucinations, but they had been seen as part of an extended and violent
reaction by an elderly woman in bad state of health to the earlier
stomach upset. Why should it have crossed anyone's minds that
there was a second poison at work here?

And looking at the symptoms, the easy access to the deadly
berries, it had to be possible that the poison used was deadly nightshade. Alice had thought so, and Susan agreed. Colette's grandmother had died at this time of year, when the berries of deadly
nightshade were readily available. Susan had seen them in the
woods and in Torri's garden. Anyone in the group could have
picked them.

They must have stolen the book the night of the party and then
poisoned Colette's grandmother. No, she needed to think about
this. They stole the book, and added something to the punch to
ensure a mild outbreak of food poisoning. Colette's grandmother

had gone down with the same sickness as the others. However, later on, she was much worse as a result of being given the stronger, far more deadly poison. No one was going to look for a second poisoning, especially as the doctor signed off her death as the result of her heart problems.

But how had someone managed to poison her while avoiding mass poisoning of the other residents in the home?

33

The next morning, Susan went down to the beach, and was pleased to see most of the group were there. She was keen to see if she could find out where they had been the night of Nikki's fall.

The dogs were all off lead and those who'd not seen Nathan since Nikki's accident were full of questions.

'How is Nikki then?' asked Beatrice.

'She came home yesterday evening,' explained Nathan. 'She has a huge dressing on her forehead but she's all right in herself. She'll be bossing me about again today, I reckon.'

'But why on earth was she walking so close to the cliff edge in the dark?' asked Robert.

'I don't think she was thinking straight. She was quite upset about things that had happened,' said Nathan, glancing at Susan. 'Although I realise now I was a bit harsh on Susan. I need to explain that Colette's grandmother gave me the brooch as a present for Nikki. That can all be proven, the brooch was not worth anything. Nikki also admits to going down to the cove, she has told the police now and also told them that although she saw someone, she didn't recognise them.' He paused, took a breath.

'She did seem upset when we had a drink on Wednesday evening, she'd not been to drama, which is not like her,' said Beatrice. 'As I was leaving the hotel, I saw her getting her coat and asked her where she was off to, and she asked me to go with her. We talked until we reached the Falaise Hall and then she asked me to go. I really didn't want to leave her, but she insisted, so I went on home. I wish I'd stayed with her now.'

'I wondered where she was off to,' said Torri. 'I saw her disappearing off through the door, but I had some reading to catch up on, and Trystan was off to practise something in the kitchen.'

'She told me you got there very quickly,' Susan said to Nathan.

'Yes, it was lucky. I was in the shed, but I had my mobile.' He looked away.

'The main thing now is that Nikki is safe and recovering,' Robert added.

'Yes, thank you,' replied Nathan and he looked around at the group. 'Now, I'd love to invite you all to a champagne tea tomorrow. Nikki and I have something very special to tell you all – come about three.'

Susan could see he was very excited and wondered what was happening.

As the others walked on, Susan noticed Robert hang back to talk to her.

'How are you?' he asked.

'Feeling pretty guilty about what happened. I should have been more careful about how I confronted Nikki. I really upset her, and even alerted someone else to information she had.'

'Nikki should have told the police she'd been down there when Colette was found. Has she been able to give any description of the person she saw?'

'No, not as far as I know.'

'She may have imagined it, it's very dark down there.'

'Now, I have found out something very interesting about one of the items Colette's grandmother was hiding away. It turns out it wasn't the brooch that was so valuable.'

'Was it the locket?'

'No, it was the book. I think it might have been a very rare copy of an early Beatrix Potter story.'

'Wow, that's incredible. So now you're thinking that someone stole the book. Do you think Colette knew about that?'

'I don't think so, but whoever stole it may have been scared that Colette was on her way to discovering what had happened.'

'Unless you can find this book, I don't see how you can prove any of this, and now we've ruled out the lip gloss, you're no closer to figuring out how someone could have actually forced Colette to ingest shellfish.'

'Ah, I've had an idea about that as well. I think I know a way Colette could have ingested the shellfish, apart from the marshmallows. If someone had taken the time to spread fish oil or a rich, concentrated fish stock like the one Trystan made from shellfish along the rim of one of those cigarette papers she used, she could have licked the paper, completely unaware of the danger she was in.'

'But why would Colette need to accept a roll-up paper from someone else, she'd have had her own, wouldn't she?' asked Robert.

'No, remember when we were all at Steephill Cove that afternoon with Colette? Torri or Trystan sat close to Colette and one of them asked to borrow her roll-up papers... that was it, one of them spilt their drink on them. Colette wouldn't have had her own papers that evening, maybe the killer saw that and at that moment got the idea for how they would kill Colette?'

'But would she have accepted them from someone?'

'Why not? The person was known to her, she had no idea what they had in mind.'

'But there was no evidence of people having been smoking there.'

'But if this was the method, the killer would certainly have taken away all traces of them.'

'Yes, I have to concede that. I suppose it's possible. We know Colette smoked roll-ups and a few of the group do, don't they?'

'Exactly. Nathan, Torri, Trystan – I've seen them all rolling cigarettes.' She smiled at him. 'We're really getting somewhere now, aren't we?'

'You certainly are finding out a lot, I have to admit that.'

As they were leaving, Beatrice invited Susan round for coffee. When they arrived at her house, Susan was shocked to see a For Sale board outside.

'You really are going?'

'I have to. I don't feel at home here any more. It's okay. I never stay in one place long.'

In the living room, Susan noticed a number of cardboard boxes, some already filled.

'You're packing already? You've not had an offer, have you?'

'Not yet, although I'm hopeful about the man who is viewing later. No chain, looking for a quick move, the estate agent said it's looking very promising.'

'Look, Beatrice, I'm not going to say anything about your past. You don't have to leave.'

'I think this is best. Now, let's give these dogs something to eat and then I'll put the kettle on.'

Beatrice went out to a utility area to feed the dogs and Susan walked around the room, it felt so bare.

All the sewing things were packed away in boxes, she could see the plastic drawers with the neat, colour coordinated squares of fabric.

All the pictures had been taken down, only grey outlines and

darker paint showed where they'd been. The urn and all the ornaments and antiques had been packed away, even the books, she
noticed, were in a box. Susan was about to go and check the box
when Beatrice returned.

However, they were interrupted by the ringing of the house
phone and Beatrice went to answer it, explaining, 'Sorry, it could be
the estate agent so I'd better take it.'

Once Beatrice had disappeared into the hallway, Susan went
straight back to the box with the books. She knelt down and started
to examine each one, but she could find no sign of a small children's
book. She did, however, find a copy of a newspaper dated 15
February 1952 and started to read about the funeral of King George
VI taking place at St George's Chapel in Windsor Castle.

She was so engrossed that she didn't hear Beatrice return. 'Are
you looking for a book to borrow?' she asked Susan.

'No, no, no. Sorry. I was reading that newspaper—'

'That was a birthday present from Nikki, amazing what
happened the year you were born, isn't it? I know it was a nice
thought, but it made me feel ancient.' Beatrice screwed her eyes up.
'Why do I get the feeling you are having more than a casual peek in
that box?'

Susan got up quickly. 'Sorry, I always love nosing among other
people's books, see what they read.'

Beatrice looked at her sceptically. 'No, you're still asking questions, still suspecting everyone. I suppose you did discover that
Nikki had been down at the cove. Who'd have thought that?'

Susan was watching Beatrice carefully for any signs of nervous-
ness or anxiety but saw nothing.

'I know, and I think Nikki may have recognised the person down
there but is too frightened to say who they are. I don't think her fall
was an accident.'

Beatrice stared at her with cold eyes. 'So now not only do you suspect one of the group of killing Colette, but you think they could have attempted to kill Nikki as well to silence her. I was watching you on the beach earlier, noting what everyone was doing when Nikki had her accident. I guess you've realised I was the last person to see Nikki.'

Susan felt the tension between them growing. There was challenge and defiance in Beatrice's words.

'You have never explained where you were the night Colette died,' Susan said quietly.

'No, it's a matter of principle, it's private. I didn't kill Colette. I didn't push Nikki; you have to take my word for that. I'll be gone from here soon, and that will be the end of it.'

'But you have to see how it looks, Beatrice. If you are innocent, then why not tell me what you were doing?'

'Because, as I said, it is my personal business. You are not the police, Susan, you can't demand I tell you anything.'

'You can't always run away.'

'I can try. Now, I need to get on.'

Taking the hint to go, Susan called Libs and Rocco and put their leads on and Beatrice walked with her to the front door.

'Houses can take months to sell, you know,' said Susan. 'Don't you think you are packing up a bit too soon?'

'I plan to go on Monday morning, and leave the house in the hands of the estate agent. I have removers coming in the morning to pack up and put everything into storage, and then I shall leave the place empty.'

'But why the rush?'

'When I make up my mind, I like to get on with something. I have Nathan and Nikki coming around for a meal this evening, we shall talk through the business side of it. I'll join everyone for one last walk on Monday morning and that will be it.'

'I'm sorry you're going.'

'I'm not, it's time to move on.'

Susan left Beatrice and returned home.

Later that day, she decided it was time to see if there was any way she could get to talk to Torri on her own.

Susan approached the hotel by the side path, which led her to the quad. There was nobody about and she walked over to Torri and Trystan's lodge.

She leant over the new fence and yes, there they were, going over now, those black shiny berries she'd been reading about.

'The garden is starting to lose the autumn glow now, isn't it?'

Susan turned to see Torri.

'Hi, I was admiring your garden again.'

'I love it at whatever time of year it is.'

'Am I right in thinking those are deadly nightshade plants?'

Torri looked surprised but answered, 'Yes, they are one of the reasons I have this fence up. They are beautiful but deadly, like quite a lot of nature, when you think about it.'

Susan shot her a look. 'I was reading all about it the other night. It mentioned that painting of Beatrice's, *Woman with a Mirror*. She told me you knew all about the painting.'

'I knew about it from doing an art history course at the local museum in my teens. It's amazing what you remember, I guess hearing about the women putting such poisonous substances in their eyes was pretty memorable.'

'Well, despite their horrible story, the berries and the rest of your garden look very beautiful safe behind a fence here.'

'Thank you. Nathan has been a help. He's so knowledgeable, isn't he?'

'I certainly learnt a lot on that walk he led.'

'So, what are you doing around here today?' Torri asked. 'Can I help at all?'

'Um, yes, actually, it's you I came to see. I realised things were quite difficult last time we chatted and wanted to see how you were.'

Torri looked sceptical but invited Susan in.

'Do you know what this champagne tea tomorrow is about?' asked Susan.

'No idea. I've not talked to Nikki since she came home last night. She should be resting, not organising parties.'

'I went to see Beatrice this morning. She is definitely selling up, then. I don't blame her. Nathan said you and Trystan were having the same thoughts?'

'Trystan and I have had a long talk. I confessed about the letters. I think it made him understand how desperate I've been and with everything that has happened, he's warming to the idea of moving to Portugal. He's so changeable, though, we'll see what he says next week. Would you like a coffee? Oh, and I've made some fruit tarts, do have one.'

Torri made the drinks and brought her over a plate of tarts. Susan stared at the red, dark blue and black berries, nestled in a pastry case. It looked beautiful, but there was something about the berries that unnerved her.

'That looks gorgeous,' she said.

'Thanks, eat up,' encouraged Torri.

Susan put the plate down but sipped her coffee. 'I saw you took some of your special egg custard tarts up to the party at the nursing home. Did you make them when you worked there?'

'Oh no, but I made these, the residents loved them. I have added a crème patisserie now, but they are very much the same. I use berries I can harvest from my garden now but don't worry, I'm very careful.' She grinned.

'I was chatting to the doctor at the party at the nursing home, he was remembering there was food poisoning the night of your leaving do.'

'How odd, why on earth was he talking about that?'

'I brought it up, I'd been asking Alice about Colette's gran, I just wondered how she died.'

Torri's eyebrows shot up, but there was no blush of shame or guilt. 'She had heart problems, didn't she? I remember the food poisoning; it was pretty mild. We had been given the night off catering; they used people from outside. I told them that would teach them to stick to us.'

'So, you didn't do any of the cooking?'

Torri shrugged. 'No, as I said, they had people in. If I remember, the food poisoning came from the uncooked fruit punch but it didn't make anyone too unwell.'

'Apart from Colette's grandmother.'

'But she died from heart problems.'

'You remember it then?'

'Of course, it was so sad. I'd known her a bit, she had a sweet tooth like Colette, I used to take her the odd slice of cake.'

'Or fruit tart?'

Torri stared down at the untouched fruit tart next to Susan. 'Hang on, where is this all leading?'

Susan took a deep breath. 'I was wondering if you happened to give Colette's grandmother one of your fruit tarts the night she died?'

Torri scowled angrily at Susan. 'Are you suggesting I gave her some kind of food poisoning? Why on earth—' Her eyes lit up. 'My god, that's what all those questions about deadly nightshade were about. You think I am some kind of sick person who goes around trying to kill off old people—' She paused, her face changed, her expression cold and hard. 'No, this is to do with that damn jewellery box, isn't it? You think I stole something the night of the party, and then killed off Colette's grandmother so she'd not tell anyone? But have you forgotten, Susan, the brooch wasn't worth anything, and in any case, it had been given to Nathan earlier in the day.'

Susan swallowed hard. 'Actually, there was something else worth stealing.' As she spoke, she watched Torri very closely, but saw no change.

'I think you'd better leave now. I told you before, Susan, you need to be very careful. One day, you'll go too far with your nasty threats and accusations.'

Susan was shaking now, but Torri hadn't finished. She leant over and took a large bite out of Susan's tart. 'Well, look at that, I wasn't trying to poison you, who'd have thought it.'

Susan stood up. 'I'm sorry.'

'Get out, and just remember what I said.'

Susan practically ran out of the lodge, and once outside stopped to catch her breath. This time, there was no doubting the threat in Torri's words.

She rushed home, shut the door, her heart racing, fear squeezing her so tight she could hardly breathe.

She stayed in the house all day and the dogs had to make do with visits to the garden. She wandered around with them, pulling up the odd weed, picked up a few apples that had fallen from the tree and some blackberries from the self-planted bush at the edge of the garden.

At night, she closed the curtains, locked the doors, and kept the lights on when she went to bed. Time moved on but the fear never left her.

She lay there, listening, alert. Someone had been in her home twice, she'd been pushed on that cliff walk, she could have died. It wasn't too late yet, she could back off, keep away from it all. Nothing she did would bring Colette back, it was the past, and maybe that was where it should stay.

34

The next morning, Susan was relieved to find that the fear had loosened its grip. She knew that however scared she might feel, she had to keep searching for answers about Colette's death.

Looking at her clock, she saw it was only six in the morning, it would be dark outside, but she had to get up and she knew exactly where she needed to go.

Susan dressed, went downstairs, packed a flask and some fruit she'd picked the day before in a small rucksack. The dogs were out of their beds, wagging their tails, excited at the prospect of an early walk, although a bit surprised when they were taken to the car.

She drove along the dark streets, only a few cars passed her, people going to or coming off shifts, she guessed. She drove into the car park at Steephill Cove and walked down the hill. She had her torch but realised there was enough light now to walk without one. Once at the bottom, she took the dogs along to the gate, around the corner and along the esplanade to Castle Cove.

Once there, she let the dogs off their leads and sat on a large boulder, looking out to sea. Unlike dusk, she loved the twilight dawn. To her left, far on the horizon, she could see the light getting brighter as the sun crept its way to the horizon. And when it did, she sat watching in awe as it displayed all the autumn colours of the woodland across the sky.

She breathed in deeply, and then as the colours mellowed, she poured herself a drink and opened the small plastic box with her fruit in.

As she sipped a coffee, her mind went to Colette. She'd last sat here in the dark but someone had taken away the privilege of waking to another day. Who had done that? Who had been down here, given her the cigarette and watched her die?

Susan closed her eyes and tried to imagine Colette here, on her own. But, of course, she hadn't been alone.

Susan looked out to sea, she felt so close to the answer, but it kept slipping through her fingers. Who in the group had been down here?

She shook her head, feeling no closer to the answer. The dogs came over, ready to go home for their breakfast, and she started to pack her things away. As she did, however, she breathed in and for some reason she was taken back to Colette sitting on that seat in the garden that Saturday evening. What was she missing? And then the conversation came back to her, and she realised that there had been something very significant that she had been ignoring all along. Put that with what Kathy the nurse at the home had said as well... it had to be possible.

Susan started to walk back along the esplanade. As she looked over towards Steephill Cove, she realised something else, of course, why hadn't she seen it before?

Susan returned home with fresh resolve. She was looking forward going to the hotel that afternoon. She ate her lunch, sat down, tried to read, but time dragged. She had so much to do, so many loose ends to tie up. She was very close to finding the killer now, she could almost feel their breath on her face. She shuddered, admitted she was scared. It would be foolish not to be and yet this was something she knew she had to do.

As she walked to the hotel, even though it was only three in the afternoon, the sky was darkening, and the wind whistled up from the sea. Susan was glad to arrive at the hotel, which looked warm and welcoming.

'We are out in the conservatory,' said Nathan, who came from behind reception. 'Let's go through.'

Susan went with him but as she approached, she was very surprised with what she saw. The room was full of balloons and a huge banner declared 'Just Married'.

Nikki came over, grinning. 'We didn't feel we could go without some kind of celebration. Nathan and I were married yesterday afternoon!'

Nikki was wearing the red taffeta dress Susan had seen hanging on the tailor's dummy in their room and she had the red patchwork bag slung over her shoulder.

'You look lovely. I remember seeing that dress on the dummy in your room, I thought you were keeping it for Christmas.'

'I know but I finished it a week ago, thought what the hell, I love it, and I think it made the perfect wedding dress.'

'Tell me all about the wedding.'

'Well, we changed into our wedding gear, covered them with our biggest coats and grabbed two unsuspecting guests and dashed to the registry office. A few quick photos on our phones and we were back and changed for the evening service. How about that!'

Susan blinked. 'That is incredible, many congratulations.'

Susan heard the popping of a champagne cork and they were all given a glass.

Nathan made a short but loving speech, then a waitress from the restaurant came and offered plates of cakes and cups of tea.

Slowly the excitement receded, and they started to find seats and chatted to each other.

Susan sat next to Torri.

'I know this is very exciting,' said Torri, 'but I am very hurt Trystan and I were not invited to the wedding. We've been friends for a long time. It's a bit of a kick in the teeth. And what about their family? I would be devastated if my daughter did this, wouldn't you?'

'I don't think so. We went to Fay and Zoe's civil ceremony, maybe they will have a wedding one day, it's up to them. It all costs so much money nowadays, I can understand people keeping it quiet.'

'When I get married, everyone will know about it.'

Susan smiled. 'And I shall come and throw confetti.'

Nikki came over and sat next to them. 'Now, Torri, don't tell me you are miffed at not being asked to be a bridesmaid.'

'Of course not,' replied Torri stiffly and walked away.

'Oh, god, I've upset her, haven't I?' said Nikki. 'Still, she'll get over it. Maybe I'll ask her to make a cake sometime, see if that helps. I need to keep her on side. Trystan was weakening the other day about this move. I hope he's changed his mind again, but you can never be sure of anyone, can you?'

'How are you feeling?'

'Nathan is looking after me well, fusses about my medication, keeps trying to make me eat. He's even got Torri making little pastries and tarts, but I'm just not hungry. He's a good man, really.' She glanced over at the patio, where Nathan stood rolling a cigarette.

Nathan gave them a wave and then took a drag on his cigarette. Susan saw Torri go out to join him and he handed her a cigarette paper, which she used to roll her cigarette. Torri started the ritual, taking a paper, folding it, carefully sprinkling just the right amount of tobacco on the fold, rolling it, and then running her tongue along the edge before finally completing the act of making the cigarette.

Susan felt a hand on her arm. 'Are you okay?' Nikki asked.

'Sorry, I was miles away. You were saying you didn't feel like eating? I shouldn't worry, your appetite will come back soon. In fact, avoid pastries, you could try a little soup or something lighter.'

Nikki smiled. 'You're right. Now, I just need to go and speak to Robert.'

Susan was looking around for someone to go and talk to when she saw Beatrice come over and then sit in the seat vacated by Nikki.

'Nikki and Nathan look very happy; I love her dress,' Beatrice commented.

'She is so clever, and that bag you made matches it perfectly.'

Beatrice frowned. 'I didn't make that bag. By the way, the man who came made an offer, it should all go through very quickly.'

'But doesn't that mean you could get more? Prices around here are climbing all the time.'

'I don't care, I've made up my mind. I have a flight booked for tomorrow evening.'

'I thought you were driving somewhere.'

'Oh, yes, sorry, yes, I'll be driving off. However, I will see you in the morning for a final walk on the beach.' Beatrice looked at her watch. 'In fact, I need to get on back and organise a few things.'

With that, she stood up and quietly left.

Nikki came back over to Susan. 'Beatrice left quickly, is she okay?'

'She's gone back to pack.'

'Wow! She's taking this offer, then? We went round last night, she's in a rush to get away, isn't she, I wonder why?'

'Some people never seem to settle in one place for long.'

Susan heard a loud buzzing.

'Is that your phone?' Nikki asked.

Susan opened her bag, took out her phone. 'No, it must be you—'

Nikki laughed. 'Sorry.' She picked up her patchwork bag and started to rummage inside. 'This bag from Beatrice is very pretty, but everything gets lost in it.'

Finally, she found her phone. It was a text message which she began to answer.

While she waited, Susan began casually looking at Nikki's bag, admiring the sewing, even wondering if she could persuade Beatrice to show her how to make one. But, of course, Beatrice would be gone soon. Susan started to examine it more closely, could she work out how it had been made and try to teach herself? There were a lot of squares of different kinds of material, cotton, crepe, damask and velvet. They were all different shades of red, but then one in particular caught her eye, and that was the red velvet material. On the edge was a small piece of gold embroidery and she knew where she'd seen that before. Her heart leapt. Good god!

Nikki finished her call and replaced her phone in the bag.

'That bag—' Susan stammered. 'You said Beatrice made it, but she claims she didn't.'

Nikki blinked in surprise. 'Yes, she did, she gave it to Nathan to give it to me. I forgot to thank her. Maybe she'd forgotten making it, she makes loads of these things. I saw a pile at the WI sale.'

'But this is different to the others, it had so many different colours and types of material.'

'I had told her I wanted something like that, though. I'd discussed it with Nathan, he has a good eye for these things. Is something wrong? You look quite pale.'

'No, sorry, my mind is whizzing around, all this excitement of your wedding, Beatrice moving and everything. So, tell me, when do you think you will be back at work?'

'I've already started. I'll be manning reception tomorrow; Nathan is off to some big auction on the mainland tomorrow. He said he'd seen some model of a James Bond car in mint condition, boxed and everything, he is very excited.'

'He enjoys the auctions?'

'Not so much now. He tends to do that more online. He picked up some books and models online and he may sell them on, he has a pretty high reserve price on them, though, but he's prepared to wait. He always went with Beatrice to the auctions, but I don't suppose she will want to go tomorrow.'

Nikki grimaced, rubbed her ankle.

'It is hurting?'

'It's sore, yes.' She looked over at the cakes. 'You know, I really fancy one of those little sandwiches now, a cucumber one would be really light, wouldn't it.'

'Then I will get you one,' said Susan, smiling, and went to find one.

When she returned, she picked up her bag. 'I'm just popping to the ladies', I won't be long.'

35

Susan left the room quickly and went back to reception. This was going to be her only chance, but she needed to be quick.

There was no one in reception, just a note by the bell telling people to ring if they needed someone.

She went to the cleaners' room, there were two key safes, and she knew the one with the room keys in. Remembering the code, 4321, she pressed the keys, it opened, and she grabbed the keys hanging up and stuffed them in her pocket.

She went behind reception and out of the back door that led to the gardens and Torri and Trystan's lodge.

It was floodlit, and she felt very exposed. After checking no one was around, she quickly made her way to the lodge. Her hand shook as she opened the door.

The first thing she was greeted by was Max, who came running over to her, wagging his tail. She smiled, put on the light, and immediately felt better.

'You're not to tell anyone I was here, okay?' she said.

She went over to the bookcase and quickly worked her way through the books, paying particular attention to the leather-bound books, remembering that Wendy had told her that leather covers could be made for a rare book. She opened each one but there was nothing. She glanced around, there were no other books, she couldn't stay longer, she had another room she needed to search.

Susan reached into her pocket, there were always a few dog treats loose, and she gave some to Max.

'I'll see you on the beach soon,' she said and left.

She checked around again, there was nobody about. Susan quickly re-entered the hotel and then went upstairs to Nikki and Nathan's flat.

Once inside, she was again greeted by a dog and this time it was Duke. He walked quietly over to her and greeted her in his usual understated way. She patted him and he returned to his bed.

She headed straight for the bookcase and started with the children's books. She took each off the shelf, opened it, but she found nothing. She went through the rest of the books, but still nothing.

She went into the kitchen, glanced around. From what Wendy had said, the kitchen wouldn't be a good place to keep a rare book because of the temperature variations, but then she saw the wine cooler. She went over and looked inside, no, nothing.

Susan ran into the bedroom, rifled through the books on the bedside tables, but again there was nothing. She was aware time was getting on. As frustrating as it all was, she had to get back.

Before she left, however, she went over to Nikki's sewing corner, it was as messy as before, with bits of thread on the floor, and patterns strewn around. Susan guessed that Nikki must be deciding what to make next. She idly picked up one or two bits but then she quickly checked the boxes, there were no squares of material anywhere.

She couldn't stay here any longer, and so, after giving Duke a treat, she left.

She ran quickly and noiselessly down the thickly carpeted stairs and went over to the cleaners' room.

She returned the keys to the key safe and then looked at the other safe, it was quite large enough to keep a book in, she needed to see inside it. What was the code? She tried to imagine a code Nikki might use, her birthday was the obvious one, but apart from knowing it was in March, she had no idea. She could hear voices, she had to leave, Susan closed the door and was just turning round when a voice asked, 'Are you okay?'

Startled, she turned to see Nathan.

'Yes, um, thanks.' She glanced around and saw a photograph of a butterfly on the wall. 'It's beautiful, isn't it?'

Nathan smiled but he was still looking at her curiously.

'I'd better get back to the party,' Susan stammered. 'Um, congratulations again.'

She ran back into the conservatory and went straight over to Nikki. 'I think the dogs need a walk now, so I'll leave if that is okay.' She looked around, waved her hand at the banner. 'Many congratulations again!'

'Thank you, see you in the morning.'

'You're well enough to come to the beach?'

'Of course, I'm off to drama this evening. The show must go on!'

Susan walked home and immediately found the leads. Rocco and Libs jumped up, excited.

The wind was whistling between the houses, and it pushed them down the hill towards the beach.

Once there, she let the dogs off and they ran wilder than ever, chasing the wind. She looked over and saw Nathan walking towards her.

'I didn't expect to find you down here,' he shouted, his words fighting with the wind.

'A quick run for them. It was lovely to have the party today, did you enjoy the wedding yesterday?'

'It suited me, I'm not one for fuss.'

'Of course, do you think you might get away for a short break?'

'Not now, we'll find a week sometime – I suggested Portugal but Nikki said we had to wait.'

'You both deserve a rest.'

'Thank you.' He looked around. The grey-black clouds were starting to join together, forming larger, darker masses above their heads. The white foam rode high on the waves. 'It always feels a bit ominous when the clouds gather like this.'

Susan looked out at the rough sea, the waves were enormous this evening and she could make out dots of people in wetsuits surfing.

'That's really dangerous, isn't it? What makes them go out in the dark in this weather?'

'It's all part of the thrill. Conquering the sea and the waves, it's a fantastic feeling.'

She saw his eyes, bright with excitement.

'I've never understood people risking their lives for thrills. I like a quieter life.'

'Ah, but that's not quite true, is it?'

She realised he was looking at her in a very serious, concentrated way.

'What do you mean?' Susan asked.

'You are prepared to stick your neck out; I don't know if it gives you any kind of rush, but you are doing it. You've not given up on investigating Colette's death, have you, and that means you suspect one of us. I thought you were bored but maybe you enjoy the excitement of it all.'

'I don't enjoy thinking one of my friends could have done such a terrible thing, but I feel I owe it to Colette to find out what really happened to her. I've been proved right about there being someone else down there with her, Nikki has confirmed that.'

'It could have been someone walking their dog, she says she didn't recognise them.'

'But do you believe that? I was thinking about Nikki's fall, she told me you appeared quite miraculously, I was wondering how you happened to be up there so quickly.'

'She phoned me, and I went straight there, it's no mystery.'

'She had quite a miraculous escape, though, didn't she?'

Susan couldn't quite pick up the strange intonation of his words. He was very close to her and suddenly she was aware they were alone on the beach.

Susan felt a few spots of rain on her face. 'I'd better get these two back,' she said and called Libs and Rocco. Nathan called Duke at the same time, and they began to walk off the beach and then climb the hill.

'Have you got anything on this evening?' he asked.

'No, quiet night in, how about you?'

'Nikki is out at drama; I think I'll tuck myself away in the shed. We've not many people staying, I've someone on the bar, he'll listen out for it. Now, I meant to check, have you had your locks changed since the break-in?'

'I had them changed the next day.'

'Good.' He smiled down at the dogs. 'We don't want someone making a mess again, spilling cereal on the floor and the like. Even worse, we don't want them coming in while you are asleep. I can't imagine either of these two are much good as guard dogs. I bet someone could give them a treat and walk straight past them, and rummage around upstairs. They'd have to mind out for the creaky step second from the top, though, eh? You be careful, even with the locks changed, someone can always get in.'

Susan stared at him. He had just admitted to being the person who had broken in, she was sure of that. Why was he doing that? Was he warning her that he would come again or just telling her how easily someone else could?

Seemingly unperturbed, he continued, 'Right, I'd better get back, us married men can't just stay out as long as we like.' With this, he walked away.

Susan went back into the house, and found herself checking the door, putting on all the lights.

She made a drink and then tea for the dogs, and planned a quiet night in. Before she settled to watching the TV, however, she wanted to see if she could work out a code Nikki might use for the safe. In a flash, an idea came to her. No, not her birthday. That was too obvious.

Susan ran upstairs and she found Colette's things. She took out the newspaper cutting about the opening of the hotel, 13 October 2012. That could be it. The safe she'd opened had used four numbers... maybe it was 1312? It could be, she would have to try it out. But when would she be able to get back in there?

She was mulling this over when she received a message from Beatrice.

I have to talk to you before I go, there is something I need to tell you. Please come to the bench at Falaise Hall, I am up here now. xx

Susan concerned, sat up, and replied:

What is wrong? Would you like to come here?

No, please come here, it's peaceful up here.

Susan replied 'Okay' and went to find her coat.

It seemed a strange request, but she was worried about Beatrice, she sounded desperate.

As she got her things together, Rocco and Libs looked up from their comfy beds by the fire.

'You two stay here in the warm.' They both flopped back down in their beds, and she left the house.

Susan went over to her car but before she got in it, she looked up the road towards the hotel.

It was seven o'clock, Nikki would be out at drama, and Nathan had said he was working in his shed. Would she be able to go and look in that cleaners' room again and try out that number?

Susan walked quickly up to the hotel and entered. There was no one in reception and she went straight to the cleaners' room.

She put on her gloves, pulled the door behind her, switched on the light. What was the number? It needed eight numbers.

She tried 13102012 It didn't work, damn, 20121310, no, how about the American way of writing the date, 10132012. She pushed the numbers, this had to work, and yes, the door opened.

Susan's heart was racing, had she finally found the book? However, the excitement soon drained away, inside were simply more keys, just as Nikki had said.

Susan was so disappointed, she closed it all up, and left the room. There was still no one about, only a few people having a drink in the bar. She wondered where Duke was, up in the flat, out with Nathan or of course there was his bed in the office.

Her heart started to race again. The office. The safe. She quickly went along to the office. It was in darkness and this time she daren't use the main light, unsure if Nathan could see into the office from his shed. Using her phone as a torch, she went over to the safe, what was Nathan's birthday? Think. Yes... 140175. She opened it easily, and she rummaged inside, nothing.

Despairing, she closed it up and crept out of the room. However, she turned off her phone too soon and fell over a large cardboard box.

She got up quickly and wiped herself down but as she did, she suddenly remembered that pile of boxes over in the cupboard in the cleaners' room, the ones left by Beatrice. It was only a chance, but she had to check them out.

Fortunately, there was no one in reception and she went back into the cleaners' room. Remembering there were no windows, she switched the light on and went over to the boxes. They seemed quite light, looking inside the first few, they seemed to be full of packing materials. However, when she opened the box right at the back, she found something very different inside.

She looked down on a large, heavy-duty safe. She tried to pick it up, but it was far too heavy and then she noticed she could lower the flap at the front of the box to reveal the front. The lock was a digital keypad, and so once again she was confronted with trying to guess a code. She started to try Nathan's birthday but stopped. No, Nikki had said these boxes were put here by Beatrice. What might she choose? Then it came to her, the date on that newspaper – 15 February 1952. She tried various combinations and when she was just starting to despair, she got it: 15195202.

Her hands shook as she opened the safe. Inside, she saw one item, carefully wrapped in a leather case, and knew she'd finally found it. Without moving it, she carefully opened the case and yes, there it was. Using her phone, she took photos, but then she heard voices outside. Quickly she returned it, closed up the safe, and waited. People were talking in the reception, she opened the door slowly, saw a couple leave the hotel. Glancing around, she saw it was empty, and quickly she walked out of reception and left the building.

Susan was shaking but triumphant, she had found the book.

She ran back to the car and, once inside, quickly checked her photos. As she did, she enlarged one, saw something she hadn't seen before. Her heart thumped against her ribcage; this was it.

Without giving herself too long to think about it, she drove to the Falaise car park. Once she'd arrived, she stepped out of her car into the darkness, she could hear the sea bashing against the rocks below and pulled her coat around herself.

She was going to use her phone light but decided the torch she kept in the car was much brighter and so found that and switched it on.

The brightness illuminated the path in front of her, and she was able to see clearly where she was going, and she quickly arrived at the shelter. She could see them waiting. She took a deep breath and went straight over to them.

36

'I wasn't expecting you,' Susan stammered.

'No, sorry, I thought I'd surprise you.' Nikki held up a phone. 'I borrowed Beatrice's phone.'

Susan switched off her torch and pushed it into her pocket.

'But what happened to drama?'

'Ah, I showed my face at half six, and then said I had to pop out at the shops. We can't be too long.'

Susan sat down; she noticed Nikki was wearing a rather old-fashioned overcoat.

'I brought us a drink.' Nikki lifted up her flask and poured some into the flask cup, some into a spare cup which she handed to Susan. 'Have a fruit tea, it'll warm you up.'

Nikki's dropped her voice and became very serious. 'The reason I came was that I needed to talk to you in confidence. The more I think about the night I fell, the more I'm convinced you are right, I am sure now that someone pushed me and what's more, I am pretty sure who that person is.'

'And who is that?'

'I know you are friends with her, and I hate to say this, but I think it is Beatrice. She insisted on coming with me when I went for the walk that night, and although I watched her walk away when we arrived here, I am sure now she turned back and followed me along the path. I remember the push from behind, and smelling perfume. When she came to the party earlier, I smelt it, it all came back to me.'

'You believe Beatrice wanted to kill you?'

'Yes, I'm sure of it.'

'But why?'

'Because, and I am so sorry to say this, but she is the person I saw down the cove that evening with Colette. I know I said I didn't recognise the person, but I'd not wanted to get her into trouble. I was certain she'd have a good reason for being there. But then when I realised it was her who'd pushed me, well, there could only be one explanation, couldn't there?'

'But why would she have wanted to kill Colette?'

The wind dropped, the waves below lapped quietly, a cloud drifted in front of the moon, it was very still and dark.

'When Beatrice offered to invest in the hotel, I checked her out and found out a few things about her. Her husband is not dead, he is in prison for a particularly nasty armed robbery. She appears to have been innocent of this and that is why I went ahead and accepted her investment, but I've always been a bit wary of her. She is so secretive; she lies a lot.'

'But none of this is a reason to kill Colette, is it?'

'I think it is. I think she is pretty desperate to keep it a secret, and I have a feeling Colette might have found out about him.'

'I agree.' Susan told Nikki about the photograph, and her own investigations into Beatrice. She saw Nikki sit back, relax.

'I knew I was right,' said Nikki. 'Listen, I've been thinking about all that marshmallow business, and I had an idea. How about if the fish oil was in a paper for a cigarette? I kept wondering about

Colette and the marshmallows and then I was watching Torri one evening, and thought of the cigarette, I was wondering if you saw the same earlier today?'

'I did.'

'Exactly, now I know Beatrice doesn't smoke, but it's very easy to get hold of papers and tobacco. She cooks with Trystan's fish stock; she could have doctored the papers with it. And I know this is going to sound incredible, but Nathan and I went for a meal with Beatrice last night and I had a good mooch among her boxes and you won't believe this, but I found a packet of roll-up papers, stuffed down the side of a box.'

'No! Did you touch them?'

Nikki grinned. 'I've seen too many crime programmes to do that. No, I took a photo and left them there. The other thing I found, however, is far bigger.'

Susan sat wide-eyed. 'What was that?'

'I looked among Beatrice's sewing squares and found some red velvet squares which I am pretty sure are from Colette's red velvet pouch, she showed it to me once. I don't know why I didn't see it before... she used some on the bag she made me! Again, I left it there. The thing is, Susan, do you think I should go to the police?'

Susan nodded slowly. 'Yes, I really do.'

'I thought you would say that, maybe you would come with me. I think I'd better go soon, with Beatrice obviously planning to do a flit. I shall tell them everything.'

Susan put her head to one side. 'Will you?'

'Of course.' Nikki frowned. 'What's the matter? I thought you'd be pleased to have justice for Colette.'

'But it won't be justice if the wrong person is blamed for her death.'

Nikki pinched her lips tight, lowered her head. 'What do you mean by that?'

'I mean that I don't believe Beatrice killed Colette, all those things you found at her house could easily have been planted by someone.'

'You just don't want to believe it's her.'

'The thing is, Nikki, I know who the real killer is, I know who you saw that night you went to the cove.'

Nikki crossed her arms tightly around her body. 'And who was that?'

'The fact is you didn't see anyone. In the same way no one pushed you up here, did they. That fall was all very carefully staged. You chose a place to slip, somewhere with a handy tree, gashed yourself with a rock before you did it.'

'Why would I do something as stupid as that?'

'The point of the fall was to bolster up your story that you had seen the killer at the cove, the story you hurriedly made up when you made the blunder revealing you had gone down there.'

'But I did see someone.'

'It is impossible to see anyone from the gate at Steephill Cove. You can't see Castle Cove from there, you have to walk around the corner.'

Nikki blinked fast. 'I made a mistake – I must have walked a bit further on.'

'You did, in fact, you walked all the way to Castle Cove. But the only person you met was Colette and you went there to kill her. I should imagine you put her at ease, told her you'd come to confess about the brooch and explain. Now you needed to get to her bag, you had to find a way of distracting her. Maybe that was when you offered her your pocket telescope to look up at the stars?'

Susan glanced at Nikki, saw the look of astonishment, yes, she was right.

'While Colette was preoccupied, you took your chance. You removed the red velvet pouch from her handbag. Now you needed to check you had the EpiPen. You looked quickly inside the pouch, but the zip was broken, and it was kept together with a rubber band. You took this off and saw the EpiPen, shoved everything in your pocket.

'After this, you offered her a cigarette paper, maybe joking you'd taken up smoking again and pinched some of Nathan's papers. These, of course, were different, they were laced with rich, concentrated stock made of shellfish, but the flavoured paper would help mask the taste. You watched her roll a cigarette, lick that lethal edge of the paper. Did you get the idea when you saw Torri ruin Colette's papers at Steephill Cove earlier? I am guessing you had a Plan A, maybe the marshmallows, but this was easier, wasn't it?'

'You really believe Colette would have taken anything from me?'

'Not food, but a cigarette at this point, yes. You'd have said anything to put her at her ease, maybe even offered her a promotion, and then you walked away.'

Susan felt her throat muscles start to tighten, the next words were not ones she wanted to think about, yet alone speak out loud. 'It wouldn't have taken too long for the reaction to set in, but you weren't far away. You would have heard her gasping, shouting for help, seen her collapse, frightened, in pain, and you did nothing. You could have saved her, but you chose to do nothing.'

Susan paused, swallowed the anger that burned her throat. 'And then, when you saw she was unconscious, you went back to her and removed the cigarette butt. The EpiPen had fallen out of the pouch, but that didn't matter, the main thing was to make sure they found it on Colette, and you put it in her bag, put the opened packet of marshmallows in her pocket, using one to coat the inside of her mouth. And then you left, raced back to drama. You didn't think for one moment anyone would look for the pouch, you got home, and quickly cut it up into small pieces and put it with your sewing materials. I'm sure you thought that was very clever.'

Susan stared intently at Nikki, looking for a reaction, desperate for a hint of regret or shame, but there was nothing.

Nikki had one eyebrow raised, her eyes were wide but cold, her lips straight and narrow.

'This is all very interesting, but I would have to have had a very strong motive to do something like this. So, what do you think that could be? If you want to go back to the Colette's grandmother, well, we know the brooch was worthless, in any case, it was given to Nathan. I had no reason to steal anything from her. As for any secrets she had on me?' Nikki threw her hands up. 'There was nothing. If you think Nathan had an affair with Colette, you're wrong – I think that was on your mind when you told me about the roses and the song?'

'It had crossed my mind, but of course I know it wasn't Colette.'

Nikki looked at her sideways. 'So what were those flowers and that song about? Any idea?'

'Oh, yes, we both know who it was, the fact it was a Welsh song should have told me straight away.'

'So, you know about Torri. I'd been worried for a while; I could see the way Nathan's mind was working. I wasn't committing, and Torri is pretty enough, getting nowhere with Trystan and, best of all, wanted to run off to Portugal.'

'But you didn't want him to do that? You seemed quite reluctant to get married, and then it was such a small affair, so unlike you.'

Nikki laughed. 'I know, what a joke. No, I wasn't bothered about getting married, but I did it to keep Nathan.'

'You love him that much?'

'That's a bit of an exaggeration. The most important thing about our relationship is our partnership in the hotel. Now would be a disastrous time for him to quit and want to sell up. We would lose so much, and I've worked too damn hard for that.' She hesitated.

'Anyway, this has nothing to do with Colette, you haven't found any motive for me to want to kill that girl.'

'Ah, but I have, there are two, in fact. The first was to stop her revealing your theft from her grandmother. Not the brooch. No, you stole the locket and the book.'

'The locket wasn't worth anything.'

'No – I did wonder why the thief kept hold of it all this time. Maybe it was for insurance, a useful tool to frame someone one day. As it was, you used it to buy yourself time. You knew Colette wouldn't be satisfied with the locket, but you needed a time to get Colette on her own. Anyway, back to the book, that was what you really wanted.'

Nikki turned, there was no smile now.

'And why would I want to steal a scruffy old children's book?'

'Because it was a very special book. It was one of the first private print run of Beatrix Potter's book *The Tale of Peter Rabbit*. To everyone else, it was a scruffy old book, but you knew, didn't you – what did I hear one sold for? Twenty thousand pounds... and it may be worth even more now. That's a lot of money.'

'You have no proof of this whatsoever.'

'But earlier this evening, I found it, in a safe, in a box, in your cleaning room.'

'Not among those boxes of Beatrice's! I don't believe it—'

'It was there, in a safe, hidden in the box.'

'Beatrice hid it there?'

'No, I know it was you, Nikki.'

'But the code for the safe—'

'Beatrice's birthdate, I saw on the newspaper you gave her.'

'You can't prove I put it there—'

'I photographed it and when I checked that, I saw something else, a single hair, one long red strand of hair.'

Nikki's eyes were suddenly bright. She smiled again but now it was like a child keen to show how clever the words tumbled out. 'I knew the first time I saw it; I knew how special it was. I pulled open that drawer and looked inside, there was that awful brooch, the locket, and the book. I couldn't believe what I was looking at, didn't anyone else realise just how much this book was worth?'

'You were looking in the box when Colette's grandmother came in.'

'Yes, I closed it up, said I was cleaning, but I think she saw what I was doing.'

'She told Colette and Alice she'd seen someone looking at the jewellery box, but of course she never named you. She did say she'd seen a glint of something, she said she didn't trust you.'

Nikki gasped. 'I never knew.'

'No, she hid it well, but she knew deep down she couldn't trust you.'

Nikki scowled. 'Don't you judge me. People have always let me down, I learnt early on to only trust myself and, yes, money. Money doesn't lie.' She lifted up her engagement ring. 'See that? What hurts about that is not its size, it's how it makes people like Beatrice look down on me. If I'd had a whacking great diamond, she'd have respected me. That is what money can buy.

'When I saw the book,' she continued, her voice shaking with emotion, 'I knew it was the way, for the first time in my life, to have a decent amount of money of my own, it would be my insurance. If everything went wrong with the hotel, if Nathan walked out on me, I would survive. I was desperate to find a way of getting hold of that book without Colette's gran making a huge fuss. If she started describing to people the book that had gone missing, someone would soon realise how valuable it was and I'd stand no chance in selling it.'

'No, my friend was telling me the real problem with stolen antique books is selling them on, and with something as rare and valuable as this, there were bound to be questions about where it had come from and so you devised a new plan, didn't you?'

'I only had a few more weeks working in the home and having easy access to Colette's grandmother's room. I decided to steal it the night of our leaving party. It was fortunate that her grandmother died the day after I left.'

Susan scowled. 'Fortunate? I don't think luck had anything to do with it. I said you killed Colette for two reasons, one was to cover the theft of the book. But you knew it was only a matter of time until she unravelled something far darker and more wicked and that was the fact you murdered her grandmother.'

'Oh, that's ridiculous.'

'Oh, no, and I'll tell you how you did it. It didn't take that much planning, did it, adding a mild emetic from the medicine cabinet to the fruit punch? The real poison you'd prepared early from the berries of the deadly nightshade plant growing next to Torri's lodge, the same poison as used in *Macbeth* and by the woman in the painting you gave to Beatrice.'

'You noticed the Titian? Torri told me about the woman and the belladonna, it's what first gave me the idea. I thought it was best to get rid of the painting, though, it was quite fun seeing it on Beatrice's wall.'

'I saw it, but it was Alice who showed me the significance of it.'

'I don't know how on earth you thought of the deadly nightshade, the doctor certainly didn't.'

'Interestingly, it was that painting that you handed on to Beatrice that first put me onto the idea of deadly nightshade, well, Alice, actually. I looked up the painting, read about the use of the poison and the symptoms – hallucinations, a racing heart, all things that got lost in the other reactions Colette's grandmother was having. I knew anyone could get hold of the berries, but how on earth would you have used it, that was my next problem. And then when I was down in the cove, I smelt the berries, it took me back to Colette telling me about the fruit teas her grandmother had each night in the home. You took her the fruit tea every night, didn't you, and after the party, Kathy told me you kindly offered to tidy up. But, of course, you had another motive. And that was to give Colette's grandmother her tea. Settle her tummy after the earlier upset.'

For the first time, she saw Nikki look uncomfortable.

'You can't prove any of this, it's a load of speculation.'

'Oh, I can. Let's take Colette's murder. There is the patchwork bag with the pieces of material from Colette's red velvet pouch.'

Nikki threw her hands up and laughed. 'Beatrice made that, most of the squares of material come from her stock. If anyone is going to be suspected because of that bag, it will be Beatrice.'

'But you made a mistake. You made that bag in your sewing area, which is far from tidy. I was looking earlier; you have bits of cotton and material all over the place. In fact, I picked up a tiny piece of material that I could swear was red velvet. I don't think a forensic team would have a lot of difficulty finding evidence of that red velvet pouch in your flat. And there is the most damaging piece of evidence, as I said, the book in the safe with your hair on it.'

In a flash, Nikki reached to her side and produced a walking stick, and whipped off the wooden sheath to expose a short, sharp, lethal dagger.

37

Nikki's eyes were wide, wild. 'Recognise the dagger?'

Susan didn't dare move. 'Beatrice's walking stick?'

'That's it, one of her collections. She'd going to take the blame for this, for your murder and that of Colette.'

She held the point of the blade to Susan's throat. Susan instinctively moved back.

'Don't move. Remember I'm a nurse, I know exactly what I am doing. I'm not going for the jugular. What a stupid expression that is, it's a vein, and no slitting your throat like in the movies, trying to slice through all that cartilage. No, the point of this dagger is exactly in place to pierce your carotid artery. You will bleed fast, you will die quickly, you should be grateful.'

Susan held her breath, Nikki's face was so close, she could feel her breath on her cheek. She could see the collar on the coat, the brown corduroy.

'Why are you wearing Beatrice's coat?'

Niki have her a pitying smile. 'When I kill you, there is going to be a lot of blood. I think this coat will be found in a bin not too far away. Poor Beatrice.'

'But why would she kill me?'

'Because you'd worked out she killed Colette. When the police come to tell me about your death tomorrow, through my tears, I shall let it slip that Beatrice was so scared you'd discovered that she'd killed Colette. There are going to be a lot of clues pointing her way, it will be fun watching the police find them.'

The wind was building up again, Susan could hear the waves crashing angrily on the rocks in the distance. 'But it's not a game, is it, Nikki? You have taken the lives of two people.'

'Colette's grandmother only had a year or so, at the most, probably a lot less, and Colette's life was such a mess, she was nothing.'

'As Colette said, "The kind of person no one cares about, the kind of person who walks out of a room and is forgotten"?'

'Sad but true.'

'No, not true. Colette and her grandmother were part of this world. They lived, loved, touched people. Remember the sermon at Colette's funeral, the story of the mayfly... only a day's flying life and yet so essential to others.'

'Oh, god, that sermon—'

'Colette and her grandmother loved and were loved. Go to the beach, every grain of sand makes up the beach we walk on, every star up there up there makes the night sky beautiful. Take one away and the world is poorer. You have robbed the world, Nikki, with your actions, you have stolen from the universe.'

Nikki blinked. 'Don't you start preaching at me.'

'You don't need me to do that, guilt is running through your veins – you will never wash their blood off your hands. You won't ever forget Colette, or her grandmother, and they will never forget you.'

For a second, she felt the point of the dagger ease. She grabbed her torch from her pocket and shone it straight into Nikki's eyes.

Nikki fell back and screamed. Susan got up and was about to

run when Nikki recovered and came at her with the dagger, no cool plan this time, just a frantic attack.

'Stop!' a voice shouted through the darkness.

Nathan came running over and grabbed Nikki. 'Enough, you must stop now. The police are coming, it's over.'

Nikki crumpled onto the ground, started to sob.

Susan could see the flashing of lights and stared at Nathan.

'Thank you, oh, god.' She burst into tears. 'How did you know we were here?'

'I have had a tracker on Nikki's phone for a while now. It's how I got up here so quickly the night she fell. Ever since Colette died, she has been waking up screaming, she won't tell me what has happened, but I've known something was very wrong.'

'And yet you married her?'

'I loved her. She was always the one for me.'

'When did you suspect something was wrong?'

'I'd had a feeling deep down for a while, but the day when we went to scatter the ashes, I knew for certain something was very wrong. Nikki would never have told Colette about the brooch, she'd never have taken the risk of digging all that up. I also knew she couldn't have seen anyone from the gate. I put the tracker on her phone when we got back to the hotel. I was watching it that night, saw she'd left drama and came up here. I hid and watched her pick up the rock and injure herself and then carefully let herself down the side of the cliff.'

'And yet you seemed so convincing when you spoke to me the next morning.'

'I still didn't want to believe she was a killer. I thought if we were married, having me and the hotel would be enough. But I was a fool. I'm not sure anything will ever be enough for Nikki.'

The police came to join them, and Susan watched as Nikki was led away.

EPILOGUE
APRIL 2016 – THE FOLLOWING SPRING

Susan drove to the village that was soon to be her new home and parked outside the house she would be moving into in two weeks' time. This was the first home she'd ever bought on her own and she already loved it.

Her house back in Ventnor had sold quickly, but it had given her the push she needed to finally sort the place out. It was hard to be leaving Ventnor, but at the same time, it felt easy to move here. This place was where her story started, she was coming home to her roots. But it didn't feel like an ending, no, it was a new beginning.

She put the keys in the ignition and drove past the village shop, the pub until she arrived at Bishopstone nursing home.

Susan entered the home, signed herself in and went straight to the room.

'Susan, how lovely to see you again,' said Alice.

'I'm sorry I've not been for a while. I've just been to see the house, it's perfect, you must come for tea as soon as I'm settled.'

'I would love to. Now, tell me, is there any news about Nikki? Her case must be coming up soon?'

'Yes, she confessed to the stealing of the Peter Rabbit book, but not the murder of Colette or her grandmother. The police, however, seem to be building a good case now for the murder of Colette. After her accusations against Beatrice failed, Nikki tried to pin things on Nathan. However, once they knew where to look, the police knew what they were looking for, and it was amazing what they found – the threads of the velvet material from the pouch among her sewing things, and even a cigarette butt with traces of fish oil and Colette's DNA on. Nikki had just pushed it into her pocket and forgotten it. The point is she never thought she would get found out.

'The last thing I heard was that Nikki was planning to confess to Colette's killing in the hope of getting a lighter sentence, who knows what will happen. She is denying anything to do with the murder of Colette's grandmother, however, and Robert doubts they will ever build a convincing case for that.'

'No, I thought they might not, but I am glad we know the truth of it,' said Alice. 'Now tell me about the others.'

'Well, Beatrice and Nathan are now officially in partnership at the hotel.'

'I'm glad she stayed.'

'She had applied for a divorce, and yes, she is building a new life here. People have been more understanding than she expected, particularly as they see her commitment to working hard at the hotel and all that brings to the community.'

'And Torri and Trystan?'

'Oh, Trystan has been awarded his first Michelin star. It's so exciting. He's finally had his test and has hearing aids; Yvonne has moved over to work in the restaurant with him.'

'And how is Torri feeling about that?'

'She is reconciled to staying here for some time, at least. She's been for counselling, her and Trystan are to be married in the summer. The patisserie side is taking off big time and she is working with a local bakery to extend that.'

'Do you know what Colette's uncle plans to do about the book?'

'It will be sold at auction and some of the money raised will pay for a seat to be placed as a memorial down by Castle Cove to Colette. Wait, I have a photograph of what we are having made.'

Susan showed Alice the picture of an intricate stone carving of a mayfly, and underneath, the words 'Colette, a precious life, never forgotten' engraved.

'That's beautiful,' said Alice.

'We have permission for it to be set into the wall opposite the slipway at Castle Cove.'

'Perfect.'

'And the rest of the money will go to a children's counselling service.'

Susan took out her phone. 'Now, I remember once saying to you that we would talk of happier things. Well, this has to be some of the best news I could bring you. This is a photograph of my beautiful new grandchild; she has joined the world.'

'Oh, that's wonderful.'

'It's a baby girl called Jamari, which apparently is a Native American name meaning "a woman warrior". A great name, I think.'

'It certainly is, and very fitting for your family.'

Susan shared more photos and then walked over to the window, looked over at the downs and the sea. 'You have a lovely view, how are you settling over here?'

'The move has worked out well. I have restricted my daughter to one visit a week, she'll wear herself out otherwise, but the staff are very kind.'

'You don't regret moving from Ventnor?'

'No, after everything that happened, I think I needed a fresh start.' Alice grinned. 'Not bad at ninety-one! How about you? Leaving the place you lived for forty years must be a wrench.'

'I've realised I can take all the important things with me, and my roots are over here on West Wight. I can't wait to take Jamari down to the beaches here that I went to as a child and, of course, up on the downs, it will be wonderful.'

'But what about Robert? He can't be happy to see you move?'

Susan smiled. 'It's not actually that far, is it – I think I will still be seeing him and, of course, Gem Gem and Dougie.'

'When you're settled, do you think you will find a new dog-walking group?'

Susan laughed. 'I might not rush into that, but I have already been asked to join the village choir.'

'Ah, I knew the grandfather of the young man who is running it now. You'll find it an interesting group.'

'I shall look forward to it.'

Alice leant forward and smiled. 'The main thing now is to keep out of trouble.'

'Of course. Mind you, if anything were to crop up, I'll always know exactly where to find you.'

ACKNOWLEDGMENTS

Firstly, an enormous thank you to you, my lovely readers, for taking the time to read *Death at Castle Cove*, and thank you for all the messages of support.

A huge thank you to my wonderful publisher Boldwood, and the whole team for your outstanding dedication and hard work. A very special thank you to Sarah Ritherdon, for your insight, knowledge, and kindness, and yet again taking a very messy first draft and enabling me to craft this story. Thank you also, to all the editors for your exceptional work, the cover designer and everyone involved in bringing this novel to life.

I would like to thank Darren Claydon from the Isle of Wight Ambulance Service for your invaluable insights and help with plotting the scenes at Steephill and Castle coves. A huge thank you to you and all your colleagues, for your commitment and tireless work in caring for the community here on the Isle of Wight.

There are quite a few dogs in this story, and I'd like to thank all the owners for allowing me to use the names and descriptions of their very special dogs. Thank you, Diane Lister, for allowing me to mention Libby (Libs), Pat Pearson for Rocco, Pauline Trimmings for Gemma (Gem Gem,) and Fiona McGregor for Dougie. All these people are members of the fabulous group, Cocker Spaniels on Facebook.

Also thank you to Harriet for allowing me to mention Biddy and Ruth and Tom for Duke.

I would like to say a huge thank you to island photographer

Steve Gascoigne and Sharon of Available Light Gallery and Gifts here on the Isle of Wight, for again generously donating a stunning mounted photograph for the publication day competition.

A huge thank you as always to my gorgeous family, my husband, and children, Thomas and Emily, for their unending support and encouragement.

Thank you to everyone on Facebook, Twitter and Instagram, writers, and friends. Your kind words and support mean so much to me. Also thank you to the wonderful group of bloggers who work tirelessly reading and reviewing books and offer so much encouragement to writers like myself.

Thank you so much, Deryn Edwards, for adding a touch of magic with your wonderful narration of the audiobook.

MORE FROM MARY GRAND

We hope you enjoyed reading *Death at Castle Cove*. If you did, please leave a review.

If you'd like to gift a copy, this book is also available as an ebook, hardback, large print, digital audio download and audiobook CD.

Sign up to Mary Grand's mailing list for news, competitions and updates on future books.

https://bit.ly/MaryGrandNewsletter

Explore more gripping thrillers from Mary Grand...

 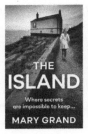  

ABOUT THE AUTHOR

Mary Grand is the author of six novels and writes gripping, page-turning suspense, with a dark and often murderous underside. She grew up in Wales, was for many years a teacher of deaf children and now lives on the Isle of Wight.

Visit Mary's website: https://marygrand.net/

Follow Mary on social media:

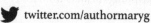 twitter.com/authormaryg
instagram.com/marygrandwriter
facebook.com/authormarygrand
bookbub.com/profile/mary-grand

Poison
& Pens

POISON & PENS IS THE HOME OF
COZY MYSTERIES SO POUR YOURSELF
A CUP OF TEA & GET SLEUTHING!

DISCOVER PAGE-TURNING NOVELS FROM
YOUR FAVOURITE AUTHORS &
MEET NEW FRIENDS

JOIN OUR
FACEBOOK GROUP

BIT.LYPOISONANDPENSFB

SIGN UP TO OUR
NEWSLETTER

BIT.LY/POISONANDPENSNEWS

Boldwood

Boldwood Books is an award-winning fiction publishing company seeking out the best stories from around the world.

Find out more at www.boldwoodbooks.com

Join our reader community for brilliant books, competitions and offers!

Follow us
@BoldwoodBooks
@BookandTonic

Sign up to our weekly deals newsletter

https://bit.ly/Boldwood9Newsletter

Milton Keynes UK
Ingram Content Group UK Ltd.
UKHW042251140224
437856UK00002B/3

9 781804 269077